TOPAZ

IS DENIABILITY ENOUGH?

RICHARD ROBINSON

SPELLBOUND BOOKS

PROLOGUE

THE SOUND OF RUPTURED METAL FROM THE PARKING BAY GAVE WAY TO a horrific explosion as the Fiat burst through the hydraulic doors and its fuel tank spectacularly detonated. The flames burst high into the rafters of the warehouse and the press and terrified MI5 agent sprinted to the back of the room. The double doors leading to the main room were then kicked open and standing there was a single gunman in a paramilitary balaclava. He held a pistol and in one shot killed the policeman, who was already prostrate on the floor from the impact of the car exploding. The gunman then looked around the room, he stared over at the assembled media with his gun still raised and without blinking picked out the agent who took a shot to the head and immediately collapsed.

Topaz knew that they were safe behind the metal fence at the top of the viewing gallery. They needed to stay quiet and motionless but all three were still peering over the balcony, transfixed on the scene. Jones was sure one of the journalists had noticed them but the horror of the unfolding situation had kept their attention away from the figures hidden in the rafters.

"Where is he?" shouted the gunman, with a clear and unmistakable English accent. Topaz recognised the voice.

CHAPTER ONE

Jones hated heights. In the days leading up to the start of his new employment as a labourer, he had imagined fetching and carrying, sweeping up, and even mixing cement. But scaling a large country house on a trembling over-extended ladder to re-point a chimney wasn't part of the vision.

His two colleagues, both older, wiser, and much better versed in the art of banter, found his inability to swing his leg over onto the top rung of the ladder whilst gripping a bucket of wet cement hilarious. Jones had been stuck up there in the same position for almost 15 minutes, gripped with fear and trying not to look down.

Worse still, was the fact that he was horribly hungover. He'd spent the previous evening in the Seven Stars waiting for his three friends to emerge from the cinema. They'd gone together to watch Braveheart but at the last-minute Jones opted to see an entirely different film from everyone else. It was an attention-seeking move. He had a desperate need to be different from the crowd and had opted for an arthouse movie with Korean subtitles. On realising it was almost incomprehensible, he walked out and ordered a Kronenberg from the pub opposite. This became four or five Kronenbergs and by the time his friends arrived from Braveheart, he was hammered. Jones lied to his friends about the 'astonishing' Korean film and how they were too corporate and brainwashed to appreciate its brilliance.

But at the top of the ladder, sixty feet up, he just couldn't force his 18-year-old body to teeter over that huge drop and his head was spinning. The nightmare was over in a flash when the more heavily tattooed of the two men grabbed his shaking leg and thrust it on the second rung from the top. There was laughter. Jones felt foolish. This job wasn't for him he quickly decided.

At one point Jones saw himself cascading down the ladder as he momentarily slipped down a few rungs but once he'd steadied himself, he was safe. And he climbed slowly down to the floor. His Walkman, previously clasped onto his back pocket, dropped gently onto the shingle below and he glimpsed the foreman rolling his eyes. It hadn't been a good start to the week, and he still had a beery aftertaste.

"You'd best mix the cement and stay on the ground, we haven't got time to babysit you," the foreman announced at the bottom. Or Caddick, as the lads called him.

"I'll take a length of rope up and you can attach the full bucket and we'll pull it up. Unless you're scared of the ground too?" He added, with a grin.

"I'll be fine," Jones replied, picking up his cassette player and looking for damage. With Caddick looking on he quickly grabbed a trowel and threw a pile of concrete dust into the bucket and started mixing. The foreman started up the ladder with a thick rope tied around his waist.

"I'll chuck the rope down when I get to the top, you attach the bucket. Can you manage that?" Caddick called down.

Jones ignored him.

Behind Jones, a grey Volkswagen pulled up next to the builder's archaic Bedford van and the shingle crackled under the tyres. An older man in an ill-fitting business suit stepped out of the car and strolled over to Jones, he still had the remains of breakfast ketchup on his lapel. Instead of looking at Jones he focused upwards and watched Caddick take confident steps slowly towards the summit and the ageing chimney stacks.

"You must be Jones, I'm the Site Manager here, and you are about to win the award for the shortest employment tenure with us," he announced. Jones looked shocked.

"Your mother's been on the phone," he said, finally looking at Jones.

"You're to go home and pack. They've found you a university place, but you've got to leave today. I'll drive you back home. It seems your exam results weren't quite appalling enough for a permanent job with us!" He laughed.

As they both walked towards the car, the end of the rope landed a couple of inches from the bucket. Followed by some howls of derision from the roof above. Jones shrugged his shoulders and looked up at Caddick. They won't miss me, he thought.

They barely spoke on the journey and Jones' mind was in overdrive. It was the summer of 1995 and Jones assumed he had crucified his chances of a university place by drinking his way through sixth form. His drinking had reached Olympic standard and he barely revised for his 'A' Level examinations. His parents had almost tied him to a chair and made him apply to various universities via UCCA despite Jones' pleading that he didn't care. Life was easy and there was plenty of time to make plans. The bottom of the application barrel must have been reached, he assumed. Somebody must want me and I may as well give it a crack. He reached for his Walkman from his back pocket and pushed play on a cassette by The Smiths.

Jones was a chancer and stumbled his way successfully through school life. He occupied his time by doing the bare minimum in studies and the rest of the time playing his records or walking to the pub with his friends. He was average in height, had average brown hair and was averagely attractive. He lived in a small commuter-belt town in South-East England and was the only child of two London-born parents, who both worked in local government. They were attentive and interested in his life but he often needed to dumb down some of the more leftfield elements to save their feelings. They weren't aware of girlfriends, alcoholism or the occasional dabble with narcotics in the park. He was happier with them in a state of careful ignorance and that left him free to experiment Life was just fine and dandy.

He'd had countless menial part-time jobs. He'd assisted the milkman in the dairy, had swept up hair in the hairdressers, had helped set up computers in the local newspaper office and had even written a few articles for the newspaper. And whilst he enjoyed being industrious outside school, he'd only succeeded in using the money to swell his record collection and in enhancing his reputation as a generous and reliable drinking partner. The thought of leaving home and creating new networks, following an academic career and changing his lifestyle was a shock to the system. But at the same time, scaling a ladder and re-pointing a chimney needed swerving, and for this he was grateful.

On arriving home to his proud parents, he learned quite how much of the barrel they'd scraped before his application was successful. Two fee-paying international students had their visas rejected at the last minute and therefore a place in the BA(Hons) course in Communication Studies at Milton College was his. He barely remembered applying. The last three months were hazy, at best.

His parents, perhaps too enthusiastically, helped him pack ready for a meeting with his tutors the following morning and the imminent start of term. Jones wondered what nightlife existed in Milton and how quickly he could recreate his charmed lifestyle. He was in the car and heading down the motorway less than an hour after arriving home. His parents, sitting in the front seats, were keen to pass on their advice about campus life but Jones put his headphones back on and un-paused The Smiths 'Strangeways Here We Come' tape on his Walkman, the title seemed oddly prophetic.

Milton College, formerly the Milton Tech and Secretarial College, existed deep in rural Gloucestershire but boasted a bustling market town centre with good transport links to the nearest city. Jones had also fortuitously nabbed the final bedroom in the student halls a mere five-minute stroll from the campus but less happily he would be sharing that bedroom with two other freshers in an old-fashioned dormitory.

The nearest city was Cheltenham and this was the home of the Doughnut. The odd-looking structure served as the base for Government Communications Headquarters (GCHQ). This was the intelligence and security organisation responsible for providing signals intelligence and information to the government and armed forces of the United Kingdom and very hush-hush. It was an organisation which, for most of his young life, Jones had never heard of. He simply assumed intelligence meant whatever Magnus Magnusson could crowbar out of petrified contestants on Mastermind.

CHAPTER TWO

Milton wasn't one of the great Universities of Britain. There were no magnificent statues of former Chancellors in the gardens, busts of Queen Victoria in the hallways or rooms named after Prime Ministers who were amongst the alumni. No, according to the prospectus, Milton was a 1930s college originally designed for local girls to learn shorthand, to touch type in rooms filled with rows and rows of typewriters. The photos showed uptight-looking women in round spectacles teaching secretarial etiquette to the masses. Its heyday was undoubtedly in the 1950s when women were no longer housewives and homemakers, they had proven their talents during the Second World War and whilst misogyny and chauvinism were still the go-tos for the men returning from the war (and wanting their jobs back), this was probably a turning point. Albeit a very slow one. Milton was, for a while, competing with Wimbledon Ladies College as the gold standard for secretarial skills.

By 1995 the glamour had long gone but the original carpets and furnishings hadn't. Leaving a kind of musty smell which was perhaps comparable to the stench when Howard Carter opened Tutankhamun's Tomb. However, not everything that remained from the glory days was tired and obsolete. One such example was Virginia Curry, a shorthand tutor par excellence, who had been teaching Pitman's Shorthand since the dawn of time and probably taught Pitman himself. She was quite simply brilliant at her job and could spot a great mind, a potential star or hidden talent amongst the herds of inadequates that otherwise frequented Milton's woodworm-infested corridors. The pool of talent was particularly dry of late though and the question of her possible retirement had even been mentioned by Virginia when breakfasting with her husband, Charles.

One further fact that eluded 99.9% of those who attended the rebranded and gently modernised Milton College, was that Virginia Curry was married to Sir Charles Curry, a retired Director General of MI5, former station head in multiple locations across the globe for Her Majesty's Secret Service and retained recruitment sergeant for the Secret Intelligent Services and GCHQ. This meant that Milton was not just a home for more mothballs than the nation's branches of Woolworths, but also home to the most dedicated recruitment and training base for spies in the United Kingdom. It was an enormous clandestine operation hiding in plain sight.

Milton College simply continued to exist and to shape the UK's future espionage networks without appearing to do much more than teach rather antiquated Communications degrees, a few token Media Studies qualifications and a dozen other useful but outdated qualifications. Including shorthand, naturally. Most left with their certificates and being none-the-wiser and that meant they had failed to impress the Currys but had done enough to please the examination boards.

Virginia, this particular Tuesday morning, was scheduled to meet a long list of new students who were joining the Communications Studies undergraduate course.

She acted as a tutor for a carefully selected dozen or so which she handpicked based on her almost unique intuition for skills, patterns of behaviour and potential. Gone were the days of all-female groups as males had been admitted into Milton since the early 1980s but she liked to prioritise any female recruits. They were the best spies, she considered. However, as shorthand tutor for the Communications Studies course, she was able to run the rule over the whole cohort, as the syllabus demanded at least 120 words per minute of shorthand proficiency by year three. That was rather like writing at warp speed.

At precisely 10.32am, there was a knock on Virginia's door and she immediately summoned in the latest candidate. Jones was dressed in a pair of unwashed beige jeans, an untucked navy-blue polo shirt and some tired-looking brown loafers which had clearly been around the block a few times. Jones sniffed and was quickly awe-struck. The room was probably three times the size necessary for a meeting of this type and was empty aside from the table, two chairs and wall-to-wall fraying brown carpet revealing antique wooden floorboards.

His nose was still full of dust from the previous night of unpacking into the student halls, which were relics from a bygone era of questionable provenance. Jones had barely slept, not just from nervous anticipation for his first day on campus. But also, from the umpteen strong coffees he downed to stave off the aftermath of the hangover.

As he walked in, still clutching his appointment letter, his brain was armed with questions about the location of the local launderette and when he'd be receiving his student grant and wasn't expecting the careful interrogation planned by Mrs Curry. His attire, not the tailored sharp suit one would expect from a keen-to-impress new student, was the first negative mark on his file.

"So," she started, peering over her glasses, "please introduce yourself and give me some background about why you chose Milton College."

"I'm Jones," he began, not proffering a first name, as he barely used it. "And I didn't really choose Milton College, it chose me. You see, I came through the clearing system and this appears to be the only route available to me. My exams were really not my finest hour."

"Nonsense" she replied and hastily leafed through Jones' file and CV. "You're an all-rounder. You've done a bit of this and that. You've even had some stories published in your newspaper. You showed some real promise there. Let's drop the confidence-bashing stuff. What is your ambition, Jones?"

"I'd always fancied myself as a football reporter," he announced, which resulted in an almost silent sigh from Virginia. "But I'm keen to learn and develop before I make any decisions about my future. I've been quite fortunate to get myself on the academic ladder and therefore I'm focused on being sponge-like and soaking up information and skills. This is a real opportunity. Milton College already seems like an exciting prospect."

This rather earnest response won him a few ticks in Virginia's boxes. And there was something about Jones which she had warmed to. It was true, he was an all-rounder. Someone who was truly keen on being industrious and keeping busy across a range of activities. Neither of them knew quite whether this was going to shape itself into something meaningful or, like most who Virginia peered over her glasses to examine, whether Jones might just leave with a certificate to frame and a career in a provincial newspaper writing up births, deaths and marriages.

"Tell me about your journalistic career, young man," she asked.

"The Editor of my local newspaper asked me to help set up his computer systems in the office. To replace all the typewriters. It was easy. Sixteen machines, three printers and a server and a large Winchester disk. I had it all up and running pretty quickly."

"That's impressive. How did you land this opportunity?" she inquired.

"I was working behind the bar in the local pub. And the Editor, well, he's a bit of an old soak. I think I was the only person he knew that had ever used a computer. We got talking one night at the pub and I showed up and sorted it the very next day. He gave me £20 and two weeks on the paper as a trial."

"Fascinating," she replied and wrote his whole answer down phonetically in Pitman's in her shorthand pad.

"Never call anyone an old soak, Jones," she said. "Most journalists pick up all they need to know from the local pub. It's where everything happens and all walks of life intertwine. You're an example of that. It's just one or two Editors and journalists who get rather too accustomed to the public house. Listen and take heed, as my father used to say. Wars were probably won and lost from information picked up in pubs."

"I wrote a piece on dropped kerb stones for the paper. I know that sounds very dreary but I had to research all the measurements and legislation to write the article. The Editor put it on the front page. I was surprised. I think most of the other journalists were pretty annoyed too," added Jones.

To his amazement, Virginia pulled out the article from her file.

"Yes, it's a rather well-constructed piece. Your research was comprehensive. Frankly, I think that sealed the deal for your admission here. Let's leave it at that, shall we Jones? You'll see me again tomorrow and I think I shall be your contact point around the College. You can ring me on this number if you need me." She passed him a rather formal-looking gold embossed business card and smiled at him.

"Get yourself a suit, a shave, and stop with all that drinking. Smarten yourself up and you might get somewhere," she strolled over to the door and opened it wide. Jones shook Virginia's hand and headed out. He was relieved.

As Jones walked past the long queue of other students, he overheard a pushy father say to his besuited son in parrot-fashion. "Remember what I said to you earlier, son. You'll need to be sponge-like, thank her for the opportunity and mention how fortunate you are to get onto the academic ladder at Milton College." That ship has already sailed, thought Jones. And headed in the wrong direction towards some cleaners' cupboards, quickly correcting himself as one or two of those waiting sniggered.

As he walked towards the exit of the college something caught his eye. Right up in the heavens of the college ceiling up high. It was like thread or a long spider's silk which seemed to shimmer in the edges of the ceilings like infinitesimally small Christmas decorations. They were everywhere and seemed to lead nowhere initially.

As he walked through the corridors and tried to find his bearings, he noticed that he was alone in finding this odd thread interesting. Everyone else scurried around the college from room to room like worker ants but he gazed upwards and was totally unable to shift it from his mind. What on earth were they for? He followed the tiny lines up a flight of stairs and noticed how they seemed to all congregate into a dusty box in the ceiling. The ceiling itself looked newly painted and the box had hinges and a grate which seemed to be some type of inlet. The threads then merged into one thick black wire and he followed that further along into another quiet corridor where there was a flame-red door with a frosted glass window that seemed to be the final destination for the strange threads or wire. Too thin for telephone wire or computer cabling, he thought, and walked away back down the stairs into the main throng of activity filled with men and women in business attire. He stood there, in a wardrobe that looked like he'd just walked out of the amusements at Butlins, and scolded himself, and then looked for something to eat.

He followed the sign to the refectory and grabbed a notebook from his back pocket. He needed a reminder to stock up on food and provisions for the dormitory. He'd left his Walkman at the Halls earlier in an attempt to formalise his appearance but realised this was in vain when he saw the number of expensive-looking dapper suits on show. She was right, he did need to smarten up, he was a little unshaven but he was clueless as to how she noticed the last remains of his Sunday night hangover. Underneath cheese, butter, bread and lager he scrawled razor blades in his notebook. But right now, he needed a bacon sandwich and to sort his life out.

The refectory was busy as it was heading towards lunchtime. There was a long servery with individual stations for sandwiches and salads, cooked meals, pizzas, old-fashioned puddings and hot drinks. There were also three large vending machines for fizzy drinks, crisps and chocolate. There was no bar, which was probably a good thing, he surmised. If Virginia can spot a two-day hangover, I'll need to be savvier with my drinking etiquette.

He nudged his way into the long queue for sandwiches and was immediately struck by two pairs of eyes staring at him from a table immediately opposite the sandwich station. They were figures that he would have instantly avoided at school or perhaps, to his shame, probably gently bullied. They were wearing matching brown blazers and smart trousers with turn-ups, probably chosen by their parents, and hairstyles that involved a kitchen bowl and pinking shears. Yet oddly, he knew without question that these were his roommates who were absent from the Halls last night. Aside from their shared shopping habits and floral ties they also seemed to have the same insecure gaze which probably came from others teasing them.

He smiled over at them assuming that they'd seen him last night and they waved back cheerily. It was only then that he realised that whilst they were indeed modelling clothes found by their parents at 'Man at C&A' he was possibly the only person in the queue or refectory who looked like he did. And for the first time since arriving in Milton he realised he was the outsider. At the top of the queue, he held his anger when he discovered they'd run out of brown sauce for his bacon sandwich and decided to get acquainted with his roommates. Civility is the way forward here, Jones, he decided, and pulled up the spare chair on the table.

After brief introductions and some small talk around the state of the Halls (archaic, they all agreed) Jones began to learn a great deal about the course. It appears Tom Marsh and Carl Kelly had done their homework and were researching different aspects of the core syllabus. Carl was combining his thumbing through the Media Ethics programme literature whilst selecting his favourites from a box of Cadbury's Animal Biscuits and then biting their chocolate heads off and sharing the results with Tom. The two seemed to find this unspeakably funny.

Tom was a tall man with cropped wavy hair and very shiny shoes. He spoke quickly and laughed nervously at the end of every sentence, almost as if he was hoping no-one would notice he'd said anything at all. Despite being the taller of the two, he was eagerly looking to Carl for agreement and positive affirmation. Carl was in charge. He was shorter, with styled curtained hair that was greased back on either side with enough petroleum-styling wax to make him a fire hazard. In the five minutes they'd spoken, Carl had attempted to finish almost all of Tom's sentences and had almost certainly emptied the box of Animals. Jones wondered whether the two of them had ever spent any time in female company or away from their parents.

What was undoubtedly useful for Jones was their almost encyclopaedic knowledge of the course and the timetable. And with the revelation that they didn't start lectures until the next day at 10am, Jones decided to find a pub, dragging the two boys along for good measure. A course reading session, if you will. In the five-minute walk between Milton College and the Halls of Residence Jones inspected a few candidates for an acceptable local. And at the same time, Carl had slipped off to a newsagent and was brandishing a Wham bar and a bag of cola cubes. The winning hostelry was The Jericho, a small back street boozer with two rooms and an alluring selection of real ales and lagers. Jones treated the boys to a pint of Carling and he settled on a Stella. A man's drink.

Three and a half hours and four pints later, Jones had discovered that Carl could down a pint in less than ten seconds, that they were both enormous fans of Status Quo and had season tickets for Norwich City Football Club. They were also both stony broke until their student grants appeared and he was accepted as part of their little gang primarily as the cash cow. It was an arrangement he could live with until more useful friends emerged. Perhaps tomorrow. After an eventful short walk back to the Halls, with both singing Quo songs with much gusto, the boys slept almost instantly. Jones on the other hand took a walk around the Halls to get acclimatised to his new surroundings.

Whilst his quick walk around the grounds yielded nothing in terms of new faces or a Hall Bar (there wasn't one), it did rekindle his interest in the long threads he saw back in the main corridor. Just outside the Halls was a long set of cast iron railings which terminated at the entrance to a cellar. The cellar looked like the abandoned entrance to an old public convenience with the base of the cellar door divided into two small staircases. He stepped down the three or four steps and gazed through the gaps in the locked metal doors. Beyond the doors, the threads were bunched into small groups for about ten feet and again vanished into a black cabinet. He wasn't sure why this odd cabling had piqued his interest quite so much and he made a mental note to ask Virginia Curry about his discovery.

CHAPTER THREE

Two brand new Land Rover Snatch vehicles were parked outside a nondescript supplies hut in Enniskillen, Northern Ireland. Drivers passing on the A4 heading towards Tamlaght would have immediately spotted them, but these hefty, armoured vehicles were so normalised in public life that nobody would have turned a hair. The political climate was fraught, talks were ongoing, and the Americans had waded into discussions to end the generations of sectarian fighting, known as the 'Troubles', but confidence was low and another stand-off was inevitable.

Behind the supplies hut was a smart black minibus with room for twelve passengers. It had been ferrying around a group of young adults who were being trained to join a new intelligence unit which had been shaped using the best brains from both the great Universities and some specialist colleges scattered around the UK. Entry tests were exhaustive, training was precise and measured every aspect of performance and aptitude. These were future communication operatives and field agents. Some would end up in the Secret Intelligence Service, some in GCHQ and others on detachment to various intelligence corps across the Armed Services. Another group would not quite make the grade and these could end up anywhere, including such civilian roles as Risk Analysts for the Insurance Industry. So, for many, failure was not an option.

The group had been code-named YCU. The Young Communicator Unit. And whilst this might sound like a step up from the Scout Association or the Boys Brigade, the somewhat unconvincing name belied an ambition to ensure the United Kingdom continued its excellence in targeted communications.

In the backroom of the supplies hut sat ten focused young adults. It was a mix of males and females from a variety of ethnic backgrounds. But the gender and the colour were immaterial. These people needed to be the communications machinery that made the future of British Espionage tick, and the future, not just in these islands but across the globe, was more challenging than ever. The cold war almost felt predictable compared to signals across the world in 1995 with the rise of China, whispers from the Middle East and the horror of the Balkans still so murderously complicated.

The whitewashed walls were punctuated by speakers, a pull-down display board, and maps in varying degrees of detail. Leading the meeting was a slight man in a long dark trench coat with a stubbly ginger beard and thick glasses. Aside from the group of note-taking trainees, were three male officers. Two in dark Royal Ulster Constabulary uniforms and the other in a green military uniform emblazoned with the Royal Irish Regiment badge. They were joined by a further female attendee dressed simply in a suit and she stood next to the trench-coated man.

"Today you face your most significant challenge yet and, as you've been briefed previously, will involve the use of breathing apparatus, blanks and explosives. This scenario will be the closest you've all come to a real-life or death situation and I need to underline that this is a pass-or-fail moment." He looked around the room and tried to catch every eye.

"This scenario has been planned in great detail and under the guidance of our colleagues from the RUC, RIR and MI5," he turned and nodded towards the three visitors.

"Within forty minutes of Belfast, there is a suspected safe house or storage depot for a paramilitary organisation calling itself 'Red Line'. Its roots are unknown and the only intelligence we have suggests they are seeking to make Northern Ireland a standalone nation, neither part of Ireland or the UK but with some very suspect allies. We know nothing regarding the leadership of this organisation. What we do know, is that Red Line is utilising safe houses to store previously unheralded dirty bomb making materials. This has been smuggled into mainland UK from Cuba and transferred to Ireland using refrigerated lorries coming in through Larne and Belfast Ports."

The trench coat man pulled down the display board and switched on a grey projection unit. His eyes still calmly assessing the room.

"Whilst this is an exercise and great care has been taken to ensure your safety, you should be aware that this is a real-life scenario. Our friends in the RUC have intercepted two lorries filled with Scottish Lamb and containing large drums of Agent Orange." He pointed to the screen showing images of two large blue bins of white powder amongst lamb carcasses with officers wearing protective HAZMAT suits.

"Agent Orange is a hideous outdated weapon of war. It's an herbicide and defoliant chemical used by the US military as part of its chemical warfare programme, known as Operation Ranch Hand during the Vietnam War," the screen changed to some imagery of Vietnam and fleeing civilians in a forest setting. He pushed the presentation on and showed diagrams of chemical formulae.

"It is a mixture of equal parts of two herbicides, 2,4,5-T and 2,4-D. In addition to its damaging environmental effects, traces of dioxin found in the mixture have caused major health problems for many individuals who were exposed as well as their offspring. So, it doesn't just harm the target but their families too." The next slide showed graphs and a few photographs of classified documents.

"The government of Vietnam says that up to four million of their citizens were exposed to Agent Orange, and as many as three million people have suffered illness because of it. The United States government has described these figures as unreliable whilst, at the same time, documenting cases of leukaemia, Hodgkin's lymphoma, and various kinds of cancer in exposed US military veterans. And this is still out there folks." The screen then showed deformed bodies and packed Asian hospital wards.

"Finally, before anyone goes away thinking this is all about stupid yanks, it's worth pointing out that Agent Orange was first used by the British in Malaya during the Malayan Emergency. They were the guinea pigs for the Agent Orange attacks in Laos and Cambodia during the Vietnam War. This ghastly shite is out there, ladies and gentlemen, in our streets and brought here by Red Line using contacts in Cuba and Russia. This may be a training exercise, but the threat is real.

"Red Line is not a fictional group and part of my role, outside leading your studies, is determining who they are and their intentions. Knowledge of this group is very strictly 'eyes only' and you are being trusted with highly classified real-life information.

"Your task is to locate the safe house or storage depot, clear the area and ensure that this chemical weapon does not become part of the Red Line armoury. The chemicals are dummies, they cannot harm you, but this will be an ideal opportunity to test your hazardous materials training and working in HAZMAT suits.

"You all have your briefing packs; you all know the drill. You will move back into your two groups and we will rendezvous at the safe house, once you've located it, at 2100 hours on Wednesday for a full debrief. Otherwise, use the call signs and numbers on your handhelds to get support."

There was a brief huddle as the trench-coated man shook hands with the officers and he reached behind a folding table for a wheeled suitcase.

He turned to the female MI5 operative and gave her the same briefing papers as the assembled trainees.

"I'll be back here in a few days. I have recruiting to do and I'm dealing with some assessments in England. Can you be my eyes and ears? I'll be available throughout on the phone in the college, you have the number." The operative nodded and the trench coat man disappeared through the back doors, wheeling his case behind him.

CHAPTER FOUR

Jones was up with the lark. The boys were already watching cartoons on Kelly's black and white television and laughing sporadically whilst eating coco pops from green plastic bowls. There was excitement in the air.

Day one was an induction session at Milton College. The entire cohort was introduced to their tutors and lecturers in a large hall and the College Principal gave a welcoming speech. The man in question looked like an angry version of Captain Birdseye but he certainly had the gravitas and guile of a College Principal. There was a hush when he spoke and a respectful applause when he finished but the contents of his speech were instantly forgettable as was his name.

Jones had misjudged the dress code again and had arrived in beige chinos and a white untucked Ralph Lauren shirt. His fellow students had opted for Bank Manager chic, and he wondered how he'd missed the memo. Tom and Carl seated themselves away from Jones perhaps in an attempt to avoid being infected by his smart-casual ethos.

After a gruelling presentation from Mr Singh, dressed in a brown warehouse coat, white shirt and yellow woollen tie, who led on Modern Technologies and Communication Ethics, Virginia was poised to take over. Mr Singh had mad professor vibes and conducted his entire speech with a smoker's pipe in his right hand, occasionally waving it for effect. Jones found him fascinating. Once Virginia took the lectern, she divided the cohort into two groups. She, in turn, was dressed in a long red dress emblazoned with poppies and paired with a long chain of pearls around her neck. Her half-moon glasses were perched right at the end of her nose and her short fair hair bobbed up and down as she read through a list of names from her clipboard.

The Emerald Group disappeared into an adjoining room with Mr Singh and Jones noticed a large tome of information was handed to the group as they entered the side room. Tom and Carl were amongst the stragglers who made their way out of the main hall and looked excited to receive the large bundle of tagged documents. Emerald appeared to be around three-quarters of the whole cohort and was an almost 50/50 split between male and female. What remained was the Topaz Group and this was Virginia Curry's selection.

"Right, Topaz" she announced.

"You're with me and you'll be learning about communication under pressure. You'll be trained on how to tailor your methods of reporting and communicating to distinct audiences and deadlines. You will learn about signs, codes and ciphers. All of you are physically fit, most of you speak a second language and there'll be something unique about your abilities that will come to the fore over the next six weeks." Virginia looked into the eyes of every one of the assembled fifteen Topaz group members.

"The Emerald Group will be shaped into a high-quality research unit. By the end of the six weeks, they'll understand how to guide and respond to changes in the environment and conditions to get the right result. They will be your eyes, ears and brains but they'll be in the back room. You'll be the front-line." It was at that moment that an alarm bell went off in Jones' head. This was going to be tough and it was becoming apparent that this course had very little to do with being a football reporter and much more about being in a war. Either reporting on one or in one, he decided.

Jones didn't speak a second language. He wasn't necessarily fit but he had the frame and the aptitude to get fitter. The mention of a unique attribute was troubling him but he put that to the back of his mind and let the information wash over him. He listened intently, wrote rapid notes and found himself truly engaged in the process of becoming a communications scholar. Virginia Curry gave way to Mr McNally, a broad Ulsterman who described the basic theory of coding, ciphers and signs. McNally was ginger, pale and dressed like it was 1972.

"Information plays a big part in our daily lives," he began. "Every day, we exchange information with various degrees of importance. It could be something as simple as tonight's dinner menu, or as critical as when to attack in a war. It has the power to turn a piece of clandestine news into a headline or converts a losing battle into a winning one. This is why making sure that information reaches its intended target without being leaked is crucial. This can be done using ciphers."

McNally paused, scratched his stubble and looked over the top of his glasses as if examining each of Topaz for contraband.

"So, what's a cipher?" he continued. No-one jumped to answer.

"A cipher is an algorithm that can encrypt or decrypt a message or signal. A cipher transforms a message, called plain text, into something called ciphertext, which is a message that has been scrambled with a certain key. By using a cipher, even if someone manages to find a way to obtain your message, they wouldn't be able to make sense of it. So, whether you're using shorthand to dictate an article to your editor or using a cipher to send your position, this is vital stuff."

He reached behind a long black curtain at the back of the room and pulled out a large cardboard box full of small purple books. Every member of Topaz was given one and McNally, dressed in an unseasonal black leather trench coat with brown flared trousers and battered brown leather shoes, moved back towards the lectern.

"This is your everything," he started, holding up the book. "It is your constant wee friend. For reasons that will become clear." His huge eyes darted around the room and waited for the group to look back in his direction before continuing.

"Go back to your digs. Read it, remember it. Retain that knowledge and there will be a quiz tomorrow. Come back here at 8.45am with a bag packed. You'll need winter coats, yes, I realise it's summertime, and enough clothing for around four days. I'd stay off the wine or beer tonight lads and lasses!" he laughed and looked to Virginia, who joined him in a quick upper-class guffaw.

"Importantly," Virginia added from behind McNally, "say nothing to anyone about your instructions for tomorrow. Not to Emerald or any other groups in the college or at home. Believe me, we'll know."

There was a sense of palpable excitement in the room and as he looked around the faces in the Topaz group, people looked back and smiled nervously. This was a group of strangers that would soon get to know each other very quickly. Jones leafed through the book. In small lettering at the front, it simply said 'Almanac 1995' and the rest of the purple cover was empty. There was no publisher's name or even 'Made in Taiwan'. The rest of the book was laden with page after page of maps (both global and tiny city maps of the UK), information about population sizes, a series of graphic illustrations of the human body, flags, chemical elements, weights and measures, historic family trees of Kings and Queens and even a list of Oscar Winners going back deep into the past. Bizarrely, there were a few chapters from Rudyard Kipling's 'Kim' right at the back in a small subscript font. Otherwise, it was a comprehensive handbook of useful information and the book itself fit neatly into his back pocket. There was a grudging acceptance that the Walkman had to go into retirement, for now.

McNally and Virginia took a flurry of questions about tomorrow's escapade without giving anything useful away. Yes, people would need some money, their wash kits and medication. No, we wouldn't be travelling to the Antarctic and there would be no sight-seeing. A slight, freckled woman with a mass of strawberry blonde hair held up a mobile phone. She was quickly informed it would need to remain with Virginia as would any other communication device, like a pager.

Jones met up with the boys in the refectory. Carl had managed to acquire another box of chocolate animal biscuits and Tom was making his way through a lasagne. Mr Singh had broken Emerald into small research groups. Each had a specific task focused on patterns of information. They had press clippings, notes from meetings, dialogue from ministerial addresses and numbered paperwork on case studies and incidents. Jones tried to grab Tom's folder, but he snatched it back. "Important information," said Tom. "Eyes only" and he smirked nervously. He went on eating his lasagne. There wasn't going to be a group trip to the Jericho tonight, Jones assumed, and walked away from the refectory with his bacon sandwich in a paper bag. HP sauce was liberally applied.

Jones planned a solo pint before heading to a quiet space to read the purple book. On the way, he found a payphone and called his parents. His mother was at work as an accounts clerk in a district council and she answered the phone professionally. Jones diligently explained his induction and meeting Tom and Carl. But he found himself stopping before saying too much else. He certainly didn't mention tomorrow's mystery and instead mentioned a field trip to a provincial newspaper. He was used to lying to his parents to spare their feelings, but this felt like an altogether different untruth. She, in turn, passed on news of his grandparents' ailing health and his father's recent 180 in a pub darts match.

The Jericho was totally empty when he wandered in. He ordered a half of Carling and then straightway changed the order to a pint. The landlord filled the glass and wandered back to his crossword. Jones loved the serenity of the place, and he sat in silence reading the book. Only the ticking of a grandfather clock in the adjoining lounge bar broke through the quiet. Jones loved trivia, he enjoyed retaining information and was fantastic at pub quizzes. He was delighted that he'd swerved the Emerald project. Two, three, four hours passed, and Jones had read the 'Everything' book on several occasions. The landlord asked a few times whether he wanted another beer but Jones decided to moderate his drinking this evening and he kept it down to three pints. God knows whether Virginia or McNally would be smelling his breath or interrogating the landlord.

He quickly read the Kim chapters but struggled to read the font size on a few of the pages. He began wondering what use his new-found appreciation of the existence of Lesotho (entirely landlocked in another country), the fact that there were 236.588 millilitres in a US cup or that there is an Australian company that turns dead bodies into ocean reef, might be? But soaking up information might be a worthy skill.

Wandering back to the Halls of Residence he spotted McNally leaning outside another pub across the road. He was still in the leather trench coat, smoking a cigarillo and the remains of a pint sat on a nearby table. He remembered the cigarillo smell from his childhood when a favourite uncle smoked them religiously. It was a reassuring memory of home. Jones half thought about joining him for a pint and discovering the Talbot Inn, but he wasn't on solid ground at Milton College yet and McNally didn't look like he wanted company. So, Jones carried on back to the dormitory where he found Carl air drumming to 'Caroline' by Status Quo and Tom reading the Beano. It was only 8pm and he perched on the corner of his single bed and carried on reading the Almanac and gathering a few clothes together for the trip. He slept soundly, even with Francis Rossi and Rick Parfitt for company.

CHAPTER FIVE

It was less than twenty-four hours since the two teams had left Enniskillen and had been transferred back to their Barracks outside Belfast to go through the technical notes and briefing from the trench-coated man, or Declan, as he was known to the YCU teams. The team leader of the first team was Isadora, a mixed-race woman from Solihull who had passed her GCSE maths and science exams at 12-years-old. She had already located the likely location of the safe house and, ahead of schedule, was planning to use the Land Rover Snatch to drive to the site with two fellow team members to undertake a recce. This wasn't a necessity, but Isadora was a perfectionist and a competitor.

However, such was the excitement from her team that, despite a heated argument, all five wanted to go on the road trip to the location. After all, this was simply a recce. They'd look through windows, perhaps confirm the entry points and look at what community safety measures might need to be explored. There would be no need to keep a communications post back at base and the hazmat suits could be left in the lockers. All of that could wait until the real deal tomorrow evening.

With that logic agreed and the team dressed in dark clothing, handhelds charged and equipment readied. A map was drawn to the location and as they would be going through army check points on their way out of the barracks, they picked up their blue identification passes. The warmth of the July sunshine was still palpable as afternoon gently headed towards dusk.

The team had worked closely together for almost three years now and whilst discussions and disagreements were common, there was enough mutual respect and friendship to ensure these were quickly forgotten. Isadora, for all her genius, was often accidentally hilarious as extreme academic prowess was not always a marker of supreme common sense. That said, she also liked to drive and that's why she practically burst out of the front door of the Barracks and into the front seat of the Snatch. The remaining four, three men and another female slotted into the back seats.

The location was in Limehall, a very rural spot. The map suggested some kind of brownfield site which left many unanswered questions about the terrain and position. The briefing and technical data included two intercepted ciphers, in theory from Red Line's operatives to their smugglers who brought the chemicals over from Larne. This gave them the Limehall area and precise coordinates from an Ordnance Survey Explorer Map of Mourne and Down.

Isadora very cleverly worked out that the ciphers had used the same coding as the fabled Zodiac killer's last two ciphers which puzzled California police for more than 50 years. A French engineer famously cracked the code which revealed the killer's name, and he sent his findings to the FBI and San Francisco Police Department. Neither commented, citing the ongoing investigation. But GCHQ had already long unravelled the mystery and had been using the cipher in practical tests for years. Isadora guessed this particular Red Line cipher was the work of Declan. There was optimism amongst the team that their opponents hadn't worked out this little teaser yet.

The Land Rovers were the go-to vehicles for the RUC and the YCU had access to two silver unmarked Snatch models. They were powerful, could handle a variety of terrains and whilst they were not completely bomb or bulletproof, they gave the best protection possible for these young recruits. That's not to say the two teams didn't abuse the luxury of these cars a little, one of the Beta team had even taken their vehicle into Belfast for a booze run earlier. And the tutors were none-the-wiser.

The journey was less than ten minutes and the Snatch glided easily along the uneven roads leading to the yard. Tall fir and spruce trees lined the route as they headed off Limehall Road onto a bridleway with a large raised grassy verge separating the tyre tracks. It was clear that this route had been used recently but was so overgrown that it seemed otherwise untouched. The bridleway rounded a series of corners before Isadora noticed a clearing ahead and what looked like the remains of an allotment or market garden. There were broken greenhouses, an overfilled skip, which looked as if it was being reclaimed by nature, and a small parking area with weeds poking through cracked bare concrete.

The predominant sound was summer. Birds chattering in the late afternoon sun, a wood pigeon calling out its commands and the odd rustling of insects and small mammals. Nature was returning and the yard was peaceful.

The Land Rover was parked a generous fifty yards away whilst the team inspected the site. Declan had mentioned blanks and breathing apparatus and whilst this was only an exercise, Isadora wanted to be absolutely on the mark when preparing her summary report. So, the team spread out and carefully surveyed the surroundings. It became quickly obvious that nothing was hidden amongst the broken glass and potting containers in the greenhouses. Aside from a pile of disused bags of compost and piles of redundant shingle, the centre of the site was just a wasteland. Had Isadora got her cipher coding wrong? Was this a mistake?

Ten minutes passed whilst they slowly examined the curtilage of the former allotment and whilst passing some overgrown fruit trees, Isadora discovered two stables. Again, both looked immediately empty, and the floor was dangerous for her to walk through as the concrete floor was cracked, uneven and had large sections of the base missing altogether. There was a visceral smell coming from the right-hand stable and Isadora half expected to see a decomposing horse carcass. Instead, more rotting wood and old feed bags.

Isadora called out to the rest of the team and three were quickly in view. Two of the men were sorting through the waste materials looking for anything hidden amongst the bags and the woman was walking towards Isadora and writing notes in a small book.

"Where's Craig?" She called out, scanning around her for the final team member. There was no immediate response or reply from her colleagues.

"I'm over here," A man's voice called. "I think I've found something." And the four members of the team clambered through the weeds and tall grasses and made their way to the stables. Isadora held back and shied away from that horrific smell. And then, just when they were in touching distance of the young man, all peace was shattered.

There was a noise, an almost unfathomably fierce and loud blast. It was as if suddenly all of the oxygen had been vaporised from the air around. Followed by an enormous flash of light and a further terrifying explosion. Isadora felt an incredible force of physical impact as if she had been shoved hard to the ground and simply couldn't recover. Everything hurt. She put her hand to her face and felt grit stinging her skin. And then suddenly, total silence. Isadora had been deafened and everything else, her sight, the smell, the atmosphere, was incoherent and puzzling. The final sound was the muffled noise of the Snatch car alarm going off in the distance. Isadora had an insatiable need to sleep.

Two, three, four minutes passed. Slowly pieces of rotten wood, plastic bags and paper came floating down to the ground, still burning. There was a reflection of flames on the remains of the greenhouses, turning everything red and angry. A crow started cawing in the distance as if laughing at the terribleness of it all. The agony and insanity of the situation.

Isadora staggered tentatively to her feet, her clothes hanging in shreds off her. She was feeling shaky and almost mesmerised by the scene. She was having trouble seeing and her ears felt like they were stuffed with cotton wool. She moved towards her team and the scene became all the more bewildering as she realised. This was death, this is what they'd been taught could be the end result.

Without even registering the annihilation in front of her, she moved towards the Land Rover and away from the scene of tragedy. There was nothing left to salvage, no hope. She opened the car door, collapsed over the front seats and was instantly unconscious.

CHAPTER SIX

Jones had only ever flown once in his life and that was to Majorca when he was 15 years old. So, arriving at Gatwick with the Topaz group was another surprise. A vintage Bedford minibus with the former Milton Tech and Secretarial College branding fading on the side pulled up outside the terminal with relative ease. McNally and Virginia had sat randomly amongst the group in the bus, and they were joined by another member of staff, Mr Armstrong, who sat up with the driver. He was probably in his early thirties and wore a full navy blue Umbro tracksuit and black Hi-Tec trainers. Armstrong was blonde, muscular and chiselled. And one or two of the female members of Topaz looked joyous about his addition to the ranks, although he did appear to have the annoying habit of running his hands through his blonde hair every five minutes as if he was auditioning for a Timotei advert.

For once, Jones had dressed appropriately for the trip as his jeans and green polo shirt combination was very much in keeping with the rest of the group. Only the strawberry blonde woman, now without her mobile phone, was dressed for business in a sharp suit and knee-high black boots. Maybe she knew something? He'd packed lightly but ensured his brown parka and a scarf made the trip, rolled up in the base of his backpack.

As they were herded through the terminal building, McNally handed them each a brown envelope with the vaguest details of accommodation and a blue UK passenger document. Jones was surprised to see that his already featured a recent passport photo and he was left to sign at the bottom. He looked up on the destination board to see their next stop was Aldergrove Airport, north of Belfast in Northern Ireland and presumably McNally's home ground.

Northern Irish politics was turning a corner, but peace was still a pipedream and the mainstream media painted a picture that would concern the majority English Topaz group. As they touched down at a cloudy and dismal Aldergrove, Jones peered out of the aircraft window. It looked cold. Perhaps this is why McNally insisted on winter coats in July.

Aldergrove Airport was only barely set-up for civilian aircraft, a small customs channel and a deserted WH Smith greeted the 15 youngsters and McNally strode purposefully towards the exit with his trench coat flapping around his midriff. Ahead of him, customs and Army sentry points. With such scarce facilities, hopes of a jumbo Toblerone and a duty-free pack of Silk Cut were quickly extinguished. This was a military airport and most of Topaz, if not all, would never have come across armed soldiers or police in the UK. Whilst they faced limited checks, it was a wake-up call for the 18-year-olds. Just as the group was coming to terms with the location and had collected their luggage from the carousel, Virginia waved her arms in the air to call the group together and soon after McNally and Armstrong started calling together pairs of the Topaz group and shuffling them off into awaiting taxis. They reeled off the surnames and taxi numbers and one by one Topaz made tracks.

"Jones and Richmond, taxi number 14" came the call from Armstrong. Jones quickly spotted his partner. It was the strawberry-blonde woman with the business suit. And, as Jones quickly spotted, a fairly enormous suitcase which would better suit a family of four travelling to Los Angeles for a month. Still, it was only a journey to their accommodation, Jones put any concerns to the back of his mind.

As each of the Topaz group paired off, aside from a sole group of three, Armstrong and McNally ticked each name off on a clipboard and Virginia chatted to the taxi company representative at a purpose-built kiosk by the exit. Two soldiers stood watching and a few more were playing fruit machines by the taxi desk, smoking and flicking the ash into trays which littered the tables next to the kiosk. Every soldier sported the same moustache and a look of abject indifference. Welcome to Belfast.

As the Value-Cab taxis raced off the rank, Jones quickly noticed that they were going in different directions once they'd navigated the terminal car park roundabout. Some were travelling off towards Belfast and others were taking country roads further into rural Northern Ireland. Jones quickly started to memorise the signs and gain his bearings. The signs suggested Aldergrove was some way from Belfast. He saw directions to Muckamore, Templepatrick and Ballyclare. But then once he was beginning to follow the route confidently, the driver doubled back on himself, and Jones saw the airport building again and a few other taxis with Topaz students in the back. Jones scrambled into his backpack and found the purple book. He was almost certain there was a city plan of Belfast amongst the maps as well as some tourist information.

His partner, Jenny Richmond, was getting carried away chatting with the taxi driver. Mr Brian Legge, as his licence card revealed, was blessed with another impressively bushy moustache. Brian had almost run through his entire life story with Jenny and he talked at an alarmingly quick pace. She was struggling to keep up but within the brief holes in conversation, as Brian took a breath, she pretty much revealed everything about herself. It was to be short-lived white noise which was simply an irritation as Jones tried to fathom out what felt wrong. He stayed quiet and wasn't in the least surprised when the driver simply parked the taxi next to a farmer's field, switched on his hazard lights and handed Jenny a manila envelope. She tore it open, and Brian peered over her shoulder with interest.

"Welcome to Northern Ireland. Make your way to Thiepval Barracks in Lisburn. Arrive at exactly 00.01am tomorrow, wear your winter coat on arrival. You may not use currency with the Queen's image to pay for items and you must not mention the challenge to members of the public or armed forces. You are to remain with your partners at all times. Do not tip or bribe the Taxi Driver."

Jenny looked at Jones with astonishment. Brian moved to the boot of the car, a silver Ford Cortina, and fetched their luggage. Richmond's large suitcase was going to slow her down, as were her knee-high heeled boots. Jones fancied a pint and slung his backpack onto his shoulders. It was 5.45pm and the Northern Irish weather was undecided on its next move.

As the Cortina and Brian vanished into the distance, Jones sat on the grass verge and hastily began to work out where he was on the city map. Jenny looked forlorn and watched Jones as he traced his finger along the line of the main road into Belfast.

"Exactly how far away are we from the Barracks?" she asked.

"No idea," Jones replied. "And neither Aldergrove Airport or Lisburn appear on this city map in the purple book. I think I memorised the route from the airport but we are going to have to find some local knowledge."

"How the hell are we going to do that? Have you ever been here before?" she asked.

"Absolutely not, but if we find a local community, we might find a pub. We'll get some answers there" he added and pointed at the chimney pots in the distance. Jenny picked up her case and harrumphed.

It took them almost three-quarters of an hour to walk into the nearest village. Jones was beginning to tire of Richmond's incessant moaning about her clothing, the weight of her luggage and the task. But McCracken's Bar, a small building with green wooden slats covering the exterior, was open and Jones could hear the fantastic buzz of drinkers and humour. The only issue was one of the rules. The image of the Queen was on all of their currency and neither was confident that McNally's spies weren't everywhere.

Jones pushed open the door and the assembled throng barely noticed their presence as they stepped inside. A few heads turned next to the bar and one of the older gents, sporting a faded grey fedora, checked out Jenny and her red hair. Jones and Richmond had brought the average age of the clientele down considerably, and Jones felt at home immediately. A short, bearded landlord, halfway through pulling a pint of stout, called over to Jones.

"How can I help you, fellas?"

"Do you take luncheon vouchers?" Jones enquired, to Jenny's astonishment. He pulled the royalty-free slip of paper from his wallet and offered it up.

"Do we take luncheon vouchers? That's quite the question." The landlord burst out laughing.

"Yeah, no bother. We'll take anything here. What will you be having?" Was the response. Jones looked across the bar with relief and made a quick choice. The Kilkenny looked like the local favourite. Jenny, on the other hand, was trying to gain

Jones' attention and urgently bring his thoughts back to the task at hand.

"I've only got a fiver on this voucher," he said, absent-mindedly and nodded towards the bar. "What are you drinking Richmond?". She remained silent and in the interim Jones ordered two pints, two pork pies and a packet of crisps. £1.40 a pint was a steal and the pies looked homemade. He located a table with two chairs. He'd drink the second pint himself if Jenny wasn't keen.

"What on earth are you doing?" She demanded. Her face was red with indignance.

"It's simple, isn't it? I'm winning friends. What would be the point of two strangers barging in here and expecting answers? Plus, look, two pints, food and no sign of the Queen's image anywhere" He explained quietly, looking pleased with himself.

Ignoring Jenny's displeasure, Jones noticed an AA map on the wall next to the payphone. The payphone was in use, with a small elderly man in deep conversation around horse racing. Jones could make out the discourse fairly clearly. The older chap was writing down horse names and odds on a small sheet of paper and asking questions about the current form. The whole pub was decorated in equestrian memorabilia and images of horses and jockeys dominated the décor. The only exception was a few prints of motorcyclists in 1970s racing garb.

Jenny had moved closer to the map and had found Lisburn. Just to the east of Belfast and down a bit. Someone had burnt a hole in the Perspex sheeting covering the map with a cigarette. But most of the route was still visible. It was a long journey on foot and there was no indication of where the barracks might be. Jones supped his pint and stuffed a large chunk of pork pie into his mouth. Retrieving his purple book from his pocket, he looked for walking distances and map keys.

"That's at least a four-hour walk from here," Jones announced, with a mouth full of pie. "It's getting on for 6.30pm now. It's certainly do-able. But do we want it to be doable? There must be an easier option." Jones looked around and sitting behind Jenny was a younger man, eating a crisp sandwich and flicking through a newspaper.

"Excuse me?"

The gent turned around, as did a few other locals within hearing distance.

"I don't suppose there's a train station locally?" Jones asked.

Before the younger man could speak, the chap with the fedora chimed in.

"There's not been a station in Muckamore since 1961. My father was a porter there. You'd need to get to Antrim now. And that's quite the trek. Where are you heading?"

"We've got to get to Lisburn. We're meeting family" Jenny replied cagily.

"Antrim to Lisburn is well over an hour by train. But Jasper works down at the Down Royal racecourse, not far from Lisburn. You won't need the train then. Hey, Jasper, when are you heading back to the stables?" Fedora man shouted across to the man on the phone.

"Will you be quiet?" Jasper shouted. "I'm busy here on the phone. What is it?"

"Do you fancy taking a couple of English down to Lisburn? I reckon they're lost. Are you lost, fellas?"

Jenny and Jones both nodded in unison.

"Aye. I'm leaving in about an hour. But, no bother, you'll have to sit in the back though. You can bung me a fiver for fuel." And Jasper went back to his phone call.

Jones sat back in his chair and opened the crisps. This was

shaping up nicely. Even Jenny sucked the froth off the Kilkenny and Jones saw her shoulders drop. Fedora man dismounted his bar stool and headed towards the gents. On the way, he caught Jones' eye.

"Don't let Jasper drink too much in the next hour. He's a handful after a few shandies, your girl might need to be on her guard."

"I'm always on my guard!" said Jenny "And I am certainly not his girl!"

In the intervening hour, Jones and Jenny Richmond became better acquainted. Her strawberry blonde hair ("It is NOT ginger!") sat upon a pale freckled face with no discernible make-up. She was shorter than average, maybe 5'1, with a very slender, boyish figure. Smiling, however, wasn't her thing.

She was a year older than him and had taken a year out after sixth form to work in Dolcis, the shoe shop and then she'd headed off to the French Alps for the ski season. He didn't ask whether she'd been skiing or was a chalet maid, which he'd heard was particularly lucrative. She lived with her Mum in Bermondsey and the family wasn't short of a bob or two. Jenny had a boyfriend who worked for British Telecom, 'high up' in marketing. She was nervous that he didn't have a clue where she was. "We speak every day" she'd explained. Jones was interested to learn that Milton College was her first choice and she'd heard "extraordinary things" about how good the course was. After their chat, Jenny had vanished for about twenty minutes whilst Jones sank pint number three.

His more pressing concern was his lack of acceptable currency, as his sole luncheon voucher was gone. It was a gift from his mother who'd been given the vouchers for a local authority time management course. In another feat of ingenuity, he persuaded the young chap with the crisp sandwich to exchange three local fivers (two Northern Bank, one Ulster

Bank, Her Majesty not pictured) for three Bank of England £5 notes. He used the first one to buy another round.

The pub was lively and instantly homely with around twelve locals chatting constantly, Jones regretted the need to get to Lisburn for 00.01am as he could safely have stayed there all night. Meanwhile, Jasper had only briefly put down the receiver on the payphone, to order another pint with a Bushmills chaser, and had written out lists of information which looked like Egyptian Hieroglyphics. It had now been an hour and twenty minutes since the pair had been promised a lift. Still, thought Jones, no dramas.

On Jenny's return to the bar, she looked like a different person. She swapped the business suit for a pair of jeans and a brown long-sleeved t-shirt. Her hair was pulled back behind her head into a thick ponytail which resembled a sunburnt pineapple. Her long boots poked out the top of her large bag and instead she was wearing bright white Gola trainers.

"I'm ready," she announced. And as if on cue, Jasper shouted a loud, slightly slurred cheerio to the locals and headed into the car park.

Jones peered into the front seat of Jaspar's battered Land Rover Defender and noticed it was almost completely full of bags of carrots and sacks of feed. There was no room for either Jones or Jenny and barely room for Jasper in the driver's seat. Noticing Jones' curiosity, Jasper pointed to the horse trailer at the back of the vehicle.

"That's what I meant by the back, take it or leave it." And he unlatched the door. The previous residents had left their mark with some gusto and Jenny's white trainers were unlikely to remain so for long. They clambered in, awkwardly, and Jenny looked horrified as she danced around the piles of brown stuff. They sat in the far corners of the horse box with their bags between their legs.

"Right," said Jasper. "Hold tight, you're not supposed to be in the back of these things and the suspension is dreadful. And, if I'm altogether honest, I'm a bit drunk. But I'm sure it'll be grand." And with that, he slammed the ramp door and re-latched it. Jones laughed heartily, that Kilkenny was working its magic.

As the Land Rover pulled away the pair were immediately slammed into the side of the box and then thrown forward. Jenny narrowly missed the poo.

"Oh God, I think I'm going to be sick."

It was almost total darkness inside the horse box. Light filtered through some of the wooden slats near the top shutter of the door but otherwise it was devoid of useful light. Jones had planned to use the journey to find out more about Thiepval Barracks from Jasper. How to get there from the racecourse and some local knowledge. But he was aware that he didn't want Jasper to think they were anything other than English students looking to meet up with relatives. Was Thiepval a village? Or just the name of the military HQ in Northern Ireland? Who knew?

The two barely said a word as the box hurtled along the roads, occasionally juddering left and right, stopping sharply and then shaking violently as the Land Rover picked up speed. Jones guessed they had hit the A30 when the road felt more even and secure, and he bent down to peer through a hole. True enough, he could see the countryside speeding past. And more intriguingly when they stopped briefly at a filling station, he heard young English voices. Perhaps the rest of Topaz had simply walked? With the time now approaching 9.15pm, Jones felt confident they'd aced this task and all that was left was finding the barracks.

Jenny had closed her eyes for the majority of the journey. Jones had checked on her occasionally as she squatted awkwardly on the hard floor. She couldn't possibly have slept, the terrain and suspension meant that was impossible. He knew she blamed him for the challenging journey, but a four-and-a-half-hour walk would have sapped their souls. Jones guessed she simply wanted to keep quiet and avoid conversation. On the other hand, Jones had been able to lay down with his body pressed hard against the wheel arch in the middle and he was able to rest a little.

After nearly an hour in transit, the Land Rover came to a stop and he heard the car door slam. Richmond's eyes were wide open now and they both expected the doors to be unlatched any second. But the sound of Jasper's boots momentarily headed in a different direction. They stared at each other through the gloom and then suddenly they heard the gentle patter of water hitting the ground. Jasper was relieving himself and time stood still whilst the two youngsters worked out whether this was unspeakably funny or just unspeakable. To Jones' surprise, Jenny started laughing.

Soon enough the Irishman opened the back doors and Jones and Richmond clambered out carefully. Jenny's pristine white trainers were caked in mud and manure and Jones' trousers were thick with hay bedding.

The Land Rover had stopped at a large stable complex. There were tens of dark wood stables with horses looking out serenely or munching on straw hanging from bags next to the stable doors. The horses even smelt expensive. Every stable had a coloured name badge and a few still had tack propped up or draped over the doors. Jones expected Jenny to feel right at home here, but she looked unimpressed.

"You'll need to head out through the back field," said Jaspar pointing at a gate in the distance.

"It's about a twenty-minute walk into Lisburn from there. Do you know where you're heading?"

"No, not really," said Jones. "But we'll make a call from a phone box when we get into town and meet up with our relatives. He rifled around in his pocket and pulled out the Northern Bank £5 note.

"That'll do nicely." Jaspar chirped. And the pair walked towards a white gate, the horse's eyes followed their journey with interest.

CHAPTER SEVEN

No-one was expecting Isadora's team to jump ahead in the task and when Barracks Alpha Briefing Room and the common areas were empty it was assumed they'd decamped into Belfast or Lisburn for a meal or a few drinks. There was no shortage of hostelries locally and the people are amongst the friendliest you could hope to meet. Despite everything.

With the weather now set fair and the coolness of the evening becoming ever more evident, Virginia Curry took her early evening gin and tonic to a makeshift garden table in the grounds of the Barracks. Armstrong and McNally had borrowed a civilian vehicle to see if they could locate any of Topaz as they made the arduous journey back from the airport. It was a four-and-a-half-hour walk but that's if you knew the way – and none did. The trial was more of a test of ingenuity than stamina, which would come later. But she wasn't heartless. She had a soft spot for her recruits and these moments when they were taking their baby steps in the field worried her greatly.

Being stuck in her ways, Virginia stuck to the same brand of gin and the same time for her imbibing it. Whilst the saying goes that it is always 5 o'clock somewhere, in Virginia's mind, the 9.45pm gin was a critical part of her routine. However, she was troubled by the thought of those 15 youngsters lost somewhere in a field near Belfast or walking next to a busy motorway. But this was nature's way of sieving the wheat from the chaff, and Charles, her ex-spook husband, had always liked to recruit the sneaky Machiavellian ones.

From the back window, she could see both the block containing the Briefing Rooms Alpha and Beta and the atrium containing the officers' mess and canteen. She loved the hum of activity and the feeling that she was making a difference to young lives but times were changing and even Charles' years of experience were being superseded by new tradecraft and technological advances.

With Isadora and her small team out of sight, the second group were milling around in Thiepval Barracks in Briefing Room Beta and were struggling with the cipher. Their team was led by a Welsh genius called Ewan and his approach was one of an absolute research methodology. Ewan was assisted by his self-proclaimed deputy leader, Rachel, who was the polar opposite. Rachel went on instinct and even after almost three years of gruelling training, she trusted her gut. All of their research led them to believe the safe house was in an industrial estate in an area of Belfast called Lennoxville, they could see on the map that the whole site was marked as wasteland. And further research from the Barracks' vast library suggested it had been derelict for many years and there was a nearby disused hospital that was crumbling after years of neglect. The site was an obvious option but Ewan hadn't cracked the cipher and there was little to gain from simply sitting on their hands and waiting for inspiration to come. Rachel had drawn a map of the area using the Ordnance Survey detail, complemented by a few aerial shots available in the library. She had also found the closure dates of both the former two-storey furniture depot and the hospital on microfiche. But the aim of the exercise was to unravel the cipher and that was the key, in so many ways.

Virginia saw the group pack the second Land Rover Snatch full of equipment and all five clamber inside. She had personally mentored Rachel and she raised her glass to her as she saw her jump into the front seat and slam the door shut.

When the Snatch raced off through the checkpoints and out of sight, Virginia ambled back to her base, a small administration office and picked up the handheld.

"Declan," she radioed, "Your Beta team have disappeared off the base. I told you Rachel would crack that cipher. You're losing your touch." There was a crackle on the line as she waited for his response.

"Oh, I don't think I've quite lost it yet, Virginia. I've left quite a scattered trail of breadcrumbs this time. But I'm not sure why they're bothering this late on a Saturday. I'd be in the mess now, probably three or four pints deep," he replied with a laugh. "We'll be back soon." With that, the handheld went dead.

The road between Lisburn and Belfast was notoriously busy and traffic was creeping as they approached the Ormeau Road. The streets were still littered with Union Flags, Northern Irish flags and then after a few blocks that changed to Irish Tricolours and green, white and orange kerb stones. And then, every so often, a Petrol Station with a parade of shops attached, a few pubs and seemingly hundreds of fast food joints. Everyone was quiet in the Snatch, this was simply a punt and Ewan secretly hoped that something about the location would give away the cipher and he could claim some small personal victory. Rachel was excited to just get out of the building and into real life but was also edgy about failure. Still, they had all day tomorrow to continue the quest if necessary.

As they pulled off the main road and through a rather run-down unionist part of the city, they could see the waste ground and the former hospital, utterly dilapidated and vandalised. The street light shone out as if illustrating a piece of bizarre modern art. Beyond that, they could see a large stretch of open ground and then the furniture depot, all in darkness. But Rachel could see the remains of an old clock on the front of the building, the hands were frozen at a quarter past eleven.

"Hold on," said Ewan. "11/15 is mentioned in the cipher. But I assumed this was a reference number or an American date. We might be onto something here."

In the back of the Land Rover, they studied Rachel's map and Ewan gave each member of the group a zone to investigate. They had torches and a fervent commitment not to touch anything until Ewan was present. Whilst the rest of the team carefully pulled back the metal barricades to get into the bottom of the hospital, Ewan and Rachel headed further towards the depot and clock. The silence was unnerving but the noise of an occasional car passing back on the main road was enough to break up the feeling of solitude. There was even the fluttering of wings in the darkness, which could either be birds fleeing their roosts high up in the rafters or bats making their first moves into the looming darkness.

The bottom of the clock house entrance of the depot was sealed and boarded by thick wooden panels and none of the original windows had survived. It looked impenetrable and Rachel shrugged her shoulders at Ewan as they tried in vain to shine their torches through a gap in the boards.

"Nothing doing," she said. "Let's see if we can get through the fence and in through the back."

But the fence had also been fortified by more wooden

boarding and this was covered in thick black paint. The only entrance point through the fence was via a small hole dug underneath, perhaps by a dog or fox. Ewan summoned one of the three other team members to help and they roughly kicked and dug at that hole with their hands, having left the spade behind. Rachel was able to slip underneath before too long.

"Use your handheld and let me know what you can see," Ewan said, head poking under the hole. "And be bloody careful." Minutes passed as Rachel shone her light around the former car park and back exit. She noticed a cellar door or chute and one of the metal latches was hanging free.

"I think I've found a way in," she announced via the handheld. Ewan quickly turned his volume down as her voice echoed in the darkness.

"Jesus, this place is still perfect inside. It looks like they moved out yesterday. There are loads of telephones, television monitors and... Eeek! rats! Loads of them. I hate rats. Let me see if I can open the front door. Get the other two over. We need to give this place a thorough going over."

Ewan grabbed the attention of the remaining two members and beckoned them to the clock house entrance. He appointed one lookout and waited for Rachel to open the door.

"I can't." They heard her say, handheld off. "It's stuck, but it's off the latch now. "Chaps, can't you all push? Maybe it's painted shut? Can you hear me?"

All four broke through the front door, with one remaining outside. Ewan managed to quickly get acclimatised to the dark and saw each of the team members with their torches blaring into the whiteness of the former reception area and then inspecting the piles of abandoned materials. There were carpet rolls piled together as if awaiting collection and two huge boxes of upholstery foam strewn in the storage area towards the back door. This looked like the home for the rats as hundreds of tiny eyes looked back from the torch lights.

Ewan noticed a small spiral staircase to the right of the building. And used his torch to point this out to the other three. Just as he did so, his handheld crackled into life.

"Ewan? Are you receiving me? This is Virginia at the base."

"Yeah, I'm receiving you. Go on." The voice echoed through the empty building.

"Is Isadora's team there with you? According to the checkpoint they were there a few hours ago. I've tried all of them."

"We've not seen them since lunchtime. They are not here and we have no idea what's in their briefing. You'd best speak to Declan." Ewan registered concern in Virginia's voice. However, he was untroubled, they had Craig in their team and he was famed for his astonishing drinking prowess. Isadora would have cracked their cipher and they'd be having a whale of a time.

When the line went dead, the group scurried upstairs and immediately spied four large containers in each of the distant visible corners of the L-shaped room. They looked like water butts and Rachel's immediate thought was that these were leftovers from the furniture depot. But on turning the corner Ewan quickly developed a different picture. With row after row of large green packing boxes covered in clingfilm, these almost covered the whole of the wall. Something felt wrong. These were new and even had fresh packaging labels on them. But closer inspection revealed that the boxes were simply filled with polystyrene balls. Each could be picked up by hand easily and confusion reigned. Nothing in the room or the empty depot suggested a safe house, bomb-making facility or even an armament store. Ewan motioned with his torch to head back down the stairs but Rachel was already heading over to the far corner to check out the water butts. As she got closer she tripped over something hidden amongst the debris on the floor and all hell erupted. There was a sickening firebomb that tore the top of the building apart.

All four containers exploded instantly and the whole of the upstairs of the depot was immediately engulfed in fire. It was an instant burst of vivid colour, a jarring and deafening sound, the immense splintering of shattered glass flying as the boards burst from the side of the depot. The plastic and chemical smell combined with the horrid metallic taste would be the last sensation the four would-be SIS operatives would ever comprehend. Rachel was killed instantly as she took the full force of the blast but the other three would have survived if the implosion of the building hadn't driven the ceiling, metal rafters and window frames on top of them.

A lone Beta YCU was waiting outside and as he picked himself up and assessed his shrapnel injuries, one to his face, he realised that the very worst had happened. His mind was immediately taken back to a session led by Declan McNally last year. He thought about the lessons he'd learned from that session and how that would now shape his future.

That session illustrated how chemical fires can cause dramatic fireballs. These were in sharp contrast to military explosives designed, say, to penetrate armour or bunkers. These result in mostly ballistic force, throwing up a lot of dust and debris and only a very brief, bright flash of light as detonation occurs. These were nothing in comparison to the enormity of a chemical fireball. He knew he'd just witnessed such a fireball. The explosion sent out a shock wave and whilst he had been pelted with debris and was struggling to cope with the dust and smoke, his mind was alert enough to recognise a dirty bomb and his first thought was to find cover, to clean himself thoroughly and to pray to God. Then, and only then, did he realise that his colleagues of the past three years had gone.

This was no exercise, no dummy mission, and this was meant to happen. In the space of six hours, the Alpha and Beta teams of the fledgling YCU were either dead, dying or indeterminably injured. And yet such was the regularity of explosions in the area, that even those who heard the blast less than a mile away carried on their Saturday evenings and simply waited for the sirens to come.

CHAPTER EIGHT

Jones was now less than an hour away by foot. He knew he could sit comfortably in the sneaky category which Charles so adored but he was also pretty proud of his ability to find alcohol in a desert. And this, as Jones and Jenny circumnavigated a field filled with wheat, was part of the motivation that spurred him on. In Northern Ireland, he'd read somewhere, you're never more than five miles from a pub. And there was lots of time before they were due at the Barracks. He spied a golf club in the distance and knew golfers love the refreshment found at the nineteenth hole. Perhaps a quick one? Jenny wasn't looking too enamoured by the prospect.

The sign ahead read Mazehill and Limehall with a turning to Royal Links Golf Club and the summer dusk was still warm enough for Jones and Jenny to build up a sweat, it had been a long day. As they walked the final few miles towards the town centre their legs ached and yearned for rest. Still unclear of the precise location and with Jenny persuasive enough to divert Jones' attention away from the golf club and presumed bar, they headed towards a gasometer they could see in the distance. The landscape also slowly revealed church spires and the top of a small tower as they approached. The view reminded Jones of home and this triggered a realisation that he was so far away from his parents. It felt odd that they had no idea where he was or what he was doing. Jenny, it seemed, was having similar thoughts.

"If there's no map in the phone box, I could ring my boyfriend. He's got hundreds of detailed maps at home. No-one would ever know," said Jenny.

"Let's not. No-one is supposed to know we're here. I'm guessing it's a project based on our ability to use our initiative. The last thing I want is to be drummed out due to cheating. Let's head into town. We just need to find a friendly soldier." Jones got the feeling Jenny Richmond was testing him.

If it was soldiers they were looking for, Lisburn had a vast selection. A forty-minute walk revealed that whilst Lisburn was a relatively small Barracks town it was very much a combined community. People were going about their business and the army fatigues simply blended into the civilisation. The Bunch of Grapes, on Belfast Road, was their first stop en route as they headed in from the countryside. Inside the pub was empty. A young bartender was leaning on the bar smoking and reading a magazine. She appeared surprised that she had customers and immediately focused on Jenny's huge bag, with the boots sticking out of the top.

"Tourists or recruits?" she said, almost bored. "Only we don't tend to get tourists here and hikers don't tend to have bags like that" pointing at the suitcase.

"Neither. We have family here. Big birthday bash. Oh, and two pints of lager and a packet of dry roasted peanuts please." Jones immediately sat down and made himself at home. Jenny looked exhausted and there was still an odour of horse manure in the air. The last of his fivers was handed over.

"English though," the barmaid continued.

"Yeah, English. My Mum works at the Barracks, in the kitchen," he lied. "Are we far?"

Ten minutes later and a map had been drawn on the back of a Smithwick's beer mat. It was approaching 10.30pm and the pub was only thirty minutes from closing. But the barmaid had taken pity on them as they were gifted two rather sorry cheese and ham sandwiches that were left from lunchtime. Pubs were the answer to everything.

As Jenny stared out into the shadows through the public bar window, a blue Ford Mondeo pulled up. Jones joined her and they stared in apprehension as they realised it was McNally and Armstrong who were exiting the vehicle and neither looked jolly. Armstrong had changed from his navy tracksuit to a pair of jeans with a figure-hugging black roll-neck sweater but McNally was still in the long coat. He had just casually thrown his cigarillo end into the grass verge. Fortuitously, they didn't appear to notice the pair through the window as they strolled into the lounge bar and were out of sight. Moments later, they reappeared with two large takeaway beer containers and several packets of crisps.

This was perfect timing for Jones and Richmond to make their final assault on the Barracks and head back into the countryside. They meandered up the main road, staying close to the footpath and counted the several military vehicles as they headed up the hill. As they took a sharp left the rural landscape opened up again and they saw fields of allotments as they took a footpath eastwards into the gloom.

Jones wasn't keen on the dark. And with no torch and Jenny's heavy bag to carry it was a struggle to follow the barmaid's instructions on the beermat. They'd swapped mainly as Jones' conscience was triggered when Jenny tripped down a small bank of bramble clinging to her baggage. She didn't find it funny. They kept a tall communications tower as their reference point as the town lights disappeared further and further away. The two devised a game to keep spirits up. It was Jenny's idea to run through an A-Z of world nations and kept score. They were still arguing about Palestine's place in world geography when Jones saw flashing hazard lights in the distance.

They came across a short path leading past a few derelict buildings. And Jenny came across a single black shoe in the middle of a grass verge between tyre tracks. The flashing lights illuminated the path as the gloom turned to darkness and the Jones was craving the townscape again and the predictability of the ground underfoot. Jones noticed Jenny had stopped and was staring wide-eyed at the shoe.

"Jones, Jones....." she called. "My God, there's a foot in this shoe and blood." She immediately retched and looked at Jones' horrified face. She rubbed her hands quickly down her jeans as they immediately felt dirty.

"Put it down, Jenny. Let's report this when we get to the Barracks." Jones said breathlessly.

For a moment, they stood staring at the shoe and Jones' mind ran through a series of next steps in panic mode. This was the fight or flight signal he'd heard about at school. He needed to get away from this discovery quickly.

All of the darkness, the flashing hazard lights and the change of temperature made Jones grab Jenny's arm momentarily, as if pulling her away from danger, and run further along the path. They hurried past the flashing lights of the Land Rover and then continued along the narrow path away from the eeriness. Jenny's bag suddenly felt full of stones and heavier than ever. The grass was, by now, up to their knees in places and Jenny simply couldn't stop and take a breath. She needed to be away and had no interest in what more was to be discovered. Jones felt his heart pump faster and faster. He felt the sweat dry and cold on his face and had two thoughts. What was this? And how can he find out more?

As they reached the top of a small hill and looked behind them, Jenny panted as she sat on Jones's backpack, Jones could see another set of car lights joining the Land Rover and within their two-minute recovery time, all of the car lights went off. No more flashing in the distance. The pair watched as two torches flashed across the night sky. Jones didn't believe anyone knew they were there and he told Jenny as much, but she remained silent. Jones' watch flashed 11.35pm. They had thirty minutes and they made their way back onto the road and into civilisation.

There was an almost instantaneous need for the pair to hide, even though there was every chance that other members of Topaz would be arriving along this lane heading towards the Barracks. They even ducked behind some small hedges when cars went past, full beams blaring as they headed towards the top of the hill.

For a while, they sat at a bench overlooking a children's play park. There was a small flickering light overlooking a large industrial-looking metal slide. Insects were buzzing around the bulb. Jones wanted to talk about what they'd just seen, but Jenny still looked bewildered. The day had been challenging from the start but to come across something so horrific was a punch in the guts. In his mind, Jones was already planning the conversation with Virginia.

As the time ticked by they both silently picked up each other's bags and walked to the gates of the Barracks. The entrance was busy with cars and military vehicles still moving in and out, drivers would be stopped by a couple of officious-looking soldiers, who would either look at a clipboard or look at their passes and wave them through. Another two soldiers would appear and thrust a long pole with a device attached underneath vehicles, clearly looking for explosives. This pattern repeated itself on three or four occasions as the pair moved round to a pedestrian entrance and were stopped by a soldier with a lime green beret. They were asked their surnames and the name of their organisation, after some thought, they gave the organisation as Topaz and the soldier, requisite moustache in place, escorted them down a gravel path next to a large brick building into a portacabin. The pair were surprised to be on their own, Jones checked his watch and it was unequivocally 00.05am. Twenty seconds later, the moustached soldier arrived with two manila envelopes and then silently left the building.

"Welcome to Thiepval Barracks. Change into your winter clothes and walk through the door in front of you. Leave all luggage at the back of the room. Carefully find a seat and wait for the film to start. At the end of the film, there will be questions based on observation and understanding. You are to remain alert and vigilant."

There were two doors facing them and they were blacked out. There was no sign of what was beyond. Both Jones and Jenny Richmond were exhausted but the horror of the shoe was still etched in both minds. Jenny was still frantically wiping her hands down her jeans as if covered in blood but they seemed spotless. Even though they barely knew each other, Jones was worried about Jenny and wanted to urgently speak to someone about the find.

Quickly, they changed clothes and Jones found an aged navy hooded jumper and his winter coat. He threw the jumper on over his polo shirt. He did it up tightly and looked round at Jenny. She had removed her brown long-sleeved t-shirt and was rooting through her oversized bag in her bra. Before pulling on a fawn jumper with a snow scene on it and a pair of gloves.

"Do you think we'll need these?" she held up the gloves to

him and he stifled a grin as his brain recognised the insanity of the situation.

"No, I think you're fine with the skiing jumper and a massive coat. In the middle of summer. Don't you?" He smiled, and fleetingly she smiled back. "It's going to be okay, you know? We'll get through this." Without further words, they pushed their bags to one side and walked through the double doors into darkness.

CHAPTER NINE

In Lennoxville it had taken just eight minutes for the police to arrive and two Land Rovers from the British Army had also pitched up. A police cordon had been erected at the end of the road and a small crowd had built up. It was past midnight now and although the temperature had dropped, most of the locals peering over the police tape were in short sleeves and holding a beverage. There was a local working man's club a stone's throw away and it was getting near chucking out time so a few had congregated, beers in hand. An elderly couple with their small excited dog stood next to the derelict hospital and there were whispers about a gas explosion, there would be much debate about this for many months in the local community. But there was a definite difference in the Lennoxville explosion, this wasn't a mortar or Semtex. This was a fireball, this couldn't have been the work of terrorists. Could it?

Preventing the locals from seeing the immediate scene was an ambulance. It had been parked diagonally outside the remains of the clocktower building but far enough away for the police, with a temporary floodlight and torches, to properly examine the scene.

"So, tell me again son, there were five of you. You're one of five students from England and you were examining the building as part of a training exercise. But you didn't have permission, is that right?"

The young man in the silver space blanket nodded at the bespectacled police officer, who was writing notes on a small pad. The man's hearing was beginning to recover and he was running through his emergency routine, drummed into him by Declan, about what to say when questioned unexpectedly by RUC plods.

"Can you give me the names of those inside the building when it went up? And who should I contact at your college?" The officer continued.

"I've told you all I can," the young man quietly responded. "To be honest, everything is a blur. I never went inside. I never saw the interior of the building and I've got no clue what led to the explosion. It was a simple exercise for my communications degree around following map references and looking for a location. I don't know why they went inside."

"This is all very odd." The policeman turned to the paramedic and nodded as he exited the back of the vehicle. He picked up his radio and started talking loudly.

"My Chief Inspector will be here shortly, she'll want to speak to you too." The officer shouted back into the ambulance. But the ambulance was already prepping its journey to Belfast City Hospital. Although the young man would have preferred Lagan Valley Hospital as this was closer to home. But, incredibly, aside from some temporary deafness, a nasty shrapnel wound to his face and a few cuts and bruises to his right arm he felt fine. The shock and emotion would come later.

As another RUC officer moved the tape aside for the ambulance to make its departure, the Chief Inspector arrived in an unmarked Silver Vauxhall Cavalier. In just twenty minutes she would be told that there were four bodies in the remains of the depot and there was a troubling powder which had been sent off for analysis. The police had donned hazardous material equipment but initial evidence suggested there was no need to evacuate the local area. The possibilities ranged from a terrorist armament store which had been booby-trapped in some way using low-level chemicals, a targeted explosion using an unusual charge or a simple gas explosion triggered by a lit cigarette or naked flame. Nothing was off the table until the crime scene examiners arrived.

Chief Inspector Orla Massey, four years into the role with the Royal Ulster Constabulary, had seen tragedy and witnessed the savage loss of life due to sectarian hatred. She'd also seen the normal, everyday homicide too in a career that had started down south. But something appeared off about this. These were college students, or so she had been told, and she couldn't immediately quantify why these would be targets. There was no warning, no obvious motive and absolutely no intel that had suggested anything in Lennoxville was likely. This was generally a peaceful district and whilst nothing surprised her, something didn't add up.

In the short term, she needed to get a briefing from the on-call pathologist, find out the names of all four of the dead and start the process of informing next of kin. She made a mental note that she needed to get hold of the college quickly and understand why they were there. This would help in keeping the press off her back too. And as if on cue a television crew had arrived on the scene and were setting up next to the derelict hospital.

One phone call, on her bulky new-issue Carphone, drew the curtain back on the 'students' and their role. Somebody back at base had joined the dots from the briefing in Enniskillen to this fatal explosion. Suddenly they were targets and this could very well be a planned hit. The Young Communicator Unit rang a vague bell in the back of Massey's brain and she hated dealing with MI5. They were normally English, difficult, and somehow untouchable.

"Bloody hell, how in God's name am I supposed to deal with that? They were just kids! Can you get me the local MI5 liaison officer and can someone get Thiepval Barracks on the telephone? Tell them they've lost four of their trainees."

In an ambulance careering at 40-50mph up a deserted Lisburn Road, Stephen, the sole Lennoxville survivor picked up a crackling from his handheld device. He immediately assumed this was the ambulance radio, but on holding it to his ear he could pick up faint noises and cries.

"Help me, please help me. I'm hurt. Is anyone there?" and the crackling, whistles and fuzz swallowed up the female voice. Quickly silence was restored.

"Hello, this is Stephen from Beta group, who is that? Can you read me?" but to no avail. The red battery light on his handheld was flashing and he was surprised that it had survived intact at all. Stephen held onto the side of the stretcher and thought that someone else might have heard that cry for help. But, with the rest of Beta dead, Alpha similarly embroiled in tragedy and Virginia, McNally and Armstrong out of reach, the cries went unheard.

CHAPTER TEN

The blacked-out doors led through to a large room, three times the size of the original portacabin but with similarly blacked-out windows. Desks were laid out in examination style, rather like Jones remembered from his GCSE nightmares and there was a large pull-down screen positioned centrally. They opted for seats next to each other, they were at least an arm's length away and there was a strange feeling of disconnect for Jones. There was a curious amber or orange light coming from the very front of the room and this was just enough light to use the pencil and paper laid out in front of them.

He looked around the room, remembering that fifteen students made the trip to Aldergrove, he noticed there were only twelve remaining. Three somehow hadn't made the cut, maybe they'd got lost or hadn't arrived in time? The two students in front of him looked very dishevelled and he wondered what on earth had happened to them on the four-hour walk. In the meantime, he focused on waiting for one of the tutors to walk in and deliver instructions, so he could explain about the shoe and the bloody foot.

Rather like a cinema experience, the projector spluttered into life and displayed a further message.

"This is a public information film. Please watch the film very carefully and await questions at the end. This exercise may be repeated."

The film then whirred into life and he watched with interest as his colleagues across the other tables leant their arms on the table, heads in hands but pencils at the ready, as the subject matter became clear. It was, unbelievably, water purification systems in Nairobi, Kenya. And from the word go, the technical detail was extreme. Right the way down to the size and the shape of the filtration systems and the gauge used to measure rainfall. Jones rapidly wrote words down, just little prompts and when Jenny caught his eye with a questioning look, he motioned that she ought to do the same. Although he could tell just from her mannerisms that she was still recovering from the horror of it all. The film was at least 45 minutes long and his body was beginning to long for rest. Not necessarily to sleep, but just to stop thinking and registering what was going on around him.

At the end of the first 45 minutes, a series of questions appeared on the screen. One after the other. This was technical detail, facts and figures, locations and simply the rudiments of the film's basic premise. But as the final question appeared on the screen, two things occurred to him. Firstly, that he was finding this devastatingly easy and secondly that the room was getting noticeably hotter.

After a break of two minutes, the second film appeared on the screen. This time black and white and the subject matter was tin mining in Cornwall. The narrator's voice was slow and deliberate, it was a film from the 1950s and in a Pathe News style, just without the trademark upbeat music. Again, he followed the dialogue carefully, wrote keywords and awaited the questions. It was 02.30am but, for some insane reason, he was exhilarated. Jenny, on the other hand, was struggling. Similarly, the following film about the Beeching Report for Rail Reorganisation in the 1960s also wedged firmly in Jones' head and the answers came thick and fast. He began to associate individual facets of information with words or pictures and when the questions came it was firmly implanted and retrieved easily. This was a part of his brain he had never used before and an odd discovery at 3.30am in an almost pitch-black converted portacabin.

For the first time since they arrived in the room Jones saw real people, not counting his fellow students, of course. Virginia looking her normal focused self, arrived almost silently in the room wearing a summer dress accompanied by another impressively moustached soldier. She walked to the front of the room as the next film whirred into life and with obvious care, woke up and removed three students from the exercise. Jones could see a look of sympathy on her face as the three were slowly led away. He half pitied them and half envied them, a bed awaited and a new day.

The temperature had been hiked up a notch again and Virginia walked around the tables and placed achingly small glasses filled with water on each desk from a small tray. And once again, she vanished into the dark. The film concerned the formation of the Okavango Delta in Southern Africa. He saw another pair of shoulders slump ahead of him as the film reached its grindingly slow crescendo and more highly technical questions, only answerable through unswerving dedication to the film or detailed notes, appeared on the screen. Jones could feel that his polo shirt underneath his hooded jumper was wringing wet and he could also feel the backs of his legs where he'd been sitting on the plastic chair collecting sweat. He was uncomfortable but felt resilient. Virginia reappeared and two further of the Topaz group were escorted out, one of whom was almost carried from the room by the soldier. There were now seven students in the room, Jones and the flagging Jenny Richmond, and a quick headcount suggested three other women and two males.

There was a moment in Stanley Kubrick's 'A Clockwork Orange' when the main character, Alex, eagerly takes up an offer to be a test subject for the Minister of the Interior's new Ludovico technique. This is an experimental aversion therapy for rehabilitating criminals within two weeks. Alex is strapped to a chair; his eyes are clamped open and he is injected with drugs. He is then forced to watch films of sex and violence, some of which are accompanied by the music of his favourite composer, Ludwig van Beethoven. Alex becomes nauseated by the films and, fearing the technique will make him sick upon hearing Beethoven, begs for an end to the treatment.

Jones, had this vision in his head when suddenly the film turned to Nazi atrocities during WWII. It was a graphic illustration of the horrors of the forced medical experiments inflicted on people of the Jewish faith at Auschwitz-Birkenau. Several major perpetrators were never tried for their crimes, among them Josef Mengele, a doctor at Auschwitz. He'd learned a little about this during his GCSE History but was keener in those days to vanish to the school fields for a few disco biscuits and to drink White Lightning Cider and bottles of Castaway mixed before regular 'technicolour yawns' behind the cycle sheds. This horror focused his mind but he was careful to try to compartmentalise the absolute savage cruelty of the experiments against the need to simply retain facts to answer questions. The watching was tortuous and the listening was vital. And he noticed that Jenny had decided to close her eyes to ensure the listening took priority. Jones' brain was now accustomed to the facts, the systematic storing and filing of information before retrieval for the questioning at the end. But he was slowly baking and was craving the water in that glass and the feel of cool air. But he knew he couldn't experience either until this task was complete.

The horror show was finished and he'd learned a great deal and the world, he hoped, had moved on from this ghastly chapter. Back in Thiepval, Jones noticed that Jenny's eyes were still shut and with the end of the questioning looming he broke cover and kicked her table leg. Waking her up instantly. She stared at him almost pleadingly to just let her sleep, but they'd come too far and surely the exercise was coming to an end. Virginia circled the room like a raptor looking for prey and escorted two more souls to their fates – whatever they may be. A cool breeze and a nap might just be worth it though.

There were now five and Jones was soaking wet, even his trainers were squidging as he moved his toes. The temperature was now almost unbearable. Jones dipped his tongue in the water and let the moistness wet his lips. Jenny quickly copied him and shrugged her shoulders. The film started. It was the history of the British Leyland car plant and nationalisation. Oh great, thought Jones, my Dad used to have an Allegro. And he tore off another sheet of notepaper and settled in. It was now nearly 5am and in-between films he could hear the dawn chorus outside. Jones had never remained awake this long. Or at least, not without the significant narcotic intervention provided by 'Big' Alan whose office was the gents' toilet in the Wheatsheaf back home. Jones kicked Jenny's table leg again as she nodded off and he was rewarded to see her eyes widen quickly.

The plight of British Leyland was a sorry affair and there was undoubtedly blame to be apportioned to the government of the day. He found himself pushing the pencil and paper to one side and simply soaking up the information, almost like a challenge to himself. But also, as he looked down, he found the tiredness was affecting his ability to cope with the light of the room and his eyes were struggling to focus. He wasn't about to fall asleep, he knew that, but he was beginning to wholly rely on his ability to retain the information. Jenny's head was in her hands, propping her head up whilst she stared, half transfixed and half comatose, to the screen.

The last of the questions appeared on the pull-down screen and Jones had finished his notes when Virginia appeared once more and suddenly the five became three.

To Jones' surprise, the lights went on. There were to be no more films. The immediate brightness of the luminous strip lights which flickered into operation hurt Jones' eyes and he looked around the room noticing a sea of empty desks. Half-written notes and tiny plastic beakers of water littering the room.

"What now?" Jenny whispered, her eyes watering as she rubbed them to acclimatise to the light. As if answering the question, Virginia appeared.

"Jones and Richmond," Virginia announced in her jolliest voice, a remarkable feat for almost 6am.

"I think you've made quite an impression on our assessor. You are our only survivors." A bearded man in a brown parka stood up from the far corner of the room and walked towards Virginia silently acknowledging her as he did so. So, the assessor was the third person in the room. He must have been taking the scores. Jones' mind was now finding thinking painful.

"Jones," she continued. "You should know that in my twenty years of seeing this test take place, you are amongst our highest scorers in the questions. You were incredibly close to full marks. Having two survivors is also monumentally rare, so whatever you two did today in reaching the Barracks has given you a head start."

She perched on the edge of the desk directly opposite them with a half-smile. "I think it's bedtime now, don't you? I'll get one of the team to show you to your bedrooms." Virginia reached into a carrier bag by her feet and pulled out two glass bottles of Perrier water. Jones had never been so pleased to see a non-alcoholic substance.

"Actually," quickly added Richmond, "We need to show you something." And as if the plug had been pulled on her batteries, tears began to stream down her face. Jones too, found himself struggling to contain the emotion.

"We think there's a body down the lane. It's about a 15-minute walk." Jenny continued.

Virginia, without a word to Jones and Richmond, quickly walked through the blacked-out doors holding them open. "We'd better round up some troops and head down there. I suggest you find some more appropriate clothing and I'll talk to the night shift here. God, I hope you're wrong."

And whilst the pair clambered out of their sweat-drenched clothing, Virginia Curry scurried back through the portacabin door. There was no air of urgency, it was simply focus and thought that hung in the air. Jones and Richmond had no intention of sleeping until this was over.

It took Virginia, Jones and Jenny just 15 minutes to walk down to the bridleway. The night shift was short staffed and it was agreed that the Military Police and the RUC would be called once Virginia had confirmed the hazy detail delivered by Richmond.

Jenny had changed into a short green summer dress and Jones back in jeans and a polo shirt. The cool morning air was refreshing. Birdsong sound tracked their slow, silent, walk to the scene and yet nobody felt the need to add to the explanations as they got closer to the site. Tiredness ravaged their every thought and yet their senses seemed oddly crystallised. Jenny had previously explained three or four times what she had seen, the foot, the flashing hazard lights and the other car appearing – followed by torchlight, but she dreaded coming back to nothing.

They walked 100 yards down the overgrown access to the site before the scene opened up to them all. The foot, still where Jenny had found it, the terrible acrid smell hit them immediately, then the pieces of debris and paper strewn as far as the eye could see. Soon after, the sight of the Snatch vehicle, windscreen blown out and driver's door wide open. Passing the Land Rover and clambering over the remains of the car park they could see a scene of utter devastation.

As Virginia peered into the Land Rover, she saw small deposits of blood covering the backseats and an equipment pack opened and items scattered in the footwells. She had made the connection, she knew this was the Alpha team, young adults she'd had breakfast with earlier the previous day and had interviewed for their chance in the front line. But she held her emotion, held her tongue.

Jones walked further into the scrub, past the high grass and weeds and quickly saw the bodies. It was a sight he instantly knew would be etched into his mind forever, so much so that he called over to Jenny and Virginia Curry to stay back. Both, intrigued, immediately wished they'd followed his advice. The horror and brutality of the explosion was incalculably gruesome. Only one of the three bodies, the furthest away, appeared fully intact and a handheld communications device was still uselessly in the hand of the deceased man.

Virginia, who had realised the body count was one short, quickly made the call to the Barracks and the RUC. Within twenty minutes the place was crawling with life. Like insects slowly pulling apart roadkill. Soon nature and silence would return to this place but the shadow of the explosion would never leave.

Chief Inspector Orla Massey arrived to examine her second multiple fatality in less than a day and her notebook was already almost full. She was under-resourced and under pressure and there had been none of the trademark media announcements claiming responsibility. Maybe these were to come but as she walked, head bowed, accessing the scene and liaising with the crime scene examiners, her head was buzzing with tangents and half-information. Her fortnight in Greece would need to be cancelled.

Within half an hour, Jenny and Jones were back in the Barracks and had been directed to two bedrooms adjoining the now silenced Briefing Rooms. However, they laid huddled together on a double bed, still fully clothed, windows wide open and the curtains blowing with the gentle breeze. Their eyes shut tight as they held tight onto each other. No words were required and no invitations for closeness were sought. This wasn't romance. This was survival.

CHAPTER ELEVEN

By lunchtime the following day, the dejected souls of Topaz flew back into England and Milton College ready to be welcomed and subsumed into the Emerald group. Those who hadn't survived the endurance test had been released back to Milton and their dream was over. Topaz was now a group of two and they remained in another part of the UK with a wholly different train of thought. Within the next twenty-four hours they were due to join the other ten YCU members who had been under Virginia's guidance, or that was the plan. That now wouldn't be happening.

The news of the two incidents in Northern Ireland had been on the lunchtime news but no-one had made the link. The story was delivered in a tone which almost hinted at a tired narrative rather than the reckless ending of lives. Families, who hadn't realised their relatives were training in Thiepval were yet to hear news of their loss. That was to come.

Emerald's newbies would learn the rudiments of communication studies and ethics that would make them solid research officers and a subset would be trained to undertake covert surveillance. But they had failed Virginia's rather unique endurance test which analysed their ability to think innovatively and to retain information to build a brief under extreme conditions.

None of this bothered Tom Marsh and Carl Kelly who were busy following dots on a screen in a college teaching studio. Carl had ensured his blood sugar ratio prioritised the latter with another box of Animal Biscuits (beheading them was still raising a titter too) after a long seminar with Mr Singh on pioneering work in GPS technology. Tom, sitting to his left and equally absorbed by the screen, had been promoted to team leader in their current exercise.

They were following a GCHQ case study which identified a 'foreign' agent in a packed shopping precinct using only his mobile phone signals. This was fledgling technology as mobile phones were unwieldy and basic. But the signals and locations were becoming fantastically useful. This was a defining moment in SIS training, almost in the same sphere as the invention of radar in the past.

This technology had developed to such a degree that the handheld communication devices used in GCHQ and MI5/MI6 had rudimentary, but effective, GPS equipment installed. But this wasn't the case in YCU, they had very basic handheld radio equipment which simply acted as communications device. Almost like a CB radio with no power cord. But the YCU handhelds were still drained of battery incredibly quickly.

Both Alpha and Beta Teams from Thiepval had been issued entry-level handhelds and the other units belonged to Virginia, McNally, Armstrong and Mr Singh, who, incidentally, had hand-built every one of the devices to his exacting specifications.

But for Mr Singh, the basic nature of the YCU handhelds represented a challenge. He decided to utilise his genius to create his own GPS utilising US satellite technology, but not telling them, and certainly not informing Virginia or McNally. It was a labour of love but in Mr Singh's mind he was giving YCU the best as well as testing out his unique skills.

He had a sprawling workshop at Milton and a brain that throbbed due to the weight of ideas lodged in it. He had long known that covert surveillance would become easier in the future. This, he surmised, would be due to the general public's appetite for mobile phones – and these already had low-level signals that could be triangulated to reveal their location. The technology was there and being used in Cheltenham and he was simply 'experimenting' with it using his wonderful little handhelds. This was Mr Singh's big secret.

Tom and Carl were Tiggerish in their approach to problem-solving and although the rest of their cohort were either at lunch or discovering the hostelries of Milton, they were keen to share their findings with Mr Singh. Their exercise required them to use GPS technology to plot a map of where the fictional foreign agent was likely to be located now. And they had cleverly worked out that the agent was in a car park underneath The Barbican Centre in central London. That's where the signal had dropped and there had been no sign of it since.

So, with a box of Animal Biscuits in one hand and an Our Price bag full of paperwork in the other, Carl Kelly left Tom alone and hurried off to locate Mr Singh. He had been last seen heading upstairs to his office and into the maze of equipment stores and filing cabinets filled with the information and briefings that made Milton College tick. Halfway up the stairs, past Virginia's dark cubby-hole office and the Principal's meeting rooms, he noticed the long threads that had so fascinated Jones, the worm-like silk threads that were too small for telephone lines or computer cabling. Like Jones, he followed them up the stairs, along a dark corridor and towards the red door with the frosted windows. They were an oddity, and Carl's inquisitive brain wanted to know more. He also wanted to ensure he knew this information before Tom, as Tom's promotion to team leader had irked him more than he'd cared to admit.

As Carl strode purposefully towards the red door, a young female computer technician walked past in a brown lab-coat, Carl had often seen her around college and was captivated. But Carl suffered from an in-built awkwardness around women he found attractive, and in a moment of almost slapstick failure he attempted to confidently smile at the technician but instead his legs seemed to forget their traditional right/left walking pattern and tripped on a loose carpet tile. Retaining hold of both the biscuits and the record shop bag, he lunged headfirst straight through the red door, breaking it open, and landing messily in a pile of cardboard boxes. The technician let out a loud burst of laughter and was gone.

Mr Singh sat in a large leather chair beyond the boxes smoking his pipe and looked startled. The room was full of screens, machines and work benches. And the long threads disappeared into the back of a series of junction boxes immediately above the bank of black screens. The work benches were alive with electrical equipment, soldering irons and drills. At the back of the room was a large table with a game of 'Test Match', the cricket version of Subbuteo, in process. Still further back was a set of bunk beds, a small kitchenette and an exercise bike.

"What on earth are you doing in here? This is private! This is……." Mr Singh stopped, shook his head, and realised that Carl was struggling to get to his feet and had hurt himself. He helped Carl onto a chair next to the bank of screens. "Are you okay? No bones broken?"

"This is fantastic! You're like Q from James Bond, only with Subbuteo! What are all these screens for? And all these wires?" a torrent of questions flooded from Carl as Mr Singh turned and looked for a First Aid tin.

"Oh God! Twenty-six years I've been working diligently, and no-one has ever been in here. And then you! And your clumsiness. And it is all over!" Mr Singh sighed, gave Carl the first aid tin, and moved one of his slips to gully on the Test Match green baize. He quickly checked his fielder at deep third man before focusing back on his anger. He took an almighty drag from his pipe and pointed it at Carl.

"What were you doing up here anyway?"

"Tom and I finished the exercise, and we need some more work. Everyone else has gone," Carl shrugged. He had rolled up his left leg and was using some witch hazel to gently dab a graze. There was barely anything wrong with him, but his behind-the-scenes trip to Mr Singh's secret lab was an eye-opener. He couldn't wait to tell Tom.

"Those wires, above the screens, they're everywhere around this part of the college. What do they do?"

There was another moment of deep contemplation as Mr Singh sucked loudly on his pipe.

"Very well, I guess you're in here now. But mum's the word? If I hear this stuff repeated, you'll be doing nothing but map-reading exercises for the next six months. Am I clear?"

"We're clear," nodded Carl, and he jumped up from his chair. The injury quickly vanishing.

Mr Singh walked to the back of his lab, urging Carl to follow and pulled back a shabby bright red curtain. Behind was a large dumb waiter, a relic from when the College was a stately home, and Mr Singh climbed inside, squeezing his head just below the top of the door. After a few minutes, the dumb waiter arrived back in the lab and Carl gingerly clambered inside. It was a thirty-second journey to the top of the building and Mr Singh stood ready to help him out.

As he appeared out of the hole in the brickwork, he realised he was right above the entrance hall to the college but two storeys up and around sixty feet from the ground. And he used the opportunity to take a look down as Mr Singh followed him. He could see The Jericho pub and The Talbot Inn, the small parade of shops leading to the student halls of residence plus the confectionary shop and in the distance the train station. It was quite the view of English suburbia.

The threads had been pinned together onto the brickwork in small clusters. Then, before they pivoted upwards they had been colour-coded and directed into aerials about the size of a shoebox, but with a long protruding arm.

"This is my little secret. We have fifteen handsets. Each of these boxes communicates with a satellite high up in space and bounces the signal back from wherever that handheld might be. It needs work, the equipment drains the battery and it's not always 100% effective. But, in theory, I should be able to pinpoint exactly where our teams are within a given radius. It's effectively my own GPS system." Mr Singh explained, with pride.

On returning downstairs from the roof, Carl was shown the screens linked individually to the aerials. And how the prototype thin fibre optic cables, utilising power sources all over the college and even in the sub-station in the old public toilets near the Halls, provided uninterrupted electricity. Mr Singh, knowing the team were in Northern Ireland, showed Carl his GPS signal as an example, ensuring their locations remained confidential.

"If anyone found out what I was doing here, I'd almost certainly lose my job. But I'm not snooping. I'm inventing. And this type of information could be of national importance. One day, I'll get the call back from Cheltenham and my services will be in demand again." He added, with some sadness. There was a story here, but Carl wasn't going to ask any more questions, he was already fascinated enough.

As an extra flourish, he also revealed a small black and white television in the corner of the room that was receiving an Indian Television feed. At that moment, the flickering set was showing a Bollywood film and it was in the throes of a set-piece dance routine.

"Another little benefit from my prototype cables," Mr Singh smiled. "I get a little taste of home. And the cricket's on later. It's heaven!"

Mr Singh switched the screens off and sat back down in his chair. It's as if his lifetime of work was leading to this moment. The inventions and the cleverness of it all. But he was expecting to reveal his inventions to someone higher up the food chain than a first-year communications student.

Once the prototypes had been proved 100% effective, he had been planning to unveil it all to Virginia Curry, who agreed on the installation of the threads believing they were updated telephone lines. She knew he was clever but Mr Singh was aware that Milton's GPS would never have been agreed. Lying to her about telephone lines, and even using his technicians to help install them would crucify his career. For now, he revelled in finally revealing his prototypes and hoped Carl would keep schtum.

"Before I disappear, Mr Singh, could you show me one more thing?" And Carl nodded at the Test Match Cricket Subbuteo.

"Why on earth didn't you say? Do you play?" And the most unlikely of friendships was forged thanks to the power of plastic cricketers and a marble ball.

CHAPTER TWELVE

In Briefing Room Alpha at Thiepval, Virginia Curry was explaining the events of the last forty-eight hours to Jones and Jenny. Today was the day the two recruits were due to meet their second- and third-year colleagues. They were due to be a team of twelve and Jones and Richmond would have been separated into Alpha and Beta.

Instead, the room was almost empty. The sole survivor from the Beta Group, Stephen Finch, had finished receiving hospital treatment and he was awaiting a decision on his release back home to recuperate. . The Group Leader from Alpha, Isadora Brown, the shining star of the YCU, was still unaccounted for. She had either died in the blast or was elsewhere, Virginia suspected the former. They were awaiting Chief Inspector Orla Massey anytime and McNally and Armstrong were busily clearing and bagging the personal effects of the dead students. Lockers were stripped and bedrooms were cleared and cleaned. Ewan, Rachel, Isadora and Craig were all year-three trainees and were expecting to make the first steps into a more formal role in SIS if the opportunity presented itself. The excitement and ambition of at least eight

SIS trainees had been extinguished by two horrific deadly explosions.

Declan McNally's exercises were the issue. Both Alpha and Beta had found the correct safe houses and the remaining cipher, hidden within the two locations, would have led them to a final base in Templepatrick – where both teams would have been de-briefed and moved on to the next exercise. Yes, there were booby-traps planned to heighten the reality but both teams had arrived a day early and McNally hadn't even finalised the final cipher let alone booby-trapped the venues.

The YCU was a clandestine project. Whilst Virginia and McNally had the support of the RUC and Royal Irish Regiment and Thiepval Barracks staff had a degree of understanding, they had a duty of care over the YCU and something was wrong. Someone had either leaked the locations or there was a mole or moles within the group. Red Line or another paramilitary group had ripped apart the future of SIS but no-one had claimed responsibility. No one was carping or accepting the plaudits and this was odd.

In the meantime, life had to go on. Jones and Jenny had already spent time with Virginia fixing their cover stories. Jones was in Journalistic training for a regional newspaper in Dorset and Jenny was working in the Houses of Parliament as a trainee press liaison for an under-Minister. The parents had been dutifully proud and they were to expect regular letters and calls. Jones heard the relief in his mother's voice when she picked up the phone and he almost felt this permitted him to continue in this new life.

Jenny had been faced with a far more emotional dilemma. Her boyfriend, Jason, 'high up in Marketing' for British Telecom had taken a dim view of her being out of contact for three days. He would have been apoplectic if he'd realised Jones and Jenny had slept together for the past two nights, even though this was mainly due to Jenny's repeated nightmares. Jones had been the perfect gentleman. Jason had given Jenny the ultimatum of meeting him tonight at 9pm to discuss the relationship and her lack of calls. This was playing on her mind, as there was no way she'd be back in Bermondsey by 9pm and had no intention of doing so.

As Orla Massey arrived at the white-washed walls of Briefing Room Alpha, she was followed by McNally and Armstrong. It was a warm day and three desk fans were cooling the air from a series of small pedestals at the top of the room. A coffee percolator was gurgling away and cups were liberally spread across the long briefing table. Virginia had pinned a map of the area on the wall and highlighted the sites of the two atrocities. She had also tried to sketch out their likely routes from Thiepval. The Chief Inspector introduced herself around the room and sat down at the head of the table as those gathered filled their cups. Jenny, a non-coffee drinker, had found a glass of water and watched on with Jones.

"I'm sure I don't need to explain to you all how delicate this situation is. We are dealing with the deaths of eight young people who were part of a covert training academy based between here and several specialist colleges in England. I have had to seek the blessing of MI5 and the army to even interview you all," she continued.

"It has taken me the best part of two days to even work out who you all are. And even now, I'm not entirely sure I have all the facts as MI5 doesn't seem to have personnel records and some of you don't seem to officially exist. And yes, I'm talking about you, Declan McNally." McNally, the only person in the room in a coat, nodded sympathetically and sipped his coffee. Massey stood up.

"Virginia Curry, you're officially a shorthand tutor for Milton Secretarial College. But you're not. You're a spook.

Declan McNally, you're a former SIS operative from Derry who retired from active service in 1991 after injuries sustained during a car bomb. Joseph Armstrong, you're a former marksman turned Army Physical Training Instructor on detachment to this unit, again retired from active service with the Marines due to a training accident in Serbia and there's you two." Massey smiled at Richmond and Jones.

"You're the newest recruits to a unit and you found the key evidence that led to the first explosion in Limehall. To be clear, I am completely aware that you are all spooks, training to be spooks or something similar. But, Mr Jones and Miss Richmond, I have every sympathy for your predicament and you are not suspects. Should you wish to return home or to college, we can arrange interviews back in England."

"We're staying here," Jenny responded quickly.

"They'll be doing basic training here for the foreseeable future, Virginia and I will be returning to England tomorrow to undertake tutorials for our other cohorts." Explained McNally in his likeable Derry drawl.

Massey, still standing and locking eyes with McNally fired back, "I'm afraid you won't be going anywhere Mr McNally, other than back to the police station with me to answer some questions. You too, Mr Armstrong. I suspect nobody can provide alibis for either of you and you both have motives that I need to explore."

"Motives?" Spat McNally. "Are you saying that because I'm Irish and Catholic, I must want to kill a group of English kids training to work covertly? And what about Armstrong?"

Armstrong opted out of the conversation. McNally had done his talking.

"No, I'm not. What I'm saying is that the British Army destroyed both of your careers. And look at you now. Working at some bizarre spook kindergarten? Maybe you're frustrated that they had glittering careers ahead of them and yours are history. I need to explore that angle and find out where you were when both explosions took place."

"Anyway, this isn't just a multiple murder investigation. I am fully aware that this is also currently a missing person enquiry too. I will also need to talk to you all about Isadora Brown – whereabouts unknown." Massey took another swig of her coffee, she'd lost count of how many she had inhaled already and waited for Armstrong and McNally to follow her out.

"Let's get this over with." Armstrong half-shouted. And within a matter of seconds McNally, Armstrong and Massey had left the room. Virginia smiled sympathetically at her two colleagues as they were led away by two RUC constables who had appeared in the hallway leading from the Briefing Room to the exit. They were escorted to a vehicle waiting in the front. The room fell silent again.

"You don't believe they did it, do you? Why would McNally or Armstrong purposely set up exercises to kill their own teams?" Jones asked Virginia.

"No, I don't believe they did anything of the sort. But we must let the police do their job. I'm astounded that the policewoman only fleetingly mentioned the missing girl. Maybe we should roll our sleeves up a little. Are you game? After all, they'll be no basic training here without your instructors and I'm going nowhere." Not waiting for a reply, she marched back to the coffee machine.

"Where do we start?" replied Jenny.

"We must find poor Isadora. Either we find her and ensure her parents are given the news in an appropriate fashion, or she's alive and unable to contact us. Either way, we must retrace her steps and get some answers. In the meantime, we need some help," said Virginia. "And I have a reinforcement in mind." And with that, she vanished into her study.

Jones and Jenny walked back to the scene. The police tape was still up and forensics were still examining the area. What occurred to Jones immediately was the lack of focus on the second car, the car that arrived when Jones and Jenny had run away from the scene. Someone had switched off the hazard lights on the Snatch Land Rover. Also, the blood on the back seat. Whose blood was that? And why would they be bleeding in the Land Rover when the explosion happened at least 200 yards away? That had to be someone either recovering from the blast or hiding. Or both.

With absolutely no clue what they were doing or what they were looking for, Jones and Jenny followed the path from the explosion right the way up to the children's playground. Seeing nothing of any interest, they walked along the sides of hedgerows and verges looking for anything interesting. Perhaps she had walked from the scene to look for help? Jones grabbed a stick and imitating what he'd seen on the television, he moved the grass aside to look along gorse bushes and brambles. Jenny investigated the whole area around the industrial-looking slide and the green children's see-saw. There was nothing whatsoever. No more blood, nothing tangible that would link to the missing trainee.

Jones looked over at Jenny as she searched through the undergrowth and weeds near a vintage green roundabout. He did not doubt that this is the closest he'd ever been to a woman but wanted to avoid the pitfalls of a 'holiday' romance. Even though this was far from a holiday and romance wasn't even on the cards. Was it? He was exhausted but exhilarated at the range of emotions running through his head. He was trying to quantify the shock and horror of the sights he'd seen, this was still in his mind's eye when he tried to sleep. The enormity of the change in his life from being an 'also-ran' or average Joe back home to this feeling that he suddenly had an enormously important role to play here in Ireland and with this mission. He felt an overwhelming urge to get closer to Jenny when he had barely known her 24 hours previously. Even though he had no idea whether these new feelings were real, or simply the human need for company and closeness as he came to terms with everything.

As if hearing this thought process, Jenny beckoned Jones over and they sat on the same bench where they had rested on the night of their grim discovery. They sat close to each other, and she touched his hand. He responded with a smile.

"I'm going to tell Jason it's over." She announced. "Don't get me wrong. This isn't about you. I barely know you. But I do know that I can't give Jason what he wants from here and I can't live with the guilt of letting him down all the time. I want to give this absolutely everything. And if we develop into something, then so be it," she looked at Jones and he simply nodded.

"If we develop into something then that's fine by me too." Jones gently squeezed her hand.

"So, it's just me, you and Virginia now," he laughed and they walked back along the path, knowing this would be a brief respite before even more new horizons.

They had barely walked twenty paces when they saw Virginia walking towards them. She looked shaken and despite the sunshine looked cold, with her arms folded across her as she walked.

"I have some news. We'd better get back to base."

CHAPTER THIRTEEN

"My name is Isadora Brown, I was born on 5th November 1973 and today is Friday 21st July 1995.

I am a trainee in a specialist unit in the British Secret Service for young people learning covert communication.

I am injured from an explosion which was planned and executed by Red Line.

Red Line is demanding that Northern Ireland becomes free of British influence and reinstates a border with the Republic of Ireland to become a republic in its own right with its own freedoms.

I will be held unharmed until Monday 24th July when I will fall to my death at 12 noon.

This can be prevented by donating £2m sterling to Red Line in used Northern Bank notes. You will be informed of the drop site on Sunday.

I have not been harmed and my injuries are being treated. But you have been warned that Red Line will have no hesitation in killing me. This will be a message to Britain to stay out of Northern Ireland."

The film ended and the Briefing Room immediately fell

silent. This was a development no-one had expected and Virginia looked shocked and upset.

Virginia turned off the projector and pulled up the screen. She then quickly provided a summary to the assembled team, who had been supplemented by a uniformed Military Policeman and the guard who brought the package in. The film had been played on an ancient projector as it had been an old cine reel that had been left at the gates of the Barracks. It was marked for the attention of the YCU. It was in a tatty manila jiffy bag and the address had been scrawled by Isadora herself, that much was clear.

The film was grainy and her face punctuated an almost pitch-black scene behind her. This was the first time either Jones or Jenny had seen Isadora and he was immediately impressed by her resilience. She spoke carefully, fluently and whilst she was obviously reading a script, this was not a face in torment. She was injured but up for the fight. And this made him all the more determined to play a part in her release.

Isadora was wearing a white t-shirt and there was bruising above her right eye. There was no other obvious sign of harm and the camera never panned anywhere away from her face as she delivered the narrative. Virginia announced that both McNally and Armstrong had been released after questioning but were not to return to Milton. They'd be back in Thiepval soon. There was good news from Stephen Finch who had finally been released back home to Bangor for a period of recuperation.

Virginia explained that the film would very soon be couriered to Massey who would liaise with the Military Police and involve MI5. The package and the reel could be fingerprinted and the CCTV on the front of the Barracks checked. She guessed that the RUC would need to call upon many more resources to mount the search for Isadora as well as look into Red Line's financial demands. She could be anywhere and the Garda and

British Police would need to be informed and engaged. This was becoming messy and incomprehensible for Jenny and Jones. Virginia noted that there was a dead trail to the Red Line group. Only a handful of people were aware of its existence and McNally's attempt to build a brief on them for SIS had only gleaned fragments of information.

Red Line's ultimatum was a few days away and there was little Jenny and Jones could do, having not even started training. But what they did have was the world wide web which, although a mystery to many in the Barracks, had pages and pages of chat and information. Jenny had a working knowledge from her father's export business and Jones knew the basics. At the back of the room sat three modern PCs and a large printer. There was a dial-up connection, which was also connected to the Briefing Room Alpha line, therefore they'd be immediately cut off when the phone rang. But this gave them the base for some research.

Jenny logged on and began scouring message boards and any chatter about the explosions, including the news reports across Ireland and back home.

In the adjoining briefing room, the Military Policeman took a statement from the guard who had received the package and he headed off into Belfast with the reel. In the meantime, Virginia had been joined by an older man, perhaps in his early 70s, with a grey beard in a spotless black pinstripe suit. He arrived holding the biggest bunch of flowers Jones had ever seen and a warm smile which radiated confidence.

"A reinforcement has arrived," Virginia announced to the almost empty Briefing Room. "This is Charles, or to give him his proper title, Sir Charles Curry CBE. My husband."

Charles wasted no time in getting a full briefing from Virginia. He sat on one of the briefing room chairs with effortless charisma absorbing information and occasionally smiling and nodding to ensure full confidence. Jones could already tell they were quite a partnership.

And whilst Jones and Jenny were instantly relieved that their numbers had swollen, Jones was more delighted that Charles quickly whisked them all away to the Bunch of Grapes in Lisburn for a 'spot of lunch and a catch-up'. It was achingly hot outside and there were only wisps of white cloud in an otherwise perfectly blue sky. Everything feels better from the inside of a pub, thought Jones.

Virginia had driven the short distance in a bottom-of-the-range blue Ford Mondeo which she had been using during her stay and Jones quickly understood why she had taken the wheel. After just twenty minutes of arriving at the usefully quiet Bunch of Grapes, Charles had already ordered and quickly dispatched two neat Bushmills' Black Bush and had ordered a third. Virginia was sipping tomato juice and both Jones and Jenny were cradling pints of Harp Lager because nobody had said they couldn't. And Charles was paying. All four of them ordered Irish Stew, the special, and this was yet to arrive but massive chunks of wheaten bread and salted butter were positioned in the centre of the round table.

Charles cleared his throat as if about to make a speech at a banquet.

"I realise I am new to the case but I would urge you all to remain calm. The constabulary here are well versed in dealing with issues like this and they'll have the support of a range of other teams and agencies from across the UK and Ireland," he announced, taking a large pull from Bushmills' number three.

"It's important that you know that whilst I may be retired, I am still well connected across the different agencies and I will be helping join the dots, so to speak. You will also have a role to play, but very much in the background." He continued, quickly glancing at Virginia who looked composed.

"And that's another reason why I'm here. With Mr McNally focused on other things, I will be taking you through your basic training and that will start over the next few days." Charles made way for Virginia who was poised to interject. He quickly pulled out a packet of small cigars and dragged over a metal Guinness ashtray.

"Charles has an incredible background and this is a real opportunity for you both. I'm just saddened that this has happened in the face of such tragedy. Isadora is such a gem and we have such high hopes for her, and yet we've lost eight others whose families will soon feel such pain. Therefore, we have to keep the YCU alive through you. But in Charles, you have the very best tutor and mentor, believe me." Virginia was emotional but hid it as she immediately took a swift sip from her juice.

Jones had an odd feeling that meeting Charles might be life-changing but for now he was focused on other things. Primarily, drinking his pint and listening to the ongoing dialogue from the other three about the explosions and kidnapping. Jenny was sitting facing Virginia and he could tell there was a bond developing there. Virginia championed female recruits and with Isadora somewhere unknown, Jenny was in a good place to listen and enjoy the one-to-one coaching from Virginia. Jones needed the same from Charles.

"You appear to have a phenomenal recall, Mr Jones," Charles said as the stews arrived. "In fact, I'm not sure I've seen better. Where did this come from?"

"I'm really not sure," replied Jones, nervously. "I wasn't aware of my powers of recall until I did the test. It was as if I was able to slip into another gear as my body fought the tiredness."

"Quite," Charles responded as he dipped an enormous hunk of bread into his stew. "I think you will find those powers of recall, as you describe them, incredibly useful as you undertake your training. And the service will make good use of them too." And Charles picked up his glass again.

"We just need to work on your physicality and something called tradecraft. I'll explain all this in the next few days to you both. Being able to do it all in context, with this situation we have here, it's a real positive amongst the awfulness." And as if to bookend the conversation, Charles put his spoon down and walked to the bar. Jones stole a quick reassuring glance at Jenny but she was in deep conversation with Virginia.

Today has been a biggie so far, he thought. Isadora's deeply troubling ransom film, McNally and Armstrong carted off to the police station, Charles Curry personally mentoring him and Jenny finishing with her boyfriend. All kinds of doors open and challenges ahead. He swigged back the remains of his first pint and strolled over to join Charles at the bar, eager for a first refill.

CHAPTER FOURTEEN

JONES HAD BARELY SLEPT. NOT ONLY BECAUSE HIS BRAIN WAS FULLY engaged with the nightmare of the last 48 hours and the horror of Isadora's kidnapping, but also due to terrible indigestion from eating and drinking far too much in the Bunch of Grapes with Charles and Virginia. The early afternoon meal had extended long into the evening and Jones was now regretting it.

He had collapsed into bed and immediately slept, with Jenny wrapped around him, but something had stirred him at 3.30am and he'd been wide awake since. Jones had always struggled with the fuzz of ideas and theories trapped in his head and this, he believed, was why he self-medicated with alcohol. To stem the tide. But the tide had become a torrent recently and as he stared at himself in the mirror he could see the tell-tale signs of exhaustion.

"You need a black coffee," Jenny suggested, standing behind Jones and checking her complexion in the mirror. Jones was wearing a pair of Jenny's jogging bottoms as makeshift pyjamas and they'd crept up his legs to almost recreate MC Hammer's parachute pants. Jenny smiled at the image.

"I'm fine. Honestly. I just need to get my head into this new job. I'm surprised you slept so well. Didn't that Jason stuff play on your mind?"

"That's a conversation for another day," she said, looking to change the subject. "It's a line drawn, at least in the interim. I can focus on what we're doing here and poor Isadora. I'm up for this." As if to underline the point, she playfully pushed Jones out of the bathroom and shut the door.

"I'm having a shower now," she called from behind the door. "It's not long before we're off to Bangor to meet Stephen Finch. Poor guy was lucky to have survived."

"Bangor?" Jones said quietly.

"Yeah, you were too busy trying to chat up Charles to listen and I'm not sure you should be trying to match him on the Bushmills intake." Jones then heard the water from the shower jet hit the tiled floor and Jenny pulling across the curtain. Perhaps he should curb the spirits, he thought.

Jones was just assessing the possibility of grabbing a half-hour shut-eye when there was a knock on the door.

"I hope you're up and ready. I'm driving you two down to Bangor soon and we're pushed for time. Get your arses up. Aye?" McNally was flustered and impatient. God knows how they'd dealt with Massey's questioning and ferrying around the two newbies wasn't going to improve McNally's mood, Jones thought.

"We'll meet you at the canteen in fifteen minutes," Jones called back, realising that meant no time for a shower for him today. He grabbed Jenny's least floral deodorant, as his was back in Milton, and coated himself in it before opting for yesterday's wardrobe.

"I'll get you a bacon sandwich and a coffee and meet you in the canteen," he called through the shower door. "We have fifteen minutes," Jenny swore loudly in response.

Thiepval Canteen was full to the brim with soldiers eating

and smoking. The air was a toxic mixture of Ulster Fry and nicotine, but this didn't deter Jones. He headed straight for the back of the queue and was dead set on a heavy carb and caffeine uplift to banish the sleep deprivation. McNally and Armstrong were already seated towards the entrance to the Officer's Mess Bar. McNally was grinding another cigarillo into the ash tray and Armstrong was reading the Belfast Telegraph and drinking tea. The debris from two breakfasts sitting in front of them. Jones enjoyed people-watching but one thing stood out from the hubbub in the barracks, everyone was chatting happily and there was a general buzz of positivity. Aside from McNally and Armstrong who looked like two strangers, sitting in silence.

This oddness continued long into the car journey, after Jenny had finished her bacon sandwich en route. It was only a half-hour trip from Lisburn to Bangor and the scenery was stunning. Crystal blue clear skies met rugged coastlines interspersed with picture postcard beaches and little unspoilt villages. Jones noted there appeared to be an off-licence in every community as well as pubs everywhere. There was little sign of any sectarian issues aside from the odd union flag fluttering in the wind, tied to lampposts and aerials. There was no chatter in the car and the radio was silent.

As the blue Mondeo swung around the roundabout which led to Bangor town centre, Jones could see the marina ahead and rows of yachts and fishing boats lined up in the distance. The town was busy with a mixture of shoppers laden with bags and holidaymakers in multi-coloured beachwear and winning smiles. This felt light years away from the Troubles and the endless political skirmishes. McNally pulled the car over and lit up.

"Right. You're about to meet your other team member. He's a wee bright button is Stephen, but he still struggling with the shock of the explosion. Virginia thought bringing you here would cheer him up and perhaps bond you all a little. Does that make sense?" McNally watched as Jenny and Jones nodded before Armstrong chimed in.

"Importantly, you must not mention the Isadora situation. We don't want to panic him or rush him back to the unit. He must recover at his own pace. That was a hell of an explosion, and he lost his whole unit." Armstrong continued.

"The service has paid for him to spend a week or so convalescing in the sunshine. You're meeting him in the amusement arcade." Armstrong pointed across the road at 'Barry's Fun Time' with its abundance of flashing neon lights. Jenny suddenly looked buoyed by playing the slots and began ferreting around in her jeans pockets looking for loose change whilst McNally blew smoke out of the window. Jones was amused at the proposition of a group of spies in an amusement arcade, it somehow felt surreal.

"Hold on," Jenny interrupted. "What do you mean we're meeting him in the amusement arcade? Where are you off to?"

"We're using the range at Palace Barracks, near Holywood," Armstrong replied. "The last thing Stephen wants is us hanging around like a bad smell and we must ensure our firearms skills are up to date. Wish him well for us. We'll be back at 4pm and will meet you here."

McNally handed Jenny and Jones a £10 note each and motioned for them to open the door.

"Thanks, Dad," Jones laughed. And they both watched as the car reversed out of the layby and headed back away from the marina and town centre. Stephen Finch stood in the entrance of Barry's, his arm in a sling and with a sizable bandage on the right-hand side of his face. But he was smiling and seemed immediately pleased to see them. He held out his good arm and shook hands with them both. Stephen was athletically built with short-cropped brown hair and with a pale complexion. He looked gaunt from tiredness.

He had a military-style green shirt over his shoulders and was wearing a purple band t-shirt. Jones made out the band name 'Therapy?' from above his sling. This was a positive, they were a little shouty for his liking, but anyone that liked guitar music must be on the right track.

Jenny quickly offered her sympathies.

"Stephen, I'm so very sorry for the loss of your friends. I just can't imagine what you're going through. How are you feeling? How's the recovery going?"

"I'm okay" he replied, looking at the ground and appearing to lose himself in emotion momentarily. "My arm is almost healed now. It just aches. I have a piece of shrapnel embedded in my face and that's being removed soon. I've been quite lucky really. I just can't stop thinking about the others."

Stephen had a gentle Northern Irish accent and sentences seemed to tail off before they had properly concluded, almost as if Stephen was still debating how to finish them. Even though this was Stephen's manor, Jones felt that Stephen was like a lost child, looking for someone. Jones found himself struggling to break into the conversation as this thought reverberated in his head. He was just staring at Stephen Finch as Finch himself looked down at his feet and avoided eye contact.

"McNally and Armstrong dropped us off," Jones finally conjured up. "They're using the range at Palace Barracks."

"Ah, I wasn't expecting them to sit and hold my hand anyway. That's not McNally's style. Armstrong is a new name to me." Stephen briefly looked up at them both before ploughing on with the conversation.

"Palace Barracks you say? They torture people in there, you know? The army, they torture the paramilitaries." Stephen continued matter-of-factly. "That's the rumour anyway. It's the most hush-hush place in Northern Ireland. None of us have ever been in there. I mean, my team, they were never invited. It's home to MI5 round here, so you'd think we'd be on the guest list. I found the whole thing bloody intriguing," Stephen added.

"The whole hierarchy is a mystery too. There's an enormous black fella called Clive, he's the head honcho. The chief. Divides his time between Thames House and Palace Barracks. You know you've made it if you meet big Clive."

"Nope, I've not heard of Palace Barracks before today," Jenny replied, trying hard not to look shocked by the statement. "We're new to the area and we've not even started basic training yet. So, I think meetings with big Clive are off the menu. In fact, the two explosions mean there's just the four of us now anyway." Jenny explained, veering the subject away. "We are the entirety of Topaz" added Jones.

Jones and Jenny glanced at each other wondering where the conversation might go next. They'd dropped quite a big clanger by mentioning four members of Topaz. Isadora's name was the missing piece of the jigsaw, but fortunately, no one saw fit to bring her up. Stephen was still staring downwards and Jones wondered whether he was still in shock.

"Okay, shall we go and throw some of British Intelligence's money into fruit machines?" Jenny forced a laugh and Jones, followed half-heartedly by Stephen, made their way into the flashing and buzzing arcade.

A young woman was desperately trying to manoeuvre a pushchair containing a sleeping toddler up the steps to the arcade and Jones rushed over to lend a hand. Jenny smiled as she noted that the young woman had been making a far better fist of lifting the pushchair up the stairs than Jones, who was already red-faced with effort. As Jones placed it down on the top step, the child woke up and started screaming.

Jenny gave Stephen her £10 note and they queued for change. Stephen inspected it slowly. Inside the arcade there was an assortment of life. From teenagers in tracksuits shiftily checking the reject trays at the bottom of the fruit machines, to older women propped up on stools slowly feeding their tuppences into one-armed bandits and a few surly looking security guards looking out of sorts in bright yellow polo shirts. The electronic noise was deafening and yet the cashier at the change kiosk looked more bored and emptier than Jones had ever witnessed in a living soul.

Few words were spoken as the sad cashier handed out two pence and ten pence coins in plastic cash bags. As Jenny and Jones found their way to a row of two pence coin pusher machines, Stephen stood facing the other way at a 10p fruit machine.

"He's a bit weird, isn't he?" said Jones, quietly.

"Wouldn't you be? If you saw your entire unit blown to bits in front of you?" Jenny replied, briefly stopping slotting the coins into the machine and staring at Jones. "I mean, let's face it, that was a life-changing moment. He'll be thinking about it until the day he dies."

As Jones realised he was running out of coppers, he turned and scanned the room. Stephen had vanished from view. Jenny reached over and handed him another bunch of two pence pieces, and he absent-mindedly cascaded them into the machine, with limited return or real motivation. Five minutes later, Stephen reappeared. Jones felt a tap on the shoulder and turned to see Stephen miraculously balancing three polystyrene cups of tea in one hand, using the damaged hand in the sling to keep them steady.

"Hey, I'm sorry but this place really isn't doing me any favours and I'm probably terrible company. But let's have a cup of tea and a chat. There are some seats over there in the corner."

Jones quickly grabbed the top cup off Stephen and registered a change in his tone.

"Great idea Stephen," replied Jenny, a touch too enthusiastically, and they followed him to a large empty room with seats overlooking the marina. As they sat down, with Stephen on one side of the four-seat plastic table and Jenny and Jones on the other, Stephen finally made proper eye contact.

"I'm guessing McNally has sent you here to gee me up? Perhaps help me on my road to recovery? Well, I appreciate the gesture. I really do. And I think seeing some new Topaz faces will give me a wee bit of motivation. But I'm not coming back any time soon. I'm broken and I think my reluctance to engage with the whole Agent Orange operation has probably saved my life."

"What do you mean? What was the Agent Orange operation?" asked Jenny.

"The two groups were given a series of ciphers which were supposed to lead us to an endgame. Both groups had different locations and we would then rendezvous and de-brief at a safe house after we'd cracked the ciphers and found the locations. McNally, who loves a code, really upped his game with the task and we were pretty clueless until Ewan suddenly had a brainwave and bundled us all in a land rover and into Lennoxville. But I just couldn't do it. My confidence is so low. I'm was so anxious, I volunteered to wait outside." Stephen took a sip of his tea. He was now almost totally focused on Jenny.

"Agent Orange is a horrible chemical weapon created by the Americans. Part of the task was to locate it and ensure we gathered intelligence on the group who were going to use it. Perhaps in a dirty bomb or a chemical explosion. But it was just supposed to be an exercise, not the real thing. So, the bomb in Lennoxville is either the work of McNally, which seems plausible, or is it some kind of bloody clever hijack of the YCU task through a mole? I know who my money is on.

"You two are innocents. You've come along and witnessed this whole tragedy. But I would strongly suggest you get yourselves back to college and enjoy the safety of the English countryside. It's going to take me some time to get my mind right and get back to YCU, if ever. But I certainly wish you two all the best." Jones found it difficult to believe that in one sentence Stephen accused McNally of blowing up his own trainees, but then in the next admitted he might come back to YCU to work alongside him.

"I'm sorry about how you're feeling. I can't imagine how this must be playing on your mind. But I'm struggling with your theory on McNally. What's his motive to kill so many of the YCU?" Jones asked, managing to distract Stephen's gaze away from Jenny for a moment.

"There's a story going around that McNally's father was an informer. That he came from a catholic part of Belfast and was paid by the Brits to inform on the paramilitaries. Declan McNally watched as his father was shot by terrorists when he refused to admit it. This is why McNally works for SIS, he was taken in by the British Army and trained as their own. Even though his whole family are nationalist republicans. Where I come from, such a miraculous transformation isn't possible. You're born a Catholic and you're raised in a nationalist community. There's no Road to Damascus moments. He's just been waiting for the right time."

Jones was beginning to feel out of his depth in this conversation. He had not formed a solid opinion of McNally and realised that he had never used religion or nationalism as a basis for his like or dislike of another human being. But Stephen had an issue with McNally and the scorn hadn't finished.

"I'll tell you this for nothing. Virginia is one of the classiest people I've ever met. She's wise to the point of being too clever. But even she had a blind spot for McNally. He's effectively hiding in plain sight and that's what has cost me all of my friends in YCU and my future." Stephen dissolved into tears and Jenny rushed around the table to comfort him.

Jones saw the enormity of the conflict in Finch's brain. He had survived a bomb blast that killed the rest of Beta and blamed the incident on McNally. He was also teetering on the brink of calling time on his YCU career rather than wanting to avenge the dreadfulness of the killings. Jones also guessed, with Bangor a relatively strong protestant heartland, there was already no love lost between McNally, the Catholic and Finch who grew up with union flags fluttering everywhere. Or perhaps Jones was massively overthinking it and needed to stop looking for patterns. Maybe the poor bastard had shellshock and Stephen was blaming the easy target.

Stephen wasn't actually crying. He was staring, almost motionless, at the wall in front of him with a terrible pained expression on his face. Jenny, now seated next to him, was talking calmly about how well he'd done to start the journey of recovery and how she was looking forward to welcoming him back to Topaz. Jones could tell she meant it and he was growing more and more impressed by her ability to roll up her sleeves and tackle issues head-on. Nevertheless, it was now nearing lunchtime and Jones wanted to check out a local hostelry, he was a sucker for a seaside pint.

"Jesus Christ," exclaimed Stephen loudly. "Do you see that fella over there? He was almost a dead-spit of that politician? You know? The American? Maybe it's him. And the hat, he's a Raiders fan!"

Jones and Jenny looked round behind them and back towards the alleys of fruit machines and amusements. There, playing a one-armed bandit, wearing an orange branded baseball cap was a non-descript gent with black-rimmed glasses and smoking a cigarette. He was the only man in the immediate vicinity and Jones did not see any similarity to anyone of note. Perhaps, thought Jones, he might be a passable Jerry Lewis, the American comedian but certainly no famous politician. Jenny looked at Jones and shrugged her shoulders.

However, Stephen had suddenly found new life and raced over to the man, shaking his hand and chatting enthusiastically. Jones saw the gent point outside to a car and Stephen was smiling and talking animatedly to his companion too, possibly his wife.

"I think I'm cracking up," said Jones. "Can I suggest we end this bizarreness and take a walk down to the beach?"

"It's the first time I've seen Stephen smile all day," replied Jenny. "Let's give him a little more time, it looks like he's made a friend. Perhaps Stephen can show us the sights of Bangor?"

Jones stood up, downed the rest of his now tepid tea, and walked back over to one of the machines. Rifling through his pockets, he found a few coppers and played the slots whilst trying to eavesdrop on Stephen's conversation. The intrigue was short-lived. The older man with the baseball cap couldn't get a word in edgeways, as his wife spoke very quickly at Stephen. Jones picked up that they were holidaying in Bangor after visiting their daughter at Ulster University. They were from the Republic and had barely visited the north due to all the 'nonsense', as she put it. Jones threw the last of his coppers into the machine and walked back to Jenny, who had her head down looking at tea leaves.

"What does our future look like Richmond?"

"I predict that an impressively styled female will attempt to excuse us from this meeting and you can go and quench your thirst. In short, I don't think our visit to Stephen is helping him or us and we ought to disappear." Jenny walked over to Stephen and Jones followed, he was still trying to see the similarity to any US politician.

"Jones and Richmond, meet this lovely couple. They're here from the North Coast on a wee trip away. And look, he's an Oakland Raider's fan! He's even been over to see them play." Stephen was grinning and the tension and emotion had been swept away. After Jones and Jenny exchanged pleasantries, Stephen took a little step away from the couple and half-whispered to Jenny.

"Go and take a walk. Enjoy Bangor, it's a beautiful town. I'm sorry I've been so up and down. Hopefully, we'll work together in the future and I can begin to put all this behind me. But you're a wee dote, thanks for caring, Jenny." Stephen squeezed Jenny's hand and she smiled at him in return.

As they walked away, Jones was feeling relieved that the awkwardness was over. Stephen called out "Say Hi to Declan for me" and the two headed out of the doors into the sunshine.

"That's in my top five weirdest meetings. And that includes when my mum asked me to get Christopher Biggins' autograph at a local panto. What was all that about?" Jones asked as they strolled down the hill towards the sea.

"He's messed up. But he's alive and he's not been kidnapped. I think we park Stephen for now and hope he's part of the gang in the future. But I just feel as if we're wasting time here. Isadora has been playing on my every thought since that film came through. And we were playing slot machines. Why? Maybe Charles and Virginia just want us out of the way?" Jenny stopped momentarily and climbed up the steps leading to the sea wall. Jones could see an attractive-looking pub next to the RNLI office, with some seats outside.

There was a cool breeze blowing off the sea and, once they'd taken their seats outside the Marine Bar, Jones watched a young family play in a small triangle of sand that the incoming tide hadn't yet reached. There was a small boy in a light green bathing costume who was giggling as his father was helping him build a sandcastle. Jones and Jenny watched as the sea moved closer and the family moved to the steps but let the child play on as the space on the beach got smaller.

Jones took a significant swig from his pint of Harp Lager and briefly thought about his grandmother. She was a pub landlady and used to take her punters on regular summer trips to Southend. They'd charter a bus and Jones would tag along during his school holidays. It would always end up with some of her regulars drinking too much and there'd be a fight or some commotion on the journey back home. But ten minutes later they would all be singing and laughing before falling asleep for the rest of the journey. He didn't miss home, he decided. But he did miss his Nan. Jones smiled. The weather had stirred a memory of him and his favourite green pair of trunks and the wonder of a seaside beer garden.

As they sat and watched the sea and chatted about Isadora, Stephen, Red Line and the new personalities they'd met, Jenny became aware that Jones' eyes were shutting. Even in between sentences Jones was struggling to stay awake. She moved his pint away from him and gently nudged his head onto the table in front of him. She pulled off the brown sweatshirt, which she had tied around her waist, and placed it underneath his head as a pillow. Within five minutes Jones was snoring gently and Jenny let him rest. From her vantage point she was able to keep one eye on him whilst taking in the beauty of the landscape. All this sea air would mean she'd need an early night too.

CHAPTER
FIFTEEN

In Belfast, behind the requisite fortified steel cage at the Knock Road Station, Orla Massey had finished typing up her notes of the interviews of both McNally and Armstrong. Whilst the Isadora film had thrown a catastrophic cat amongst the pigeons it was inconceivable that either could be ruled out. McNally was shaping up as the standout suspect.

The booby trap in Limehall could have been placed there anytime up to 48 hours before detonation and she was urgently seeking dog walkers, hikers and local landowners who might have seen cars or visitors in the vicinity over the past few days. She had despatched a team of constables and reserve constables to question those living nearby.

She was already on her umpteenth coffee of the day and was still riled from having to cancel her fortnight holiday to Kefalonia with her partner. She had requisitioned a large blackboard from Divisional HQ and was rapidly trying to pull the many strands of the past 48 hours together. It wasn't easy and she had little help. She had one inspector, two sergeants and a team of eight constables, as well as a handful of reserve constables assigned to the case as more resources were sought. A specialist unit dealing with kidnapping was also being lined-up and en route. Helicopters were also on standby, there were RUC helicopters and one from the Garda Síochána would be politely requested if they needed to investigate closer to the border.

McNally and Armstrong had given each other as alibis but had only arrived in Northern Ireland less than nine hours before the first explosion. The timing made their guilt less plausible, but Massey felt she was missing something obvious. And, if Massey was being frank, she didn't like McNally much. He had the look and the smell of a terrorist and all of the YCU and MI5 guff wasn't hiding that smell at all well. Armstrong, on the other hand, was what the Americans like to call a 'jock'. All chiselled cheekbones and an impressive six-pack but with the brains and vocabulary of a confused hamster. He would need more thought.

In Lennoxville, the crime scene examiners still hadn't conclusively identified the chemical that led to the fireball but there were no noxious gases onsite, and the area was no longer sealed off. That said, it wasn't unusual for significant explosive quantities to simply enter the atmosphere and leave little trace in the immediate aftermath of an explosion. The Explosive Ordnance Disposal Specialists (EOD) remained on site and she awaited their report. She was interested that the range of the blast was much larger than Limehall, as Stephen Finch, who was standing over 120 feet away from the detonation site still required hospital treatment. There were two CCTV cameras from the adjoining road but the quality was so poor that the Abominable Snowman, Lord Lucan and Shergar could all have lit the fuse in direct sight of the cameras, and no-one would know. Cars had gone to and from the site in the days leading to the incident, but no registration plates were visible. One eyewitness mentioned a vehicle arriving hours before but these vehicles were common place in the area and this would need further verification.

Finding Isadora safe would help tie up many loose ends but most intriguingly, how did her blood get on the back seat of the Land Rover Snatch? Who was driving the other vehicle on site around 11.45pm on the day of the incident, as described by Jones and Richmond?

The difficult job of informing the families was taking place in the evening, utilising MI5 liaison with local county and metropolitan police constabularies across England, Scotland and Wales. Only Stephen Finch was local, and his family were simply being told of his initial hospitalisation for observation. The cover story was a mini-bus accident in Hampshire where all eight perished. And MI5 were hastily mocking up a scene with photos and eyewitness reports. This, of course, would be hideously unpicked if Isadora's film made it into the news. And that was the current pressing issue.

Both BBC Newsline in Northern Ireland and RTE from over the border had run the story in great detail but hadn't, as yet, connected the sites or the deaths. Likewise, national newspapers across the UK had registered disgust at another terrorist outrage in Northern Ireland and even the US Peace Envoy, Fred Martinsen, had described the events as "mindless killings". A sectarian murder in Strabane had added to the flurry of interest but that had been almost instantly claimed by a unionist paramilitary group as a revenge killing. Orla Massey's brain was on overtime trying to join the pieces of the madly scattered jigsaw and to keep the media out of the loop. It was an almost impossible task.

The most irksome and confusing part was the absolute silence from the paramilitaries. Both the RUC and MI5 had received no intelligence from their various snouts or informants that either side was involved, and this was rare. Not unheard of. But incredibly rare.

McNally had helpfully provided a few observations about the almost unheralded Red Line group. In his opinion, they were not linked in any way to the tiny and obscure Ulster Nationalist movement who had fielded a few candidates in recent elections, unsuccessfully. Instead, McNally thought Red Line had different allegiances altogether. Local police intel drew a blank and this was a worrying sign for Isadora Brown.

As Massey's thought bubble was about to burst onto the chalk board, her desk telephone rang.

"Chief Inspector Massey, I have a call for you on line two."

"Who is it please constable? I'm madly busy," replied Massey, sharply.

"It's a fella called Charles Curry. Says you'd like to talk to him" the Duty Officer responded.

Orla immediately pushed the flashing button on line two.

"Hello? Is that Chief Inspector Massey? Yes? This is Charles Curry, we've not met. But I am working with the YCU at Thiepval and would just like to run a little theory past you if you can spare the time?"

Massey wasn't altogether sure she could spare the time but was grateful for any thoughts on a caseload that was becoming rapidly foggy.

"Of course, Mr Curry, I've already met your team at the Barracks and I'm very sorry for your losses. It must be a horrific blow."

"Thank you, Chief Inspector, those sentiments are greatly appreciated." Charles Curry was in Virginia's bolthole office in Thiepval and smoking a cigar. He was pacing thoughtfully around the small room.

"I won't use up too much of your important time, Chief

Inspector Massey, but I think I can offer some advice. In my forty years with the service, I find myself almost unable to be surprised by the depths humanity sinks to in order to make a political point. However, I think we might be plumbing new depths here."

"Go on, Mr Curry, please," Massey instantly recognised that she was dealing with someone with either a very high opinion of himself or with real gravitas and she was keen to work out which. She had also grabbed a pencil and her notebook to take down the conversation.

"I am going to make my observations succinctly, as I am not altogether convinced that this conversation isn't being recorded," he paused for an answer but nothing being forthcoming, he ploughed on.

"I would like to suggest that Red Line is a false flag organisation. I do not believe there is any significant body of support for Northern Ireland as a standalone republic, free from British Government intervention and killing the notion of a United Ireland. I think this is the work of another major power trying to undermine the work of the US Peace Envoy and simply trying to mischief make. And I think the word 'red' is perhaps significant here." Again, he paused, this time Massey responded and silently cursed for not working this out for herself.

"If I'm not mistaken, Mr Curry, you're suggesting that our friends in Moscow are trying to dismantle any steps on the peace process by simply stirring up trouble? That Fred Martinsen's work will be unpicked? And atrocities like this will make us all question whether peace is ever possible?" Massey quickly wrote Russia in big letters on her chalkboard and then rubbed them out, realising her colleagues might think she was insane.

"I'm suggesting that much like President Clinton is proposing a Third Way to find consensus in politics, our friends have found a third way in Northern Irish politics to achieve the opposite and to utterly destabilise. However, Chief Inspector

Massey, I would also suggest that this means Red Line is not a movement or a paramilitary front, but more like an individual lone wolf paid by the Russian Government or KGB at an arm's length to simply be Machiavellian. But with these terrible consequences."

"Mr Curry, I am very grateful for these theories and who am I to challenge them? As conspiracy theories go, this is as believable as the next. But surely this is a job for your friends at Thames House? Surely MI5 or MI6 would be crawling all over this?"

"You'd think so, wouldn't you? But some politicians are so keen to attend the funeral mass for the cold war, that there might be some rose-tinted spectacles being passed around in Thames House or even the Pentagon. Therefore, we may have to prove this link ourselves and in doing so you'll get the biggest collar of your career, and we can ensure there are no more Red Line attacks. Am I making sense, Chief Inspector Massey?" Charles Curry finished his cigar and flicked it into a metal wastepaper bin.

"Yes, I think so, Mr Curry. But I have my Chief Superintendent to bring onside and you will know that there are other agencies already involved in this. I absolutely want to follow this angle through but I can't do it without alerting almost everyone." Massey was thinking out loud and scanning the room for other ears. The conversation was almost certainly not being recorded but she was aware this was a big call that she needed to make.

"I assume that Declan McNally is amongst your list of suspects? Well, I think we can disprove his involvement, but in the meantime perhaps you might let your colleagues and other agencies believe that a little longer?"

"You mean stall for time? Give my Superintendent a false lead? What about Isadora Brown?"

"I am completely on your wavelength, Chief Inspector Massey. Everything I am doing is to expedite the release of Isadora. Can you simply give me 24 hours to elaborate further on this theory and perhaps that will enable us to bridge the gap between the bombings and the kidnapper? Thus, bringing this drama to an end, with luck."

"I haven't ruled out McNally anyway. So, it's not a false lead and therefore you have your 24 hours, Mr Curry. Perhaps you might give me conclusive evidence that McNally wasn't involved about this time tomorrow? But in the meantime, we will continue to use all our resources to find Isadora Brown's location. Her life is our priority," explained Massey, desperately attempting to hold some of her ground.

"Perfect. And to ease your path with the kidnapping, I can probably locate the ransom funds in less than 24 hours. But let's hope it never comes to that. Oh, and our other casualty, Mr Finch, has now made a decent recovery and met our two new recruits today, so there are some positives. Goodbye Chief Inspector." And before Orla Massey could respond, the phone was dead.

Massey's coffee was cold. But at least her brain fog had lifted. It's the bloody Russians, she thought, interfering bastards, and cursed again.

CHAPTER SIXTEEN

CARL HAD LEARNT THAT THE OBJECT OF HIS AFFECTION WAS A LAB Technician called Wendy. She was single and not averse to the odd dalliance with a student. She had been a student herself a mere 18 months previously. Mr Singh had been most forthcoming with this information. Carl had caught her eye a few times in the refectory and they had also bumped into each other at The Jericho during last night's Karaoke and Pound A Pint night. She was blonde, petite and had a pixie-haircut as well as a few interesting piercings. Carl was smitten and buoyed as he genuinely believed he stood a good chance.

The other thing that Carl had learnt was that Mr Singh was truly excellent at Test Match, the Subbuteo cricket game. England, under Carl's command, were regularly dismissed for single figures, and India had once scored 400 before declaring triumphantly. So much talent exuded from Mr Singh, that he had allowed Tom to join Carl in a few games over the course of the past few days and therefore he too had been allowed into 'Mr Singh's lair' as they had nicknamed it.

The lair itself risked coming under rare scrutiny from the Principal. He had received a letter from the local council explaining they were considering re-opening the public conveniences adjoining the college. They had been closed for many years now and they backed onto the electricity sub-station. This was a disaster as the sub-station was Mr Singh's clandestine power source. He would need to tidy it and hide the prototype fibre cables as a matter of urgency.

Therefore, a plan was hatched to kill three birds with one stone. Firstly, after dark, Tom and Carl would help Mr Singh re-route his cables away from the public zones of the conveniences. This would ensure the secret of his handhelds, Indian TV, and other inventions would remain safe. Secondly, Mr Singh would ask Wendy to help too, feeding her some cock and bull stories about the college's electrics. He'd pay her a little overtime to keep her happy and she would coordinate efforts into the junction box at the top of the stairs with Carl. Thirdly, and perhaps most importantly, Carl would get to spend good quality time with Wendy. She, in turn, would probably reject him. And Carl would then stop talking incessantly about her. It was a win-win-win.

At 22.00 hours, Mr Singh, Tom, Carl and Wendy mustered outside the lair ready for 'Operation Re-Route'.

"Okay everyone this is a simple task. We need to ensure the rerouting of the cables into the college from the sub-station," Mr Singh briefed the team.

"Carl and Wendy will be upstairs at the junction box. You will need to carefully disconnect each of the cables from the junction box, one by one, and add an extra six feet of cable. This will enable Tom and me to feed them through a new route. You will need a delicate touch as the cables are fragile," he explained.

"You'll be fantastic at this, Wendy. Your hands are so delicate." Carl smiled pathetically at Wendy. Wendy returned with a withering look which hinted at almost immediate repulsion.

"Wendy, I'm going to give you this handheld device and I will communicate with you when each cable is ready to be disconnected. You'll need each extension ready soldered. Okay? Understood?" Wendy nodded at Mr Singh and thought of the overtime payment.

As Carl readied the soldering iron and kept a look out at the top of the stairs, Wendy started measuring the six feet lengths of cable and waited for the handheld to come to life.

Tom helped the tutor carefully break into the public conveniences and dragged the wires individually away from prying eyes and into a freshly drilled cavity created by Mr Singh. The whole operation took about an hour. Each time the cables were ready to be moved the team downstairs radioed up to Wendy and Carl to re-connect at the junction box. The handheld died just as the job was completed.

During that hour Carl had tried his best moves on Wendy. He explained his love of Status Quo and Norwich City, showed her his trademark underarm farting technique and had brought a stash of Chocolate Animal Biscuits. Biting the heads off with gusto to cue hilarity. Wendy was stony-faced. Carl had behaved like an annoying little brother and being a polite sort, Wendy desperately tried to let him down gently. But she got the feeling that subtlety wasn't going to work.

When Mr Singh and Tom arrived back upstairs, she couldn't get away quickly enough. Throwing her mini rucksack over her shoulder and hot-footing it down the stairs. A few pints at The Jericho and then she'd be meeting friends at a nightclub, her evening was planned nicely.

"I think that went very well," smiled Carl. "We made a good team and I think this is the beginning of something interesting. How did it go downstairs?"

Ignoring him, Mr Singh pushed the red door open, and the two boys settled in the leather chairs. Bangla TV burst into life in the background and the ageing tutor grinned happily. He sparked up his pipe.

"Brilliant, brilliant!" He beamed. "Now we need to check whether the handhelds are working correctly. Let's use the one up here as a reference point. Carl, where's the handheld you were using with Wendy?"

Carl quickly flailed around his pockets and looked outside the red door but to no avail. The set was nowhere to be seen.

"I'm sorry Mr Singh, I think Wendy has taken it with her. Shall I go and chase after her? It wouldn't be a problem."

"No!" chorused both Mr Singh and Tom, almost harmonically.

"It's fine. She can return it to me tomorrow. But we can still use her location now to check whether the cables have been connected correctly. Let's see, handheld twelve is on screen six. Let's check out where my GPS tells us she is."

Mr Singh switched on the screen, and there it was. A flashing blue circle indicating Wendy's location. She was just heading over the road between the newsagents and The Jericho. Carl was a regular customer for his chocolate fix, Wendy was more likely to be buying rolling tobacco.

"This is brilliant, Mr Singh! You're a bloody genius. And especially bearing in mind the handheld died about 20 minutes ago. Is there a separate power source for the GPS?" Carl enquired.

"The handheld died? Are you sure?" Mr Singh asked. "There must be some residual power somewhere. That'll explain the GPS being operative. It'll switch off soon. Let's finish the day with some Test Cricket and perhaps a small whiskey?" And he switched the screen off and headed to a makeshift medicine cabinet.

The three congregated around the green baize and Mr Singh

cracked open the Jim Beam and poured it liberally into plastic cups.

"Thanks for your help lads, cheers! And remember, Mum's the word!" And the three plastic cups disappointingly smashed together.

Less than an hour later, being a fair-weather drinker, Mr Singh was asleep on the bottom bunk. The lads had almost drunk him dry and were giggling. England had already been dismissed for thirty-eight and Tom suggested they made their excuses and headed out of the lair.

Like a lightbulb to a moth, Carl couldn't help but switch on-screen number six. The blue light flashed. Wendy was still in The Jericho and after looking knowingly at Tom, his friend attempted to bring him to his senses.

"Don't be a cretin Carl, she's well out of your league mate. This is basically stalking. Let's go back home and play some Connect Four. Best of five?" And with that, the pair disappeared back to the halls.

It was a chilly night in Milton, the temperature had dropped as it was now heading towards midnight. The night air had quickly increased their drunkenness. The boys were in short-sleeves, and they decided to pop into The Talbot for a nightcap. The pub was having a lock-in and Tom and Carl quickly recognised a few students and tutors happily propping up the bar. They indulged themselves with another nip of whiskey, this time a more expensive Jameson, then carried on back to their accommodation with almost a Ready Brek glow of alcoholic warmth. Tom was cheerfully inebriated after at least six with Mr Singh, but Carl was worse, secretly hating his disastrous moments with Wendy and feeling sorry for himself.

The pair fumbled for their keys as they casually stepped over two second-year students who hadn't quite made it back to their rooms. They were slumped on either side of the door with four empty bottles of White Lightning for company. As they passed a still noisy common room, the payphone at the end of the corridor rang. Tom, half-sprinted in an ungainly fashion and picked up the receiver.

"Hello, Roadkill Café, you kill it, we grill it. How can I help you?!" And both Tom and Carl dissolved into hysterical laughter, not bothering to listen for a response. When they had regained their composure, which seemed like minutes, Tom tried again.

"Hello, sorry about that," he laughed again. "Who are you looking for?"

"Hello," said the caller. "This is Jones, I'm looking for Tom Marsh or Carl Kelly. Is that you? And if it is, you're not as funny as you think you are."

"JONES!" shouted Tom, before more booming drunken laughter. "Where the hell are you? And why are you calling us at midnight?"

"Well, I'm calling you at midnight because it's the first chance I've had. I've been out all day at the seaside. I'm surprised you're up if I'm honest. And secondly, I need my stuff sent over here. I'll be away for a little while. It's a PO Box number. Go and get a pen, and I'll give you the address." Jones patiently explained, realising they were both drunk, but hardly one to criticise the 'over refreshed' pair, especially as the sea air had caught him rather off guard earlier.

"We were about to play Connect 4" added Carl snatching the phone from Tom. He motioned to his friend to go and find a piece of paper and a pen, using the medium of drunk mime. If Jones ever needed a reason to complete harrowing basic training, this conversation would be the clincher.

"You'll never guess what. I have some female interest. She's an absolute belter!" exaggerated Carl, with Jones humouring him whilst he waited to give the PO Box number.

"Not only that, but I know exactly where she is! Right now! That may sound creepy. Which I guess it is. But Mr Singh has put this GPS gizmo in the handhelds and I can locate her at will! Obviously, I won't though. Because that would make me a stalker." And Carl put his finger to his lips making a ridiculous shushing noise, to no-one in particular. Tom was still hunting paper, or possibly asleep somewhere.

"Mr Singh, right? He's a legend. He lets us play Subbuteo cricket and he's got this amazing bank of screens which tells him where all the handhelds are. The man is a genius. He's a lightweight though. We easily drank him under the table." And, with that, Carl put the phone down, hanging up on Jones, and headed three paces towards his room.

He then quickly ambled back and picked up the receiver again, only to hear the dialling tone.

"He's gone. That's just rude." Carl shook his head and walked back to his room.

Back in Thiepval, Jones was still gnarled by Carl not taking down the PO Box number. Jenny was asleep back in the Barracks dormitory rooms after her taxing day in Bangor and the whole significance of the GPS conversation was lost on him. As he ambled back to his room and carefully slid into bed next to Richmond he wondered how much longer he'd need to live out of an overnight suitcase. He and his clothes were beginning to smell.

Jones could hear the distant hum of cheerful bonhomie from the Barracks Mess Bar and wondered what Isadora was doing now. Someone he had never met was playing a crucial part in his life. He settled down and attempted to close his mind to it all. Richmond was now snoring.

CHAPTER SEVENTEEN

In Briefing Room Alpha, McNally, Armstrong, Charles and Virginia had rendezvoused early. Charles explained his role moving forward and Declan McNally smiled nervously as he realised how significantly Sir Charles Curry outranked him. Charles was dressed for action in a tweed suit, a green woollen tie and brown brogues that required a small mortgage for mere mortals to purchase.

"We need to ensure that young Jones and Jenny Richmond are given the best possible training and accept that YCU might be a team of four for a while. I am determined to play a positive role in finding Isadora Brown and I'll put a call into Stephen Finch later now that he's convalescing at home, I hear Jones and Jenny paid him a visit"

"McNally, can you utilise absolutely any intelligence you might have on Red Line and keep me fully briefed? I need you confined to Barracks unless it's absolutely critical to leave. If that's the case, you brief me. No vanishing acts. I think we all realise that you're the prime suspect with Orla Massey. But we know otherwise. We just need the evidence. Am I making sense?"

"Aye aye," McNally responded. "I'll be here and doing my bit. No bother. I'll put my ear to the ground. Thanks for your confidence, sir."

"Armstrong, put Jones and Richmond through their paces with the physical training modules, starting this morning. Neither appears to be a glorious specimen but let's test that theory. I've spoken to the Royal Irish Regiment Second Battalion, and they'll be doing some exercises in Newtownabbey later in the week, I suggest you join them with our two recruits. But don't let them get hurt. And don't get hurt yourself! Understood?"

"Yes sir," replied Armstrong. "I'll go and get them from the mess after we've finished here and see how fit they are." Charles nodded in response.

Armstrong, a former marksman, looked as if he was going to enjoy putting them through their paces.

"Finally, Virginia, can you undertake the modules on ciphers and signals from McNally's course text? I'm sure Declan won't mind talking you through it." Virginia quickly agreed and looked to McNally who was likewise in agreement.

"If Chief Inspector Orla Massey comes here, she talks to me only. I want to ensure we have one solid method of communication. And I have shared an interesting theory with her that she's currently wrestling with, we will see what she does with that information." Charles then smartened his tie and stood up to his full height, looking down on the assembled team.

"One last thing, please remember I am on your side and I'm here to support this unit. So, if anyone has anything you want to tell me, now would be a good time. I will not tolerate any secrets or nasty surprises further down the line. You have been warned."

The room fell silent. Charles dismissed the team and Virginia gave her husband a supportive smile. McNally poured himself an enormous black coffee and vanished into one of the small admin offices, ready to make some calls. Charles had set out his stall.

Jenny and Jones were still in the canteen area next to the mess. Jones had devoured an Ulster Fry and was battling with the notion of a white pudding. It tasted great on top of a slice of potato farl covered in Chef Brown Sauce. But Jenny had ruined it by explaining its contents. She, on the other hand, had opted for muesli and a small pot of banana yoghurt. She had offset this healthy option by adding an enormous custard apricot Danish to her plate. Jones silently caught Jenny's eye and pointed out Armstrong looming large, making his way through the scattered dining tables.

"Hello you two, how's breakfast?" Armstrong announced himself, dragging over a chair from a nearby empty table. "There's been a slight change of plan."

Jones was looking bedraggled. With no irony intended, he was wearing a 'Meat Is Murder' t-shirt. It was emblazoned with The Smiths' LP artwork and the collar was frayed as his beard growth caught on the edges. He hadn't shaved since his arrival, and he urgently needed a refreshed washbag.

Jenny, on the other hand, was already in sports casual mode in black leggings, a white t-shirt and her hair effortlessly bound together in a ponytail. Her large overpacked case had paid dividends. She looked awake and ready for action.

Armstrong continued. "Jones, I suggest you head back to your bedroom and sort yourself out. You look like a wreck. Do your ablutions, grab yourself a shave and wear something more appropriate for a young man at a British Army base. Jenny, go with him, read a book or something. I'll see you outside Briefing Room Beta in an hour. We're going to test your physical ability."

"Air hockey?" asked Jones glibly, which was ignored by both Armstrong and Richmond.

Back in the dormitory, Jones borrowed a clean brown t-shirt from Jenny and shaved with her pink lady shave, much to her hilarity. He even borrowed a little of her hair-styling foam to make himself a touch more presentable. The crowning glory was his further use of her floral Impulse deodorant to repel the smell of his repeated alcoholic exertions. He made a mental note to phone the lads back at Milton College to get his stuff sent over, this simply wasn't sustainable.

Armstrong was already jogging on the spot, with his navy tracksuit top and tight black Hi-Tec training shorts, when they arrived. Jenny quickly smiled at the sight and Jones followed her eye. But he was much more concerned about the run ahead than any tiny feelings of jealousy. He was never going to be Armstrong and didn't want to be. He just wanted this over.

Both Jenny and Jones were given an almost empty green rucksack and they were strapped to their backs. Without any further discussion, they headed off around the large drill field at the back of the Barracks. At every fifth lap, Armstrong, who had joined them on the run, added a small sandbag to their rucksacks. Jenny was very quickly ahead of Jones and shared the same weight on her back. She paced herself and her running style was easy and relaxed. Armstrong was no Drill Sergeant or Regimental Sergeant Major, he urged and supported rather than seeking to embarrass and demean. It was about 24 degrees in the summer heat and the sky was again perfectly clear. The lack of breeze and the humidity were making Jones sweat heavily and he attempted to keep up with Jenny who was a good deal fitter than him.

After twenty 400-metre laps, roughly five miles in total, Armstrong brought them to a standstill. He doubled the weight in their rucksacks and handed them bottles of water.

"You have two minutes rest time. And we start again. Don't drink too much of that water, there'll be no time for a toilet break. Jones, is that pure alcohol seeping out of your pores, lad?"

"You have Sir Charles Curry to thank for that," Jones wheezed whilst taking a swig from the bottle. His hands were on his knees. "We were in The Bunch of Grapes a few days back. Great meal and too many lagers. It was the same place we saw you and McNally on our trek here from the airport."

Armstrong looked at Jones in disbelief. "You saw us in the pub on day one? About what time?"

"About 11pm, I guess. Why? Is that important? You were in the Mondeo."

"More important than you'll ever know! You two might just be our alibi. Start running in about thirty seconds, no shirking. I'm going to speak to Charles and Declan." Armstrong quickly vanished back into the barracks.

"Right, come on," called Jenny. "You heard him, no shirking!" And she dashed off around the circuit once more, her now heavily-weighted rucksack bouncing up and down as she jogged away from him. She completed a solo circuit and watched as Jones struggled to catch his breath.

Jones half-considered throwing a few of the weights into the hedge and sprinting after her. But instead, he watched her hit the 300-metre mark and ran alongside her.

"You're a cheating bastard!" she laughed. "But it's fine. Let's do this together." Even though she could easily have sprinted off, she matched him stride for stride as they ran around the drill ground. After they'd completed the seventh lap of the circuit, they saw two figures walking towards them. It was Armstrong and Charles Curry.

As they got closer and the pair ran around the corner of lap eight, Charles Curry loomed and immediately looked like a fish out of water. He was still dressed in his Tweed suit and must have been boiling in this hot summer weather, thought Jones.

Charles unfastened his jacket as he approached and waited for them to coast to a stop.

"When I did this, back in the 1950s, we had to run around a parade ground carrying a telegraph pole above our heads. In groups of four, of course. Still, that was National Service, I suppose." Charles looked thoughtfully around the field as if acclimatising himself, before turning to the other tutor.

"Mr Armstrong, I think we might cut this short; I know you two will be devastated," Charles stifled a grin, knowing Jones was close to exhaustion.

"One of Massey's team will be here later to take statements from you both about what you saw at the pub in Lisburn. If we're very lucky, this will clear McNally and Armstrong of involvement in the Limehall explosion. As there would simply not be the travelling time between the airport, the Barracks and the pub to also set up such a complicated device."

"This is a vital piece of the jigsaw," Charles smiled.

Armstrong quickly removed the weights from Jenny's rucksack and set them down on the grass beside her. He repeated the exercise for Jones and they unfastened their rucksacks.

"We have a briefing at 16.00 hours and I suggest you get yourself some rest time," Charles added. He and Armstrong strode back to the Briefing Rooms, Armstrong easily carrying the significant weights in either hand and leaving the pair with their rucksacks. They followed behind, still catching their breath, but now feeling a sense of being part of the solution.

As they lagged behind Armstrong and Charles' purposeful striding, Jenny looked at Jones.

"Look, with all the hubbub in Bangor and trying to find Isadora, I haven't properly mentioned my conversation with Jason. I've been trying to process it."

"Oh," exclaimed Jones. "It's none of my business, please

don't feel that you have to tell me. But I did see you chatting on the pub payphone. How did he take it?"

"I'm trying to tell you, Jones! Well, Jason was furious and he's made me agree to meet him when I get back to talk things over. He just can't accept that this is the end. But I have no idea when I'll be back, and I have this awful feeling he'll come looking for me in London or go and worry my parents. He'll blow my cover."

Jones slowed a little and watched into the distance as Charles was in deep conversation with Armstrong. He was pointing out the supplies huts, the equipment stores and the NAAFI like a tourist.

"He won't blow your cover. He has no idea where you are and you're not easily contactable. Tell your parents you've broken up acrimoniously and that you need some space away from Jason. The last thing you want is them worrying." Jones looked concerned and he made sure Jenny could see he was taking this very seriously.

"You're right. I'll ring them later. Maybe a little time and space will help Jason move on too. I have a new life to lead but this must be difficult for him."

"Give it time," reassured Jones, suddenly feeling like a mature thinker. But he was beginning to rely on Jenny and he loved her company. He could imagine Jason must be apoplectic.

There was time for the pair to grab a coffee from the canteen before they changed. They sat in the same seats as for breakfast as Jones was still struggling to catch his breath after the session with Armstrong.

"I'm thinking that enormous fry-up this morning was probably a bad move Jones! Perhaps stick to the rabbit food to start your day, otherwise I'll be running rings around you!"

"Well, I wasn't to know. It was quite the bombshell this morning. And yesterday's sea air didn't help either. I need to get fitter" he grimaced as he swigged his coffee. Thiepval coffee was hardly restaurant quality.

"But Tom and Carl, my roommates from Milton, were absolutely smashed last night. I had to ring them when we got back, I need my stuff shipped over" he continued.

"Those two are like toddlers, you know. One night, when I first arrived, they spent an entire afternoon watching Danger Mouse and Bananaman episodes on video. Tom was honing his impressions of Penfold and Baron Greenback. Carl likes colouring in. You couldn't make it up. It's like a kid's club."

Jenny laughed loudly. "How on earth did you cope? Don't tell me you didn't join in?"

Jones shook his head innocently and put down his coffee, laughing. He liked seeing her face erupt with humour. It reminded him that they were both still in their late teens and that what they were doing was extraordinary.

"I only phoned them as I really need some clean clothes, some shoes and my wash bag. Otherwise, I'd have left them to their Kerplunk or whatever. The way things are going I'll be borrowing your clothes forever! And Impulse just isn't my brand!" Jones added, still laughing.

"Anyway. I got a little bit of college gossip. I didn't catch all of it but the Emerald tutor, Mr Singh, has apparently put some kind of system in the handhelds which has enabled Carl to stalk a girl. He knows where she is 24/7. It sounds horrific."

"He's done what? Isn't that illegal?" Her face switched to concern.

"Have they put cameras in the ladies' loos too? That poor woman. Stalking is dreadful behaviour and Mr Singh agreeing to it? You know, I hate to say this, but you really ought to tell Virginia about that. Or at least mention it? Isn't she Mr Singh's boss?"

"You're right. I'll speak to her. I don't know the first thing about handhelds. But I'm not keen on Mr Singh and Carl being weird. Right, let's head back." Jones emptied his coffee cup and stood up.

"Briefing at 4pm, we have two hours! Let's get back on the internet once we've changed. Do you need to borrow my mascara or anything? Maybe some blusher to highlight those reddened cheeks?" And the pair walked back to the accommodation block, with Jenny smirking.

After they'd changed, with Jones now modelling the long-sleeved brown t-shirt Jenny wore on the trek, they logged onto the internet in Briefing Room Beta. The dial-up connection was awful and Jenny spent some time hopelessly staring at a blank screen. Jones, after realising the joint effort would be a waste of time, disappeared to the on-site library and trawled through books and references to Ulster Nationalism, which were quite few and far between.

Exploring microfiche of newspaper cuttings he learned that this 'third-way' approach was a very minor school of thought in the politics of Northern Ireland that sought outright independence of Northern Ireland from the United Kingdom without joining the Republic of Ireland. Thereby becoming an independent sovereign state separate from both.

This form of Independence had been supported by some groups, like factions of the Ulster Defence Association. But it was such a fringe view that it was neither supported by any of the political parties in the UK nor the Republic of Ireland. However, there was one name that caused Jones' alarm and it was a blast from the past. The National Front.

The British National Front was a neo-fascist political party in the UK and had its heyday in the 1970s. But even then, never returned an MP, only a few councillors in English local authorities. Jones found a document entitled *Alternative Ulster – Facing Up to the Future*, which laid out plans for how independence could be achieved and how the independent state would function. The document Argued that Ulster represented a nation distinct from the rest of Ireland and Great Britain. But whilst this was intriguing, and the words 'neo-fascist' concerning, there was little to suggest a campaign so vociferous that it would involve bombings and chemical explosions. Sure, the National Front had been involved in significant violence in the 1970s and 1980s but this would be an almighty leap, especially when the organisation itself seemed to have significantly shrunk in size, even in its heartlands.

Jenny, still frustrated by the dial-up, had managed to look at some basic chat rooms about Northern Ireland and the troubles. And whilst there was a real community of thought online, there was nothing about Red Line or links suggesting likely candidates for the explosions. In fact, there was more talk of mysterious 'outsider' groups and what possible effect they might have on peace talks. She had only really learned that people active on the web, even those using the platform to speak anonymously, had no knowledge of Red Line. If the Isadora film was leaked, she thought, this would be an altogether different story.

When Jones and Jenny met back in the Briefing Room there was a feeling that they'd learned plenty about the context of the issue but nothing whatsoever about the incidents themselves. Which, coincidentally were exactly the same conversations going on in Knock Road RUC station, where Orla Massey had drawn more blanks than a circus gunfighter.

Charles Curry had called her and explained the alibi given to McNally and Armstrong by the pair, but Massey hadn't needed to drive the thirty minutes from Belfast to Thiepval to get statements, as the bartender at the Bunch of Grapes had also now verbally confirmed the story. Statements would be taken later. This was progress.

Charles, as he prepared for the 16.00 briefing, was ever more confident that his version of events was the most likely and Massey was joining his thought process. The problem was, both Charles and Massey had no way of proving it. It was simply a theory.

CHAPTER
EIGHTEEN

ISADORA BROWN HAD BEEN THE SHINING LIGHT OF THE YCU SINCE HER first appearance in Thiepval. She arrived after swapping from a military training college in Sandhurst and was a year older than the rest of the team. The assessors at Sandhurst had called her a 'machine' but that was just as much for her training ability as her analysis and problem-solving skills. Her transfer was a no-brainer.

Isadora believed she wasn't cut out to be a soldier but whilst diminutive in size, at only 5 feet tall, she had been a fierce competitor with an enormous academic ability to boot. Virginia guessed that when Isadora sussed out she was never going to be a Marine or in the SBS, she opted to join the SIS ranks. She simply wanted to be the best. Therefore, she quickly bonded with Virginia. Virginia and Charles saw her as not just the stand-out female candidate but the stand-out candidate, full stop. And that was significant praise when male SIS entrants were still the significant majority across the whole service. Even McNally rated her.

With the two teams, Alpha and Beta, toe-to-toe competing

to be the leading YCU group and undergoing such rigorous training methods, she had proved her leadership skills time and time again. Much to Ewan's chagrin, the Beta Team leader, who simply didn't have her mettle. Isadora's four brothers, all older and all from a military background, were the likely reason for her ruthless competitive nature. And nobody in her family believed a word of her cover story, that she had changed careers to become an Operations Executive for a Cruise Liner. But it did explain her long absences from her family home.

From Isadora's current location, she could hear the sound of water in the small hours. She assumed this was the sea and she could often hear the aggravating cries of seagulls. This was when the streets below fell quiet from the buzz of the traffic and the people, going about their everyday lives. They were blissfully unaware of Isadora and her current plight, she hoped. Even with death a real possibility she had her service head firmly on. She did not want to be a statistic but nor did she want to cave in. In these hours of danger, she was just as professional and determined.

She was lying face up, with her arms and legs tied together but she was not blindfolded or gagged. She was cold, having had the majority of her outer layer of clothing blown off in the blast, she was in a white t-shirt and the little remains of her black combat trousers. A large gaping hole slit her trousers from the left knee up to her thigh and her t-shirt was a few inches too small to cover it. When the wind blew, she felt the cool July air during the nights and she shivered.

She had shoulder-length straight black hair and she knew she had blood, debris and white chemical detritus all over her face and head. She wanted to be clean, she wanted to scrub the dirt and the smell of the explosion from her body. She hated the smell of the white t-shirt he had given her to cover her modesty, it smelt of cigarette smoke and cheap deodorant. Her kidnapper had forced it over her head as he woke her when she arrived here, she guessed he'd found her unconscious at the site. She remembered the bomb. She guessed that she was the only survivor but she was still addled after an incalculable amount of time stuck in this room.

Isadora had a desperate need for perfection and feeling prepared. But that was impossible and for now, she was solely focused on staying calm and thinking about her next move. From her position, she could see only grey breeze-block walls in a room that couldn't have been more than six feet by four feet small. But the wind swirled and any movement was echoed. It made her ears hum. There was a door behind her head, and if she manipulated her body she could see its silver locking mechanism and thick black hinges.

Any minute now he would arrive and sit in silence whilst she drank from an old wine bottle full of water and she awkwardly ate another tasteless white bread, cheese, sandwich. It was definitely a man, even though no words had been exchanged, he had a male physique and even smelt masculine. He had black clothing, an unseasonal thick black sweater, black jeans and Dr Marten-type boots, a woollen balaclava with the face cut out and black sunglasses that disguised his eyes. There were no gloves and that omission meant she could see he was Caucasian, with no rings or jewellery or any tattoos. He was just an average man who had kidnapped a 22-year-old SIS trainee and hidden her God knows where.

She knew she was up high and that the room was either on the roof of a building or at the top of a flight of stairs. She felt a breeze when he opened the door and the noises from outside were far more pronounced. The energy and the birdsong. There was even the unfathomable sound of whirring machinery which she just couldn't identify.

Remembering her training, she told the man everything

about herself. In order to build a bond. She told him about her life in Solihull, her brothers, her difficulties at school being the only mixed-race child in her class and she told him she had a very serious sexual disease called 'Blue Waffle' just in case he thought about raping her. He hadn't responded to anything. He simply waited for her to eat the sandwich, drink the water and, on two occasions, he had blindfolded her and let her urinate in the corner of the room.

In the right-hand pocket of her tattered combat trousers was a large item, which she had been unable to reach. It made her feel even more uncomfortable. It was either her purse, which she assumed he would have confiscated, or her defunct handheld communications device. She couldn't tell. But the handheld had died some hours ago and he already knew who she was, somehow, so her identification in her purse was no help.

She knew the clock was ticking. But, on the other hand, surely every police patrol and other agency was looking for her? As the hours passed she grew ever more concerned and her fortitude waivered.

She felt a little pride in adding 'fall to my death' in his pre-written film script to help pinpoint her location. He either hadn't noticed or cared. But despite her problem-solving skills, she had no clue where she was or who he was. White, average build, dark clothing and poor sandwich-making skills were hardly watertight identikit materials.

The door was about to be unlocked. The slight squeak of the hinges would come first and then the sound of his boots moving outside. She could already hear the sound of him sniffing slightly as the carrier bag with her food rustled. It was almost always a white Shell Station carrier and one of the transparent loops, reinforcing the bag, had come loose.

She'd once read a book which talked about a hostage flirting outrageously with her kidnapper and building a veil of intimacy that way. She couldn't bring herself to do that. But perhaps she could embarrass him? She could force him to make an unplanned move that would reveal himself in some way. Use the 'chains' of her capacity in some twisted manner. She could, but she might sound like an idiot. Still...

He paced heavily into the room, put the bag down, and locked the door behind him. There was no key on the inside, just a bolt. The man then grabbed Isadora by the shoulders and sat her upright. He was gentle and effective, rather than brutal. He then pulled an ancient-looking flick knife from his trouser pocket and slashed at the duct tape on her wrists. Before rebinding her at her forearms and passing her first the white cheese sandwich and then the wine bottle. It was a bottle of pinot noir from 1992. A good vintage. The water was much less enjoyable. But she swigged a little from the bottle but just enough to keep her hydrated as she was dreading urinating in front of him again, she'd prefer to do that in the darkness, much later. The moment had come.

"You know," she said in between chews, almost retching at the insanity of what she was about to say. "Some women like being tied up. And, whilst I've not considered it before, this is actually really turning me on. All this bondage. And the tightness around my wrists and bare legs. It's quite a thrill." He looked at her, he'd stopped what he was doing and was listening.

"Oh my God, this is quite embarrassing. I'm really turned on. Perhaps this is what I've always fantasized about?" And then forced a smile adding, "Is this why you're doing this? Do you love bondage? Do you want me to call you Daddy?" Isadora laughed, slightly mockingly, looking for a reaction.

The words jarred as she spoke. She hated using sexual words as a tool but time was ticking and he wasn't interested in her backstory. There was a brief moment of silence. Isadora took another bite from the sandwich and looked up at where his face and the eyes were hidden. She was repulsed by what she'd said. But equally energised.

The man reached into his left-hand pocket and pulled out a scrap of paper and an Argos catalogue pen. He scrawled the words 'don't push it' in capitals with his left hand and pushed it towards her face for her to see. And then in a split second, he quickly turned and furiously smashed the wine bottle into the far corner of the room. Water splattered up the grey walls and tiny shards of glass scattered across the floor.

He was angry. He turned the paper over and wrote something, and then instantly scribbled it out with the small pen. He carefully replaced it with the words 'twelve hours' and showed her. Again, in capitals. He snatched the half-eaten sandwich from her and left, powerfully slamming the door shut. The boom of the door closing echoed around the room. Maybe she had embarrassed herself and gone against the very core of her being, but she had certainly got a reaction. He's left-handed, he's probably Anglophile and he's got a short temper. Useful intelligence.

But then, as Isadora began to compute her findings from the past two minutes, he returned with a dustpan and brush and cleared up the broken glass, putting the pieces into the carrier bag. As he bent down to sweep the remnants of glass from the floor she saw the label on the back of his underpants. It read 'John Lewis'. It all felt surreal to Isadora. Why the hell was he clearing up?

Isadora knew she wouldn't see her kidnapper again tonight. His next planned visit would be very early in the morning. So, she laid flat on her back on the slate-cold bench and closed her eyes. Hoping that by some miracle she would sleep or a solution to her predicament would present itself. The night would close in soon and she would listen for the gulls and the sea. She hadn't given up.

CHAPTER NINETEEN

MR SINGH HAD NEVER REALLY BEEN IN TROUBLE BEFORE. HE HAD BEEN a diligent student and took his work incredibly seriously at Milton College and beforehand as a Research Assistant for GCHQ, just up the road in Cheltenham. GCHQ hadn't understood Mr Singh's worth, or that was his theory. However, when the call came from Virginia Curry, who had been made aware of his GPS system and Wendy's stalking episode, his heart had sank. He briefly considered deconstructing the lair in anticipation of his P45. But he decided he would hear her out first and assess his options.

Somebody had made a complaint about him to the College's Personnel Department. The allegation was that he had created a device which enabled a student to successfully stalk a female member of staff. And this put her in danger. Virginia had underlined that he would need to explain his actions or face a disciplinary procedure. Mr Singh, who was in his early sixties, had both parents alive and well and living in the small town of Jaunpur in Uttar Pradesh, a state of India bordering Nepal. And they would be horrified to learn of any disciplinary for such matters. He would be a disgrace. That would be intolerable in his family and in Jaunpur generally.

Nevertheless, he'd decided his best strategy was to hold his hands up and explain that he had indeed made such a device but the stalking was coincidental. He would never dishonour a woman and certainly not a fellow member of staff, like Wendy. Frankly, though, he was much more concerned that Carl or Tom had breached his confidence and after so long with the lair being his little secret, this saddened him.

It was coming up for 10am in Milton and Carl would be showing up any second to finish a game of Test Match and assist him in setting up a photocopier that Mr Singh had found in a skip outside the local branch of Lunn Poly. A squirrel had made its home under the lid, but he had long desired a personal photocopier and fixing it would be a challenge. If he still had a job in an hour's time.

The phone rang in the lair and Mr Singh stared at it anxiously for a good three seconds before deciding to pick up the receiver.

"Hello, this is Mr Singh."

"Good morning Mr Singh, I'm sorry to be ringing you in these circumstances but I would like to discuss a complaint made against you anonymously. I'm afraid the Principal is engaged at the moment, so I am dealing with this issue on his behalf." Virginia Curry was brutally professional. But Mr Singh had seen the Principal literally moments before in his study. He had been swigging tea and dunking hob nobs, so he guessed Virginia had volunteered to grill him.

"Now, not to put too fine a point on it, you have been accused of stalking a young female member of staff using the handheld communications device. Can you please explain yourself?" Mr Singh was beginning to sweat.

Virginia was sitting bolt upright in her chair, with her desktop fan blowing the early morning heat around the room. She had pressed the speaker button on her yellow desk phone and was making notes whilst Charles was reading GCHQ files in the background. Charles was half-listening to the conversation and was always impressed by his wife's ability to deal with difficult situations. He knew Virginia was incensed by the notion of stalking.

"I admit it, I'm sorry. But I never meant any harm and never intended to use the device to stalk anyone, female or otherwise, unless in the cause of national security. It is simply a Global Satellite System chip I placed in the handhelds to ensure we can locate them, either when they go missing or to locate the user on a map on my computers here." He explained.

Charles stopped what he was doing and stared at Virginia's desk phone.

"Mr Singh, this is Charles here, we'll get back to the disciplinary issue in one moment. This was a prototype GPS? Did it work?"

"Oh yes, my invention was a great success. In terms of the chip working and being located on a map. The clever thing is that my GPS chip does not require the handheld to transmit any data, and it operates independently of any telephone reception." Waiting for the next question, Mr Singh had briefly slowed the feeling of panic in his chest.

"What I'm saying is, I meant to test my invention and had no idea a student would be using this to track the position of a female staff member. This system uses US military data provided by their satellites, I'm simply piggybacking, and this is not illegal. The United States government created the system, maintains and controls it, and makes it freely accessible to anyone with a GPS receiver. But we never had any idea of its real capability until now. But I'm sorry I've caused a problem."

"I understand Mr Singh. You say a student was using this to

track the position of the female staff member? Who was the student and has he been reprimanded?" Virginia intervened.

Mr Singh looked around the room and noted that Carl, who had arrived early to continue a game of Test match, was sniffing one of his pipes. His childlike mannerisms were no excuse for the stalking issue though, he silently decided. Although he also knew he'd handled this badly.

"It was a student called Carl Kelly and he is here with me now. I was planning on disciplining him myself." Carl, like a rabbit in headlights, put the pipe down and sat in one of the chairs facing the bank of screens.

"He's here with you now? Can you please put him on the telephone?" Virginia asked.

Mr Singh, head slightly bowed, passed the telephone over to Carl. Who was doing a passable impression of Munch's Scream.

"Carl, this is Virginia Curry. The notion of you using a handheld device to reveal the whereabouts of a female member of staff disgusts me. You must realise this is abhorrent behaviour and we will now be starting our college disciplinary process." Carl looked distraught as Virginia underlined the severity of this situation.

"Mr Singh will explain this process to you in more detail. However, I believe the member of staff in question is unaware that this incident took place and I am also conscious that identifying the nature of Mr Singh's prototype would be harmful to the project. Therefore, we will need to ensure a suitable reprimand for this behaviour. I will detail this in a letter to you once the process has been completed. Please pass the telephone back to Mr Singh."

"Yes, I am so sorry, Mrs Curry. What I did was horrible." Carl passed the phone back to Mr Singh and adopted a rather concerned pose on the leather chair.

"Mr Singh, on no account can Carl Kelly be allowed to cause your technician any further concern, either consciously or mistakenly. Can I rely on you to deal with that?" Virginia heard the tutor quietly agree but Charles wasn't finished.

"Mr Singh, Charles here again. When will you be installing this chip on the handhelds we are using out here in Northern Ireland? When do we get to test them?" Charles was beginning to put the pieces together and was trying hard not to sound impressed by the prototypes. Mr Singh gulped hard.

"I'm dreadfully sorry Sir Charles. But they already have the technology installed. I should have sought permission from Virginia. I was not snooping but I appreciate I should not be aware of your whereabouts. I realise this is a grave error of judgement." Mr Singh awaited the sound of further professional disappointment and the lecture about the Official Secrets Act.

"Let me get this straight. You're saying that GPS is available in all of the handhelds that are in use. All fourteen of them? You can log their position on a map now? Instantaneously?"

"That is correct Sir Charles, as I said, I'm most terribly sor......." But Virginia interrupted him. "Can you tell me the exact position of handheld unit four, belonging to Isadora Brown? And is it active? Is the battery dead?"

"By some quirk of fate, it appears the battery on the handheld can hang onto some residual power after the unit has been drained. But I have no idea how long that residual power lasts. Let me test this theory." He switched his bank of screens on.

At just that moment, Tom walked through the door of the lair. He was carrying three cups of tea and a large bacon bap, brown sauce dripping onto the carpet. As the screens whirred into life Tom placed his breakfast down and looked over at Carl, the admonishment on his face was clear. However, at that moment, Tom and Carl saw all the GPS locators flashing on the screen for the first time and were fascinated.

"You are handheld number two, Mrs Curry and you are at Thiepval Barracks near Lisburn, Northern Ireland. As we anticipated. Numbers one and three are also in that area two. I am thinking these are Mr McNally and Mr Armstrong?

"You are correct, Mr Singh. But what about Number four?"

"Number four is offline, that is Isadora Brown. I'm sorry. There has been no location for that device for days. In fact, four, five, six and seven are all offline. They were all Alpha Teams devices. But eight is powered and so is twelve. Let me just check where they are."

"Morning, Mr Singh," said Tom, quietly as the tutor carefully interrogated the screens.

"You two are not supposed to see any of this" Mr Singh responded through hushed tones, with his hand over the mouthpiece on the receiver. "Now, go and sit over there and let me sort this." Tom walked away feeling slightly scolded. Neither knew that Mr Singh could be saving lives with this information.

"Number eight appears to be in the centre of Belfast. Great Victoria Street, near the railway station. I think it's the Europa Hotel. It's not moving. Number twelve is in Great Victoria Street too. Do you have two of your recruits staying at the hotel, Mrs Curry?"

"Good Lord!" Charles Curry exclaimed. "Hold that thought."

Virginia Curry, dressed for summer and certainly not for sprinting, put the receiver to one side of the phone, kicked her shoes off and dashed out of her administrative office and down to the canteen next to the mess bar. There at the front of the busy queue were McNally and Armstrong, both with plated Ulster Fry breakfasts on a tray.

"McNally, how high is the Europa Hotel?" She called across the canteen. Waving at him madly as she spoke.

"Tall enough." He shouted back. "Maybe about 150 feet. Why?"

But they had both grasped the issue before McNally had finished the sentence. Armstrong and McNally calmly placed their trays on the counter in front of them and mouthed 'sorry' to the canteen staff, before they very quickly joined Virginia near the entrance, after another slalom of apologies as they circumnavigated the canteen tables.

"It's Isadora, right? Is that where she is? How do you know?" said Armstrong frantically.

"Too many questions!" she replied breathlessly. "There is so much more to this. Follow me please, gentleman. Let's head back to Charles, he's in Briefing Room Beta on the phone with Mr Singh."

All three dashed back through the Briefing Rooms to Virginia's makeshift office. McNally was wondering how the hell Mr Singh had managed to crowbar his way into this operation when he wasn't cleared at any level for this type of information. He was a civilian tutor.

McNally and Armstrong quickly joined Charles and Virginia in her small office.

"Mr Singh? This is Charles Curry. Are you still on the line? Can you hear me?"

"Yes, Sir Charles, loud and clear." Mr Singh was still none-the-wiser of the jigsaw for which he was unconsciously providing some of the missing pieces.

"Listen, old chap, by hook or by crook you have managed to pinpoint the location of a member of the YCU team who has been missing for some days. I can't say more than that. Except that lives are at risk. How confident are you with your information?"

"I have been looking at the data here since you put me on hold a few minutes ago. I am confident that handhelds eight and twelve are in the vicinity of the Europa Hotel and there is only one other operational device and that's number fourteen. That is showing live at a small outbuilding near Lisnabreeny and Cregagh Glen. Do you know where that is?"

"Aye aye," quickly interrupted McNally. "it's owned by the National Trust of Northern Ireland. That'll be a storage facility or maybe a garage. There are not many buildings there."

Armstrong was delving around at the bottom of a drawer next to the entrance to Virginia's office and found an Ordnance Survey map. He quickly spread it onto the table and McNally put his finger directly onto the Glen. "It's on the way to Belfast from here, literally twenty minutes on the A23. I know the area well. It's got a view of the city and it's also possible someone could fall from a great height there. But it's not as high as the Europa."

Charles said goodbye to Mr Singh and strode purposefully to use the phone in Briefing Room Beta and update Orla Massey. Virginia remained in her office and gently reassured Mr Singh that he wasn't in trouble but she would speak to him once the dust had settled. The call ended soon after.

Charles briefed Orla Massey who was still waiting for clearance for a helicopter search. He explained there were two possible sites to search, the Europa Hotel and Lisnabreeny and Cregagh Glen. Both were high enough but the Glen looked more likely to be a small storage base. He conceded that Isadora could still be held in either location.

The only puzzle left was the second handheld, still alive and reporting a position near the Europa. This was either another member of YCU or Isadora somehow had two handhelds in her bag and was simply poised to bring them back to the Barracks once rescued. It would have been Isadora's style to hold onto useful equipment.

As Armstrong and McNally ran to the car park to requisition a Land Rover Snatch, Jenny peered her head out from behind the shower curtain in a bedroom a few short paces from the canteen. Jones was lying on the bed reading a book about Signs and Ciphers given to him by Charles the day before.

"I was just thinking." She shouted through the half-opened bathroom door and over the sound of the hissing water.

"If Mr Singh has created a tracking device out of the hand-helds. Do they not have the same equipment in the handhelds used here? Couldn't that be used to find Isadora?" She had been washing her hair for what felt like three hours now and Jones was feigning interest.

"You what?" He called back.

"Bloody hell. I'm so stupid!" And Jenny quickly jumped out of the shower and burst into the sleeping area. Jones wasn't expecting nudity so early but wasn't about to complain. She hastily got dressed and explained her theory to Jones, who only partially listened and only vaguely understood. He threw the book on the bed and grabbed his trainers.

Within five minutes of her epiphany, Jenny was standing in front of Virginia, hair dripping wet and unnaturally flat to her head. Jones nodded intelligently as she delivered the new angle.

"You're ten minutes late to the show," said Virginia. "I'm impressed you worked that out but we now need to give the police time to do their job. McNally and Armstrong are off to the sticks to check out a location," she added. "Isadora is in one of two places. We feel certain about that now."

"Wouldn't it be good for us to see the whole thing take place?" said Jones, clearly eager to see some action. "This kind of real-life scenario has to be the ultimate training package."

"I agree," Charles quickly added. "But this is a definite 'look but don't touch' scenario, understood?" "Which one of you two drives?" And Jenny raised her hand. Virginia threw her hand-held number nine routinely kept at the base and suggested she grab some keys from the Barracks reception.

"Take the main road into Belfast, park in the city centre near the main train station and we'll meet you there. Remember to observe only. I'll let Massey know you're on the team." Added Charles.

They were only five minutes into their journey when the handheld burst into life.

"This is McNally. This is an all-stations alert. Charles, I think you should see this." He gave directions to the Glen to the team.

Jones, still fiddling around with the tape player in the Land Rover and desperately trying to soundtrack their journey with his 'Louder Than Bombs' cassette, turned to Jenny and suggested a detour. The Glen wasn't far away.

CHAPTER TWENTY

Sir Charles Curry had heard the McNally announcement on his wife's handheld. He had to make a few phone calls before he left for Belfast with Virginia in the Ford Mondeo lent to them by the Barracks. He was arranging the ransom funds, just in case. And whilst Massey was beginning to accept his theory about Russian involvement, Charles had also alerted a few friends in MI5 and MI6 for 'off the books' assistance. There were still enough friendly spooks who were able to see past the recent Russian peaceful overtones, or that owed him a favour. He had arranged a rendezvous en route at a safe house in Ormeau Road to pick up a duffel bag full of Northern Bank currency, although he was convinced he'd be giving it back by sunset unused. But he needed the surety, just in case, as he had little faith in Massey's team, who had not covered themselves in glory so far.

However, there was another thing playing on Charles' mind. There appeared to be zero chatter about Red Line, nothing from police informants and nothing from his friends deep in the secret services. Maybe he was wrong. Perhaps Red Line was just an angry young man acting as a lone wolf? Someone with a grudge? But if that's the case, how did McNally pick up intelligence on them? He shared these thoughts with Massey before the Currys walked to the Barracks car park. Massey was trying to arrange an armed support team at the Hotel but had failed in locating the ransom money from Headquarters. She also still hadn't successfully requisitioned air support. This was a far cry from the Belfast of old when Army helicopters swooped over the city with searchlights looking for any sign of trouble.

It seemed a vulnerable young woman possibly falling to her death was not a priority for the Royal Ulster Constabulary but, then again, Isadora didn't officially exist. She was a trainee spook and the police were already beginning to bend to the public relations needs of the job, focusing on quick wins, rather than SIS missing persons. That wouldn't win them many plaudits.

Jenny and Jones quickly found the gravel path leading to the bottom of the Glen and parked in a small car park covered in grey shingle. Jones could see a pathway to a large wooded glen and in the distance an estate and green fields. As they walked closer to the estate and a collection of small buildings they saw McNally and Armstrong's Land Rover.

The whole place was unspeakably stunning and they walked quietly taking in their surroundings and contemplating what might happen next. Was Isadora here? They guessed not. An understanding was slowly being developed between the pair that meant words weren't always necessary.

As they walked on, a National Trust sign pointed the way to the summit of the Castlereagh Hills on the edge of east Belfast. The path hugged the sides of the Glen and they climbed through pools of sunlight cast by the trees. Some were tall and others overhanging. There were still displays of asters in white, lavender, and deep blue next to the paths and wild flowers dotted around the grassy banks.

As they reached the outbuildings and the first signs of life, there were the whistles of birds and the gentle sounds of a waterfall. McNally was standing, hands on hips, near the edge of a walkway. They could see a row of sheds overgrown with nettles but with a side-door half opened.

"I wasn't expecting to see you, do Charles and Virginia know you're here?" McNally half-heartedly questioned Jones and Jenny, as Jenny carried on walking, ignoring the query.

"We heard your call," Jenny called back as Jones searched for a response. "It said all stations and we assumed that meant us too. Charles and Virginia are on their way."

Jones shrugged his shoulders and he joined McNally as they walked towards the building. McNally was wide-eyed and edgy.

"Don't touch anything. Armstrong found the handheld in a pile of clothes here. We'll leave it all in situ so the RUC can fingerprint and bag for forensics." And McNally pointed in the far corner of the abandoned storage shed. "What's concerning me though, are these barrels."

There were four large blue barrels, each with a white lid and with polythene packaging wrapped around two of them. They were unused. The other two had been opened and there was evidence of white powder around the lid and on the cracked concrete flooring. Armstrong was writing down the details listed as the contents of the large blue containers. The labels were faded and those on the used barrels were all but torn off. But beyond the packaging, Jones could just see 1,3,5-trinitro-1,3,5-triazine emblazoned below the hazardous and explosive material warning logos.

"My guess is that these are full of RDX. Which is Royal Demolition Explosive and pretty bloody lethal stuff. And there's a load of it here. It's not Agent Orange, thankfully. The problem is that there's so much missing. You'd never use that amount for the two explosions in Limehall and Lennoxville.

There's another bomb somewhere." McNally picked up his handheld.

"I didn't want to broadcast that over the handheld, as God knows who is listening in. But Charles will need to speak to Massey and get a team down here sharpish. We're now looking for another device or devices somewhere. But that still doesn't tell us what substance created the fireball in Lennoxville."

"Armstrong, could you have a dander around for a telephone? There's an old Youth Hostel down the way. Maybe there's someone in there? We need the police here as soon as possible. Can you wait here for them?" Armstrong dashed off towards the estate.

"Let's use your car and get into Belfast. We really ought to get to the Europa. I don't think there's any doubt about where Isadora is being held now. Armstrong can brief the Currys. Unless one of you two wants to wait here for them?" Jones and Jenny shook their heads quickly in disgust, like toddlers refusing that final spoon of cauliflower puree. McNally was certainly fired up, he was dusting down his skills and slipping back into operational mode.

Within five minutes they'd made their way back along the track and to the vehicle. Jenny immediately threw her keys to McNally, not just because he was certainly a more experienced driver but because he was also a native. He proved that point instantly by putting his foot on the accelerator and coasting through the gears onto the A23 and headed down the Cregagh Road. Jones was relegated to the back and sat between the two front seats watching the quick progress.

Last night, Jenny had mentioned that McNally gave her the creeps. He could see why. McNally wore the same long trench coat, even in the summer heat, with the same punished loafers and brown trousers. Either he kept a wardrobe of replica clothes or these were his only options. And now he was seated downwind to McNally he could smell the dirty fibres of the coat and a stale smell of sweat. His unkempt ginger beard looked like it had been thrown at his face and only just landed. There was also the pronounced stench of the cigarillo smoke and as he careered faster along the single-carriageway into the city, McNally lit one up.

As they turned left onto Albertbridge Road, Jones saw the city for the first time. Belfast was a thriving but divided community. Whilst there were signs of political progress, the divisions were still obvious and army vehicles and checkpoints were a common sight. He has seen signs and graffiti along some of the redundant buildings referencing the release of Lee Clegg, a paratrooper with the British Army, who had been released from prison on the orders of the British Government. Clegg had received a life sentence for killing a Catholic civilian. This had caused uproar in the nationalist community. Jenny turned her head and gazed back on intricate murals that covered the side of houses but in the next second, there were burnt-out cars and damage to the street from recent rioting. However, life continued, children were kicking a ball down a side street, there were a few scattered market traders and then the sprawling commercial area loomed large as they headed over Albert Bridge.

As they made their way through the city centre, Armstrong radioed in to confirm that he had briefed Massey, who'd been preparing a team to recce the Europa, and shown the Currys the chemical stash. Charles had confirmed McNally's suspicions, there was a lot of RDX missing for two explosions. Little was said over the handheld, just enough to explain progress. McNally, in turn, gave nothing more than an acknowledgement in reply, by this stage he was too busy trying to locate a parking space with a view to the Hotel, instead, he gave up and suggested they sat in a former railway tavern called Robinson's. This was a useful vantage point. They could see the Hotel and the entrance to the thoroughfare to the main train station. They all ordered Beamish and settled in, waiting for something. Maybe a helicopter or a cue from a radio message? Whatever it was, they waited in silence, with only Jenny's uncouth slurping breaking the quiet.

For what felt like an hour, the table remained silent and only the occasional questioning looks between Jones and Jenny broke the deadlock. McNally chain-smoked cigarillos and nervously looked at his watch waiting for news. Jones started to kill the time by watching cars. He started to memorise car registration plates, makes and models. He managed ten initially but was then blown off course when an elderly man in a beaten-up brown Hillman Imp broke down in the middle of the street and the car backfired loudly. Both McNally and Jenny rose to their feet and watched the commotion out of the window and Jones momentarily lost concentration. The man seemed in some distress and Jones, recognising something of his own grandfather, walked over and helped push the ancient car to the side of the road next to a bookmakers. A few other bystanders helped out too. The scene was over in about five minutes and the gentleman walked off to a payphone to summon help. However, the sound of the backfiring car still resonated in Jones' head and he walked over the road, towards the thoroughfare to the train station, to simply stretch his legs and clear the brain fog.

The sun had momentarily vanished into a mass of angry clouds and the temperature dropped a couple of degrees. Jones, in his polo shirt, suddenly felt under-dressed and looked across the road to see if he could spot Jenny and McNally. But these few moments of alone time allowed him space to assess the situation. He ran through the events of the past week or so, and whilst he did he forced his hands into the pockets of his jeans to add some degree of warmth. There was a canopy over his head in the passageway leading to the station and he leaned on a wall underneath and watched some smokers light up and chat loudly about the state of the shopping centre.

This bizarre stand-off was a complete waste of time, he suddenly decided, and with someone's life at risk and the clock running down, something had to be done.

The Europa Hotel was an easy ten paces from where he stood. McNally, in one of his rare conversations, had told the pair that it was Europe's most bombed hotel and this was mainly due to being the home from home for visiting politicians, envoys and journalists in the height of the Troubles. There were precious few hotels left. But the Europa still stood tall and proud. And in a fit of reckless bravado, Jones turned and walked towards the hotel entrance. If only to sneak a peek through the windows. There were no signs of Massey's team but there were employees milling around looking to escort paying residents in and usher the uninvited out. Jones wasn't going to get any further without some quick thinking. He began to imagine Jenny and McNally staring at him through the window in Robinson's wondering what the hell he was doing. In all honesty, Jones wasn't at all clear either but couldn't sit on his hands.

He double-backed on himself and walked through the thoroughfare to see if there was an obvious back entrance. Behind the shops and beyond the canopy was the entrance to the Europa car park. Which looked, initially at least, like an underground facility but there was no immediate pedestrian entrance from the thoroughfare exit. Instead, he quickly darted down the vehicle slip road signposted 'exit' and through a set of service doors. The doors had a small sign claiming to be alarmed but as they were already partially opened he guessed this was an old sign.

He was now on the bottom floor of the Europa car park and could easily be mistaken for a hotel resident looking for his car.

But no cover story was necessary, for now, as the bottom floor was entirely devoid of human activity. It was at this moment, as he spotted the customer lift dead ahead, that he realised he had no handheld and had absolutely no way of getting in contact with Jenny, McNally or the Currys. If he stepped into the lift from here, he was solo and vulnerable. Any failure from here would probably mean he was on a plane back to Milton College to eat chocolate animal biscuits with Carl. As this thought resonated, the lift suddenly chimed and sprang open. Two well-dressed middle-aged ladies in long pastel summer trouser-suits stepped out. One was in lime green with a large gold belt and the other in pink with a thin white linen jacket. There was a small rat-like dog under the arm of the woman in pink. They showed little interest in Jones as their eyes scanned the bottom floor looking for something or someone. As he was about to walk past them into the lift, one tapped his shoulder.

"Excuse me, young man, is there a taxi rank on this floor?" the pink-suited woman stepped back and looked him up and down. He guessed she was trying to work out whether he was an employee or not. There was a sign immediately to the left of the lift door which pointed out that the taxi rank was on floor three. But Jones decided to use this information to his advantage.

"Ah, no I'm terribly sorry ladies. The taxi rank is on floor three. Would you like me to show you up?" And without any response, he guided them back into the lift and pressed the button to floor three.

"So, are you enjoying your stay? Is everything satisfactory?" Jones put on his best received pronunciation and quickly felt rather silly. But they responded in kind, they were either English ladies that lunched or were heading out on a business meeting. But the dog, which looked permanently petrified, seemed an unlikely addition to a business lunch.

"It's a beautiful hotel. And the staff have been marvellous. Of course, my husband and I are in the presidential suite and therefore we have been delighted with the excellent service afforded to us." The lady in green smiled. The dog looked at Jones wearily, as if about to join the conversation.

"The presidential suite is our best standard of accommodation. It's my day off today but normally I'm one of the guest services executives and we have a long waiting list for that suite." Jones was becoming skilled at thinking and lying at speed. Jenny would be impressed. But she was probably now furious, he quickly remembered.

As the lift shuddered to a halt on floor three, he could already hear people outside the doors waiting to get in. But, as the doors flew open, a fire alarm immediately sounded in the hotel. It was unnervingly loud. So much so that the dog, chose that exact moment to projectile urinate all over the white linen jacket. A hoard of onlookers dashed into the lift to avoid the scene. The lift door closed, mainly rammed with men in grey business suits.

"Oh Treasure! You poor little dog! Did that alarm frighten you?" The green-suited woman spoke as she was quickly dabbing her friend's white linen jacket with a handkerchief. "Young man, do you realise loud noises scare animals? The hotel should pre-warn people about such alarms." The pink-suited woman added, nonsensically. The alarm continued. Jones could barely hear himself think.

"Why don't you take the jacket off, Madam? I will see that the hotel dry cleans it and leaves it freshly laundered in your bedroom. I can only apologise." And he smiled charmingly at the two, whilst gently stroking the dog's head. Who was looking slightly less bemused now.

"Barbara, that's not such a bad idea, you know? It's a warm day out there and I haven't brought a jacket. Let's get away from this horrendous noise! Why not give it to the young man and we can carry on to our mini-cruise on the Lagan?" And without any further debate, Barbara, in the pink, handed her sodden jacket over to Jones. And he pointed them along the white faux-marbled passageway towards the taxi rank. As they passed him, the lady in green handed him a £5 note and winked.

"I might see you later, I'm in 936, opposite Barbara's suite." And with that, she quickly scampered after her pink-suited friend. Jones was slightly shocked by the invitation but was still coming to terms with the ongoing fire alarm.

Jones quickly checked the jacket over and found to his absolute amazement that Barbara had left her room key card in one of the pockets. The only issue was, that the plastic card was blank aside from the name of the hotel and a telephone number. But if the green-suited woman was in 936, it shouldn't be too much trouble to find.

He raced back along the corridor following the signs for the stairs. His only sight of a member of staff so far had been a man in a full blue boiler suit, but with the name of the hotel stitched into the lapel, who was clearly in maintenance and he was amongst those entering the lift with the grey suits. Therefore, he could safely assume his presence was largely unknown. On finding the winding staircase, he quickly sprinted up five flights of stairs, checking the numbers on the doorways as he completed each circuit. At 700 he was exhausted and slowed down and took a breath. He foolishly looked over the side of the stairwell and edged back again warily. It was a long way down. And Jones wasn't good with heights.

As he re-started his ascent, three women in white and black uniforms walked past him with clothes on hangers in cellophane and others with bags of cleaning material. He wished them good afternoon in his politest voice and carried on up the stairs. The ninth floor was the first with a large double-door entrance and as he entered the hallway he could see rows of small pedestal tables with fresh-cut flowers adorning them. There were large rectangular mirrors in-between each of the doorways and the carpet was thick pile. He could hear his shoes squeak as he moved across the hall looking for 936. It was the third room from the stairwell and diagonally facing it was the Presidential Suite. With the soaked jacket in his hand and the key card in the other, Jones knocked loudly on the suite door, checking whether the husband was inside. There was silence. He knocked again, not entirely clear on what he would say if anyone was in the room.

Using the card, he gained access and slowly edged through a small entrance lobby into a large sitting room with a television built into the wall. The furniture and furnishings were luxurious and elegant. The whole suite was almost the size of his entire home back in England. However, there was little sign that anybody had been in the room aside from two cups and saucers, both thick with lipstick. He walked through the heavy pile carpet into the bedroom and saw only one side of the king-sized bed had been slept in, as cushions covering the other side were still present. Likewise, only one towel had been used in the gargantuan bathroom with a huge jacuzzi bath and double sinks. The husband either hadn't arrived yet or was sleeping elsewhere.

He opened the bathroom window and was immediately met with a view of the bottom of the car park in one direction and a row of window ledges leading to a set of fire escape stairs, seemingly reaching up as high as the maintenance tower on top of the roof.

This was either an ideal location to get up to the roof, where Isadora was being held, or he was on the wrong side of the building altogether. Only time would tell. But, he swiftly figured that he needed to make the team aware. Without having a handheld, there was only one possibility. And he was chancing his arm that this approach would work on a Saturday.

He quickly located the guest telephone, pressed nine for an outside line and then dialled the number for Milton College, a number he had memorised after repeatedly calling it to check being accepted onto the course after his horrific exam results.

"Good afternoon, can I speak to Mr Singh please." And the receptionist patched Jones through. It was indeed a Saturday, but he guessed the tutor would be on site. He wasn't to know Mr Singh effectively lived there.

"Hello, this is Mr Singh speaking, how can I help you?"

"This is Jones, I'm in Topaz and a room-mate of Tom and Carl. We haven't spoken before but I am involved in operations and I need your help to communicate with the team. I do not have a handheld." Jones explained.

"Is this a secure line?" Mr Singh queried. "I am in a hotel room on an outside line. So, I will explain briefly my location and a suggested approach and perhaps you could pass this onto handheld nine?" Jones remembered Jenny had the base spare handheld, number nine, but he also guessed that the rest of the team would hear the communication.

"Go ahead, Jones. I'll pass it on." Added Mr Singh, who was already bringing up their locations on his bank of screens in the lair. Jones began to dictate.

"I am at the accommodation and meeting Mr Clinton. There are stunning views of the vista. Perhaps other members of the team might like to enjoy the scenery too? I have had no sign of our other guests yet. Please let yourselves in."

Mr Singh, with Jones still listening in on the hotel phone, relayed the message to the team. Whilst he wasn't expecting wild adulation and praise from Jenny, he was surprised to hear her immediately call him a 'bloody idiot' with McNally quickly hushing her in the background. The call then ended.

Downstairs, McNally and Jenny had been joined by Armstrong, who had been dropped off in the city centre whilst the Currys headed to the safe house on Ormeau Road. Armstrong had already been assigned look-out by McNally, as Jenny was deemed too inexperienced to leave solo. But at the same time, for a barely-inducted trainee, McNally seemed oddly keen for Jenny to accompany him up to the top floor of the hotel to recce the scene.

Jones briefly considered switching the TV on and emptying the jam-packed minibar. But instead, he did the unthinkable and climbed nervously out of the bathroom window desperately trying not to look down at the 100-foot drop. This was, without question, the bravest and most foolhardy thing he had ever considered and had even shocked himself at his courage. He was now gripping onto the inside window handle with one hand and the other was holding onto the outside window frame, he would have to do the same twice more to reach the side of the building and the fire escape steps. In his mind, he remembered the strength he mustered when, on a Scout camp in the late 1980s, he abseiled down a climbing wall. He remembered begging the camp leaders to let him off the giant abseil. But he had made it. Today, no lines or cables were holding him in place. He was freestyling.

The moment soon came when he needed to let go of the inside window handle and this was the point of no return. The reinforced plastic window ledge was about the same length as his size eight shoes and he felt a degree of stability moving from the first ledge onto the second. But he struggled to find something from his hand to grab onto. There was only a thin wire which was attached to a small satellite dish. That seemed strong enough to carry his weight and he shifted his balance from the window sill outside the Presidential Suite to the next window and just hoped no-one was in. As, even with frosted glass in the window, it would be screamingly obvious someone wasn't going to be cleaning the windows unaided that far off the ground.

Gingerly moving across the window ledge of the second suite, he could hear someone in the bath. She was singing 'Memory' from Cats at the top of her voice and was very focused on her performance. But when she hit a painful flat at the crescendo, Jones found himself stifling a laugh before quickly remembering his predicament. He shuffled further across the window ledge and grabbed the satellite cable from suite three. There were just ten feet now between him and the side of the building leading to the steps. That would be relative safety.

Downstairs, Charles had radioed to McNally that they were five minutes away. From the safe house, he'd called Massey and she confirmed she had finally located helicopter support. The helicopter would be attempting a reconnaissance fly-over in an hour to get aerial shots of plausible locations. But from a distance, in order not to spook the kidnapper into doing something stupid. The deadline of noon on Sunday was looming but with the time just after 3pm on Saturday, they had some time to play with.

McNally and Jenny had decided they needed to either rescue Jones or support him in some manner. Richmond was a little worried about him but did not let her poker face drop for a second. This was no time for emotion. There was Isadora to think of. He could handle himself. Probably.

They opted to try a more traditional approach to gaining access to the building. McNally had phoned and attempted to book a last-minute viewing of their conference facilities. Jenny would be meeting one of their eager salespeople in the

Carmichael Suite at 3.15pm to quickly check the facilities for a potential wedding booking in September. She would then ask to use the lavatories after her tour and head upstairs, letting McNally in. Somewhere. With this plan shaped and whilst they waited for a briefing from the Currys, McNally and Jenny switched to soft drinks in Robinson's. The anxiety in Jenny's mind was growing.

Jones had hit a stumbling block in his final six feet before the fire escape. He was relying on the satellite cable above suite three being strong enough to take his body weight and allow him to swing carefully onto the steps. He had pulled and pulled the cable but it was just too loose and he couldn't risk slipping on the thin ledges. Dust flew out of the hole in the brickwork where the cable was inserted and Jones desperately needed to rub his eyes.

Instead, he found himself teetering on the ledge and removing his trouser belt to swing the metal clasp end onto the base of the satellite dish above. He then pulled the two ends together. This piece of ingenuity enabled him to swing across and haul himself onto the steps successfully. He was delighted with himself, he was working at over 100 feet and had managed to put his fears to the back of his mind. He was now anchored on the bottom step of the fire escape and felt relatively safe.

He then watched his belt fall helplessly onto the car park below, it took about eight seconds and he watched each second with dismay. For a moment the realisation hit him. He instantly froze and clung to the steps above for dear life. The bravery of the last fifteen minutes played out in his mind. This momentary panic had happened to him many times before and he just kept looking up into the sky as a coping mechanism. He counted the steps and focused on not looking down. He had done the hardest bit. These were metal steps and as long as he held on, he'd be fine. That was the mantra he repeated whilst he climbed tentatively upwards. As he finally climbed onto the flat roof and the safe ground, he saw the task at hand.

There were three service buildings, one looked like the top of the lift shaft and the other two perhaps storage units or utility cupboards. Steam and smoke billowed from large aluminium outlets on the roof and the thin shingle on the flat roof cut through his still-shaking hands. He was on top of the Europa Hotel and somewhere up here was Isadora. Somewhere down there was the rest of his team and he had to quickly shape a plan.

CHAPTER TWENTY-ONE

Orla Massey was having the mother of all bad days. Not only had she been repeatedly outflanked and patronised by a spook old enough to be her grandfather but she had also seen the Lennoxville and Limehall explosions passed over to a different team. The Anti-Terrorism Unit was headed by a man whose misogyny and chauvinism knew no bounds, Eric Rogers. Worse still, he was yet another Englishman, and her days were currently filled with pompous Englishmen with high opinions of themselves. She knew Sir Charles Curry had been delighted when she failed to raise a single penny of the ransom money and his thought process around Russian interference had now been discussed with her bosses who concurred. Her theories had been debunked some days ago. Even their MI5 liaison grudgingly admitted Charles was probably right and that the cold war hadn't quite thawed. Although many questions remained about the role of the mysterious Red Line group and the explosions.

But what had crapped on her cornflakes was the fact that a unit, who she had arrogantly described as a 'spooks kindergarten' just days earlier, had now located the likely position of

Isadora Brown. And this was maddening for a Chief Inspector who prided herself on results. Half of the YCU had never even visited Northern Ireland before let alone Belfast, and the bloody GPS signal was back in South East England. Orla Massey had even relented and started smoking roll-ups in the back yard of the Knock Road Station to take the edge off the stress.

Massey filled her lungs with tobacco smoke and exhaled deeply and as she did so a colleague appeared with an update.

"Chief Inspector, the helicopter has now been despatched and will be reporting back with images in the next hour. The kidnapper's deadline is now 20 hours away." Massey was ready to simply acknowledge the update and head back to her desk before the Constable continued.

"There's more though, the surveillance team have just reported seeing one of the trainees from Thiepval on the roof of the Europa. He scaled the side of the building after breaking into the hotel's Presidential Suite and climbing out of the window. What would you like us to do Ma'am?" The messenger looked sheepishly at Massey awaiting the predicted explosion. Instead, Orla Massey stared furiously at the constable and ground her roll-up into the concrete as if it was Sir Charles Curry's smug face.

"Jesus Christ. All we need is fecking James Bond Junior saving the day. I will have to deal with this. Get me regular reports from the surveillance team and for God's sake don't let the press get wind of this. We will never live it down." Massey stormed out of the yard and slammed the door so hard the entire building shook.

There was an icy chill. Her colleagues took cover as she sprinted to her desk to find a police radio and the keys to her car, but as she reached her desk she found a large brown folder with fluorescent yellow post-it notes attached. It contained both archive files from the RUC database and a series of black and white photographs. This was a breakthrough moment. And not a moment too soon. Suitably interested, she rethought her plan and postponed her jaunt into the city. This package of fresh evidence was now a priority and she quickly read through the detailed notes of an undeniably promising new angle. One that might repair her flagging reputation.

"Constable," she called out. And her still wide-eyed messenger replied as he rifled through a large filing cabinet. "Yes, Ma'am?"

"Get me the surveillance team on the phone. Now. And we need to watch that idiot fella on the roof. And bring Sir Charles Curry to the station as quickly as possible. I think he's going to want to hear this." And her day suddenly turned an almighty corner.

It took Massey's team twenty minutes to locate Charles and Virginia Curry, they were enjoying a chicken and bacon boxty with seasonal vegetables at Robinson's and, what looked like, a decent Shiraz. They were alone but close enough to the window to have a handle on the proceedings. Armstrong had been patrolling the perimeter of the hotel and sprinted back over the road to support. Charles slowly consumed his meal and disappeared back to Knock Road with Massey's team and Armstrong tagging along. Virginia was left with the remaining Shiraz and a handheld. In the back of the police car, Charles adjusted his Marylebone Cricket Club tie and matching pocket square and looked over to Armstrong reassuringly. He was secretly delighted that Massey had finally found a new lead. After all, he couldn't do it all for her.

CHAPTER TWENTY-TWO

JENNY WAS HARDLY DRESSED FOR THE TASK OF GETTING THROUGH ONE of the tightest hotel securities in western Europe. The knack of bombers targeting the hotel had made management understandably keen to restrict uninvited guests. Her hair had never dried properly after her quick exit from the Barracks and she was looking like an extra from Hair: The Musical. Therefore, she and McNally had contrived to use one of his shoelaces to pull her frizz into a passable, yet extreme, ponytail. And she had tidied herself up to perhaps 20% of her normal level of acceptable splendour. She did not look like a potential blushing bride and she wanted no-one on the planet to assume her future husband was McNally.

With that in mind, she waited smiling at reception, as a Sales Executive arrived to show her the dining facilities and the potential location for a wedding breakfast. Her cover was shaky. She was Jemima, she worked at Belfast City Council and she was marrying her university sweetheart. Someone she loved so much that she'd moved from Berkshire to Central Belfast. The Sales Executive quickly took her through some brochures with photos of stunning brides looking pleased with themselves and the backdrop of the Europa's impressive facilities. But the conversation took place seated around a table within a few yards of the reception and Jenny was keen to get into the main complex of the hotel.

This was more difficult than it sounded. The Sales Executive was possibly the fastest-speaking person Jenny had ever met in her whole life. So quick was her broad Belfast sales patter that she left barely any room for breathing. Let alone for Jenny to interrupt and make her exit upstairs. Jenny half expected the woman to pass out as her non-stop narrative continued unabated. But when the moment came, Jenny grabbed it with both hands.

"I'm sorry, but I must use your toilets. I've been drinking champagne all morning and it's gone straight through me. Could you tell me where they are?"

"Not a bother, the wee bathrooms are up the steps on the left-hand side. Come and find me at the reception desk afterwards, and I can take you through the menus." The Sales Executive explained.

Jenny smiled engagingly and headed up the steps towards the toilets and peered behind her to make sure her new friend wasn't following. She was fine, the coast was clear. She dashed up the corridor and swiftly found the internal stairs. Grabbing her handheld, she radioed to McNally who explained he was waiting by the rear fire escape by the car park on the ground floor. She found a list of floors and dashed to the fire exit where McNally stood. He looked typically dishevelled and his eyes bulged behind his thick NHS glasses. She pushed open the fire escape bar to let him in and she led him to the staircase which the signage suggested would ultimately lead to the ninth-floor Presidential Suite.

Much to Jenny's surprise, McNally proved himself incredibly physically fit and he sprinted up the stairs with apparent ease. Jenny was a flight behind him at one stage and she found herself struggling to keep up. But when they came across two hotel staff with gleaming golden corporate badges and formal business suits walking slowly between floors, they slowed. And she walked alongside him as they both smiled cheerfully at the staff members. Or as cheerfully as someone like McNally could muster. The ninth floor came relatively quickly and when the opulence of the deep-pile carpet gave way to the Presidential Suite door, left on the latch by Jones, they realised he wasn't there. But there was the tell-tale sign of the bathroom curtains blowing and the window wide open. Jenny could even smell Jones, with his continued use of her Impulse giving him an unusual feminine odour.

"Jesus Christ, he's on the bloody roof. Look! How the hell did he get up there?" And McNally grabbed the window handle and edged enough of himself outside to see the fire escape steps and the flat roof.

"Jones!" Screamed Jenny. "Are you up there?" And for an agonising twenty seconds there was silence before he appeared by the top of the fire escape steps, head craning downwards to see McNally and Jenny's heads poking out from the Presidential Suite window. "Can you hear me?" Jenny shouted as Jones squinted through the afternoon sun to see them.

"Yeah, It's fine. I can hear you loud and clear. But I suggest you don't shout." And he pointed towards the two windows leading to the fire escape steps. "I need a handheld, there must be another way up."

McNally, recognising the need for silence, responded with the 'A-OK' gesture and held up his hand, suggesting to wait for five minutes. Jenny poked her head out of the window and they shared a glance before she mouthed the word 'prick' and disappeared into the suite.

"He could have been killed out there. That's madly dangerous." She said to McNally, who was already heading to the door.

"He wasn't, though was he? He's done a surprisingly good job. He won't want you worrying about him. Let's stay focused. I'm going to see if I can find a way up there." McNally shut the door and Jenny went back to the window. Jenny didn't want to be the lookout and she wondered what the hell Armstrong was up to. In the meantime, Jones had vanished.

He had scurried around the top of the roof, which was divided into three sections. Jones could see the section he stood on was simply a bare flat roof covered in thin grey shingle. There was a small gantry leading to the front of the roof which he had explored for the past five minutes. He had found the gantry led to the huge hotel sign, spelling out the word 'Europa' and a small electrical fuse box. There were also two seemingly long defunct searchlights on either side of the sign, with the bulbs removed. He decided against getting too close to the hotel sign as he would be immediately visible to the pedestrians on the main street and to the crowds at the train station. Therefore, he remained close to the centre.

The third section was where the outbuildings and lift shaft were. But there was a gap of around five or six feet between the original two sections of the roof and the final section with the outbuildings. There was a sheer drop in-between. And the thought of jumping made him feel sick to his stomach. The immediate task at hand was finding another way up there and maybe McNally would jump over that gap.

He spied another set of steps on the far side nearest the hotel sign but he would have to hoist himself over the ledge to plant his foot on the top rung. The very issue he had back in England with that damn chimney. But after jumping between window ledges, this was less frightening and without much thought, he crawled on his belly until he reached the side of the building and let his legs slip carefully over the side until he found the first rung. Sure enough, after four steps there was a maintenance door which he could push open from the outside and he jumped in. The room was like the industrial zone from the Crystal Maze with long heating ducts and machinery along with rows of incomprehensible dials. But he was focused on finding a way out of this room unseen and getting McNally in. The room was empty but deafeningly loud. There were occasional signs of life from those maintaining this hidden department, with Pirelli calendars and cut-outs of newspaper cartoons littering the walls. There was a mug with warm tea teetering on top of a radiator, so one of the maintenance team was close at hand. Still, without thinking, Jones negotiated his way around the noisy room and looked for the exit on to the landing. Sure enough, a door with horizontal slats emerged from the maze of machinery and Jones was back on the internal stairwell. With no sign of McNally, he sprinted down a flight of stairs and was back on the ninth floor. He could see McNally right at the end of the plush carpeted corridor and he coughed loudly to get his attention.

Within a few moments and with barely a word spoken, the pair were back through the pumping machinery and heating ducts and the Irishman was making his way up the side of the building on the metal steps, with Jones behind him. At the top, with Jones now giddy from all of the exertion, McNally radioed to Virginia downstairs in Robinson's explaining that they were on the bird's nest. Jenny also heard the call.

Jones walked slowly across the top of the Europa roof and quietly pointed out the nearest sections. He silently nodded towards the three buildings and shrugged his shoulders. McNally whispered to Jones.

"If she's in one of them, how did she get up here without being seen? Is there a separate exit from the lift shaft in the middle?" Again, Jones shrugged and then walked right up to the gap between the sections of the building, looking down.

"After you," he said quietly and without even the merest sign of concern, McNally took three paces back and launched himself over the narrow drop. There was a loud thump as he hit the deck on the other side coated in shingle and dust. He immediately dusted himself down. His shabby trench coat was covered in grey dust. "Come on," he motioned towards Jones. "It's only a wee gap. Don't overthink it."

And Jones, wondering where this rampant testosterone had come from, took ten paces back, as far as one of the small aluminium outlets, and sprinted before jumping full-length over the gap. His heart almost stopped half way as the yawning chasm beneath him opened up. And the relief was tangible when he landed heavily on the other side. He had not made it with the relative ease of McNally but he was over. He crawled gingerly away from the edge and McNally helped him up.

"I told you not to overthink it." And McNally helped dust him down.

All three outbuildings had doors with thick padlocks, but one stood out. It was the furthest on the right, next to the lift shaft. This one had an extra padlock at the very top and bottom of the door as well as a thin wire travelling from the central padlock to an unknown location. McNally traced the wire with his eyes. It led to a passageway between the building and the shaft. On closer inspection he could see a leather holdall halfway down. He walked down the passage towards the bag and bent down, unzipping the holdall very slowly and peering inside.

"It's a booby trap," he whispered. "I've seen this before. There's a timer and a mound of plastic explosive. We can't touch that padlock. If we do it'll trigger the explosive and blow the top off the hotel."

Suddenly, from deep inside the room, they heard a cough and then a voice.

"Is that you McNally? Can you get me out of here?" Isadora had heard the commotion. He could hear she was desperate.

"Isadora! It's fantastic to hear your voice. That's the plan, sit tight please. We have a few obstacles yet. And we'll have you out of here before last orders." It was the first time Jones had seen McNally smile properly or crack a joke. But as he spoke he was edging backwards away from the holdall before surveying the rest of the building.

"Isadora, I'm really sorry, but there's a booby trap on the door. Are you tied up? Have you tried charging the door?" McNally enquired.

"A booby trap? I'm not blindfolded or gagged. But my arms and legs are bound. I pushed hard against the door but it was rock solid. And I never know when he's coming. I can't risk it."

"Isadora," interrupted Jones, "I'm Jones, we haven't met. Do you know your kidnapper? Are you hurt?"

"Nice to meet you. You're one of the new intake? My God, what a baptism of fire! I have cuts and bruises from the explosion. And I'm foggy. But as far as identifying the kidnapper, all I know is that he's white and left-handed. Oh, and he's wearing a pair of John Lewis underpants. He hasn't said a word."

"How long have we got before he comes back?" Jones replied.

"He feeds me early in the morning and around dusk and I've no idea what time it is now. I'm thinking mid-afternoon. You can do the sums." Isadora sounded incredibly spritely for such a harrowing situation.

"Ok. Just keep away from the door. We'll sort this as quickly as we can." Added McNally, before dragging Jones away from the outbuilding.

"Right," he whispered. "We need to keep her spirits up. But at the same time, we have no idea when that timer is due to go off and we can't risk triggering it by forcing the door. Let's speak to Charles and Massey and work out a plan." And they walked as far away from the trio of buildings as they could without heading back over the ledge.

At that moment, seemingly from out of nowhere, a police helicopter appeared. It swooped down so close that McNally and Jones could see the faces of the pilot and co-pilot. The vibrations almost blew the two back over the ledge between the buildings. Jones had visions of this incredible force unleashing the explosion but disaster appeared to be averted. The helicopter team had a large video camera and McNally was furiously signalling something to them. Jones guessed this was simply a way of explaining they were the good guys. It was all over in a matter of seconds and soon the rooftop was quiet again. The kidnapper, if he was close, would be questioning why a helicopter was travelling so close to his captive. Was the game up?

McNally picked up the handheld, which he'd momentarily switched off to save battery, and radioed down to Jenny and Virginia. "We have a wonderful view of a trapped cuckoo. She's rather battered and bruised but we'll need some support in taking her out of the nest. Jenny perhaps you could speak to our specialist ornithologist friends to help us."

Jones found himself thinking that for a specialist in ciphers and codes, McNally's last message was unerringly obvious to anyone listening. But he was delighted that Jenny was back in play and was looking forward to seeing her. Releasing Isadora would be a bloody successful start to his career and he was buzzing.

Back in Milton College, Mr Singh, assisted by Carl and Tom, had been keeping an eye on proceedings from afar. The two Emerald students were now partially in the loop and Virginia had been satisfied when both agreed to sign the Official Secrets Act. Although neither were entirely sure what this meant. On the bank of screens, they had seen the congregation of blue flashing dots representing handhelds swarm to the Europa Hotel or nearby, and Tom was watching the screen which showed Charles heading to Knock Road. Armstrong was carrying his handheld and this was very much alive. The fly in the ointment was the two handhelds, eight and twelve.

There had been a working theory that Isadora's handheld was blown up in the Limehill explosion. This was number four and was now out of service and probably in smithereens. Therefore, she could have grabbed two working handhelds from her fatally injured colleagues at the scene, perhaps to bring them back to the Barracks. But number twelve was now suddenly on the move for the first time. And yet Isadora was still confined. There was always a margin of error on Mr Singh's prototype GPS which meant number twelve could have been up to five metres away from number eight during her captivity. So, if Isadora had number eight but was unable to reach it, who had number twelve and where on earth was it going?

Whilst Carl and Tom watched ball-by-ball coverage of the latest India versus Sri Lanka test match on Bangla TV, Mr Singh radioed Virginia, still in Robinson's, with the update. She, in turn, attempted to reach Armstrong who had been chaperoning Charles at his meeting with Massey. With no luck.

And just at that moment, handheld number twelve's blue flashing dot alerted the Emerald team in Milton. Carl, eager to prove his worth, pointed out to Mr Singh that it was heading away from the Europa Hotel at speed on a perfectly straight trajectory across the countryside and exiting the scene.

"Surely this means handheld number 12 is on a train?" queried Carl, as Mr Singh appeared at his shoulder to check it out.

Unknowingly, Isadora's kidnapper, who had been spooked by something, had taken the handheld on the Belfast to Larne railway. For a few moments the pieces of the jigsaw edged closer together.

CHAPTER TWENTY-THREE

Hillman Imps were never the most robust of cars. They were always a little small, boxy and very uncomfortable but with useful boot space. A week's shopping perhaps or room for luggage ready for a camping trip. They were a poor man's Austin Mini.

On this occasion though it was just two kilos of RDX, a detonator, blasting caps and a fuse in a shoe box. And the result was spectacular. There was no warning and little understanding as to why anyone would detonate such a horrific blast in the centre of a sprawling suburban city. The flash of extreme light and energy was over in seconds but the devastation would be long-lasting.

This wasn't the first time of course. But this wasn't a paramilitary attack with a political endgame. This was a kidnapper creating a devastating diversion for an escape and the lives taken were simply collateral. The intense heat and incredible energy from the bomb saw the vehicle explode and somersault. It landed just shy of a bookmaker's shop which was crammed full of punters. Two of them were killed instantly and it later claimed a third victim from her injuries. She was just passing by, having dropped off some shoes for repair further down the street. Such was the horror of the explosion that in the blink of an eye, all normality ceased and all that remained was the stench of burning plastic and an odd metallic taste for the survivors. This was carnage.

It wasn't a pipe bomb or a lit rag attached to an old fuel tank. This was an evil distraction and was purely created to move attention away from Isadora on top of the Europa and allow someone to slip away to the ferry. Or that was Massey's theory later in the day.

Virginia had wandered outside when the explosion came. She had been mid-sentence speaking to Armstrong on the handheld and explaining about the possibility that the kidnapper was on the fast train heading eastwards to Larne Harbour. It had taken umpteen attempts to reach him. She was blown off her feet and around ten feet back towards Robinson's Bar. There were a host of other casualties too and the chorus of ambulance sirens were already nearing when Virginia regained consciousness. People were dazed, there were nasty shrapnel injuries, and two of the bartenders were beginning to walk round and check on people, giving reassurance. Incredibly, no-one was seriously injured in the bar, but the bookmakers was hit so badly that the building was quickly collapsing internally. Fifteen minutes after the incident there was still a dust cloud haunting Great Victoria Street and the sky had developed a deep grey hue. Even at 120 feet up they heard the blast and felt the tremor.

Minutes earlier, Massey had stopped attempting to interrogate Charles and he, in turn, had pulled down some of the barriers of secrecy the service demanded. It wasn't so much of an impasse as a mutual surrender. They were briefly joined by Jube Spencer, the RUC MI5 liaison and Belfast Office Chief who finally agreed to the sharing of personal data for all 36 of the previous YCU recruits, even those who had dropped out or moved on. Massey was never going to like Charles Curry, but she needed that intelligence.

Charles had met Spencer before and knew he was one of the good guys. He was a portly, amiable, Northern Irishman. The legend has it that his parents were so loyal to the British Crown that they named their only child after the 1962 anniversary of the Queen's ascension to the throne. Which also happened to be the date of his birth. Jubilee Spencer was born, but he was so embarrassed he quickly shortened Jubilee to Jube, often misheard or misspelt as Jude.

Spencer had also handed over all of the personnel records of current and former staff too. And this included McNally, who Massey still fancied had a role to play. But Massey didn't share the new evidence that had come to light. The contents of the manila folder that had so cheered her earlier. She decided at the eleventh hour that she wanted this information to be absolutely bulletproof before she took things any further. Although she didn't believe in coincidences, she also didn't want Charles' smugness to hit new levels if she was proved wrong again. So, she held that manila folder back.

The bomb changed her trajectory completely. She alerted the Anti-Terrorism Unit and updated their Chief, Eric Rogers, on the progress of the case whilst his emergency team were en route. There were three fire tenders and seven ambulances also at the scene. Pretty soon, news crews from the main broadcast media were unloading and beaming pictures from the aftermath around the world but with the context instantly wrong. *No one had claimed responsibility*, they said. *There was no warning*. But this was an explosion that used the ongoing turmoil in that beautiful country to create a mindless diversion. And it had partially worked. As the emergency teams dealt with the dead or seriously injured, no-one aside from

Jones or McNally was fully engaged in extricating Isadora Brown.

Jube Spencer, back on terrafirma 120 feet down, had decided to bring the Hotel General Manager into his confidence about the scene on his roof. More Official Secrets Act documents were signed and the Manager's jaw dropped when the full extent of the situation was explained. He promised every assistance, including adherence to the ongoing media blackout. This could not leak and the Manager didn't want that intrusion either.

The Manager, now fully on-side and hell-bent on limiting reputational damage, quickly moved Jenny from the Presidential Suite and created a Command Centre for the Isadora rescue in the only empty room on that floor. She was then shown a far safer route to the roof and was reunited with Jones and McNally. Jenny was tasked with befriending Isadora through the bolted door and keeping her calm and focused. This was not because she was a 'girl', they simply decided that she was the most likeable and could stem any concerns from Isadora with ease. There was even laughter from the pair when they shared their rather tactless opinions on McNally's 1970s dress-sense. The Manager had also provided the rooftop team with an impressive sandwich lunch, room service on the roof terrace was a first, he noted.

Pretty soon Spencer would be joined by Charles at the scene but he would have Virginia to worry about. She was injured and bruised but unbowed. MI5 would normally bring in significant extra resources, especially as the YCU were their own unit, and Charles had repeatedly demanded that. But with the US Peace Envoy in Belfast, the RUC were the only show in town. His only option was to bring in the Explosive Ordnance Disposal Company, part of the Royal Army Ordnance Corps. But they would expect the evacuation of the hotel and the surrounding area and this could not be achieved quickly or quietly. And nobody was sure whether the kidnapper had other eyes on the scene. If more bombs were triggered before the Sunday noon deadline, the rest of hell would break loose. Jube Spencer had effectively been put in a no-win situation.

There was also the question of the media interest in Great Victoria Street and the eyes of the world literally within spitting distance of the kidnap. So many things could go wrong. Whoever the kidnapper was had made sure the operation was as complicated as possible.

Massey had been asked to act as RUC Gold Commander for the ongoing emergency and would remain in the Knock Road Station and was therefore temporarily out of the Isadora information chain. Eric Rogers was in charge on the ground and was detailing and briefing both his team and the RUC's constables who had been dispatched to the scene. But barely anyone outside the inner circle knew about the rooftop scenario.

Charles grabbed Virginia's handheld and promised to be on full alert and engaged as the ambulance whisked him and his wife to the hospital. But operationally, he was out of the picture. His devotion to her was without bounds.

Therefore, with Spencer assuming command, a decision was made to move operations to the Hotel suite on the ninth floor, where a telephone was also available. Spencer and Armstrong quickly made use of the hotel floor plans and pinned them to the walls of the suite. They also were able to pass a prototype service camera to Jenny on the roof, which enabled McNally to photograph the bomb from multiple angles and in almost forensic detail.

MI5 were trialling Multi Media Card technology which allowed the images to be transferred to the Barracks without being developed in a dark room. Once a detailed cache of photos was assembled, Armstrong was dispatched back to

Thiepval with the MMC to liaise with the Explosive Ordnance Disposal Company. He would remain there whilst the bomb disposal team explained the task in hand giving step-by-step instructions, using Armstrong's handheld. In less than an hour work could begin on defusing the device.

Whilst they waited, a team of sniffer dogs arrived at the scene on Great Victoria Street to assist in checking for further explosive devices. None were discovered and therefore, a plain-clothed Bomb Detection Officer was also asked to take a walk through the hotel and across the landings and function rooms. It was achieved surreptitiously, with even hotel residents stopping to pet the service dog, much to the chagrin of the handler. The hotel was clear.

It was less than twenty minutes after the hotel all-clear that Armstrong made contact on the handheld. He had walked away from the soldiers, challenged with remotely disarming the device, to explain their concerns to Spencer and McNally. Jones and Jenny listened in.

"The lads here aren't keen. They can see the job in hand but they are concerned that if other eyes or ears are on the call, the button could be pressed elsewhere." Armstrong's attempts at being cryptic made everyone wince.

"Ring me in Briefing Room Alpha from your telephone in the room and we'll have to explain the steps that way," Armstrong concluded.

Jones looked towards McNally. "But who is going to be defusing the device? Do you have the know-how? You must have had training?"

"Oh aye," he responded quickly. "I've defused more bombs than you've had hot dinners. But that's why I was medically discharged. I have rheumatoid arthritis. This is why I have a desk job now," and he showed Jones his hands.

"I'll do it," Jones said, without a moment's hesitation.

"Kid, you've barely undertaken a moment's training. This is not the time for bravado." McNally responded.

"It's me, you or Jenny. Surely, it's just following instructions from the bomb disposal experts at the Barracks? I can do that." Jones sounded oddly confident.

For about twenty seconds there was silence, as McNally considered the options.

McNally picked up the handheld and radioed Armstrong. "We need five minutes to find some tools. We'll ring you from the room once we're set." Jenny looked at Jones with utter dismay and carried on her conversation with Isadora through the wall.

All that Spencer could muster from the Hotel Manager's maintenance store was a set of wire cutters, although these were far bigger than required for the thin wires to the timer, and a set of nail scissors and tweezers. Both of which were within the hotel's lost property. Chef's knives were offered and, somewhat bizarrely, a catering ladle but a set of 'snips' could not be found. Spencer himself carried his father's Swiss Army Knife with a small screwdriver that was considered useful.

Back in the hotel room, Spencer made the call to the Explosive Ordnance Disposal Company and was put through to an Ammunition Technical Officer. He gave his name as Captain Dee. There were no introductions and the weather had no bearing on the conversation. It was a straightforward blow-by-blow explanation of how this process would work.

"Mr Spencer, I understand you are going to relay my instructions to the team defusing the device at the top of the hotel. Am I correct?" He began.

"You are entirely correct, call me Jube though."

"Fair enough Jube, can I please ask that my instructions are repeated like an echo and you come back to me straightaway with any further questions? Do I make myself clear?"

"You do, Captain, go on ahead."

"Before I start the process, for your information, the wire order begins with the first of the top three wires. Always count from the top. Understand? So, wire one is the one at the very top."

"Understood."

"The bomber has left us no red wires. Therefore, I am going to begin the process by cutting the second wire next to the timer. Which is white. And then the blue wire on the bottom, the third wire. Am I making sense?"

"Absolutely. So, my first command is to cut the second wire. The middle white wire. Shall I proceed?"

"Proceed."

Jube Spencer, put the phone down and ran through the maintenance room and shouted the first instruction.

"Jones cut the second wire. The middle white wire to the timer."

Jones was crouching in the middle of the gap between the lift shaft and the outbuilding where Isadora was being held. McNally was holding the black holdall open, pulling the zip apart to reveal the whole device. Jenny was sitting at the very beginning of the gap, close to the door, with the range of instruments and tools collected by Spencer and the Hotel Manager.

"Okay. Understood." He shouted back.

He gently prized the spindle containing the three wires apart and traced the white wire back to ensure it was indeed the middle one. But, the wire cutters were too big. They could damage the two wires on either side. He sat back momentarily and looked up at the sky, regaining composure and trying to stop his heart from beating so rapidly. He sucked air in through his teeth and asked Jenny for the nail scissors. He could hear this heartbeat in his head and sweat running down his back underneath his polo shirt.

He took the nail scissors, which looked tiny in his hands, and placed the blades over the middle wire. He considered saying something heroic but instead simply made the cut but the scissors were blunt and rather than a clean cut, he had to attack the wire again. It made a loud snipping noise. The digital timer, rather like a travel alarm clock, remained bright and was illuminating the time. There was no countdown. It was simply a timepiece.

"I've cut the white wire. "Jones shouted across and Spencer dashed back through the maintenance room to the phone in the suite. There was an audible sigh from the team. Isadora was pressing Jenny for information and she simply replied by repeating "almost there" in her calmest voice.

Spencer picked up the phone. "Success, Captain."

"Okay. Move down to wire three. The blue wire. If this is successful, the digital timer should switch off as this is the power source. But it remains viable until all wires are cut. Understood, Jube?"

"Understood Captain"

"My next instruction is, to cut the third wire. The blue wire. Proceed with that command, Mr Spencer."

With that, Spencer placed the receiver down and ran back to his position. It was silence on the rooftop. Everyone remained in position and completely still as if the merest move could set something off. Still, the sun shone down and the birds sang happily as the little bubble of abnormality on the rooftop continued.

"Jones. Cut the third wire. The blue wire." Spencer was tempted to add the extra detail that the timer would then switch off. But he remembered Captain Dee's comment about being simply an echo. He leant on the side of the door and watch Jones hunched over the bag, McNally still holding the sides apart. Jones shot a quick look at Jenny, who was white and looking terrified and wondered if he radiated the same emotion.

He attempted to make the cut with the nail scissors, but they were so blunt and delicate that they simply refused to coordinate with enough force to cut through the blue wire. He picked up the tweezers and edged the wire millimetres up from the rest of the spindle and then located the tiny scissors among the tools in the Swiss Army Knife. The cut was made.

As the timer switched off an audible beep sounded that forced everyone to the ground. McNally covered the holdall with his chest and upper body almost attempting to sacrifice himself as the blast may be imminent. This showed the measure of McNally and was an image that would remain with Jones and Jenny.

In that split-second, Jones turned and stared at Jenny. There was no explosion. The clock simply blinked and lost power. The timer had been switched off. Jones was now soaked with sweat and he was finding it almost impossible to control his heart rate. Again, he looked up in the sky and counted, sucking air into his lungs and then dispelling slowly.

Jube Spencer was back at the phone.

"Captain, there was a loud beep before the timer switched off. People are jumpy."

"The beep is simply an alert confirming that the timer has been de-activated. If there is a constant beep, you'd normally need to run. But there's little point up there. Where are you going to go?"

Ignoring the last comment, Spencer asked for the next command.

"Jube, the next instruction is to cut the thick black wire. The black wire is the 'hot' wire, it carries the electricity from the breaker panel into the device. This will disarm the unit. However, please simply give this instruction – cut the thick black wire at the base of the timer which leads to the panel. Got it?"

Spencer confirmed and sprinted back to his position. He called across to the team. Still sitting in silence.

"Jones cut the thick black wire at the base of the timer which leads to the panel."

Jones looked down at the device. The thick wire was indeed significantly thicker but it was, at least, not attached to the cluster. There was only the sole top wire left on that cluster. The black wire was as thick as a kettle lead and he only had one tool that could make the cut. He wasn't feeling confident. He pulled the small sharp saw utility from the Swiss Army Knife and looked up at McNally. McNally, who had barely moved an inch since he adopted the position pulling the holdall apart, looked quizzically back at Jones.

"Yeah, I can't see any other option. But you'll have to give it some welly." And McNally smiled briefly and encouragingly. McNally looked madly uncomfortable in that trench coat in the late afternoon heat.

Jones grabbed the side of the holdall and rapidly thrust the saw implement up and down until he saw the silver wire peek through from inside and then piece by piece the cable shredded. He felt his hand throb and shake as he desperately used the saw to rip through the lead. There was one small slither of silver wiring left when the device made a quiet hissing sound.

Fearing the worst, he made the final cut and freed the cable. He ripped the device from the bag and pulled free the attached line from the door holding Isadora. And as the hissing got louder and louder, he ran to the edge of the hotel and threw the device over the edge into the car park. McNally and Jenny sprinted to join him and watched as the bomb sped down to the tarmac of the car park, Jones found himself with his hands tightly pushed together as in prayer. As the device hit the ground, there were sparks and the components flew apart. The alarm clock broke free and smashed open on the floor. There was no explosion.

Down below, as the device hit 120 feet down and smashed loudly on the ground, two ladies that lunched in pink and green trouser suits were walking back through the rear entrance to the car park.

"Barbara, did you see that? Falling debris now. This place just gets worse. You'd think they were trying to scare poor Treasure." And they walked on, the dog cradled in Barbara's arms.

McNally ran back to the outbuilding with Jones and Jenny fast behind. They quickly used the screwdriver part of the penknife to remove the hinges and slowly took the door off. The inside bolt was the last thing to give way.

Jenny ran in and grabbed Isadora, hugging the stranger whose life they had saved. She was still bound and Jones swiftly hacked off the shackles on her arms and legs. They were red raw but she was free. McNally took off his trench coat and placed it over her shoulders. Isadora didn't move whilst the team freed her, she just stared straight ahead whispering, "Thank God, thank God."

As she climbed out of the outbuilding, she screwed up her eyes to avoid the full glare of the sunlight. Jones and Jenny walked either side of her and slowly eased her back through the maintenance door. Spencer called over with his congratulations before heading back to the phone to pass on the news to Captain Dee.

Jones felt his heart beat calm and restore to a normal pattern. But he was wet through with perspiration and dehydrated. He put Spencer's Swiss Army Knife in his pocket. His fear of heights was now perhaps consigned to history.

CHAPTER
TWENTY-FOUR

It took a full three hours to get Isadora back to Thiepval after being checked over at City Hospital, where she showered and ate heartily. Massey was still finalising her work as Gold Commander for the major incident and she had despatched Family Liaison Officers to support the distraught, bereaved, families. She had also assigned a young constable to take a short statement from Isadora in one of the Briefing Rooms. There was little she could tell anyone about her capture or her detention on top of the Europa and the kidnapper had been forensically astute. The handheld was the only obvious lead and although teams had been despatched to the port and the stations en route, there was no positive update.

News of the Great Victoria Street bomb had unleashed a torrent of paramilitary theories in the media but no one had claimed responsibility. Plenty of people, across the political divide, had opinions and this simply upped the ante during sensitive fledgling peace talks. And whilst the angry theories were all almost certainly incorrect, this didn't help the families of the dead or injured.

Among those, Virginia was being kept overnight at the hospital. Both she and Charles were up to speed with events and absolutely delighted about the release of Isadora. Isadora had spoken to them both on the hospital payphone and had explained that she had no interest in going home to convalesce, she wanted to see this through and join Topaz to shape the new YCU team. Charles, who remained at Virginia's bedside, had already promised the team a celebratory meal out at the Bunch of Grapes and Jube Spencer a large pack of Cuban cigars as a thank-you for his last-minute heroic assistance. This would have been wonderful if Spencer had ever smoked.

In England, Mr Singh, Carl and Tom were providing regular updates to the YCU on where the rogue blue flashing dot was heading. It had certainly reached Larne Harbour but then the trail had gone cold. They had also been working to trace the locations of the handhelds in the weeks leading up to the Lennoxville and Limehall explosions. Massey was keen to hear that news to further her investigation. The contents of the manila file were also being slowly unpacked and pinned to a makeshift investigation board in the Knock Road Station and some of the photos hadn't seen the light of day in many years. Therefore, whilst the picture was blurrier than ever, Massey was confident that her new evidence would be the key.

It was the day after the third explosion that Massey was alerted to a call on line three. This call added a new level of complexity. It arrived from a Customs Official at Larne Harbour who had been working alongside an Explosive Detection Team, including two sniffer dogs. This was a new approach to policing and one still very much in its infancy. But explosive detection dogs had been trained to detect everything from improvised explosive devices to weapons and ammunition. They were becoming a passive way of screening people and vehicles. A

German Shepherd had discovered around 2 kilograms of RDX in an unaccompanied back holdall on the ferry between Larne and Stranraer in Scotland. But this was not a bomb, as the bag also contained a few personal items and a small amount of currency. However, whilst the bag had been hastily removed from the ferry, the sailing had been allowed to continue with members of the Dumfries and Galloway Constabulary lined up at Cairnryan Harbour once advice had been received from the RUC. The two forces had long worked closely together as both Belfast and Larne ports were prominent targets, with the HM Customs Team as the third team member.

Massey had immediately prioritised the ferry's manifest to look for likely suspects. She used the police database and Jube Spencer interrogated the list for any MI5 terrorist red flags. There were none. But savvy terrorists would be travelling on fake passports and false documentation. One RUC Officer was on the sailing and was using the onboard radio to gain instructions from the Knock Road team. But he would soon be out of his jurisdiction and could simply act as eyes and ears. Two men had piqued his interest. As he walked through the on-board canteen reserved for truck drivers and hauliers, two people stuck out as being oddly out of place. They were munching their way through a large breakfast but were edgy, sweating and continuously looking around them. As if awaiting bad news. Aside from this, they were fairly anonymous wearing old-fashioned donkey-jackets, dirty blue jeans and brown boots.

The younger of the two appeared to have a small recent injury to his face. The officer sat and observed from afar. Massey's team, after speaking to the ferry's head office, had identified them as Gregor Vinnikov and Oleg Alexinsky. They were Russian nationals who had been living in Holywood, just outside Belfast but there was little intelligence on them at all.

What made things stranger was that they were eating in the Truckers Lounge but they were listed as foot passengers and had no luggage whatsoever.

The Officer sat and observed them for the duration of their passage across to Cairnryan. He watched them become more and more jittery and anxious, which wasn't cured by their slow intake of four or five glasses of neat vodka. On five occasions, Vinnikov popped into the toilet, but he didn't use the facility provided in the Trucker's Lounge. He walked through to the area on the other deck where the rest of the foot passengers were and used a toilet there. The officer decided to follow him and watched him enter the gents on the lower deck. The Officer used a trip to the onboard duty-free as a plausible cover to watch him as a few other passengers dipped in and out of the toilet facility. Any real surveillance would have required two people and he knew he was hampered from the start. The officer quickly lost Vinnikov in the melee when disembarkation was announced over the tannoy and, after heading back to the lounge, Alexinsky had gone too.

It was no real surprise that they had both vanished into thin air at the queue for the exit when they came close to docking at Cairnryan, especially as it was so busy. But it was a real frustration for the officer. Disembarkation takes at least ten minutes and the officer used this time to identify himself to the security team and headed to the front of the queue. There was still no sign of the two Russians.

At Cairnryan, which was just a few hours sailing time from Larne, the Scottish air was cooler and with discouraging grey clouds hinting at rain. The slow parade of foot passengers ebbed their way off the boat with the RUC Officer, now out of jurisdiction and waiting to speak to the local police, searching in vain for the two Russians.

He could see the gates to the harbour and the customs

team, with a small police portacabin to the left. He headed briskly in that direction, having shown his police identity to a few crew members in orange fluorescent jackets, who looked indifferent but nodded him onwards. Interrupting him on his journey was a large lorry that was amongst the first to disembark and the familiar face of Oleg Alexinsky sitting way up in the driver's seat. Maybe he was mistaken and these were just two sea-sick passengers who were on the wrong manifest? He guessed that Gregor Vinnikov was probably sitting behind the front seats or catching up on sleep. Nonetheless, on reaching the customs desk he asked the team to search the Northern Irish-registered lorry thoroughly and was poised to radio through his apologies to Massey for wasting her time.

At the same time, in Milton College, the rogue handheld came to life and Mr Singh quickly informed McNally that it was now at Cairnryan Port in Scotland and very much alive and well. McNally made the phone call to Massey and whilst a few foot passengers had made it through customs and into awaiting vehicles, the foot passenger terminal was closed for a 'fire drill' and searches were undertaken on all of the lorries and cars as they swarmed off the ferry.

They didn't need to look far. In the back of the Russian container lorry, filled to the brim with dry pet food in large brown paper sacks, was a tiny area carved out for a stowaway. Oleg Alexinsky stood and watched helplessly as the back of the lorry was pulled apart by customs officials, he was alone. There was just a bundle of clothes, the signs of a sandwich snack, a small black handheld communication device and a small book. The book had lettering at the front which simply said 'Almanac 1993' and the rest of the purple cover was empty. This was one of McNally's 'Everything' books. In feint pencil, just on the inside of the cover was a name and just visible were the words Ewan McCarthy. Feeling around in the bag of clothes, there was a black jacket and inside the pocket were three passports – a new UK Passport in the name of Craig Finlayson, another in Ewan's name and the other a battered Irish passport with Gerard McMahon listed as the holder.

Ewan had perished at the Lennoxville blast, presumed dead. Likewise, Craig was one of those first pronounced dead at the scene in Limehall. Gerard McMahon was a mystery to Massey's team when the officer radioed it in. He was happily living in County Donegal and running a legitimate taxi company in Letterkenny. Although the Garda had confirmed he hadn't been spotted for a few days. But in July, this could be as innocent as a family holiday. There were no clear links between the YCU members tragically killed in the two blasts, the Russians, and McMahon.

Alexinsky's poor spoken English and the lack of Cairnryan Russian speakers meant that he, and the officer, were driven to Stranraer Police Station to undergo further questioning, whilst a translator was being brought in from Edinburgh.

Gregor Vinnikov was nowhere to be seen. He was not visible on any port security cameras and none of the customs staff recognised him when questioned. The initial theory was that the second Russian had made his way off the ferry concealed in the back of another lorry and was now somewhere in Scotland. But Massey was waiting for further details from Interpol and Europol to look into the background of Vinnikov and Alexinsky.

What was clear was the notion of a 'lone wolf' attack was now off the table. Ulster Nationalism also suddenly seemed an angle from ancient history. The jigsaw pieces scattered again.

In Thiepval, the newly increased Topaz team was de-briefing after 48 hours of high-octane and emotional work. Isadora had been told about the deaths of her colleagues and friends and this required the gentle tact of Virginia who was now back from City Hospital.

Jones, Jenny, Isadora and the senior team of McNally, Armstrong, Virginia and Charles were awaiting a detailed update from Massey. Armstrong, who had chiefly been brought to Thiepval to lead the physical training aspect, was keen to return to England as it was becoming clear that Topaz were now learning on the job. No more running around parade grounds; leaping around 120ft hotel roofs had done the job. Armstrong, previously a suspect, simply needed the green light from Massey before heading back to Aldergrove Airport. So, he sat in his navy tracksuit with his bags packed. Massey hadn't found anything interesting enough about him, his service history was immaculate and unblemished.

In the centre of the long table in Briefing Room Alpha was a circular machine which was a rudimentary telephone conferencing system with a mess of telephone cables leading to a small box in the corner of the room. As the team awaited Massey's call, Charles cleared his throat and addressed the small group.

"The YCU was only ever supposed to be an experiment to see if SIS could look outside the normal sphere of recruitment processes. Perhaps moving away from the big universities and the taps on the shoulder of the super-intelligent when their prowess became clear. I wasn't keen, as I've always believed that the system was pretty near perfect."

"Virginia took the opposing view. She felt everyone should be given a chance in this career and, after what's happened in the past week, I think it's high time I admitted how wrong I was. Two recruits, with no experience and precious little training, helped save the life of Isadora. And I'd like to thank you both for your incredible bravery and commitment. Jones and Jenny, we are proud to have you amongst our ranks." Jones and Jenny shared a brief glimpse, Charles' words were unexpected and appreciated but they both realised the task was only half-completed. He continued.

"However, we also need to remember the lives lost. Two groups of young people lost their lives in the most horrific of circumstances and, as yet, we do not understand why or who committed these terrible atrocities. We will, of course, have some private memorial for them here, as their families and the general public will never know their true sacrifice. The saddest part of any association with the Secret Intelligence Services is the inability to ensure public recognition for bravery or heroism."

"There will be no medals, no salutes, just a knowing look and a tearful goodbye. There'll be families grieving in England, Scotland, Wales and Northern Ireland thinking their children had been killed in a horrific minibus accident in the South of England. Virginia will fly back and meet the bereaved families but nobody will know how very close they came to serving their country and saving lives themselves."

"So, whilst we cannot honour our dead outside our own circles we will ensure their memories are cherished." Charles raised his glass of water and the rest of the team followed suit. "To Alpha and Beta Teams" and the group repeated his words. Isadora briefly put her hand to her face to deal with the emotion and Virginia offered a comforting hug. It was a few seconds of reflection before the needs of the day took priority.

As he finished, and the group settled back into their seats, the telephone conference system kicked into life. It was a useful bookend for a fitting speech by Charles.

"Good afternoon everyone and welcome back to Isadora. I'm sorry I haven't been able to meet you properly yet but the major incident team needed me at the station. I now have a brief window to give you a quick update." Massey sounded sharp, professional, and extremely tired.

"One of our officers picked up a Russian national coming off the ferry at Cairnryan, he was driving a Northern Ireland-registered lorry packed with dog food. His lorry also contained one of your handheld devices squirrelled away in a hidden compartment, along with passports and personal effects. I will fax through some details now." As she spoke, a fax sprang into life at the back of the room and Jones went over to receive the information.

"The passports belonged to two of yours, I'm afraid." Jones placed the faxed sheets in front of McNally, Virginia and Charles.

"My goodness, these are Craig and Ewan's passports. How did they get hold of them? And one of the YCU Almanacs. Did you say three passports? Who is the third?" Asked Virginia.

"It's an Irish passport in the name of Gerard McMahon but he's clean. It's a mystery. The Russian had a friend on board who's gone missing. We have detained Oleg Alexinsky in Stranraer Police Station but his fellow national Gregor Vinnikov has vanished. We have people looking for him, but he could be anywhere. And could be anyone. There is simply no intelligence." Massey signed off and promised she'd update as and when new information came to light or when forensics had finalised their work on the lorry.

The room fell silent as everyone processed the news.

Virginia's handheld echoed with the sound of interference as Mr Singh attempted to contact her.

"We've been through the movements of the GPS signals from everyone in the team. One of the handhelds has been a regular visitor to the Glen, and recce-ed the sites at Limehall and Lennoxville before the bombings. But it belonged to one of the dead men, Craig Finlayson." Mr Singh explained.

"Craig's dead," added Virginia. "I identified his body, there was no mistake."

"I haven't finished," interrupted Mr Singh. One of the boys here has worked out that Craig's handheld was also used to go to a shop in Lisburn on the day of the Limehall bomb. Perhaps in one of the Land Rovers?"

Isadora looked around the table and quickly picked up the fax, scanning for more detail on the Russians.

"Craig was with me all day on the day of the explosion. We even went to lunch together. It was one of Ewan's team who did the drive to the shops. We'd run out of wine. I can't remember who. It may have even been Ewan himself." Isadora explained.

"Ewan's body was never found, such was the nature of the explosion. Therefore, I guess he needs to be seen as a suspect. But I'm sure in the next few days forensics will confirm his remains were amongst the debris." Added Virginia.

"There's only one of that team alive now, Stephen Finch, and he appears a broken man. We could go back to Bangor and ask him about the trip to Lisburn shops and piece that day together?" suggested Jenny.

"I spoke to him yesterday and he sounded in a bad way, traumatised and despairing," Charles said, standing up and pinning the fax copies to the wall of the Briefing Room. "I'll bet you all the tea in China that our friend Stephen Finch is our bomber. And I further suggest that he may well be our missing Russian. Gregor. It just seems too coincidental to be anyone else. He's the only remaining connection. But let's just explore this theory a little before we talk to Massey. Any thoughts anyone?"

"That just seems mad," said Jenny. "I understand he's possibly the last man standing but aside from his clear dislike of McNally, he just appeared like a victim himself and with very low confidence."

McNally tapped on the table, as if asking to be let in. "We're hardly best buddies, but I know Stephen's Dad. He's a mechanic in Newtownards. I think Massey knows him too, it's a small world here. But I just can't see it. Stephen was one of the lads. Sure, he was a little quiet but he's not the force behind Red Line, he's a good fella. And damn ambitious too. I just can't see it."

The room fell silent.

CHAPTER TWENTY-FIVE

Over in Knock Road Station, Massey had found paracetamols and was drinking her fourth cup of coffee. It had been a nightmare few days and she was struggling to understand the Russian influence on the case.

She had pieced together the major elements of the investigation on a makeshift board with help from an unlikely ally. Some of the photos were from the 1920s and there were birth certificates and political memoirs of famous Irish Republicans. Jube Spencer, dressed in a smart business suit and sharing Massey's caffeine fix, was fresh from his unexpected heroics on the Europa. He had joined her and, being a part-time Irish history student, it was he who handed over the clandestine manila folder. Spencer had joined the dots in a spectacular fashion but they were an unlikely partnership.

On the board was a photo of two Irish political names from after the Easter Rising. Patrick McCartan and Rody Connolly were heroes of the Irish revolution. But both also visited and courted Russia in the 1920s as Ireland needed recognition as an independent state. However, Britain was still preventing it by having strong international relations with major states, such as

France and the US. McCartan and Connolly both had unblemished records and were faces from a vital piece of Irish history.

Spencer had proudly begun to shape an alternative timeline. And he sat opposite Massey with a few history books and a paper and pen. Occasionally pointing up at the investigation board.

"Bear with me on this," he began and Massey instantly rolled her eyes.

"With Britain so challenged by Irish independence, Irish communist and republican leaders wanted to receive support from Russia. They wanted them onside. So, Patrick McCartan was sent to Russia in 1920, followed by Rody Connolly's visit in 1921 to negotiate Russian recognition of the Irish Republic as an independent state." He explained.

"But, I'm guessing they weren't having any of it?" Asked Massey, already wearily.

"Well, the relationship never really took off. The need for international stability for both countries prevented the development of this relationship. Both Ireland and Russia were fresh from revolutions. And, in the end, Russia was in critical need of economic growth to restore itself after the war and revolution. Ireland wasn't seen as part of the future. This was an almighty blow for Ireland, for a wee while anyway." Spencer paused and looked up from his notes. Massey looked non-plussed.

"So, after a bit of a hiatus, in 1921 the trade agreement between Russia and Britain resumed. This left Ireland out in the cold and desperate for US support. Which they got. In the end. And as we know, Ireland and the US have been firm allies ever since."

"Right," sighed Massey. "That's useful history. But I really don't see what this has to do with a series of explosions in 1995. Especially as neither of us believes it has anything to do with Republicanism."

"Nope, this isn't about Ireland. This is about Russia. This is about somebody mired in the past, the deep past, suddenly being awoken to help fly the red flag and generally annoy the US. Do you see?"

Massey just looked bemused and was stirring her coffee.

"Our man Charles Curry thought the Russians were trying to blow the peace process off course by setting off a few bombs and letting the factions blame each other. He's right, I think. But there's more to it now. The US Peace Envoy, Fred Martinsen is now meeting both sides. The Unionists and Republicans. It's now becoming real and some form of peace is possible. So, they're using what remains from history to do their dirty work and scupper it all."

"I get that, in history, Russia didn't openly support Ireland on its journey to its independence. And America did. So, we now have a US Peace Envoy here and the Russians are annoyed as they don't want the US to be seen as the world's moral saviours. But you can't simply forget nearly seventy years of history and Russia rejected Ireland. And there's nobody alive from then, surely?"

Spencer pulled out a dusty photograph of a man in a green suit, seemingly shaking hands with Lenin, and then a further photo which looked more contemporary. Perhaps from the 1960s.

"Chief Inspector Orla Massey, history tells us everything!" And he banged his hand triumphantly on the notes.

"There was one man, who had accompanied both McCartan and Connolly, who had remained there from these visits. And there were rumours in MI6 and G2, the Irish SIS, that he had been turned by the KGB." As he spoke he presented the aged photo.

"His name was Bryan O'Malley, an active communist sympathiser, but ironically he was born and raised in Liverpool.

O'Malley, it seems, was Russia's man on the inside. And he acted as a sleeper here in Belfast until his death in the 1960s. He probably gave away countless Irish and British secrets to the Russians and ensured they were always in the know. He was quite the commie hero."

He then presented the second photo. It was of a man at a dancehall, dressed to the nines with slick back hair and his arm round an attractive blonde woman in a mini-skirt.

"This is his son, Seamus O'Malley. He's divorced now but it looks like he was quite the stallion back in the day! He runs a garage in Newtownards. And he has a son too."

"Jesus Christ!" said Massey, loudly, quickly establishing the link.

"His son took his mother's name after the divorce. She was Eleanor Finch," and he pointed to the photo again and then to the YCU team photo on the Board.

"Stephen Finch is what you might call a man in ultra-deep freeze. He was doing his grandfather's job by protecting and enhancing Russian interests and also perhaps earning a tonne of money before disappearing off to Russia, where the skills he's learnt at YCU will be very useful."

Massey then joined in. "So, he wasn't expecting Isadora to survive, was he? The kidnapping was maybe designed to throw us off course and after a few days of feeding Isadora, I think Finch was simply hoping to vanish in his new guise. You're a genius, Spencer!"

"Thanks, Orla, but there is much more to this yet. We may have stumbled upon his motivation but we don't know whether more are planned. As I can't imagine the explosions to date would stop the peace talks. Fred Martinsen is hardly likely to be heading home with his tail between his legs."

"No, I agree, but we need to find Stephen Finch very quickly and we don't have jurisdiction in Scotland. He could even have headed south maybe?" added Massey.

"This is a complication, Orla. But I think I have a solution. MI5 and MI6 will not officially touch any investigation which antagonises the Russians at the moment. We've been told the cold war has ended remember?"

"Right?" Massey looked quizzically at Spencer.

"But I think it could be damn good practice in surveillance and tracking to allow YCU, who have notional jurisdiction across the whole of the UK, to get over to Scotland and find their erstwhile colleague. And my team here can unofficially support that." Spencer smiled.

"I'll get Charles Curry on the telephone, shall I?" Massey said, and threw another cup of now tepid coffee down her throat. Whilst Charles' smugness was wholly unacceptable, she was beginning to like Jube Spencer, a little.

CHAPTER TWENTY-SIX

In the space of two and a half hours Isadora, Jenny and Jones were quickly and quietly removed from the Thiepval Barracks Officer's Mess, where they'd had a few drinks with Armstrong before his return to England. They'd also been given a thorough briefing from McNally as he drove them to the airport. The quick turnaround in events had surprised them but all three were excited to be thrown into the action.

They would be flying from the tiny Newtownards Airfield over to RAF West Freugh, just five miles east of Stranraer. McNally knew the airbase well as this was where he'd undertaken his armaments training in the late 1960s but he'd be staying firmly in Northern Ireland as, somewhat unfairly, whilst Massey had absolved Armstrong of any involvement in the bombings, she wanted McNally to stay put and help with the investigation. Armstrong would just be a phone call away, he promised.

Jenny and Jones had been given just ten minutes to pack some things back at Thiepval. Jones was still reliant on Jenny Richmond's vastly superior wardrobe as Carl and Tom had repeatedly forgotten to send his things across. Isadora, it seemed, wasn't his size and he couldn't purloin things from her. She was much more organised with a 'go bag' lined up ready for such adventures. The team had assembled and was en route, Jones instantly regretted the two pints of Smithwicks in the Mess, as his bladder was groaning on the journey to the airport.

"Listen, Charles has given you the green light to go and find Stephen Finch. He is not the only show in town. But Stephen appears to be the likely link, especially as he's dropped off the face of the earth."

"Let's be clear though, this is not an easy assignment and you'll be doing this with limited support. But, you know a few things. He's possibly travelling under the false name of Gregor Vinnikov or perhaps using the identification of any of the YCU fatalities from Limehall and Lennoxville. Ewan McCarthy could feasibly have survived. Stephen may have found KGB support and could already be in London, for all we know. So, this is a needle in a haystack." McNally explained.

"Stephen Finch has an Ulster Bank cash card and I have pulled a few strings with a friend in GCHQ who will brief me if he uses it anywhere. The tracing technology is new so Finch may not be aware we can do this. We have tapped his parents' phone and Massey has surveillance outside the property, so we'll know quickly if he's back home or making contact. All of the names associated with this case, including his Russian alias are on the watch list. So, if he's trying to leave the country by air, we'll know that too." Added McNally.

Isadora had been making notes. "Do we have any idea why he's headed into Scotland? Why haven't the Russians simply swooped in and taken him to Moscow?"

"Customs at Larne found a bag with two kilos of RDX lying around near the passenger terminal. I'm convinced Finch has more. The containers at the Glen had around ten kilos missing.

So, I'm guessing something else is planned. And it'll be focused on upsetting the peace talks."

McNally pulled the Land Rover over and chatted to security staff in the entrance to Newtownards Air Field, as Jones relieved himself in a nearby bush. The three were then on their own, with only handhelds for company. The security gates lifted and Isadora, Jenny and Jones walked into the tiny terminal building. They watched from white plastic chairs as McNally's vehicle indicated left and disappeared from view.

Charles had prepared each a briefing pack which included photos of Finch and his probable false Russian details. They also had the detailed historic notes, compiled by Jube Spencer, and he had also given them a number of initial lines of enquiry to work through. Charles had also given them £100 worth of currency and a list of useful phone numbers. All three had stored this information in McNally's 'Everything' Almanacs and Isadora, as team leader, held onto the currency.

As the three waited in a converted portacabin for their flight, Isadora turned to her colleagues. She was, like Jones and Jenny, dressed in jeans and a long-sleeved t-shirt with military-issue black re-enforced boots.

"I am determined to catch this evil bastard. He killed my friends and held me captive. But this cannot be all about me. I realise I'm the team leader and the most experienced, but Jones I hear you aced the tests and Jenny, you've shown yourself to be a critical thinker. We are a team now." Isadora looked fired up but Jones could see she was struggling to stay composed.

As the Cessna light aircraft taxied off the tiny runway at Newtownards, Jenny had been all but silent for hours. Jones repeatedly smiled at her reassuringly and squeezed her hand but midway through the flight, she turned to him.

"I just don't know what I can give to this. I'm massively out of my depth." And she closed her eyes.

As Jenny slept, Isadora read and re-read the briefing papers. Jones followed suit and tried to memorise the key information. Isadora watched with interest as Jones placed a blanket over the sleeping Jenny and the affection was clear.

"So, what's the deal with you two then? You seem close." Asked Isadora in an attempt to join the dots, as she started from the first page of the brief again.

"To be quite honest, I'm not sure. We have been rather thrown together. And now we have a pretty much watertight partnership. But, more than that, I'm unclear" replied Jones, as casually as he could muster.

"You ought to be careful. Relationships are pretty much impossible in the field. I've got the scars. But that's another story." Isadora continued reading

"Enjoy it whilst it lasts but we're a team on this mission. Right?" Jones simply nodded at Isadora in response. There was no doubt in Jones' mind that they needed Isadora and their desperate actions during the rescue already made her a trusted ally. This was already a team.

Jones was just plucking up the courage to ask her more about her own bruising relationship, when the plane hit a spot of turbulence on approaching the airfield. It immediately woke Jenny up and threw her bag over the far side of the passenger area.

"Don't look so alarmed, these things are notoriously wobbly coming into land. It's not a jumbo jet. You'll need to get used to this and worse!" With that, Isadora stared out of the window and they all watched the Scottish evening emerge below them.

Charles had arranged basic lodgings in the RAF base for one night and then there were planned meetings with a contact of Massey's from the Dumfries and Galloway Police - all strictly off the record. Until then, the three simply talked until the wee small hours in a dormitory bedroom and drank the best part of a bottle of rum, which Jones had borrowed from Virginia's office in Thiepval. This was bonding and Jones hoped that Jenny would gain confidence as she saw she was in the heart of the planning.

All three awoke with slight hangovers, Jones because he'd mixed lager and rum throughout the day and Jenny and Isadora because Jones had peer-pressured them both into over-drinking. And Jenny wasn't a rum drinker. She was urged strongly to get out of bed at 08.45am as they were due to pick up their Eurodollar hire car at Stranraer at 10am and they were reliant on a lift from a kindly airfield porter.

Stranraer was a busy market town and the Eurodollar rental office was just opposite one of the largest cheese manufacturers in Europe. The smell didn't aid Jenny and Isadora's hangover but Jones already had a hankering for a cheddar toastie. They'd not had breakfast yet. So, as a non-driver, Jones was relegated to the back seats as Jenny navigated Isadora to a Wimpy bar in Dumfries. The drive was over an hour and they were due to meet an off-duty Detective Constable who Massey knew. Her name was Cheryl McManus.

Whilst Jones gorged on a bender burger with extra cheese and an enormous chocolate thick-shake, his two colleagues were quietly drinking coffee and still regretting their bonding session. Jenny's handheld buzzed and she was surprised to hear the voice of Mr Singh.

"Good morning Jenny, this is Mr Singh. Greetings from Milton College. How are we all doing?"

"Don't ask Mr Singh. Let's just say Jones introduced me to rum last night and we are no longer friends." Jenny looked sternly across at Jones, who was still demolishing brunch.

"You need some soluble paracetamols and some ginger beer. My mother swears by it after a heavy night. Anyway, I have some good news for you. It'll cheer you up!" Isadora and

Jones moved closer to Jenny's handheld and listened in to Mr Singh.

"How many of you have heard of optical character recognition?" He asked. There was silence. Jones stared blankly at Isadora. Brown sauce was smeared over his top lip.

"Right, okay. OCR is a system which allows letters and numbers to be automatically collected and stored. Take for example a photocopier, when you use your photocopier to scan your documents, imagine how useful it would be if they were saved into a word processor document. And then you could edit the words or the letters?"

"Yes, I think we're with you, Mr Singh," Jenny confirmed.

"Let's take that a stage further. Imagine you could photograph numbers and letters and check them against a database. Let's say a number plate of a lorry which is wanted by a small YCU team who were looking for a needle in a haystack?" Mr Singh sounded proud of himself.

"You mean. If we got a list of the other lorries which left the ferry the same day as Finch or whatever Russian name he was using, we can perhaps locate where they were heading?" Isadora asked.

"Is that technology available now, Mr Singh?" added Jones.

"Hold on. Too many questions at once. Firstly, you could give me those registration numbers and I could check them against the prototype locations for this new technology. But they're all in England, so we'd have to hope he's heading down here." Mr Singh replied.

"The positive thing is, there is one of the trial models of this system on the A1 which stretches from the very north of England right the way into London. There are others dotted around key London routes so if he's down here, we'd know." He added.

"But there could be thirty or forty number plates off the

ferry? So, whilst the haystack is smaller, the needles are more plentiful?"

"You could say that Jenny, yes. But it's a start. And how many of those lorries had Northern Ireland plates? And I'm not really supposed to have access to these police computers. So, I'd be grateful if you didn't mention this to anyone. This is off the books, so to speak." Mr Singh said his goodbyes and the three waited for Cheryl McManus to show. She was already ten minutes late.

By the time she arrived, she was thirty minutes late but Jones had ordered another bender burger and the rest of Topaz were now feeling more human. Jenny had even attempted to eat a jacket potato. They quickly learnt that Cheryl wasn't just an old friend of Massey's - but an old flame. And she certainly wasn't over her. This came as quite a shock for the team as none had realised Massey was loveable, as she had done her best to be deliberately awkward and challenging during the last investigation. Therefore, Isadora found herself gently counselling Cheryl before extracting the paperwork from her, which was also off the record. But Cheryl was keen to help and didn't question their clandestine role, she even admitted she had wanted to be a spook herself.

"What we've got from customs is a complete list of the ferry's manifest, which includes all of the vehicles and foot passengers. I've circled a few names and my colleagues have already helpfully ruled out any regular freight or passenger vehicles." Explained Cheryl, drinking from a large polystyrene cup of strong tea.

"That," she continued in between sips "leaves eighteen cars, which I'm guessing you're not interested in, and three lorries with Northern Irish plates."

Jones scanned the paperwork and pulled out his briefing notes from Charles.

"So, none of them have the same livery as the lorry which Oleg Alexinsky was travelling in? The pet food lorry?" Jones asked.

"No, none. And there was no other pet food container on the ferry. Oh, and Mr Alexinsky is still being interviewed at the nick in Stranraer. The on-call Russian interpreter is in the room, but Alexinsky is saying nothing. Orla is waiting on Interpol and Europol to see if they can identify him from his presumably fake passport. He could be KGB. He'll be flying over to Knock Road tonight."

"What on earth was he doing in Belfast anyway?" Asked Jones.

"He was working in the Coca-Cola bottling plant in Newtownards. They rely on foreign labour. But if this Red Line thing is kosher, he would have been shipped over to support the cause. He may even have been in deep cover for the KGB but we won't know until we get more intelligence."

"Okay, this is really useful stuff. You've given us a real head start. And we'll pass on your regards to Orla Massey." Isadora said, as Cheryl picked up her polystyrene cup of tea and headed for the door.

"I wouldn't bother," she added, sadly. "I'll be in touch if we hear more." And she walked out.

Jones was the first to start rifling through the paperwork Cheryl left behind. Of the lorries with Northern Ireland plates, one was listed as 'cab only' which meant the container had been left at Cairnryan or nearby. Jones scribbled that one off the list. That left two and Jenny picked up the handheld and gave those two number plates and, for the sake of completeness, the NI-registered car licence plates too, to Mr Singh. He promised a response as soon as possible after accessing the police database.

"I'm struggling with one aspect of the series of explosions. Why was Stephen, if we presume Stephen was Vinnikov, carrying the passport of a random taxi-driver from Letterkenny? Gerard McMahon? What has he got to do with all of this?" Isadora spoke as she was fishing through her briefing pack for the photo of the Irish passport.

"Massey spoke to the Garda and they reckon he's away on holiday. What if there's something more sinister going on? Maybe we should be moving on, it feels like we're wasting time." added Jones.

"Look, let's see what Mr Singh comes back with from the registration plates and we can then plot our next move. In the meantime, could we not get Massey's team to check whether any of the cars on the ferry were taxis?" Isadora replied.

Jenny was making notes whilst leafing through the brief. "You must have worked with Stephen, Isadora?" she asked and then held up the photocopy of Gregor Vinnikov's passport. "Is this him? Can you tell from the shadowy image?" The xerox image was poor but his eyes stood out with cropped brown hair and the beginnings of a beard around his young face.

"This is going to sound weird, but I worked with him for nearly two years and yet I barely knew him. He was a background person. He was also a local and that meant he would often go home to see his family rather than socialise with us." She explained.

"Even his cover story was different. We were all at the College and undertaking our communications degree at Milton or, like me, doing a sandwich course which meant I was on a Cruise Liner away for weeks at a time. It all made sense for my family. But Stephen told his family that he was a trainee Press Officer for the Thiepval Barracks and was only at Milton to complete the media ethics part of the course. McNally sorted that out for him, innocently, I'm sure."

"Being at the Barracks so much gave him access to everything though? He knew details and operations?" asked Jenny.

"I guess so," answered Isadora. "But this is the Army and they're on alert all the time for people in the shadows. But neither they or the YCU would have suspected one of their own. I mean, who expects a cold war relic to start killing off the team? Just to create a nuisance for the Americans? I just don't know why my friends had to die for that."

"But you buy this deep freeze theory? That his grandad was an Irish double agent and worked for the KGB? And his family were awakened by the need to destroy any possible American peace deal?" Asked Jones.

"Yes and no, the deep freeze stuff makes sense. But I also think he was an outsider and was struggling for relevance. Maybe once the call came, to be a KGB hero and a prized Russian asset, it was just tempting enough to commit such horrific crimes. He must have been indoctrinated young."

The three took the hire car through the sweeping Scottish countryside intending to get to the Horseshoe Inn, a pub Jones remembered from family golfing holidays to Wigtownshire and Dalbeattie. It was in a village called Eddleston and was close enough to the border to feel both English and Scottish in equal measure.

Either Mr Singh would use the handheld and give some news about the lorry's likely position or he would do the opposite and the team would need to look north again. Jenny had suggested reminding McNally about Finch's financial records to see when his bank card was last used but that train of thought was momentarily halted when the promised call from Mr Singh arrived.

Jenny picked up the call. "I have news. And it's not altogether good. None of the lorries whose number plates you gave me have registered on the OCR machines in London or on the A1. The lorries have either not driven down to the south or have avoided the cameras."

The three looked immediately disappointed.

"But" he continued, "one of the car number plates from the ferry has flashed in three locations. On the A1 heading into London, on the North Circular Road and again just outside Westminster on the ring road. But I guess it would be moving about a lot."

"What do you mean, moving about a lot?" asked Isadora.

"Well, picking up fares or whatever. It's a taxi licence plate." Added Mr Singh.

CHAPTER TWENTY-SEVEN

Massey was half way through reading scores of forensic reports when the phone rang in the office. Unusually, someone was ringing her direct line and this meant it was either her mother or one of a handful of close friends she trusted enough to disturb her at work. It was Inspector Moira Doyle from the Garda Síochána in Donegal, someone she had known and trusted since her days at the Derry RUC office.

"Hello Orla, this is Moira, I wish I could be calling you in better circumstances."

"Go on right ahead, Moira, what's the matter?"

"It's your taxi driver, Gerard McMahon. His wife has reported him missing today. And we've spoken to his office in Letterkenny and he hasn't reported back since completing a job over the border in Portstewart." Moira explained.

"Jesus. This just gets better. What do we know about him? Anything?" asked Massey, quickly trying to stitch the pieces together.

"Nothing. Not even a parking ticket. He's a family man and has barely left Ireland. Has siblings down in Waterford and a daughter at Ulster University. No red flags, no problems." Confirmed Moira.

"The only other thing," she added "is that wherever he's gone, he's taken his car with him. It's a black 1989 Volkswagen Golf, a hatchback."

Massey passed on her thanks for the tip and pondered ringing McNally, to make the YCU Topaz team aware. But instead opted to dial Jube Spencer who she felt a little more comfortable with.

Spencer, who had just finished a round of golf at Royal Down and was slightly the worse for wear, had not made any provision for a missing Irish taxi-driver in his deep-freeze theories. He acknowledged there was no link between Mr McMahon and Russia, not even three or four generations back. Instead, Spencer suspected the taxi driver could have simply been in the wrong place at the wrong time – but for what? And where was he now?

The only positive intelligence, Jube Spencer's really big news, was that Oleg Alexinsky was a known KGB field agent who was normally working in and around the Russian Embassy in London. The Coca-Cola bottling factory was simply deep cover. This was typical for a KGB officer. MI6 had therefore provided the first real link to the Russian Secret Services. This seemed to add weight to Jube Spencer's theories. The Russian had just landed for a fresh round of questioning in Belfast's Knock Road Station, but they only had twenty-four hours. Jube laboured the point that Alexinsky rang 'loud bells' in his memory but he couldn't pin-point where he'd heard the name before. It was frustrating him enough to put down his post-golf Bushmills and drive back to the office.

Alexinsky had remained silent in all the Police and MI6 interviews and was seemingly confident that he would be deported back to Moscow rather than indicted for anything.

Massey was furious that killing innocent civilians, as well as a group of young SIS trainees, would go unpunished for the sake of diplomatic relations. But, she and Spencer would have one more pull of Alexinsky's chain before he was airlifted anywhere. Massey would just have to wait for Spencer's intelligence to come up trumps but she was already sharpening her claws.

After Mr Singh's call, Topaz had decided to make their way down south and find a central London location to track and locate the missing taxi and Stephen Finch. As luck would have it, Virginia had a bolt-hole in Stratford, east London, which was within close reach of the requisite locations. She was still convalescing in Belfast before returning to Milton College, and she'd have no need for it. Stratford was also on the same train line as Milton and a hasty plan B was assembled where Mr Singh might set up in Virginia's flat should the need arise. Jones hoped not, he was enjoying the camaraderie of their little adventure and wanted to keep things tight.

They stopped at Harrogate and then again at Bishop's Stortford for much-needed sustenance breaks and Jenny took on a two-and-a-half-hour shift behind the wheel. The seven-hour journey flew past and the conversation barely left the topic of Stephen Finch. Jones, as the only non-driver, indulged in a few motorway beers and slept on and off. He was enjoying being back in England but he was growing more and more concerned about Jenny, who seemed more distant than ever. Even when she was driving and Jones brought out the recent Now That's What I Call Music compilation cassette, she stared ahead rather than singing along with Whitney, Kylie and the Pet Shop Boys.

Jones was quickly aware that Stratford was a nearly-town. It was all laid out in front of him from the back seat. It seemed full of industrial heritage but with ghostly dwindling manufacturing zones, and boarded-up shops and warehouses. It was close enough to London but not part of it. As they crawled through the busy evening streets looking for the address Virginia had given them, it became clear that the area was commuter belt territory with a real local heart, spirit, and an incredible charm. It was as if it was clinging onto not being swept into London like a land-grab. And that seemed at odds with its years of under-investment. Those vibes were all the more palpable as they stopped at the Railway Tavern, parked the car and walked inside for directions. A night-cap seemed a sensible idea too.

A crowd of locals stared up at the television screen as the football highlights were beamed around the pub. A few men, who had clearly been there for a while, dissected the West Ham performance clinically but with a narrative that cleverly interspersed expletives with tactical nous. Jones smiled. This was where he felt most comfortable. And as Jenny chatted to the barman, looking for directions, Isadora ploughed money into a quiz machine. This was a way to disconnect from the real world. A few pints, some chat about football but with an awkward nagging feeling that somehow the girl you've bunked up with for the past fortnight was losing interest. Kronenburg should ease that little dull ache, he thought.

"It's literally around the corner," Jenny said to Jones as she appeared from the bar. She had a Guinness in her hand, he hadn't seen her partake in that particular delicacy before.

"He said we can park the car here if we want. Parking is tricky in this neighbourhood, no spaces." Jones quickly worked out that this was a mindless chat that was heading to a much bigger conversation.

"Okay Jenny, what's up? You've been odd since we landed. Is it Isadora? Because you're much more than a match for her. Have I done something wrong?" Jones grasped the nettle.

Jenny supped from her Guinness and self-consciously pulled at her hair, tightening the pony tail.

"We are less than 30 minutes from Jason's office here." She said, after a pause.

"He's been my life. And now I'm here with you, it suddenly feels like I'm cheating on him. Have we just been in a holiday romance? A fling? If this is what we are, I need to know." She didn't look at Jones. She was nervously fiddling with a Skol beermat and pretending to watch the babble on the television.

"I'm here to learn," Jones said quietly. "I want to excel at this job. I want to be the best. But the feelings I have for you are new to me. And I'm learning from them too." And he looked up at Jenny.

"I'm not Jason. I'm not some Marketing Executive with a big wage, an attractive pension and a BMW. But you and I just fit, don't we? Jesus, that's cheesy. I'm sorry." And Jones grimaced and buried his reddening face in the top of his lager.

"So, no, Jenny, we're not a holiday fling. I'm not sure what we are. But it'll be fun finding out. Don't you think?" As he finished, a glass smashed from behind the bar and the whole pub cheered.

"Promise me we'll never stop this luxury lifestyle?" She grinned and flicked the froth from her Guinness playfully in his direction. They both laughed and the tension lifted momentarily.

"Of course. But why the hell did you wait for us to get to Stratford to buy a pint of Guinness? We've been in Ireland for a fortnight!" Jones smiled and wiped the froth from his t-shirt. He bent forward and kissed her on the nose, and then they embraced. Jenny cried and Jones couldn't help but join in. It was as if a bubble had burst.

"What the bloody hell are you two crying for? "Isadora asked and she pointed to the quiz machine which was loudly spewing out one-pound coins. "Looks like the next round is on me. What are we celebrating?"

"I think I've just broken up with my boyfriend again," Jenny said and walked over to the payphone, grabbing two of Isadora's pound coins out of the machine tray on the way. "I'll have another Guinness and maybe a chaser. I've got a difficult conversation to have." And Jenny walked away.

Jenny knew Jason's number off by heart but wasn't expecting him to pick up the phone instantly. It caught her completely off guard and she still had a mouthful of Guinness.

"Jen, I've been so worried about you. Why haven't you been in contact? What's going on?" Jason asked as soon as he recognised her voice at the end of the phone.

"Calm down Jase, I'm not phoning to update you. I'm phoning to say goodbye."

"Goodbye? You're working in the House of Commons. You're less than half an hour from me. You haven't even tried to make this work. Who have you replaced me with?"

"I'm saying goodbye because I have made a new start, a new life and we have grown apart. I have been there for you every step of the way as you've grown in your job. The ups and the downs. But there has never been any time for me. You wouldn't let that happen. So, it's my time now."

"Hold on. You know I love you? You know I'd do anything for you Jen? I just can't imagine life without you. I don't want to imagine that."

"This isn't about what you want. It's about my future. Please do not ruin the life we've had by making this call more difficult than it has to be. I do love you. I will always remember our time together but I've changed. I've changed for the better. I'm going away for a little while now, it's a work trip. I will be in touch again once the dust has settled and I do care. But there is no going back."

"You know I won't let this happen. I won't let you leave me. And whoever you've replaced me with, I'll find out. This is not the end." Jason had turned nasty, as Jenny knew he would. He had been dependent on her and she was moving away. She felt a surge of courage and freedom as she looked over at Jones before preparing to sign off.

"There is nothing left that you have, that I want. And I have given you everything of me. Remember that generosity and move on. Goodbye, Jason." Jenny replaced the receiver and walked back to the table.

"You know, I think that Irish stuff gave me Dutch courage," said Jenny, putting her hand on Jones' knee as she sat at the table.

"What? I'm madly confused." Isadora said, staring over at Jenny as she forced a pound coin into the quiz machine slot.

"Yeah, me too. But I'd rather jump over that ledge at Europa again than have any more emotional conversations today. You seem brighter though, Richmond. It must have gone well?"

"Let's talk about it later," Jenny replied as the landlord arrived to serve Jones. "I'll have a Kronenburg and a packet of cheese and onion crisps" He smiled. "Everything is so much better in the pub."

CHAPTER
TWENTY-EIGHT

Whilst Topaz and the assembled forces of SIS and the RUC were desperately searching for Stephen Finch, Tom and Carl were facing the mundanity of more Emerald surveillance training and Mr Singh's signals lectures. The only bonus was the menu on Friday gave the lads something to look forward to.

The refectory at Milton College was always full on a Friday. As tradition dictated, the cooks served a fantastic fish and chips main course, and the queues stretched for miles. Near the front of the queue were Tom and Carl who were prepared to give up their lasagne addiction for the Friday special.

However, Carl was still reeling from the verbal dressing down he received from Virginia and he was awaiting a disciplinary notice from the college's student services team. He was already dreading the reaction from home. Carl desperately wanted to apologise to Wendy but he couldn't apologise openly for something she didn't know about. It was a dilemma.

It was just as this thought bubble was shaping itself in Carl's head that Wendy emerged through the double doors and instantly spied Tom and Carl near the front of the queue. Wendy, who pushed straight to the front of the line in front of

Tom, had already worked out that Carl had been warned off her by Mr Singh because of his infantile disappearing acts when she was in his proximity. She was going to make it clear that he stood no chance with her, but she wasn't immune to a bit of fun along the way. Wendy was the youngest of the lab technicians and was sick to death with the attention she was receiving from lads with over-inflated egos.

"Boys, I hope you don't mind me slipping in front of you. I have an important meeting straight after lunch and I'm already late." Wendy stood facing both of the lads, but Carl pretended to be fascinated by a Capri Sun drink he'd picked up to avoid her eye contact.

"No problem at all Wendy," said Tom. "In fact, I was going to ask your advice about a piece of work I'm doing for Mr Singh. I think I may have changed the setting on one of the map-reading programmes and I need it reset."

"I'll come and find you after my meeting, I think I know what you've done. It's an easy mistake to make. By the way, Tom, I'm hearing good things about your electronic surveillance techniques and I have an extra-curricular group you might like to join. We are looking at adapting the college's systems to make the programmes slicker and to provide more detailed results."

Carl skulked in the background with every core of his being hating this chat. Not only was Wendy impressed with Tom and wanted him to join her after-college group, but Carl was unable to get a foothold in the conversation for fear of saying or doing the wrong thing. But Wendy wasn't going to let that happen, as she quickly turned to him.

"Carl, speaking of extra-curricular activities, I am a partner down for my jiu-jitsu class tomorrow and I was wondering whether you might want to join me. Have you done martial arts before?"

Carl's brain turned to mush as he searched for the answer. Accept and he'd be seen as contravening a direct order from Mr Singh but he'd be seen as an absolute villain if he rejected her. Tom, suddenly far more comfortable with the conversation and completely unaware that Carl was facing a disciplinary, rode to the rescue.

"Tell you what Wendy, we'll both come. Neither of us has any experience but we'd be happy to tag along and help out. What do you think Carl?" Carl just gave a sheepish thumbs-up and Wendy was beckoned forward for a huge piece of fried fish to be positioned on her plate by a white-aproned member of kitchen staff.

"No problem, lads. The more the merrier I'll meet you in the entrance hall at 6.15pm. There'll be one or two other people to meet too." And after she held out her plate for chips and garden peas, she disappeared into the staff quarters at the back of the refectory.

"She's going to kick the crap out of me isn't she Tom?"

"Whilst I think this ancient art form isn't designed as a punishment, I think the likely answer is yes. And what's more, you're going to deserve it. Stalking her, without her knowledge is weasel-like and this is karma. I'll be spectating too!" Tom received the hugest piece of cod he'd ever laid eyes on, and Carl whimpered like a disappointed puppy.

CHAPTER
TWENTY-NINE

Massey had been keeping Alexinsky at the Knock Road RUC station since his arrival but she knew her time was almost up to question him. They had just twenty-four hours before the MI6 team from Thames House swooped in and the investigation was over. Aside from Jube's intel about his role as a KGB agent at the Russian Embassy, they had nothing. His passport was real, his age, even his place of birth, but Europol and Interpol had drawn a blank on anything wider or more significant. Therefore, it was a blessed relief when Spencer showed up at the station reception with another manila folder and a huge smile.

"Look, I'll be totally honest with you Orla, I either have everything or nothing in this folder. But, I'm not sure we have time for a full briefing. So, will you let me lead the interview? I realise that's normally a no-go."

"Does that mean I can blame you if everything goes pear-shaped?" asked Orla, being half-serious.

"I'm totally deniable!" laughed Jube Spencer, "I'm not even technically here! But you have my word that I'll clear up any mess I make."

"He's in interview room four. His interpreter is a barrel of laughs and he's over by the coffee machine in the hallway. Perhaps you ought to go and introduce yourself." Orla pointed down the hall to a small bespectacled man in a plain white shirt and black trousers. Spencer tightened his maroon tie and adjusted his heavily starched white collar. He meant business.

"Lead the way, Chief Inspector." Massey, with Spencer for company made her way through the oak-panelled corridors of Knock Road RUC station. Minutes later they were sitting in a dimply lit interview room with Alexinsky smoking a cigarette and looking nonchalantly into his polystyrene coffee cup. The interpreter was biting his nails and watching the small station clock above Massey's head.

"Mr Alexinsky, my name is Jube Spencer and I work for the anti-terrorism squad here in Northern Ireland," he lied.

"Upon your arrival here in Belfast I was made aware of a number of facts, detailed here in this folder relating to crimes you have committed against the Russian State. Crimes, I believe, will make deportation back to Moscow very awkward for you. Perhaps even fatal." Spencer paused for effect and then looked at the interpreter, who in turn, delivered the narrative to Alexinsky.

Alexinsky attempted to hold on to his poker face but Spencer's lines had unsettled him slightly. He spoke quietly to the interpreter and the words were translated. After speaking, he lit another cigarette and kept his head down, feigning disinterest.

"Mr Alexinsky says that you have no such record and he has nothing whatsoever to fear from the Russian State. He will not be speaking to you any further until such evidence is shown to him."

Spencer, with Massey watching on silently, delved into his manila folder and produced a photo of the white RDX powder from the Glen. It was a black and white photo and showed all four drums of chemical, including those they suspected had already partly been used in the Lennoxville and Limehall bombings.

He placed the photo on the table facing Alexinsky. The Russian smiled sarcastically at Spencer after taking a brief look at the image before reverting to his poker face and nonchalance.

"Mr Alexinsky, as you may be aware, a Russian banker called Ivan Berbakov was recently murdered through a poisonous substance believed to be smeared on the mouthpiece of his white telephone. Berbakov was a very good friend of the President. Is that correct?"

Alexinsky, now sitting upright, stared indifferently at Spencer after listening to the translation.

"According to our documents, Ivan Berbakov and his secretary, Krista Ismailova, received lethal doses of a stolen military-grade poison. And two days later both died in horrific circumstances. Now, this poison was a black-market product called Agent Orange, stolen from the KGB in St. Petersburg. I'm sure you would have heard that?"

Again, still retaining his poker face, Alexinsky waited for the translation and then shrugged his shoulders.

"The banker's murder was eventually pinned on a gang of criminals set on bringing down the Russian economy and destabilising the President. But there were several missing shipments of this product. In total, eight or nine ampoules of this military-grade poison left secret labs. This was easily enough to kill several hundred people. No?"

Alexinsky offered nothing in response.

"This substance was only known to a small circle of people, Mr Alexinsky. It was a government secret and yet we found it all here in a Northern Irish Glen. A tourist walk. The tubs of chemicals and packages containing the ampoules. That's odd, isn't it? And those blue barrels were covered in your finger prints.

"Did you steal a secret nerve agent, Mr Alexinsky? And kill one of the President's friends?"

Spencer stared at Alexinsky. And he adjusted the photo on the table. He then quickly added a photo of the victim of the Russian poisoning and then an image of the plume of white smoke above Lennoxville.

There was a silence. Massey turned and looked at Spencer. She knew the barrels had no finger-prints on them. And they were not filled with the stolen Russian nerve agent. It was RDX. Nasty stuff. But not the subject of secret British intelligence and certainly not smeared over a white telephone in Moscow. This was simply an explosive powder.

Alexinsky pulled himself up in his seat and put out his cigarette.

In near-perfect English, Oleg Alexinsky replied: "Mr Spencer you are a shyster and a liar. You know full well that those containers held only RDX. And that you cannot implicate me for the death of Ivan Berbakov. I was here in Ireland."

"On the contrary, we have evidence that you bordered a plane from Aldergrove Airport bound for a Heathrow connection to Moscow, literally days before the murder. And I will have great pleasure in passing that to my friends at MI6."

"But that is a fabrication. That is a lie. No-one will believe I am responsible!" replied Alexinsky, suddenly dropping the nonchalant persona.

"Won't they? Would you like to test that theory?"

And with that Jube Spencer stood up with Massey following his lead.

"We'll come and talk to you again in an hour or so, Mr Alexinsky. Perhaps we can dismiss your translator now. Such a drain on government resources." Spencer and Massey walked out of the room, closing the door carefully. Alexinsky's expression had changed. He was nervous.

Massey remained silent as they manoeuvred through the station corridors to her office. Spencer had stopped at the coffee machine and had bought her a black coffee in a white cup.

"Why, Jube Spencer, you sly bastard! What evidence do you have linking Alexinsky to the Berbakov murder or the theft of that poison?"

"None whatsoever. All my little invention. Let's wait an hour and see if he cracks. Let's find out where Finch and that damn taxi driver have gone."

And the pair quietly drank their coffee, while it was still hot, for a change.

CHAPTER THIRTY

In Mr Singh's lair, the tutor, Tom, and Carl were busying themselves tracing the route of the Letterkenny taxi. It had arrived down the A1 and had been picked up again on the M25 near Watford before making some stops on the North Circular Road. The car had Northern Irish plates and this was a blessing as the new-style European plates, now used in the Republic, would have been barely visible to the cameras with their tiny narrow fonts.

Until lunchtime, when Tom and Carl had vanished to indulge in a large helping of Milton College Friday fish and chips, Mr Singh was none-the-wiser about the rogue taxi and possible connection to Stephen Finch. Jenny had updated him on her handheld from the passenger seat of the hire car. He was intrigued. He had been tracking the Topaz team coming down from Stranraer and into Stratford. However, whilst Mr Singh felt more motivated than ever to be part of the action and relive his GCHQ glory days, it was concerning him that Tom and Carl were becoming like spare parts, plus Carl had blotted his copy book.

Mr Singh saw that Carl, who was becoming increasingly the

more child-like of the two, had even resorted to bringing in his favourite 'A' Team mug to the lair, eating handfuls of Animal biscuits in one sitting and energetically air drumming to a Status Quo Greatest Hits cassette. This was becoming a distraction. The lair wasn't supposed to be a den for bored students, it was his invention zone.

Mr Singh was also worried about the Lab Technician, Wendy, who he had nervously briefed earlier in the day about the stalking. This was totally against Virginia's wishes but he trusted the young technician and knew that she'd probably already guessed what the fibre-optic strands were actually for. She had been one of his most intelligent students and he envisaged great things for her. However, telling her about Carl was a bold move on his part but he was careful to avoid any discussion about Topaz and the Finch case. Wendy was simply aware of the new prototype GPS and she marvelled at the invention. She had fumed about Carl's behaviour but calmly promised Mr Singh she'd let him deal with Carl using the college's disciplinary system.

Tom was easier to handle and an incredibly bright young man. He had aced his GCSEs and 'A' Levels but would simply follow Carl around like a lost soul. Mr Singh was keen to test how far Tom could go and help him reach his potential but to do so, he'd need to test his theory of Tom's intelligence. Mr Singh even wondered whether Tom could be a potential GCHQ candidate if he wasn't being hampered by Carl.

Mr Singh had an idea. This idea grew into a perfectly shaped plan when the mystery of the Letterkenny taxi emerged. The case was complex enough but he needed all his resources when it became clear that whoever was driving the Letterkenny taxi had been followed.

Somewhere around Stevenage, a 1991 registered orange Fiat Tipo started to trace the taxi's journey. The colour of the Tipo meant it was hardly ideally placed to be clandestine. It had appeared in the same camera logs as the taxi for some time and on the final camera near the Polish War Memorial on the A40. The driver was white and fair-haired, but the camera simply wasn't clear enough to offer up any further detail.

They were in a part of London packed with entry-level but easily hackable CCTV, Mr Singh had located the taxi and Tipo in or around a run-down public house called the Black Bull in Ruislip, West London. Grainy images from the pub's car park, provided unknowingly by GCHQ, saw the taxi at one end of the overgrown car park and the Tipo within spitting distance. Nothing else of any use was visible and there were no other useful cameras within a five-mile radius.

After discussions with Charles and McNally back in Thiepval and with the Topaz team in Stratford, Mr Singh decided to despatch Tom and Carl to recce the pub the following morning. That was the grand plan, he would test them out in an operational task.

His last orders were, "say nothing, do nothing, and don't make an arse of yourselves. It is critical that you simply report on the identities of the drivers of the two cars. Then wait for further instructions."

Tom and Carl were fully briefed by Mr Singh and were tasked with taking the first train into Ruislip via the South West Trains line. Until then, the site would be monitored by Mr Singh via the grainy CCTV images and the local Met Police, who had been asked to undertake regular sweeps of the area.

Tom and Carl were understandably excited if a little anxious. But Carl had another issue to resolve first. They needed to prepare themselves for jiu-jitsu and had therefore dressed in green and yellow Norwich City shirts and black joggers. Tom was trying hard not to smile at Carl's predicament and Carl was simply keen to get this over with. The notion of karma was growing in his mind and he was expecting a pummelling.

At the arranged time, the pair saw Wendy emerge from the back streets of Milton with a few other identically dressed female friends. They were in 'Sparta Jiu-Jitsu' tracksuits with light blue branding, Wendy smiled at Tom and Carl and asked them to join the group as they walked the short journey to the college gym. It was a venue neither of the lads realised existed.

On arrival, Wendy and her friends immediately donned the traditional 'gi' and many adopted a rash guard underneath to offer further protection. A large bearded man in a blue gi walked over and introduced himself to Tom and Carl. Tom was fascinated, Carl less so.

"You must be Tom and Carl. Welcome! I'm Neale and I'm the Sifu at Sparta jiu-jitsu. You both look worried. Don't be. Jiu-jitsu is a system of close combat that can be used in a defensive or attacking manner to kill or subdue one or more opponents. No one is going to hurt you and we are simply going to teach you the basics." Carl relaxed a little. He wasn't going to be hurt, at least that's what Sifu Neale said.

"Jiu-jitsu was designed to supplement the swordsmanship of a warrior during combat. A group of techniques from certain styles of jiu-jitsu were used to develop many modern martial arts and combat sports, such as judo. So, we're going to help make you warriors! How do you feel about that?" Tom smiled and looked up for it, Carl gave his awkward thumbs-up for the second time of the day.

Carl, as he suspected, was immediately paired with Wendy and she quickly showed him the ropes. Or in this case, the floor. Repeatedly. She was firm but tried to gently teach Carl a few basic moves which she hoped would improve his confidence and help him see a different side to himself. The session had progressed an hour when the pair finally took a break. Carl was exhausted. Wendy felt this was the opportunity to have a careful chat with Carl.

"Look, I know about the stalking thing," she turned to Carl and he stopped trying to catch his breath.

"Oh my God!" he exclaimed.

"Don't panic. I'm not going to tell a soul, as I respect Mr Singh and the nature of his work too much to break his confidence. But you were a dick and you need to learn from this." She pointed out into the room and Carl scanned the session.

"These people are here to learn discipline and a skill. You need to learn respect too"

Carl nodded and adjusted his shirt as he began to regain his composure. But he still sat rather helplessly on the floor.

"Whilst I am a strong and physically fit woman, as you now know, I am also extremely vulnerable when I'm out and alone. We all are. Look how vulnerable you felt when you walked into this room." Wendy helped Carl up, as his legs were beginning to feel heavy after the gruelling session.

"Everyone at Milton is a team. And you've been given a real opportunity to learn something only a tiny percentage of the population will ever know. Don't ruin it. Do you understand?" Carl very quickly shook Wendy's hand and apologised.

"I have learned more than you can possibly imagine. I'm so sorry, Wendy." As Wendy was about to admit she was slightly amused by his underarm farting during Operation Re-Route, Sifu Neale appeared in the background.

"Wendy, your friend Tom here, he's a bloody natural" Neale pointed across the room to Tom, now dressed in a Gi and completing an almost perfect double-leg takedown on a male instructor and grinning from ear to ear.

"Can you bring him back again? I think we have someone we can work with here."

The evening ended with Wendy, Tom and Carl as well as a

number of her friends sitting in the Talbot Arms. The lads had opted for diet coke and Tom was the talk of the jiu-jitsu group in the pub. Carl, on the other hand, was still struggling from his bruised arms, legs and ego from the karma inflicted by Wendy. But, aside from the disciplinary notice, there was a little closure and a huge lesson learnt.

CHAPTER THIRTY-ONE

PUTTING TWO ENTRY-LEVEL EMERALD STUDENTS INTO THE FIELD WAS A risk. McNally had underlined that this approach had only been green-lighted as neither Tom nor Carl looked like they might be anything other than students on a jolly. And he was almost right since they had also dressed in matching Beavis and Butthead t-shirts. But there was also concern that Finch would clearly remember Jones and Jenny from the Bangor meeting. He was certainly aware of Isadora.

Tom and Carl were effectively the reserve squad, and whilst they thought all of their Christmases had come at once, the threat in Mr Singh's voice had lingered in their minds as they got onto the South Western Railway Train to London. They could not make arses of themselves. It would be a brief 45-minute trip into London and a further 10-minute hop to Ruislip and Mr Singh had entrusted Tom with a handheld and a prototype digital camera. Carl had also helpfully packed most of Jones' earthly belongings into a Safeway carrier bag, in case their paths should cross.

Back in Virginia's Stratford bolt-hole, intelligence had come through from Massey that Alexinsky was poised to sing like the proverbial canary. Massey had alerted Charles, if anything, to congratulate him for his razor-like theorising some days ago, but also because she wanted to get in there first before the 'I told you so' conversation. Jube Spencer wanted Charles on side quickly too.

Jones, Jenny and Isadora had recovered from the previous night's unplanned drinking session and Isadora was deep in conversation with McNally on the handheld. Their orders were to get from Stratford into the West End on the Central Line and await further instructions. Isadora could not risk being seen by Finch until the full plan had been activated. McNally or Mr Singh would update Isadora on all intelligence coming from the movement of the cars, the interrogation room in Knock Road or from Tom and Carl.

As Topaz made their way into the West End, via another hearty breakfast, Emerald were travelling at speed into Ruislip. Tom and Carl shared a Walkman, one in-ear headphone each, and listened to the Black Album by Metallica. Carl did more air-drumming and ate bag after bag of Frazzles from the family pack he'd bought for the trip. Tom had bought a word search book and a pack of Super Car Top Trumps. They were all set. Neither of them had yet ingrained the face of Stephen Finch on their brains from the black and white image Mr Singh had given them. And neither had considered the terrible danger they were in.

The Black Bull was a twenty-minute walk from the station and the final ten minutes was on a single long avenue with large expensive houses on either side. Every so often a bus stop would be positioned and ancient Routemaster double-deckers would convey anonymous Londoners deeper into the capital. Tom and Carl innocently strode amongst the locals, unaware of their surroundings and still enraptured by the Metallica album blaring from the Walkman. Opposite the Black Bull was a small café filled with chain-smoking and tea-drinking customers. The pair nabbed a table in the window and from that vantage point, they could see the front car park of the pub and the blue taxi with Northern Irish plates. A small privet hedge prevented them from seeing further. Carl switched off the Walkman and ordered a coke for himself and a Sunkist for Tom. With straws.

With their view secured, Tom, with zero tradecraft skills, decided to take a walk over the road to see if he could spot the Tipo. Whilst he was all too obvious in his approach, he was also fortunate that the orange Tipo was parked directly opposite the entrance to the pub and that the patio bench seats outside the Black Bull were empty. He then walked over to the taxi and memorised some key features.

He saw that the name of the Irish town had been removed from the top of the taxi's advertising light and therefore it simply read 'North Country Taxis' and the front and back seats were bare. The only sign of life was an AA Map, the remains of a prawn sandwich on the passenger seat, and a bundled-up navy blue sheet strewn over the back seat. A more effective agent would have suspected this was hiding blood or some other misdemeanour. He remembered that the Tipo had similarly been almost empty but with a large collection of Lucozade bottles thrown into the front passenger footwell. Tom simply looked over at Carl and he waved back pointing to underline the arrival of his Sunkist Orange. To his credit, Tom moved to hide behind a nearby bus stop shelter to speak to Mr Singh on the handheld to provide the update. And Mr Singh radioed through to McNally.

Topaz had opted for a public spot to await orders. They were sitting outside Burger King in Leicester Square and looked every inch the tourists that flooded the area. Jones wasn't very London savvy, although his Mother's family were born and brought up in White City, literally twenty minutes away. He used to see London family trips as adventures into the great unknown and his mother would regale him with stories of her youth at Saturday morning Pictures and the finest fish and chips in the world. He wondered what his tiny corner of leafy England would make of the past fortnight.

Jenny too appeared lost in herself but he had noticed an uplift in her mood since she had removed the shackles and guilt of her relationship with Jason. He hadn't taken it well. But it was the full stop she needed. Jenny looked fresh and had that same air of confidence that got her through the trek from the airport and the resilience test in Thiepval. However, this current mission was taking things up a notch. Isadora arrived back at the bench after a quick chat with McNally on the handheld.

"One of the Emerald lads has seen the taxi and the little Fiat at the pub in West London. But there's no sign of Finch and no clue who's in the Fiat. McNally seems to think things are about to happen. He reckons if Finch has got wind that Alexinsky is about to talk, he'll want to speed things up."

"So, in the meantime, we just wait?" Asked Jones. "Isn't it also a possibility that he's just gone to ground? If he thinks he's been found out." He added.

"Well, Jones, we either wait here and we're in prime position to make a move. Or, we chance it and join the Emerald lads in Ruislip. I'm voting for staying here." Isadora explained.

The streams of traffic made it difficult to cross the road in Ruislip but the most recent bus had obscured Tom's radio call to Mr Singh from any prying eyes. Tom was ready to sit back and enjoy a leisurely game of Top Trumps with Carl as they ate a late afternoon snack. They would simply wait for the drivers to appear, he thought, they would probably vanish into the cars and they could head back home in time for a few in The Jericho.

As Tom cautiously waited for a gap in the traffic to cross the road, Stephen Finch moved back from the window and sat on the edge of the bed in the Black Bull bedroom overlooking the car park. He was equally aware of the non-descript orange Fiat that had followed him into London as he was Tom Marsh, who he watched as he skipped back happily over the road for his fizzy drink. Finch knew that someone was onto him but he also theorised that Tom might just be a lousy car thief.

Finch had long regretted leaving the YCU handheld in the back of the lorry at Cairnryan. He'd have known more about developments then. But instead, he focused on keeping his anxious guest as comfortable as possible, awaited the possible reinforcements and watched as the clock ticked round.

CHAPTER THIRTY-TWO

In the Knock Road Interview Room, or interrogation suite – as Massey liked to call it, it had been a fair few hours since Alexinsky had seen his past re-invented before his very eyes. He had been brought back from the cells and was sitting, stony-faced, with a cigarette in his hand and a cup of water. The translator was long gone and the interview cassette recorder was unplugged at the wall. Massey and Jube Spencer strode purposely into the room and carefully placed coffee cups on the table. They'd inhaled umpteen coffees whilst they waited for Alexinsky to crack and Massey was feeling a touch giddy.

Alexinsky was the first to talk. With any notion of the language barrier long dismantled.

"I have been thinking Mr Spencer. Firstly, I am aware of my rights and yet you are no policeman. So, we are, how do you say? A little laissez-faire with my rights? Is that correct?" And he looked over at Jube Spencer.

"Keep talking," Spencer responded, indifferently.

"I have a proposal. I will answer the questions you have of me honestly. I will remain in your custody until my answers have been proven accurate. And then you will release me over the border into Ireland. And you do not mention your invented story to my compatriots."

"We are not Americans, Alexinsky. We do not agree to deals. And I have no idea what invented stories you are referring to. I have already contacted the Russian Embassy and explained the evidence we have for your crimes against Russia," replied Spencer.

"This is not the truth. You are lying to me."

Massey and Spencer made a move to stand up and end the conversation. Alexinsky looked up at the pair of them with an air of resignation.

"Alright. Alright! What happens next?" Alexinsky looked anxiously at them both.

"That depends on you," replied Massey. "You will remain in our custody once you have answered our questions. And we can discuss what happens to Oleg Alexinsky afterwards. But, as I'm sure you'll appreciate, time is of the essence. There is a missing man and a multiple murderer on the streets of London. Are you going to play nicely?"

"We know that Stephen Finch is the grandson of a Russian or Soviet sympathiser. And the KGB has reactivated him to compromise the peace talks in Northern Ireland. You can take it from there." Spencer waved his hand towards Alexinsky as if conducting his entrance.

"Your friend Stephen Finch, or Gregor Vinnikov, has been an asset of ours for many years. We helped him with his application to the British Secret Service." He began, staring at the table, not meeting Massey or Spencer's eyes.

"He has been simply waiting for the call. His grandfather. He was a great man. Yes, I believe he was one of ours too. And Stephen has visited Russia many times. He could have been a great servant of Russia. But things are changing now. We are bending and curtseying to the West. Someone has to fight the good fight and remind the Americans that they cannot be the pathetic moral saviours of the world." He snarled.

"I am a servant of my nation. But I am no servant of change. Russia will not be belittled for acceptance. However, I have a mother and father, a wife and children. Your accusation, the lies you tell, will have them killed too. Surely you know that?"

"Are they any worthier than the lives you took at Limehall or Lennoxville? What was your role in those explosions?" Asked Massey, whilst furiously making notes on a small notepad in pencil.

"Sure, I made bombs for Stephen. And I managed to route the RDX into Northern Ireland. It was not difficult. For a country so savaged by Semtex, it was remarkably easy to bring explosives on your ferry.

"But I had no idea where he was planting them. On the contrary, we believed he was leaving them at the Barracks for maximum casualties. That would seem appropriate. But he got nervous that he'd be found out. He's quite a weak Irishman. He's certainly one of yours in that respect." Alexinsky allowed himself a short cackle, before correcting himself and taking a sip of water.

"The thing is, he was a weak and spineless Irishman. He was a traitor to you. You see? But he was a strong Russian when he was Gregor. He wore that name like an iron mask. He hated being Stephen. He despised it."

Alexinsky took a drag of his cigarette and sucked it into his lungs as if contemplating his next sentence. For a moment, the room was filled with the Russian's smoke. He continued.

"It was him who wanted to kill his friends from the Barracks. The young team, or whatever. We just wanted explosions and drama. Create some questions about how committed people are to the peace process. To humble that clown Fred

Martinsen. Looks like it worked, no?" And again, he laughed. A spiteful laugh which made Massey feel uneasy.

"None of this explains why Stephen kidnapped Isadora Brown. And where Gerard McMahon is? Why would Stephen kidnap a random taxi driver?" Asked Spencer, as the fog of smoke lifted in the room.

"You want to know about the taxi driver? Have you seen a photo of him? Then you're going to have to assure my safety and the safety of my family. I am already betraying everything I stand for, as a proud Russian. I will tell you nothing more until I have that absolute assurance."

"I can assure you that we will not communicate any further with the Russian Embassy regarding the previous crimes we believe you committed. And therefore, your family is safe" said Spencer, choosing his words carefully.

"This is all trash-talk! You know I had nothing to do with the death of that banker, Berbakov. That would be signing my own death warrant. It's madness."

"I have assured the safety of your family. Please continue," Spencer added. Purposely quietly and softly to quell Alexinsky's temper.

"The young woman, she was half dead when we found her. She was unconscious. I wanted to finish her. But Stephen saw her as a bargaining chip. One of my friends at the Coca-Cola bottling plant helped us find a location to hide something. They had contacts in the maintenance team at the Europa Hotel. Again, it was all too easy. The bomb in the car was just a diversion. Then we watched and laughed as you blamed each other." This led to more bizarre snorting laughter. Which gave way to a look of anger.

"Creating diversions, that's a big thing in my world," he laughed. "You think you know everything? Is Stephen working alone now I'm here? Of course, he isn't. Your compatriots are easy to buy off, we look for a weakness and we make them an offer. But I've told you enough. I need more reassurances before I say more. Take me back to my cell."

Alexinsky stubbed out his cigarette in the small plastic ashtray and stood up. Massey and Spencer knew they'd probably pushed him as far as he would go for now and they acquiesced to his demand to be taken back to his cell. The Russian looked exhausted and forlorn. And Orla Massey couldn't quite focus away from her nagging tiredness without more caffeine, therefore the interview was paused.

As Alexinsky was shown back to the police cells in the RUC station, Spencer stopped in the middle of the hallway.

"What did he mean? Have you seen a photo of him? Why would he say that? And Finch has more help? Who?"

Massey nodded. "Yeah, he said a few strange things. God knows who is onside with Stephen now and, come to think of it, I've never seen a recent photo of the taxi driver, all we have is a picture of him at an event with his wife. I think that was twenty years old. Although I believe we have his passport somewhere. If you hold on, I'll go and find it."

Spencer stopped her. "We need to consider his trail of breadcrumbs around whether Finch is working alone. We thought he was a lone wolf. He wasn't. Could there be more Red Line members or another mole?"

"I can't say for sure, Spencer. But I'm confident the rest of the YCU team are clean. McNally was my last concern and he's come back scrupulously clean. Joseph Armstrong too, his report from his time in Serbia was verging on a gallantry medal. And the Currys are national treasures."

"Everything is a diversion," Spencer replied. "We're bound to have missed something. Let's start with that photograph."

Massey vanished back into the main office, leaving Spencer

looking for loose change to further invest in the low-quality Knock Road coffee.

It didn't take long for Massey to arrive back with a high-resolution photocopy of Gerard McMahon's passport. His grey hair was neatly parted to the right, he wore half-moon glasses and was clean-shaven. His face was thin but he looked young for his 62 years, perhaps five or so years younger.

As Massey produced the passport photo and the original family picture with McMahon and his wife at a function, Spencer compared the two carefully. It was Spencer who noticed it first.

"Oh, dear God," exclaimed Spencer. "Do you see it?"

Before Massey had a chance to answer, Jube Spencer half whispered, "Gerard McMahon, the poor bastard, is an absolute dead spit for Fred Martinsen, the US Peace Envoy."

Massey grabbed the passport photo off Spencer and ran to reception where they had copies of the Belfast Telegraph, Martinsen was on the front page. They held the two images side-by-side.

"You're right. They're identical. Why didn't we see this before?" added Massey.

"We were never going to have noticed the similarity from that old photo. So, let's recap. We have possibly the most influential individual in Irish Politics, Fred Martinsen, who's knee-deep in trying to negotiate a peace deal on behalf of the Americans. And we have a taxi driver from Letterkenny. McMahon is a doppelganger for Martinsen."

"Go and get Charles Curry on the phone, visiting hours would be over by now, and I'll ring my team at Thames House. I think we are in a great deal of trouble here, Orla." Massey held the door open for Spencer as they made their way through the hallway into the main office and both grabbed desk phones.

"Charles," Massey began. "You're not going to believe this."

After an all-too-brief call, Spencer had his orders from Thames House and they were short and sweet. With Charles Curry still on the phone to Massey, Spencer interrupted her.

"Orla, we are still on our own unless the shite hits the fan. We need the Topaz team to find out whether Stephen Finch is holding McMahon alive and what his plans are. MI5 will not engage until we know there's an urgent issue to deal with. They want to be kept appraised but they won't escalate until they absolutely have to."

Charles heard Spencer's explanation down the phone.

"Yes, there are two words for what MI5 is doing here. 'Maximum deniability'. Britain has the potential of annoying the Americans, the Russians and both sides of the Irish conflict. They're desperately hoping the issue will magically go away. So, incredibly, we are using 20-year-old novices to solve their problem." Charles summarised.

"One thing's for sure," he added. "Nobody will be telling the Americans."

CHAPTER THIRTY-THREE

Stephen Finch was in a quandary. He had planned the next phase down to the tightest detail but his friend and compatriot, Oleg Alexinsky was now almost three hours late and Finch had only booked the hotel room for one night. There was also the question of the Fiat Tipo, he had noticed the car had been following him for some time, but it was unlikely to be secret services as they weren't known for their love of orange cars that stood out a mile. It might as well have had a neon flashing light that read 'I'm following you'. Finch had a working theory as to who this might be; it was someone who he'd upset and betrayed but he also believed that his Russian friends had removed any awkwardness with a significantly-sized brown envelope. Finch had friends in high places.

That aside, he had been single-minded about his need to complete the task since he received his orders three months ago. His awakening and promise of being a Russian hero, like his grandfather, was worth his treachery to the murdered YCU colleagues that he despised. Finch's life was hollow and pointless before the KGB gave it meaning.

True, there had been bumps in the road, Isadora Brown was

never supposed to have survived and leaving the handheld in the back of the lorry was a massive mistake. Still, she was the only one left with any brains and was bound to be back on YCU manoeuvres in Thiepval. She was the golden girl and Virginia would never risk throwing her into a dangerous mission like this, especially after two such catastrophic explosions. On the other hand, it would all soon be over. All life was temporary, including his own. That was his mantra.

Finch had fed his guest a few packets of sandwiches but he appeared to be sleeping most of the time. During the brief periods when the chloroform wore off, the man appeared so subdued that Finch occasionally checked for a pulse. He would wake him up properly tonight and underline his role in the plans. People from across Russia were duty-bound to support the Motherland. This poor old boy had no choice. He would be carefully reminded that his family's ongoing survival relied on his unquestioning support. His 'wee girl' at university would be killed first, he had been told and the old boy had become very emotional. McMahon's wife had effectively explained their entire life story at their chance meeting in Bangor. It had been a gift to Finch. But Finch was unmoved by Gerard McMahon's emotion or love for his family, as this was simply a job to do. The old boy was simply a pawn in a much bigger chess game.

Finch opened a bottle of mineral water and drank it quickly. He stared out of the window and he could see along the busy road adjacent to the pub. There was a large advertising hoarding opposite and the car park was strewn with litter. He had watched the tall man run across the road after staring into the windows of the taxi and the Tipo but he appeared so unaware of tradecraft, the art of ensuring you are not seen or followed, that he suspected he was an opportunist car thief. But he couldn't be sure.

With the old man still subdued and his hands cable-tied

onto a radiator, Finch decided to check the scene. He grabbed his faded green army surplus shirt and quickly buttoned it up over his dirty white t-shirt. He knew he looked and smelt unclean and he'd shower later but that was part of his preparation for tomorrow. He might even treat himself to a beer later.

As he ran down the stairs from his room into the public bar, he took a look around. The place was all but deserted, aside from two pensioners sitting at the bar with jugs of bitter and sharing a bag of pork scratchings. The middle-aged woman who had checked him and his 'ill father' into the hotel room was serving behind the bar and he gave her a cheery hello.

He walked outside and quickly glimpsed the empty orange Fiat and noted that all of the other vehicles in the car park and nearby were unchanged since his arrival. As he walked towards the main road, he saw no large white transits or other likely communications vehicles. The road was incredibly busy and he had to wait for a bus to move off, slowing traffic down, before he nipped across the road to the café. The interior was a relic from the 1970s, with nicotine-stained ceilings and price lists clinging onto the wall with blue tac older than Finch himself. Still, he could stock up and he ordered two cheese rolls, two packets of plain crisps and a few cans of Coke. As he waited for his order he casually skim-read the front of a few newspapers, laid out on the side for customer use. All of them, the Sun, Mirror, Today, Telegraph, Mail, Express and Times led with the Northern Ireland Peace Envoy's visit. Fred Martinsen was everywhere.

He took the full colour daily, Today, over to a seat overlooking the main road and thumbed through, looking for any sign that his plan was known. There was nothing. There was talk of a storm brewing in the Conservative Party and a bounce in the polls for New Labour. There were even discussions about Liverpool paying an astonishing £8.5m for a Nottingham Forest striker. But Finch wasn't interested in sport. He wasn't a team player.

Behind him were two young men sipping cans of fizzy drink through straws and playing top trumps. They were eagerly shouting out facts and information, snatching each other's cards, whilst laughing heartily. If these were paid surveillance operatives, they must have been recruited at the Early Learning Centre, Finch thought. One was carrying a large Safeway carrier bag, apparently full of washing and the other, almost certainly the tall man who ran across the road earlier, had a half-completed word search on British Birds. Finch relaxed a little, these were students. Or tourists. But they were nothing whatsoever to worry about.

When the food arrived, he passed over his sole Bank of England ten-pound note and smiled at the young woman behind the till. As he collected the change, the card-playing lads let out a massive burst of laughter and Finch and the woman shared a 'what the hell' moment and he smiled again. It took Finch just three minutes to sprint back across the road, dodging the traffic and back through the bar. Before he reached his room, Tom had disappeared to the toilet in the café and had alerted Mr Singh.

Stephen Finch was unequivocally in the Black Bull, in Victoria Avenue, Ruislip and he was not alone. His food order suggested at least one other. News had not filtered to Milton College of the doppelgänger theory but McNally was quickly able to relay the confirmed sighting to the whole team. It was time to make a move.

Charles had radioed into Isadora to explain the full theory of Fred Martinsen and Gerard McMahon. And a plan was quickly shaped that Carl and Tom would be staying in the Black Bull in an adjoining twin room, they would watch for the movement of the cars and try to ascertain who was driving the orange Fiat Tipo. Their cover appeared watertight as two infantile students on a jolly, as this was exactly what they were.

Isadora, Jones and Jenny would set up base at a Premier Inn in Bermondsey. This was close enough to all of the major seats of power, in case any of these were his next intended destination. They surmised that Stephen Finch wasn't armed or carrying RDX, or at least not in huge quantities. There was enough left in the bag at Cairnryan Port to suggest the entire missing quantities from the containers at the Glen were accounted for. They felt they had their bases covered. But this was guesswork and Topaz were simply hoping Spencer, Massey and Charles' theories were correct.

Bermondsey was worryingly close to home for Jenny Richmond, but she'd barely be leaving the hotel room until they had word that Finch was making a move. And the perils of her love life had to be secondary. Jube Spencer was going to line up a computer terminal in their room at the Premier Inn, from his friends at Thames House. The team would be fed intelligence and detail about Finch and any likely plan. This was a software package known to Isadora as i2 and she had passed the training for this excellent package with flying colours. She had also been fully trained on the Windows 95 software that made the computer terminal easily navigable. However, with the hire car still back in the car park of the Railway Tavern in Stratford they would need to get the tube and bus to Bermondsey.

As they sat on the central line heading back eastwards, Jones whispered across to Isadora and Jenny who were sitting to his right.

"It seems to me, there is only one outcome here. Finch is going to use McMahon's likeness to the Peace Envoy to either gain entry somewhere or perhaps worse. Surely, can't we just go to Ruislip and simply extract the poor taxi driver and all of this ends?"

"It's not that simple, Jones" replied Isadora. "We all want a peaceful conclusion but we need to know whether he's connected to something bigger. We need to follow this through to bring the whole thing down and not just Finch. If Alexinsky is refusing to tell Massey the whole story, there must be something bigger."

"Like what?" Asked Jenny. "What could be bigger than murdering your friends in Limehall and Lennoxville? What could be bigger than being kidnapped and blowing up a bookmaker's in central Belfast? I don't get it."

"This is Russia, not Stephen Finch. This is nation versus nation and superpowers competing to be top dog. Who knows what's next? But we need to get a glimpse of the full picture before we make a move." Isadora explained.

"Let's see what we dig up on the system in the hotel room. I'll let you have a play on this intelligence package. Let's get some pizzas and a bottle of wine and wait for the call. You can bet that Spencer, Massey and Charles are trying to find solutions too."

It was as Topaz headed up the steps at the Elephant and Castle Bakerloo Station that Jenny's handheld came to life.

"Hello Jenny, this is Mr Singh. I've just been radioed by Tom at the Black Bull. It appears Stephen Finch has visitors at his hotel room."

"Really? Are these the reinforcements? Who are they?" Jenny asked.

"We are not too sure, but there were three young women. Dressed up for a party and then later a young man. They were probably all in their twenties. He was carrying a bottle of champagne, or so Tom says." Mr Singh added.

"And they definitely went into Stephen Finch's room?" Jenny asked looking non-plussed at Isadora and Jones. "I'm not sure Mr McMahon is up for a party."

"Hold on," said Jones. "Maybe this is all part of the plan? Is this a blackmail campaign?"

"Mr Singh, can you tell Carl and Tom to complain about the noise, trip a fire alarm or kill the power? Anything to stop this." Jones added.

"I'm not sure that's the right approach, it would effectively kill their cover and Finch will be spooked." Countered Isadora.

"It's also too late," added Mr Singh. "I've been trying to get hold of you for a while. The deed may already have been done. I'll be back in touch later." Mr Singh ended the call and the three walked slowly to the bus stop. Something had to be done.

Tom and Carl had decided that they needed to get closer to the action and decided to pop downstairs to the bar and grab a pint. They knew Finch had already seen them but the notion of them being hotel guests and nipping over the road for a bite to eat was a plausible cover. They ordered two McEwan's and a few packets of dry-roasted peanuts and waited for the next slice of the action. The party in Finch's room had been going on for over an hour now and yet it was worryingly quiet. Tom had scaled the narrow stairs up to their twin bedroom a few times to see if they'd missed anything but from their position in the bar, they'd not only see comings and goings, they would also hear any furore, such was the slow trade in the pub. Mr Singh had asked for fifteen-minute updates on the handheld on the closed frequency and they had so far remembered his instructions in-between games of top trumps and a quick thumb war tournament, which Carl won with ease.

It took another forty-five minutes for the party guests to leave. Tom reported to Mr Singh that all four left at the same time and the youngest, a blonde woman with knee-high red boots, struggled with the stairs. She looked the worse for wear. The young man, dressed in a white shirt and smart black business trousers was carrying a small white envelope. None of them looked particularly pleased with themselves, they just appeared workmanlike and focused on whatever might come next. Carl was eating Twiglets and had rather bizarrely thanked the four as they left, like an over-attentive landlord. Even Tom was baffled.

In the Premier Inn, Jenny had showered for the first time in days and Isadora was talking Jones through the rudiments of the software. It was an impressive bit of equipment, he thought. However, Jenny was barely dressed before McNally radioed in for an update.

"It's pretty simple," explained Jones, taking the handheld as Jenny dried her hair.

"Finch is in that pub in Ruislip, waiting for something. He's just had four people appear with a bottle of champagne and this looks unlikely to be a welcome home party. The two Emerald chaps are sitting in the bar waiting downstairs and they've just reported that all four left, but there's no sign of Finch or Gerard McMahon." He explained.

"You're going to have to get over there. Leave Isadora at the computer and the two of you can go and get that hire car from Stratford and head over. The two Emerald lads are untrained and God knows what'll happen there next. Their job is done." McNally replied. They could hear Charles' voice in the background.

Isadora wasn't happy. She was used to being not just in the heart of the action but also the centre of attention. She was not a backup surveillance operative. McNally calmly explained that Finch knew exactly what she looked like and it would be foolish to undermine the whole operation. Finch had only briefly met Jones and Jenny and he wouldn't be expecting them. They were untrained newbies. Isadora agreed, grudgingly. With Jenny and Jones fully briefed by McNally and Charles, they made their way back eastwards to pick up the car at the Railway Tavern. It was a forty-minute trip and Jones was dismayed that he'd be visiting a pub without stopping for a swift cold one.

The trip back on the tube was a quiet journey. Jenny chatted through McNally's briefing and they checked their handhelds were charged and operational. Jones admitted he was anxious and felt under-prepared and Jenny agreed. Neither were ready to back out especially as they knew they were so close to Finch. Someone who had ended and blighted so many lives.

As they made their way from Stratford's Central Line Tube Station, up the embankment and over the railway bridge, they could see the green-painted timbers of the pub. And as they got closer, the shape of the hire car just to the right of the building. Jenny delved into her bag for the car keys and they, once again, chatted through the action plan. It wasn't until they were within a few yards of the pub that they saw the car had been vandalised. Both back wheels were missing and the back window smashed. The car was empty and the damage was pointless but this was an unwelcome spanner in the works. There was simply no way the hire company, Eurodollar, would respond quickly enough to get them on the road and the intelligence services were deep in the background.

Jenny looked at Jones with despair and he, in turn, grabbed the handheld and explained the situation to Isadora back in Bermondsey and McNally in Thiepval.

"This isn't game over," he said, partly to motivate himself and partly because he felt this was somehow his fault. "I'll be back in touch with a plan," he promised Isadora. Whilst Jenny disappeared into the pub to find the same payphone that she'd used to end her relationship with Jason, Jones propped up the bar.

It was as if time had stood still since their last visit. The same punters, watching the same television set with the same smell of stale cigarettes and lager. Jones momentarily let the past few days sink in and downed a pint of Kronenburg. Jenny coughed loudly behind him and gave him the thumbs up and mouthed the word 'tomorrow'. She'd managed to reach Eurodollar but it'd be 24 hours before they would replace the vehicle.

Jones and Jenny sat at a corner table and people-watched. The handheld was silent and the last contact with Isadora was just to confirm that the car was dead and that they were assessing other options. Jones' list of options was pretty short. It was either get the tube to Ruislip and hang around the bar but surveillance would be a whole lot easier from a vehicle. The second option was to send Carl and Tom home and utilise the twin room to keep close to the action. Neither option was attractive.

It was when the list of options appeared to fall off a cliff that the handheld sprang into life.

"Jones and Jenny, this is Virginia, I'm sorry I've been off the radar. My recovery has been a little slower than I expected. But I overheard the call about the car and I may have a solution."

"Virginia!" exclaimed Jenny. "I've been so worried, how are you? Are you being waited on hand and foot by Sir Charles?"

"All in good time, Jenny. I'm recovering and I'm being looked after. But I think we need to get you back on the road and I have a local friend who might be able to help. Tell me, who's behind the bar in the Railway Tavern today?" Jones and Jenny looked at each other, wondering how Virginia knew they were in the pub and felt a little as if they'd been caught out. Jenny looked behind the bar and spotted who she presumed was the landlord.

The landlord, seeing Jenny's head pop over the bar, slowly made his way over from the other end of the L-shaped bar. He was a huge man covered in wonderfully intricate tattoos and wearing a distinctive red beret. His unique look was completed with a long black coat with impressive military lapels.

"Is there something I can help you with?" the landlord asked.

"Ah, that sounds like the chap. Pass him the handheld" said Virginia, listening in.

"Mrs Curry?" boomed the landlord, approvingly. Jones and Jenny looked on as the larger-than-life man chatted amiably with Virginia, like old friends. Soon enough, he passed the handheld back to Jenny. Virginia had signed off.

"I was sorry to hear your car had been damaged, love. We're normally pretty safe around here. It's a hire car isn't it?" The landlord asked. Jones had decided the gent was a cross between a mid-1970s wrestler and Frank Spencer, but he looked genuinely concerned.

"Yeah, it's a hire car. But the company can't reach us until tomorrow." Jenny sighed and sipped her Guinness.

"Yes, Mrs Curry told me. She and I go way back. She owns a little flat around the corner and we often entertain her here" The landlord quickly added.

"I feel responsible after telling you to park there and Mrs Curry is a very good customer, so I might be able to help you out."

The landlord grabbed an old Hamlet cigar tin from behind the bar. It rattled as he picked it up. After a few seconds, he retrieved a bulky set of keys.

"I'll lend you a motor. If you can get it started, you can use it. But it'll be at your own risk. There's no insurance or car tax on it." And he threw the keys to Jenny. "It's around the back in the row of garages. The last garage on the right. But don't get your hopes up. It's not much to get excited about. But please tell Mrs Curry that you're sorted, as she's a little worried about you."

Jones and Jenny practically emptied their glasses at once and Jenny shook the hand of the landlord enthusiastically. "You're a lifesaver," she said. "We'll bring it back as soon as possible."

They ran around the back of the pub and quickly found the row of dilapidated garages. The garage door was hanging off the furthest building in the block and Jones struggled to lift it. The two of them heaved the up-and-over door as far as possible to get a view of the tarpaulin-covered car. It looked like an estate from the shape of the chassis.

Between them they grabbed the long tarpaulin sheet from the base of the bonnet and slowly uncovered the entire length of the vehicle. It was a Black Ford Zephyr with a rather extended accommodation area at the back. In short, it was a hearse. Along the side, stencilled in white paint were the words 'Dead Quick' and a telephone number.

The two stared at each other briefly in disbelief before quickly sliding into the front seats and firing up the engine. It started the first time and purred. Jones found a London A-Z underneath the passenger seat and a huge bag of boiled sweets.

"Jenny, I think we've been dead lucky here."

"Shut up," replied Jenny as she manoeuvred the hearse out of the garage and through the busy car park. Every head turned as they indicated out of the entrance onto the main road.

"This is possibly the worst vehicle on the planet to undertake covert surveillance," Jenny said, smiling. "But it'll have to do." She turned to see Jones laughing heartily.

CHAPTER THIRTY-FOUR

It was late evening in Ruislip when Tom and Carl got their next sight of Finch. The lads had been entertaining themselves for a good few hours now and Carl hadn't been limiting his lager intake. He was at the stage of drunkenness where not only was everything funny, but he was keen for everyone in the bar to be his new best friend. Tom had slowed an hour or so earlier and had been a shandy drinker for the last few rounds but Carl's exuberance hadn't raised any eyebrows in the Black Bull. He was simply a typical student who couldn't hold his drink.

Finch appeared at the bottom of the stairs looking like a shadow of his former unkempt self. He was wearing crisp beige chinos and a tight-fitting white Fred Perry polo shirt. He ordered a whisky and briefly sat on a bar stool with a clear view of the Emerald lads. Carl caught the eye of Stephen Finch once or twice too often and the game was up. Finch could deal with coincidences but these two were pushing every paranoid button. The landlady, who advised Carl loudly to get some fresh air before heading to bed, was also tired of his nonsense.

Finch asked whether he could buy a bottle of whisky to take to his room and the landlady swiftly concocted a vastly inflated price to enable him to do just that. He took the bottle of Teachers and counted out some cash from a wad of Irish sterling notes. The landlady wasn't bothered about where they came from, as long as they were bankable. This sale was a nice little bonus.

Finch, a non-smoker, then motioned he was popping outside for a cigarette and leaned against the side of the Letterkenny taxi. It was a few yards away from the front door and out of sight. The air was cool now and he immediately felt a chill, he placed the bottle of whisky on the boot of the car and rubbed his hands together.

He could hear the two lads, still laughing as they exited the front door of the pub. And he called over to them.

"Lads, do you know where I might get a late-night burger from around here? Are you local?"

Tom froze. He knew that this wasn't part of the plan. He remembered Mr Singh's instructions. "*Say nothing, do nothing and don't make an arse of yourselves.*" The ship had sailed on the last instruction but he was damned if he was going to start chatting with Finch.

"Alright mate," called Carl cheerily but not entirely fluently. "We're not local but I swear I saw a kebab shop as we walked from the station."

And Carl, with Tom close behind, staggered over to Finch. As Finch went to retrieve a London map from the boot of the taxi, he called out. "Can you show me? I'd love a doner. That would make my day."

The pair wandered a few feet from the car and were ready to point out the station on the map, and in a blink of an eye, Finch swung the litre bottle of Teachers at Carl, lunging at him and catching him square across the forehead. As he went down his head and face caught the top of the boot of the vehicle and he slumped to the floor. Tom, immediately shocked by the horror of the attack, made to leave the scene but Finch was far too quick. Finch swung the bottle at Tom two or three times, just missing, and Tom attempted to use a jiu-jitsu move on Finch which surprised him and brought the Irishman to the floor. This little victory was short-lived and Finch quickly grappled Tom to the ground and it took him just two heavy blows with the bottle for Tom to be laid unconscious next to Carl and the car park was in silence again.

Finch dragged Carl off the ground and with a huge effort pushed him untidily into the boot of the taxi. Tom was lying bleeding heavily next to the back door of the car and, concerned that someone could exit the pub at any moment, he was able to shift the unconscious Tom onto the back seat. Finch was exhausted. He slammed the back door of the taxi, only stopping when he saw one of Carl's Puma trainers underneath the near-side back tyre and threw that in beside Tom. He then quickly covered Tom with a large blue blanket, which he'd previously used to hide Gerard McMahon.

He heard the front door of the pub open and he quickly snapped open the bottle of whisky. He took a large mouthful of the alcohol and then waited for the two elderly drinkers to get closer. He then dramatically spat the whisky onto the car park tarmac, instantly washing away the small spots of blood from Tom's head injury and ensuring that the pensioners looked the other way. No one wants to be in the audience for someone being violently sick on alcohol.

"You alright fella?" called out one of the drinkers.

"Yeah, I'm fine. I just need to stop drinking whisky! Good-night lads." And Finch waved them off down Victoria Avenue. Once they had turned the corner, he poured the whisky all over the floor to disperse the remaining blood and ambled casually back into the pub.

Two piles of top trumps cards were on either side of a pub

table, with a half-completed word search on European capitals. There was also a large bag of clothes in a Safeway bag. With the landlady elsewhere, Finch scrambled the cards and book into the Safeway bag and hid it underneath a bench seat farthest away from the bar. The landlady would find this tomorrow, and he'd be long gone. Finch looked at his watch. McMahon's chloroform would be wearing off in about an hour, so he sprinted to the car park and drove the taxi out onto the main road towards Ruislip Gardens and then the A40. He knew exactly where he was going.

Less than a hundred miles away, Mr Singh had switched off Bangla TV. His beloved India had lost a One Day International against Sri Lanka and his Kheer (a type of fruit-spiced rice pudding) had given him indigestion. He was looking for some Rennies when one of his bank of screens pinged in the lair. The handheld, which he'd entrusted to Tom, was travelling at speed towards the Polish War Memorial. He knew there was one of the GCHQ prototype cameras next to the Memorial and within a few minutes the Letterkenny taxi's number plate flashed up and the car sped past.

He fumbled for his handheld and first radioed Jones, who was in the front seat of the hearse next to Jenny.

"The taxi is on the move. It's heading on the A40 away from Ruislip towards Uxbridge." Mr Singh explained.

"I reckon we're half an hour away. Maybe more. How do you know he's heading towards Uxbridge? Is there another camera?" Asked Jones.

"That's the thing. Tom Marsh's handheld is also in the taxi. So, either Finch has stolen it or Tom's in the taxi. This is my doing, they were so inexperienced."

"Try not to worry. We'll get there as soon as we can. Please keep an eye on the signal from Tom's handheld and give us a location. Can you radio McNally and keep him updated too?"

Jones half-shouted back. As the revs from the hearse were making conversation difficult.

"I'll do that. And be careful." Mr Singh slumped down into one of the chairs next to the bank of screens and radioed McNally. He wasn't likely to be consoled by the brusque Ulsterman, but he knew he'd screwed up. Two well-meaning lads had been thrown into a dangerous mission they had no experience to deal with. He would pray for their safety and focus on the screens.

The screens told their own story. Around 25 minutes after the call to McNally, Mr Singh saw that Tom's handheld had stopped moving. The location was just outside the perimeter gates of RAF Northolt. It was an airbase used by both military and civilian aircraft and home to units from all three Armed Services and the Ministry of Defence. Finch certainly wanted his former colleagues to know he'd worked out he was being watched. Mr Singh immediately made contact with Charles who spoke to the Northolt team. They sent out a team to search the perimeter for a dumped handheld, only to find two badly assaulted lads.

When he received the call from Charles, confirming the discovery of Tom and Carl, Mr Singh scoured through the grainy footage from the pub car park camera and could just make out the vicious assault taking place.

The RAF ambulance crew reached the pair quickly and Carl was already conscious, although concussed and dreadfully hungover. He told the paramedics that they'd been attacked by a drunk man with a bottle at a local pub, he couldn't remember which. Carl also confessed to the medics that he was the drummer from Status Quo and he was hiding from the paparazzi. After offering autographs he passed out again but the ordeal was over.

Tom, was taken directly into Hillingdon Hospital with

advanced head trauma, he hadn't regained consciousness. Carl would undergo observation and sit with Tom waiting for him to wake up.

As Mr Singh began to piece together the events of the evening, his hacked video feed from the car park picked up two vehicles pulling into the vicinity of the pub. The low-quality footage revealed one was Finch's Letterkenny taxi, arriving just in time to give Gerard McMahon another dose of chloroform, the other was what appeared to be a vintage hearse. This had parked up a few yards behind the still baffling orange Tipo. The two flashing GPS dots confirmed Jones and Jenny had arrived in an unconventional manner.

CHAPTER THIRTY-FIVE

Along the back of the hearse were two matching purple curtains, these spanned the whole of the side windows and the back window itself was blacked out. The wooden plinth which would have supported the 'horizontal stationary passenger' was hard and uncomfortable but Jones and Jenny laid down and could get a good view of the Black Bull and the window they presumed was the location for Finch and Gerard McMahon. This was the only light on and the pub was now closed.

They took shifts in watching the window and there were occasional chats with Isadora who fed grains of detail around Finch and the ongoing case, but the lack of any movement or activity was concerning Jones. Isadora explained that surveillance is often a long, drawn-out job and he'd have to bear the long hours of nothingness with fortitude. Although he did quite enjoy the solo time with Jenny, as they'd had Isadora in tow for days now.

Jenny had nodded off at around 5am and was gently snoring, whilst Jones had perfected his flat prone position with his hands supporting his head, staring through an inch gap in the dusty purple hearse curtains. He had noticed the bedroom curtain move intermittently but the whole pub and car park appeared deserted and silent.

Jenny woke up with the sound of a motorbike careering up the main road and turning in the lane leading to the pub. There were loud impatient revs. Jones was slumped asleep, head down, in front of the inch gap and she was immediately aware they might have missed something. She shook Jones awake and he groggily pushed the passenger seat down and exited quietly through the door, with the front of the hearse hiding his movement. He dashed along behind the hedge, dividing the car park from the main road, and found a good viewpoint. He could see Finch waiting by the advertising hoarding. He was wearing a long hooded black jacket and an unseasonal beanie hat.

Jones was close enough to see the motorcyclist was riding a Kawasaki and had a luminous green vest with branding. He was a courier of some kind. Finch was chatting to him and the motorcyclist had pulled the visor up to engage in the conversation. He was passed small padded envelopes and he saw cash change hands. Jones repeated the number plate of the motorbike a few times to memorise it and watched as the courier disappeared. He sped back up the main road and towards the roundabout which led to the A40 junction. Jones needed to call this into both Mr Singh and McNally who would shape the next steps. He needed to get back to Jenny before Finch walked back past the adjoining hedge.

He slipped back quietly into the hearse and crawled under the fake floor which separated the boot space from the wooden plinth and urged Jenny to do the same. It was tight. He left the curtains open slightly to allow Finch the chance to see the hearse was empty. Sure enough, as Jones and Jenny huddled in the long space underneath the plinth, they could hear Finch's footsteps stopping to peer in through the gap in the curtains. He would see nothing aside from a well-thumbed A-Z and a half-eaten bag of humbugs. The pair held their breath and stared frantically at each other, with Jenny grasping both of Jones' hands. The minute in which he investigated the hearse seemed to last hours but once he was confident the bizarrely branded vehicle was empty, he paced back towards the hotel. Jones then knew they had about a minute to get back into position.

Jones radioed into Mr Singh first, giving the exact number plate of the J-registered Kawasaki. He then repeated the call to McNally who urged them to sit tight whilst he spoke to both Charles and the team at Knock Road.

In the meantime, Isadora made contact with Jenny. She hadn't slept. She was full of ideas.

"Right," said Isadora. "We need to take control of the situation. Finch is obviously going to deliver something potentially explosive to wreck any chance of a peace deal and therefore embarrass the Americans."

"Explosive in what sense?" Asked Jenny. "McNally seems to think all of the RDX was used at Limehall, Lennoxville and Great Victoria Street, with the remainder found at the Scottish port."

"Yeah," Isadora agreed. "But we don't know that there's no other source. And by 'explosive' I also meant something that would create headlines or drama."

Jones chimed in. "This is all to do with the party in Finch's room. We know he's a miserable bastard. And the old man is in there. This all has to be linked."

"I agree. Therefore, we need to think about locations. And I am just 15 minutes from the action here. Keep talking to me and I'll head out. Let's talk locations. Quickly." Isadora added.

"There are at least two packages. That's what I saw. So, we assume, maybe a newspaper office? Or Thames House?"

"Yes Jones, those are possibilities, but I think the biggie is the American Embassy. That's where I'd be putting my money. And that's in Grosvenor Square near Mayfair. I'll head there. Come back to me once the second target has been discussed." Isadora switched off and within seconds Mr Singh radioed back.

"He's heading into central London. It's flashed twice on the A40 but he was slowing on the way past a Happy Eater. So, with any luck, he's going for breakfast. I've also done some digging. It's a courier firm from Northwood, called Deliveries on Speed. They're kosher."

"Oh wow, Deliveries on Speed. Love the name," said Jones. "How far are we from central London?"

"About 45 minutes by car. Longer by tube. We'll need to rely on Isadora and anything we get from Mr Singh and wait for Finch to make his move." Jenny replied. Mr Singh, still listening in, signed off and the line went dead.

Half an hour or so later, Isadora walked briskly through the hotel reception and out of the main doors towards Southwark Park Road. Smiling at the receptionist on the way out, she noted they were probably the same age and Isadora found herself wondering how life could have been different. From the main road, she would either get a bus into central London or use the scarce cash she had in her back pocket to get a black taxi. It was a 25-minute journey and this was simply a punt that Finch had opted for to unnerve the Americans. The second location was anyone's guess.

It was the early morning rush hour and she was dressed in black combat trousers and a white cotton long-sleeved t-shirt. She'd grabbed a formal-looking jacket to throw over the top in case the weather turned. But it was 18 degrees outside and the temperature was due to rise. She jumped on a bus heading into the centre and clambered past a mix of commuters, parents with school children and bleary-looking students to find a window seat at the back. There she applied a little makeup and used the reflection from the window to see how successfully she'd used her eyeliner. The window was horribly smeared. Someone had scratched 'ARSE' in big letters into the glass and that made things difficult.

The bus was a sweat-box and Isadora was being diverted by a small child who was repeatedly sticking his finger up his nose and eating the contents. This reminded her that she hadn't breakfasted yet. Three stops later and with the small boy now suffering from a nosebleed, Isadora got off the bus and headed up the road towards Mayfair, grabbing a Diet Coke and a Tracker bar to allay the hunger pangs. She found an old red telephone box and turned her back on the passing hubbub to speak to Mr Singh.

"Any sign?"

"The courier flashed once going over the A40 flyover and then an old railway camera next to Acton Bridge. But nothing since. But if you were going to see him, it'd be any time now. Assuming he's had time to digest his breakfast." Mr Singh signed off.

She could see the American Embassy in the distance but had not created a strategy. She was simply keen to understand where the padded envelopes had been delivered and then discuss the action plan with the team. So, as she stood outside a newsagent eating her peanut Tracker bar and drinking her Diet Coke, fate played a huge role. Out of the corner of her eye, she saw the J-registered Kawasaki turn into the street adjoining Grosvenor Square. The rider parked up and removed his helmet. He was a young black man in black and grey leathers, carrying the package and a red clipboard. He was in either his late teens or very early twenties and looked hot and bored. As he passed Isadora, she took her chance.

"Excuse me mate, do you know if we're close to the American Embassy?" she asked.

"Wow, you're from Birmingham!" he replied in a deep Brummie accent. "What do you want the Embassy for? You're miles from home!" And as he laughed. Isadora smiled, charmingly.

"Yeah, I'm a Solihull lass actually, I've got a job interview and I'm crapping myself."

"Ah, you'll be fine. The Embassy is over there" and he pointed at the enormous building with armed guards flanking the entrance.

"I'm such an idiot, sorry. I'm being interviewed as a PA for one of the Directors," she added, still exaggerating her unusually useful accent and using her limited flirtation skills. "Want some of my Coke, you look hot!"

The courier laughed at the obvious chat-up line and took a quick swig from her can. This was going surprisingly well.

"Look, why don't you take this in for me? You'll need to sign for it though. Just write US Embassy staff in the box. And perhaps give me your number?"

Bingo thought Isadora. And she wrote an entirely different name on the courier's clipboard and wrote a random Solihull landline number on his hand. It was the number for her favourite Tandoori Restaurant, which she knew by heart. She held his hand gently as she wrote the details.

"You're saving me the nightmare of going through US Embassy security. I swear they'd strip-search me in there if they could." And he gave Isadora a quick cheeky grin. He'd be telling the lads in the office about this later.

"So, this was a useful meeting in so many ways. Let's chat soon. I have a few other deliveries nearby." He added as he took a few steps to walk away. Isadora waved and desperately tried to see the exact next address on his clipboard. But she could only make out *Aldgate, Farrar*.

When the courier walked away she gently strolled towards the Embassy, still swigging the Diet Coke. Once he'd stopped waving and had rounded the corner, she did an about-turn and headed back to the phone box, immediately radioing the rest of Topaz.

"It's me, I've been rather successful." She announced. "Not only have I managed to obtain the package from Finch but I've also made friends with a rather attractive courier called Jacob."

"You're an absolute genius, Isadora" cheered Jenny. "Have you opened it?"

"I'm about to do that now, ask Jones to radio McNally and he can be on hand if this thing goes boom."

Jones who heard the command, raised McNally and the long-distance audience held their breath as Isadora gently tore open the jiffy bag.

"Okay, I'll read this out loud. McNally, could you take down this letter word for word?" McNally gave a quick 'Aye aye' in the background and Isadora opened the first of two white envelopes inside.

"*To the US Ambassador for the United Kingdom of Great Britain and Northern Ireland,*

Fred Martinsen is a traitor and stands against everything the people of Ireland hold firm. He has used his time away from the States to commit lewd acts, to meet undesirables and to profit from money given by the very terrorist groups our nations are trying to disarm. And what's more, the British Government's secret services know about this treachery and are doing nothing about it.

The following three photos are not the only evidence. We have more polaroid photos, film and transcripts of telephone conversations of dubious activity. End these farcical peace talks. Sack Martinsen, end the US Diplomacy and allow the Irish time to find their own solutions to their own problems.

Release an official statement confirming the end of the dialogue and Martinsen's resignation by midnight or we will release the evidence to the global media.

Signed – Red Line"

Isadora then opened the second envelope to see three polaroid images of the Martinsen doppelgänger being pleasured by two naked young women, a second with the man receiving a large stack of paper currency from a figure in army fatigues but with his face covered by a black balaclava and finally, and perhaps most gruesomely, the doppelgänger in leather bondage gear being whipped by a hooded, but otherwise naked, man.

She described all three and placed them carefully back in the envelope. McNally was the first to speak.

"Isadora, how genuine do these look to you? Is there anything in them that would question their authenticity?" McNally asked.

"Nothing. The photos look watertight. He even has Martinsen's trademark smile in the photo with the currency. Finch has been bloody clever, he's even dated them on the camera to align with Martinsen's visit to London a few days back." Isadora explained.

"Right, let me speak to Charles and Massey and I'll come back to you as soon as I can. Is there anything else I need to know? From any of you?"

"Nothing from us McNally, no movement since the exchange with the courier." Jones updated.

"One more thing from me, the courier's clipboard listed his next location at Aldgate and the surname was Farrar. Perhaps we could all look into that and I'll head over to Aldgate. Jones, could you speak to Mr Singh?" And Jones agreed before signing off, leaving Isadora to find a tube station and get to Aldgate, in east London.

The second package was about to hit a doormat somewhere.

Isadora was barely halfway to Aldgate on the Central Line when she realised that the Aldgate address and Farrar could be red herrings. Couriers tend to group their drop-offs or even use other motorbiking colleagues closer to the address to make the drop. That thought was ringing in her ears when she decided to alight from the train at Liverpool Street and contact the team. But Mr Singh got to her first.

"Isadora, I'm afraid you've had a wasted journey. Farrar's is a well-known wine merchant in Aldgate and Deliveries on Speed has confirmed this is a regular booking. The next drop off could be anywhere."

She thanked Mr Singh and sat in a secluded area in the station and went through the documents again. To the untrained eye, they looked authentic and this was a tragedy for Gerard McMahon. A press leak of any kind was unthinkable, especially if it was the full story. If it revealed the link between YCU and the loss of life in Lennoxville and Limehall, it would also lead to a massive internal issue for all of the other main partners in the peace talks, as well as the British Secret Services. But all of that seemed very unlikely. There were ways and means of quelling press speculation by using the Official Secrets Act and national security considerations. This was all part of the YCU training and Charles' mantra of 'deniability'.

But, even in fantasyland, if Finch knew a press leak would destabilise the talks and discredit SIS and YCU, why wasn't he doing it? What did he have to lose? The only obvious skeleton was Gerard McMahon, the doppelgänger. Finch would be desperate to avoid McMahon's disappearance in Ireland coming to light – as this would end the whole blackmail programme. Maybe she was missing something? Was she being naïve?

If Martinsen was provably not the man in the photographs and the taxi driver's kidnapping was revealed, wouldn't it be game over? Isadora decided to speak to Charles. She knew he had a soft spot for her, as the darling of the YCU. He'd make time. She radioed him. McNally answered, Charles was meeting Massey and Spencer at Knock Road and couldn't be disturbed. Shit. She decided to bend the ear of the Irishman.

"McNally, what am I missing here? Why can't we release details of the kidnapping to the press? And just stop Finch now. Wouldn't it simply draw a line?"

"You've got to be joking. Is this why you were after Charles? Wise up, Isadora!" He replied, denting her confidence. McNally had the knack of making people feel small.

"If we release the taxi driver's kidnap to the media, they would begin to put the pieces together themselves. Finch kidnapping McMahon is a security threat. It's not just a kidnapping, it's an action from a foreign power," he explained.

"We need to kill this quickly and quietly. And you did a brilliant job getting that envelope as we now know what we're dealing with. But just because Finch looks like one of us, and we've shared a beer with him, we still need to see him as a Russian terrorist and a murderer. And we'd never leak news of a Russian terrorist to the media, would we? Do you understand? He's a bloody dangerous man."

"I get it." She replied quietly. As she pondered the next move and McNally momentarily paused to answer the telephone in Thiepval, the reason for Charles' meeting with Massey and Spencer became clear. She could hear McNally chatting to Charles on the phone in the background. After a brief pause, McNally returned to the handheld.

"Charles has just confirmed there were two further deliveries this morning, with the same photos but a different message. We're trying to get hold of the messages. One was hand-delivered to New Scotland Yard and the second to Thames House, Jube Spencer has been asked to fly over. This confirms that Finch isn't just an evil murdering bastard, but an annoying wee shite too." McNally closed the call and Isadora headed back to Bermondsey. The interception of the letter bound for the American Embassy was handy but just a little victory, Isadora was now sure the pace would hot up.

Jones and Richmond had spent the past few hours learning the mundanity of surveillance. Nothing of note had happened at the Black Bull, aside from a brewery delivery and an old lady dragging a disobedient Yorkshire Terrier around the block, the dog pausing briefly to urinate up the back tyre of the hearse. This had triggered Jones's own desperate need for the toilet but both he and Jenny were growing concerned about Finch's whereabouts and the glaring obviousness of their surveillance vehicle. So, he had to wait. Isadora had briefly radioed to explain the news about the other two packages and her belief that things would now happen. Jones wished they would, if only for his bladder's sake.

"I just saw the curtains move," whispered Jenny. "They are still in there."

Finch's head momentarily appeared in between the neon blue curtains and he appeared to be looking to the far right of the car park. The entrance to the pub. As if expecting something or someone. Not once did he look at the hearse. Almost as soon as his head had ducked away back into the safety of the bedroom, Jenny noticed he quickly reappeared.

"Look, Jones, he's wearing a tie. He's smartened up."

Jones squinted up towards the window through the thick hearse drapes.

"Yeah, you're right. He's prepping for something. I feel a bit powerless sitting here. Shouldn't we be doing something?" Asked Jones as he continued staring into the first-storey window.

"Go and stand by the bus stop. Explain to Isadora what's happening and then you're likely to get a good look at whoever picks him up. Finch seems to be expecting someone." Jenny suggested.

Without any further discussion, Jones picked up the hand-held, jumped out of the back door and hid behind the row of cars as far as the end of the car park and sprinted to the bus stop. The illuminated screen above the bus stop suggested there were another seven minutes before the next bus, but he was alone. He quickly radioed Isadora and explained Finch was suited and booted, for something.

Moments later, Finch appeared at the front door of the pub in a formal black suit and a green tie. He placed a small brown suitcase next to the front door of the pub and disappeared inside again. It was a hot late-July day and through the glare of the sunshine, Jenny could see he was chatting and smiling. Perhaps the landlady was downstairs and he was paying the bill, she thought. Finch appeared again with another small rucksack and then, from inside the pub, stepped an older-looking man. He was in a brown checked suit, a yellow shirt, a rather gaudy bitter orange tie and smart brown brogues. He wore a blue baseball cap and aviator sunglasses. The only outward sign that this was an Irishman who'd been held prisoner by a maniac, rather than the US Peace Envoy, was his painfully slow shuffle out of the front door and his obvious weariness. The doses of sleeping pills and chloroform were having a lasting effect. Finch occasionally put his arm around Gerard McMahon, clearly continuing the lie that this was an elderly relative and helped him carefully out into the London sunshine. The old man looked disorientated and vulnerable.

Jenny held her breath as Finch nervously looked around. She could just make out Jones by the bus stop and she could see he was aware of proceedings. Seconds later, an old-style London black cab appeared in the road leading to the pub and swung into the car park. The old man was slowly helped towards the waiting vehicle. Jones, furiously waved his arms at every passing taxi in an attempt to follow the cab and it looked like his luck was out, until a red Ford Escort pulled over and beckoned him into the back seat. It was driven by a very tall black man with long flowing dreadlocks and the interior of the vehicle was furnished with the green, yellow and red of the Rastafarian movement. The flag of Jamaica dangled from the rear-view mirror in the form of an air freshener, which it seemed was an attempt at masking the obvious smell of marijuana.

"Where to?" said the taxi driver in a Glaswegian accent. "I'm cash only and don't ask to see my licence."

"You see that black cab?" Jones responded, pointing over his shoulder towards the pub, as the old man was being helped into the vehicle. "Could you follow it? But from a distance?"

"No bother. Leave it with me," replied the taxi driver, with an air of utter indifference. "You're not the bloody police, are you?" he quickly added. His Glaswegian accent added a small hint of menace.

"Nah, I'm a journalist and the old man in the back is a politician. Mum's the word though. Alright?"

The taxi driver just nodded and the huge collection of dreadlocks rocked to and fro as he turned the radio up. Jones quickly identified the music as Fela Kuti's band Africa '70 and relaxed a little as he watched the black cab edge out of the car park and onto the main road.

He ducked behind the back seat and radioed Jenny.

"I'm in the red Escort."

"Yeah, I know, I saw. What on earth is that noise?" asked Jenny.

"It's what they call good music Jenny. Can you ask Mr Singh to follow my movements and update everyone who needs to know?"

"I'm on that. Be careful."

"Perhaps McNally or Charles will have some idea what the plan is here, but I'm not doing anything but following and watching. Can you pass that on?"

"Absolutely." And Jenny rang off.

Within a few miles, it became clear the black cab was heading into central London but was certainly taking its time. The driver drove slowly and carefully in the outside lane, with the red Escort remaining reliably at least five cars behind at all times.

The driver had defied the stereotype by unwrapping a packet of Marlboro Lights but was inhaling them at some speed. The smoke blew back into the rear of the car and Jones switched seats and opened one of the windows to drop a little hint that the smoke was billowing straight at him, the driver didn't take the hint and continued to chain smoke.

It was when Jones decided to stick his head out of the window for fresh air, that he glimpsed something behind him. It was just a flash amongst a long parade of vehicles heading into central London, but he was convinced he had a momentary sighting of the orange Fiat Tipo that was previously sitting in the Black Bull car park. He and Jenny had almost forgotten about it, as it hadn't moved since their arrival and it had only been mentioned by Tom and Carl in despatches. But there it was. He was surprised that Jenny hadn't called him. Jones focused on the road ahead and awaited another glimpse of the orange Fiat.

CHAPTER THIRTY-SIX

Orla Massey had been invited to a pub dinner with the Currys at the Bunch of Grapes the previous evening and, while she had been driving and therefore hangover-free, she was tired and bothered. She was already on her third coffee and was halfway through a calorific traybake, presented to her by an eager new RUC officer. It had coconut in it and she wasn't a fan. Nevertheless, she forced it down to quell the hunger and the general malaise.

She had decided, perhaps cynically, that Virginia and Charles had embarked on a dual charm offensive to try to ensure they were fully briefed on the Finch case. They needn't have worried, as she was almost completely in the dark. Jube Spencer had boarded a flight to London City Airport earlier yesterday and her one source of secret service information had gone. She felt out of the loop and isolated.

Therefore, she was thrust into the boredom of paperwork, statistics and signing off expense dockets. The life of a Chief Inspector wasn't all gun fights and super-sleuthing, in fact, her foray into the Finch case was a rarity. She was aware of the two blackmail letters which had reached Thames House and New

Scotland Yard but was simply sitting in the background acting as liaison with the Letterkenny Garda and providing guidance on lines of enquiry.

However, on a trip to the Knock Road canteen, she noticed the room was fuller than normal with several new faces milling about, drinking tea and eating lunchtime baps. She spied Eric Rogers in the corner of the canteen chatting to another divisional chief. Rogers led the Anti-Terrorism Unit and was another Englishman with a high opinion of himself. Her awkwardness around him was also triggered by the knowledge that he was one of a large contingent of RUC colleagues who would be horrified by her sexuality.

"Orla!" Rogers shouted as he saw her appear across the other side of the room. "Have you come to join the troops for a celebratory lunch?"

"Celebratory? What are they celebrating and why are there so many of them?"

"Ah, well, I shouldn't be telling you, as this is an ATU top-level briefing," he said loudly and smugly. "But we were supposed to be joining the Royal Irish Regiment to destroy a shipment of seized paramilitary arms over in Derry. The lads are celebrating an all-expenses paid afternoon off." And he laughed dryly.

"Why did it need so many of you? Surely, you're just throwing them into an incinerator and I would think even the Army could do that without your expert team," she added, purposely toning down her sarcasm a notch.

"You'd think that," Rogers replied. "But we were due a VIP audience and therefore they were being dismantled first and then incinerated. For the cameras." He paused dramatically and drank a huge swig of tea.

"You see, at the eleventh hour, they've switched the venue to a warehouse in London. It was a bit mad, if you ask me, as the arms were seized in England anyway. So, they were bringing them over here for publicity. It's all on a need-to-know basis though, Orla." Massey nodded and ignored the attempted one-upmanship.

"You said VIP guests, Eric, who are we talking about? The Northern Ireland Secretary of State?"

"Well, I really shouldn't be saying," Rogers lowered his voice and whispered. "It was that American chap, the US Peace Envoy. He's making a whistle-stop visit to the UK and this was part of his itinerary. It'll be easier now it's in London though, I should think."

"Fred Martinsen is in London?" she repeated.

"Shhhh! Yeah, he arrived first thing. He's with the PM and then moving on to the warehouse. I had a phone call from an MI5 liaison earlier this morning but aside from calling off the event here, I was asked to keep schtum. National security and all that."

"Did you get a name for the MI5 officer?" asked Massey.

"He gave me a name and a codeword," Rogers responded, he was beginning to look offended at Massey's questioning. "I'm not at liberty to disclose the codeword but his name was Masters, Adam Masters."

Massey politely smiled at Rogers but otherwise dispensed with the niceties and disappeared back into the safety of her office. Away from the pervading testosterone. She flicked through her Rolodex and located a desk number for Jube Spencer at Thames House and she dialled it quickly.

"Spencer, I'm guessing you knew that Fred Martinsen was going to an arms disposal press event in London this afternoon?"

"And a very good afternoon to you, Orla Massey, lovely to hear from you too. And yes, I had a great flight." Spencer replied.

"No, I'm not aware of Fred Martinsen doing a press junket in London. But I knew he was here to meet the PM and discuss a peace treaty. Thames House is betting that it'll be another glorious failure." He added.

"According to a source here, Martinsen is off to a warehouse to watch a large cache of arms being incinerated. It's being coordinated by a fella called Masters. Can you get hold of Martinsen's schedule?"

"I have it in front of me. He's not even here overnight. He's meeting the PM about now, it's a long session. He's then grabbing forty winks at the London Metropole before getting back on Concorde at 11pm back to JFK." Massey could hear Spencer leafing through paperwork at Thames House and she heard a tone of concern in his voice.

"Masters? Jesus Christ, Adam Masters is one of the most corrupt MI5 Officers, but he just hasn't been caught with his hands in the till yet. So, they demoted him to count paperclips until they can build a case. If this has his grubby fingerprints on it, we're in trouble. I haven't heard about any event though, but that's not a major surprise. It's entirely possible this could be such a sensitive event that I'm not part of the coordination. Although, I admit, with Masters involved this does not smell right."

There was a momentary pause as they both collected their thoughts.

"Who was your source?" asked Spencer.

"Eric Rogers, he leads the Anti-Terrorism Unit over here. So, I reckon he'd be in the inner circle locally."

"I'll speak to my chaps here and see what I can dig up on this event. I'll also get hold of McNally and find out what's happening with Topaz and I'll brief you later. Thanks for the tip-off." Spencer signed off.

Massey walked back into the canteen and found Eric

Rogers, still in situ and with an ever-growing rabble of admirers. She dramatically shooed away a few of his cronies and in her trademark passive-aggressive tone began the interrogation.

"Eric, I need anything you've got on this arms cache. We haven't got time for the Chief Superintendent to approve. Just give me the details."

CHAPTER THIRTY-SEVEN

THE RED ESCORT HAD BEEN TAILING THE BLACK CAB FOR OVER THREE-quarters of an hour and Jones had watched in surprise as the vehicle continued onto the North Circular Road and towards signs to east London. Somehow, in his head, Jones was convinced that the doppelgänger was being lined-up for a photo shoot at the Houses of Parliament or heading to the Russian Embassy. Nothing suggested a trip eastwards. The red LED on the side of his handheld was also now flashing and Jones knew this signalled the last of his battery life.

"We've been on the road a long time now, Boss. You got the money to cover this?" shouted the taxi driver over the music.

"I'll give you £100 just to continue the journey as long as it takes. You have my word." Jones replied.

"That'll do for starters, my friend!" And the taxi driver laughed, before continuing slowly behind the cab, just out of sight. Isadora had the money and he was hoping she'd make an appearance soon enough.

Just as Jones became convinced that his handheld had given up the ghost, it sprang into life. It was Jenny.

"Jones, I've just come off from McNally. They reckon Finch

is heading to a warehouse of some description. There's a paramilitary arms cache being dismantled, Fred Martinsen was supposed to be the guest of honour. But there's some confusion, as nobody from the security services seems to know much about it."

"What? How is that even possible?" Jones replied. "Hold on, Jenny."

"Mate," he called to the taxi driver. "We reckon this chap is off to a large warehouse. Where would he be going in east London? Any clues?"

"The smart money would be on the old docks. London Docklands, my friend. Major construction works are going on there but there's one or two ginormous warehouses. It's all yuppy money." Replied the taxi driver.

"Jenny, can you get hold of Isadora and see if you can both get to London Docklands? As soon as possible? And keep briefing McNally. We may need some help. My handheld is dying too."

As the black cab swung past the signs for central London, Jones could see the sprawl of the City of London in the distance and he grabbed McNally's famous 'everything' book from his back pocket. This road would take them all the way into Limehouse and from there into the new Docklands area. The warehouse had to be around there. He also calculated that if Jenny got on the central line from Ruislip, she'd be in the vicinity within the hour. Isadora was even closer at Bermondsey and would be there before them all.

Jones saw the black cab in the distance pull over into a bus stop and turn on its hazard lights. For a moment he wondered if he'd been seen. He quickly surveyed the scene behind him and there was no sign of the orange Fiat and ahead, no sign of movement from inside the cab.

"Have we been seen?" He called out to the driver.

"No, my friend. I would stake my life on it. This is such an anonymous car that he'd need to be James Bond to spot us."

Jones briefly reflected on the irony and then felt at some ease as three other similar red escorts sped past the taxi, which had also pulled over around 750 yards away from the black cab.

Five minutes passed with the cab hazard lights flashing, when a large black mini-bus with blacked-out windows cruised into view. It looked brand new and almost menacing as it made its way slowly behind the black cab. Jones could see nothing inside the vehicle, even the front windscreen was mirrored in a fashion that ensured complete anonymity.

The vehicle pulled up behind the black cab and Jones saw the nearside door of the minibus slide open slowly. Finch then emerged from the cab and briefly entered the minibus. Finch still looked immaculately dressed and there was no sign of the old man who was presumably still inside the black cab. The front door of the minibus opened and a driver, wearing a black suit, white shirt and dark sunglasses emerged. He grabbed a few bags from the back of the cab, found room for them inside the vehicle and climbed back into the front seat. Finch returned to the black cab and soon enough, the minibus indicated and continued its journey.

Jones memorised the registration plate of the cab and minibus and quickly picked up his handheld and attempted to raise Mr Singh. But the handheld was dead. The LED flashed furiously but there wasn't enough power to make the call. He hoped Mr Singh was joining the dots and was tracking the red escort as it crawled towards the location.

As the Ford Escort followed the black cab and minibus the pace slowed even further, and Jones began to wonder if not having a strategy was a natural stance for someone being trained in espionage. He was now left to his own devices and there was no time to find a phone box and call Charles or Mr

Singh. He needed the confidence of having his team around him.

As they crawled past London Wall, he scanned the pavements for any sign of Isadora. She would have left the train at Liverpool Street and run to Docklands in this direction. She was fit and intelligent. But this mind-numbing journey was piquing Jones' anxiety and the loud inconsistent beat of the driver's afro-beat music was making his heart race. He'd had one panic attack in his life, when he'd drunkenly missed the last train home, and a friend had given him breathing techniques to keep his heart rate slow, sure, and calm. He was fighting to maintain his equilibrium by breathing in through his nose and out of his mouth, letting the air flow between his teeth. It was working. He briefly closed his eyes and imagined himself back in The Jericho in Milton, Jenny next to him, pint in hand and singing along to one of his indie classics. Jones was a young man in an extraordinary situation but he knew he'd have to find some inner strength to see this through.

His moment of contemplation was shattered when the back door next to him swung open and Isadora jumped in.

"It's alright mate," she called to the driver. "I'm with him. Although he obviously wasn't looking out for me."

"Isadora, you're a sight for sore eyes. Thank God." Jones said, relieved. Isadora was dressed in a grey sweatshirt and blue jeans and carrying her rucksack.

"Oh, Jones. You're genuinely pleased to see me? That's sweet. Now help me with my blonde wig." And Isadora grabbed a short-bobbed wig from her rucksack and placed it awkwardly on her head. Jones adjusted it, half smiling. Isadora feigned anger.

"What? Finch knows what I look like; I have to change my appearance. I've got some sunnies in my bag too." She pulled out a rather stylish pair of Ray-Bans to complete the look.

"Wow," rasped the taxi driver, looking back through the rear-view mirror. "That suits you. You were born to be blonde!"

"I'm doing fine as a brunette thanks! But do keep a lookout for a mass of red hair as we get closer to East India Dock Road. She's meeting us around there. We're going to be like Charlie's Angels. Only you're going to need to scrub up, Jones!" Isadora laughed, attempting to calm Jones, sensing the anxiety of the situation.

"Remember, Finch knows what you two look like too. We're just banking on the fact that he won't have expected McNally to throw you into the deep end. Anyway. Stay calm and focused, I have your back."

As she closed the zip on her rucksack, Jones noticed a gun in the bottom of her bag. He'd never noticed it before and wasn't aware Isadora carried one. He chose not to comment but Isadora saw the expression on his face and smiled at him.

"By any means necessary, Jones. Remember? Think about how far you've come. If you can jump between two skyscrapers you can bloody well do anything." Jones gave Isadora his most reassuring grin and looked ahead through the gap in the back seats at the crawling black mini-bus.

Another five minutes would pass before they reached the meeting point for Jenny. She was standing waiting with a can of Diet Coke in her hand and immediately jumped in the front seat next to the driver.

"Another one?" the driver laughed.

"This is the full quota now," Isadora added. And as they saw signs for Limehouse and Docklands come into view, Jenny updated them on the Tipo, admitting she'd missed its departure when she was spooked by a passer-by and shut the hearse curtains. She then re-briefed them and they tried to piece together the plan but, as Jones was quick to point out, this was all reactive. They really couldn't second guess what was ahead and the Tipo was another complication.

Earlier, Jenny explained, she had received an intelligence call from McNally. He had briefed her that this was a press event where a cache of paramilitary guns were being put out of use. This was big news. But the doppelgänger's role was unclear and why the minibus? Topaz agreed to simply watch events unfold and report in, as since they were in London, they assumed MI5 would have this covered with the Metropolitan Police also in tow. They presumed everything would be aligned if and when the brown stuff hit the fan.

Jones noticed the orange Fiat in the distance again. He squinted back into the slow stream of traffic behind and could clearly see the J registration vehicle in front of a large articulated lorry. He just couldn't make out a face or explain its role in the unfolding events.

CHAPTER THIRTY-EIGHT

MASSEY HAD GOT VERY LITTLE FROM ERIC ROGERS. HE WAS UTTERLY caught up in his seniority and even after Massey explained the seriousness of the issue, he simply referred the issue upwards. Orla Massey faced the prospect of a meeting with the Chief Superintendent to get Rogers to open up.

Spencer, on the other hand, sat at his hot desk in Thames House with a mess of jigsaw pieces. A few had been joined up. He had learned that Masters had unilaterally placed a hold on the consignment of weapons, the rogue MI5 Officer had simply told Customs that they were to remain in London for further investigation by secret services. This prevented or delayed their transport to Derry for the press event.

He suspected that Masters then telephoned Eric Rogers and simply cancelled the event in Northern Ireland, using the notion of national security to keep Rogers quiet. He had partially succeeded. Rogers would have loved the feeling of being in the loop and entrusted with national secrets but he was loose-lipped enough to raise a few flags, fortunately. Likewise, Masters would have had enough contacts at the American Embassy and the CIA to remove the Derry event from Fred

Martinsen's schedule, and the press officers would have been out of the loop due to the nature of the event. Masters had found a blind spot.

Spencer had a few water cooler conversations that suggested Masters was almost bankrupt and MI5 had some serious concerns about conduct. But a recent bereavement had seen him go off the radar for a while and his enforced secondment to central administration had ended. He was therefore an absolute sitting duck for a bung from the KGB or, if he lied about his seniority, to be turned and become a double agent.

Massey's desk phone rang.

"Orla, the event is a sham. We have a rogue MI5 officer and a significant risk that this seized shipment of armaments and weapons is the target. It appears the Finch blackmail letters were another bloody diversion."

Massey swore loudly. "Alexinsky told us everything is a diversion, that's their style. We should have listened."

"We don't have time for a premortem. Get hold of McNally and Charles. Get the Topaz team to report in and be our eyes and ears. The moment we know where this warehouse is, we'll close it down using force."

"It's a press launch, Spencer. Can't we trace them and ask them where the event is taking place?" suggested Massey.

"Finch has got that covered, they've been picked up in a mini-bus. According to the national news desks, their mobiles have been taken and they've been told that the venue is shrouded in secrecy due to the consignment and the risk of paramilitaries stealing the arms. It's a genius move. But Topaz are on the tail of the minibus and Finch. We have people on the ground." Spencer was talking quickly and Massey could hear the concern in his voice, this was a major breach of security and this could be a nightmare scenario.

As the phone went dead and the two dashed off in different

directions, 400 miles apart, Massey had a nagging suspicion there was a final piece she was missing. All of this was too planned, too perfect and there must be another leak somewhere.

CHAPTER THIRTY-NINE

As the mini-bus rounded the corner leading to an eye-watering array of cranes, containers and cherry pickers, the huge expanse of Docklands became clear. On one side, large skyscrapers for luxury housing and the beginnings of hotels and a mammoth conference centre, and on the other the remains of 1970s London slowly being modernised with new warehouses and half-demolished dockside premises. In the distance, Jones could see a man standing in the road with a yellow hi-vis jacket on seemingly waiting for the party to arrive. Beyond him, was a large warehouse sandwiched between two ancient-looking brick buildings, either primed for demolition or ready for beautification for the new age. The taxi driver pulled over into the forecourt of a building contractors' car park as all three of his passengers stared ahead, watching the minibus being waved onto a half-made road into the warehouse.

"This is probably as far as I can go," the driver announced and stopped the engine. Isadora rifled through her bag and passed forward an envelope of cash, not stopping to count as she was too intent on keeping her eyes ahead. The three quickly piled out of the vehicle and within moments the red Escort had left the scene.

The black cab, following the minibus, indicated right onto the track, and the hi-vis jacketed man walked alongside and pointed the minibus towards a parking bay. The black cab's doors swung open and there was the old man, looking dapper in his American suit and baseball cap despite his ordeal. Finch helped him inside the double doors of the warehouse entrance and the black cab quickly headed away. The minibus then vanished from view as the mechanical doors in the parking bay closed behind them.

Jones, Jenny and Isadora sprinted up a rudimentary pavement leading to a pathway in front of rows of half-built business premises. There were a few builders and tradesmen on site but this construction site was off the main commuter route and traffic was sporadic. After around 500 yards the three stopped in a porchway to a building which looked set to be glazed, there were large piles of panels, rolls of insulation material and pallets of breeze blocks. Dust swirled and the plastic sheeting covering the frontage flapped in the breeze.

"We need to get in there," Isadora said as she craned her head around the porchway entrance to get a view of the building. The other two followed suit. "But this is bloody odd, there's no police presence and there's zero security. I get the idea of an anonymous event but with the ammunition involved this seems crazy."

Jones agreed. "Let's recce the building. If there's no one there acting as security, we can try to find a way in." He pointed up to the second floor of the large beige-clad warehouse. "Look, see those steps, if we can get up there we can at least get a visual inside."

"This is a massive risk," Isadora interrupted. "We have no

idea who's in there and remember, we have no formal role here. We are just eyes and ears. Let's speak to McNally."

Jenny picked up her handheld and radioed the Thiepval base.

"Hello, McNally. Finch and the old man have been joined by a black minibus and are now entering a large warehouse near London Docklands. We are going to attempt to enter the building. Do we proceed?"

"We don't have your position. The GPS systems appear to have been jammed, we have no idea by what or whom. Mr Singh had your final location as near Limehouse. We're trying to look at possible locations and get a helicopter up to look for the event. MI5 and the Met are on the case. But we believe this event has been coordinated by a rogue MI5 liaison officer called Masters and this is all a sham." McNally replied.

"Maybe it has all been leading to this? The need for Russian superiority, the blackmailing. Maybe this is the sting in the tail. This was all one targeted campaign?" Suggested Isadora.

"Remember, we are dealing with insanity here. We have no idea whether he's been toying with us or whether everything is linked. Now is not the time to go through the finer details. Can you see any police or security?" McNally asked.

"There are no obvious signs of police presence," Jenny replied, speaking into the handheld as Isadora looked on. "There's no security whatsoever. The mini-bus must be full of journalists, not police. Oh, hang on a minute, McNally" As she explained the situation to McNally, Jenny became aware of a large lorry with a terracotta-coloured container on the back. The hi-vis jacketed man appeared again.

"That has got to be the weapons," noted Jones as he squinted into the sun trying to see the driver. The driver appeared to be in civilian clothing but was accompanied by an armed and uniformed police officer. Jenny updated McNally.

"Look, you know what happened to Tom and Carl, so stay safe and listen to Isadora. She's fully trained and can guide you on your approach. However, we need to know what shenanigans are going on in there. I agree with you all, this doesn't feel right at all. But hold tight, help will arrive." McNally signed off and Isadora led Topaz back into the open and to the vicinity of the gate leading to the warehouse. They watched from behind a large reel of metal construction material.

The lorry driver was reversing the vehicle into the parking bay and they watched on as the single uniformed police officer jumped down from the cab and seemed to be communicating with the man in the hi-vis jacket. As the lorry was manoeuvred into place the large hydraulic door on the front of the parking bays began to shut. They could see both vehicles inside as the door slowly closed but, aside from the lorry driver, police officer and the man in the hi-vis, there were no apparent signs of life.

Jones sprinted away from the large reel and jumped over a low picket fence leading to the entrance. After looking around the outside of the building and seeing no cameras or security, he positioned himself behind the row of steps leading to the second-floor external entrance. He then beckoned the other two to follow. Isadora, who was annoyed that Jones' bravado seemed to be out-ranking her leadership, then made her way silently up the steps and looked through a rectangular window in the door. All she could see was a 3ft high metal divider which suggested that this was the entrance to a viewing platform. Aside from a fire extinguisher and a large health and safety poster, the rest of the area visible from the window appeared clear. She then pushed gently on the bar of the door, fearing an alarm, and once that threat was abated she entered the building. Jones and Jenny, watching her progress then sprinted up the steps and watched through the window as Isadora knelt on the floor peering into the warehouse from this purpose-built viewing platform. She caught their eye and with her finger over her lips motioned them forward into the room. The three were on their knees looking through the gap between the metal divider and a safety ledge.

The warehouse was pristine. There was a smell of fresh paint and the brown carpet which covered the floor on the viewing platform was unblemished. Below, in the warehouse, they could see an area the size of a football pitch. It was probably primed for shelving or storage, but at this time it was standing empty. There were three rows of dark grey plastic seats with space for around twenty people and a table, also empty, next to an unbranded lectern. An adjoining door suddenly opened and the man in the hi-vis jacket strolled through, talking to Finch. Their conversation was barely audible.

"You have the room for about an hour and I'll quickly run through where the fire exits and toilets are. Your guests are free to use the tea and coffee facilities in reception and if you need me dial zero on the phone in reception. Otherwise, I'll leave you in peace." The man shook hands with Finch.

"My God," whispered Jones. "This is Finch's hire. He booked this place."

Finch then placed his bag on the seat nearest the table and the three watched as he pulled a maze of wires from inside. He ducked behind the lectern and seemed to be setting up a microphone and a small camera projected towards the audience. As he did so, the door opened and another man entered the room. He was an overweight man in an ill-fitting blue suit. He had short curly hair, gelled lavishly to create a side parting and outdated bushy sideburns that curtained an otherwise bare face.

"Hi! So good to see you!" Finch called out in a passable American accent. "I'm just setting up a camera so we can record the occasion for the Ambassador here in London," Jones noted that Finch's accent veered from mid-west to New York.

"You must be Adam Masters, I can't tell you how helpful you've been. I hope our arrangement wasn't too much of a bother. I know you've been well rewarded." Masters shook Finch's hand and in a hushed voice explained. "I pulled some strings. I have a useful network, it wasn't a big ask. I also take Mr Martinsen's security very seriously and we followed your directions to the letter. There is one police officer on site to oversee the photoshoot with the arms. Mr Martinsen has a fear of people in uniforms? That's very unusual," remarked Masters.

"He was a prisoner of war in Vietnam, Mr Masters. But thank you for respecting this detail." Finch's accent was holding firm.

"This is all bullshit" whispered Isadora. "Masters seriously believes this is Martinsen? Does he think that brown envelope was for a good deed for the Americans, just off the books? That can't be right. And Martinsen was nowhere near Vietnam. This is just a ploy for minimal police attendance. What the hell is he thinking? Maybe Masters is just a useful idiot." Isadora strained to see the contents of the table.

"That camera is like nothing I've ever seen. What on earth is it? The black box next to it looks like a signal jammer to me. Finch is a clever boy," Isadora whispered.

Masters kicked his heels and watched Finch as he prepared the wires on the desk.

"Is there anything else I should be aware of here? Do you have American support for Mr Martinsen? Where is his security detail?"

Finch looked up and smiled at Masters. "We have support, there are CIA operatives stationed all around the site. Do you not have the full briefing?"

"I'm not sure......" Masters began and Finch immediately

interrupted.

"Look, whatever. We have full security coverage. And your expertise will be on show for the journalists. You can explain the seizure of the weapons and how British intelligence were heroes. Mr Martinsen will just stand for photos. He's exhausted after his red-eye flight and briefings with the PM. Your help has just greased the wheels of bureaucracy."

Finch carried on with his preparation and Masters disappeared towards the refreshments.

"Should we go and speak to Masters?" replied Jones.

"God no, he's a rogue officer and a stupid one. He's not going to welcome an intervention from YCU" explained Isadora.

Jenny, who was farthest to the right, moved slightly and could see the driver opening the door of the minibus and several people exiting the vehicle. They were all in civilian clothes and carrying notebooks, bags, and a few with cameras.

"Welcome, welcome, ladies and gentlemen of the press. Do take your seats. Thank you all for respecting our no video camera footage and mobile phone restriction. Apologies also for the secrecy around the location, but I am sure you all understand." Finch smiled as he showed the assembled press to their seats.

Masters moved to the back of the room and stood next to the uniformed officer as he began the process of unlocking the large container. The press turned to watch Masters and the officer.

"I am Adam Masters, I am a representative of British Intelligence and this is PC Keith. We captured this shipment of arms at Tilbury Docks amongst a consignment of other goods bound for Belfast Port. We believe the weapons have been purchased using the proceeds of organised crime which has led to years of terrorism and conflict in Northern Ireland. Fred Martinsen will make himself available for photographs in front of the seized equipment but please do not photograph me or the other officers, for reasons of National Security."

Suddenly from behind the parking bay, the doppelgänger appeared. Finch was whispering to him gently through fake smiles as he led him gently to the side of the container. The uniformed police officer snapped open several thick plastic security seals and then unlocked and unbolted the container. As the doors of the container were noisily pulled open there were audible gasps from the assembled press and they scrambled to take photos. The container was full of weapons and, from where the three were sitting on the viewing platform, there also appeared to be surface to air missiles (SAMs) and other weapons of war.

Masters responded directly to a media question as the photo call continued. "I can confirm that amongst this haul were several 9mm Browning, Taurus, Glock and Beretta handguns; over four hundred AK-47 Kalashnikov and AKM assault rifles; eight MP5 sub-machine guns; two RPG-7 anti-tank rocket launchers; several Soviet-made DShK heavy machine guns as well as FN MAG machine guns; eighteen military-grade flamethrowers; a large consignment of Semtex plastic explosive and most alarmingly five Strela 2-man portable surface to air missiles. This was undoubtedly one of the biggest seizures of paramilitary armaments in history."

As the press scribbled down Masters' answers, the old man grinned nervous smiles and even removed his baseball hat and glasses when the media requested. Nobody doubted the man from County Donegal on the North coast of Ireland whose only crime was an unbelievable likeness to a Peace Envoy.

Jones, Jenny and Isadora watched breathlessly as events slowly unfolded. Finch, a Russian spy, and murderer; Gerard McMahon an innocent hostage grinning hopelessly for the sake of his family and the life of his daughter, and Adam Masters, a rogue MI5 officer with a significantly filled brown envelope off the back of this press coup for the 'Peace Envoy'. Masters assumed this would be seen as landmark US involvement in decommissioning the Irish paramilitaries – with no British or Irish dignitaries in sight, but this was the creation of a smokescreen for Russian interference and US embarrassment.

As the sham continued, there was a loud skidding and engine revving sound outside. Jones turned carefully to look through a crack in the bottom of the door. And there it was, the orange Fiat Tipo. But it was now time for Finch to reveal his hand.

"Members of the press, I would like to ask Mr Martinsen to come to the stage and read a brief statement on behalf of the American Government." Finch grabbed the shaking Irishman and led him to the lectern. The old man pulled a piece of paper from his suit trousers and cleared his throat. He looked pleadingly at Finch but the silent appeal for help was ignored.

"Hello," the old man started in a gentle Irish accent. "My name is Fred Martinsen and I'm here to explain some difficult home truths. I apologise for my demeanour, I am tired and my voice is wrecked from months and months of pointless flights and ineffective meetings"

A few journalists looked at each other with utter amazement as the old man stumbled over his words. A few more flashbulbs were in evidence as the media documented the scene. There were audible gasps.

"As a Peace Envoy, I have been set an impossible task. I cannot stop a civil war. The incompetence of my government has made that impossible. Likewise, who are we to meddle in other people's problems? We are a dysfunctional state with no regard for human life and we have a history of political interference," he continued.

"The photographs you took of me standing next to the

weaponry, these are actually US-built, US-supplied or US-sourced weapons, every single one of them. Why would they want the troubles to end, when we as a nation are enabling them to continue, with our funds and armaments?" The old man, visibly shaking and struggling to stand, took a little water from a plastic cup offered by Finch.

"Finally, I am calling on the US President to end this hoax. Let the Irish have their war. Let the British sort out the problem they caused and I now stand down as Peace Envoy and hopefully consign this madness to history."

The old man had been rehearsed tirelessly and Finch smiled madly as the journalists continued to take photos and scribble notes. A few called out questions but Finch immediately intervened and helped the old man down from the lectern, which he had been leaning on for assistance.

The glare of the flashbulbs was making Gerard McMahon's eyes weep as he struggled with bright lights after days of being drugged and in captivity. Finch saw the potential for things to unravel and led the old man to the back of the room, through the double doors and into a room where the lorry driver and minibus chauffeur sat. Returning, he obligingly gave Fred Martinsen's apologies and Masters, who was utterly stunned by the speech, answered a volley of questions about the armaments to fill in for the missing VIP. However, the press already had their story. An exhausted Fred Martinsen had single-handedly killed the peace process and thrown the US government under the bus. Over four tonnes of military-grade weapons seized in UK waters bound for the North of Ireland were provided by the American military. This headline wrote itself.

Behind the scenes, the sound of revving suddenly increased three-fold and Jones whispered "That Fiat is going nuts out there. We may need to get out of here. This isn't going to end well."

Isadora glared at him and grabbed the gun from the bottom of her bag. "We stay. Or I stay alone, I've got to see this through for the Alpha and Beta teams. Finch has to be stopped. Can you see who's driving the car?"

"They're wearing a black mask or balaclava," Jones replied.

From the parking bay, the sound of ruptured metal gave way to a horrific explosion as the Fiat had burst through the hydraulic doors and the fuel tank had partially detonated. The flames burst high into the rafters of the warehouse and the press and Masters sprinted to the back of the room. The double doors leading to the main room were then kicked open and there stood a lone gunman in a paramilitary balaclava. He held a pistol and in one shot killed the policeman, who was already prostrate on the floor from the impact of the car exploding. The gunman then looked around the room, he stared over at the assembled media with his gun still raised and without blinking picked out the rogue MI5 agent who took a headshot and immediately collapsed.

Isadora knew that they were safe behind the metal fence at the top of the viewing gallery. They needed to stay quiet and motionless but all three were still peering over the balcony, transfixed on the scene. Jones was sure one of the journalists had noticed them but the horror of the unfolding situation had kept their attention away from the figures hidden in the rafters.

"Where is he?" shouted the gunman, with a clear and unmistakable English accent. Topaz recognised the voice.

Somebody from the media, clearly gave the game away with their eyes, as the gunman quickly but guardedly moved to the back of the hall in the direction of the toilets and a storage area. As the gunman burst into the back rooms, still with his gun raised he found Gerard McMahon and the driver of the lorry.

"KEYS!" He bellowed at the lorry driver, who was midway through a cup of tea and reading The Sun. The driver, in absolute panic, found the keys and placed them on the table in front. The gunman paused momentarily to look at the chauffeur and the beleaguered old man and headed back into the main room.

As he burst back into the main warehouse, none of the journalists had moved. One of them, an older woman, had a mobile phone to her ear that hadn't been confiscated and the gunman shot once which deliberately shocked her and caused her to drop the device on the floor. He was, without doubt, a marksman of some repute.

The gunman moved back to the parking bay and there, in the corner, almost attempting to hide behind the wreck of the still-burning Fiat was Finch. The gunman took two paces towards him and removed his balaclava. Isadora, Jones and Jenny could see the side of his face and could make out blonde hair and significant stubble. It was Armstrong. A man they trusted, a man who only a fortnight ago was running around Thiepval with Jones and Jenny.

"You don't need to do this, brother," pleaded Finch.

"You were never my brother or comrade. We were supposed to cause the US embarrassment but you have failed catastrophically. This is a botched operation and will embarrass Russia. MI5 already know who you are, they know that's not Fred Martinsen. I have been sent here to finish this." Armstrong's words were loud enough to travel to Topaz in the viewing platform over the sound of the flames coming from the burning Tipo.

"I was a sleeper, I wanted to remain in the background working for your Mother Russia, mainly for money. But I've been dragged out to deal with your catalogue of mistakes. I've supported you and helped you, but you are an idiot. You are a coward; a failure and you have disrespected your grandfather's memory. The world's media will now see Russia dealing with its own problems." He held the gun to Finch's head.

"You are just an animal that I need to put out of its misery."

Armstrong shot Finch cleanly in the head from close range. He died instantly. Armstrong replaced his balaclava and walked calmly away from Finch, grabbing his rucksack from the floor and throwing it into the passenger seat of the lorry.

With his disguise restored, aware of the cameras, he shouted over to two of the press team and ordered them, at gunpoint, to close the container doors. He then immediately ran around to the driver's seat and started the engine. Isadora bolted down the external stairs and across to the large reel of metal framework they had all used as cover earlier.

As Armstrong began to manoeuvre the lorry out of the warehouse, Isadora shot at the tyres of the vehicle. They were perfect shots but as Isadora awaited the tyres giving way and stopping him, all she saw were sparks. They were armoured steel wheels and bulletproof 20-chamber tyres, and her small pistol stood no chance.

As Armstrong opened the window, he called over to Isadora and fired once, hitting Isadora in the top of the leg. She spun around and fell awkwardly on the floor. As the lorry drove out of the warehouse and onto the main road, Jenny ran downstairs to join Isadora. She was bleeding profusely and suddenly the four tonnes of weaponry meant nothing. Nobody heard what Armstrong shouted but Isadora herself.

Jones sprinted downstairs and Jenny quickly pointed him away. "I've got this, go and see the old man and the rest of them," she threw Jones Isadora's handheld.

As Jones ran hurriedly back into the warehouse, a few of the journalists made their way out of the front double doors. Jones pushed past them and dashed into the back room. There, drinking a cup of tea and shaking was Gerard McMahon with the drivers.

"It's all over chaps, you're safe Mr McMahon."

"Thank goodness for that," Gerard replied. "Can I speak to my family? Can I go home now?"

Jones then pulled apart all the wires near the lectern and within five minutes two police cars with wailing sirens, an accompanying fire engine, and an ambulance turned up at the scene. The road was immediately but belatedly blocked by the second fire tender arriving close behind. Out of the back door was a figure in a short blue bomber jacket and a hoard of paperwork. He quickly introduced himself to Jones as Jube Spencer.

"Spencer," said Jones. "It was Armstrong. He arrived at the scene in the Fiat. Blew the car up and has stolen the arms shipment. He killed Masters and Finch. The whole thing was set up by Finch, he's dead over there. Where the hell were you?"

"The whole area was jammed. We could see or hear nothing. The police are already trying to tail the shipment. Where's Gerard McMahon?"

"He's in the back," replied Jones. "Armstrong picked off his targets carefully. He let the old man live but we need to get him in an ambulance. He's been drugged and held in captivity. He's a bloody trooper." Spencer nodded at Jones and walked into the main warehouse.

The ambulance crew turned their attention to Isadora Brown. Her blood loss was severe but she was still conscious and Jenny was simply chatting to her about the day's events.

"Bloody Armstrong. Bloody idiot. Just why?" Isadora said through gritted teeth.

Jube called the assembled journalists back into the main room as the fire crew doused down the smouldering Fiat.

"Ladies and gents, what you have just witnessed is an issue of significant national security. You will hand over all cameras and mobile phones and sign these forms. We will agree on what you can and cannot report once you've been debriefed. If anything goes to print without my say-so, you and your editors will find yourselves in prison. Understood?" Spencer looked for the team to acknowledge and another member of the paramedic crew began chatting to each journalist in turn, looking for symptoms of shock.

Spencer looked over at the two bodies, police officers had covered them in sheeting and they were pronounced dead at the scene. One of the uniformed policemen called out to Jones.

"This one here," the policeman pointed down at the remains of Finch. "Any clues to an identity?"

Jones shrugged his shoulders. "No idea mate. He went in there and hid at the end. The gunman found him. He had an American accent. He was running the show initially."

As Jube dished out Official Secrets Act paperwork to the assembled media, he turned to Jones.

"Travel with Isadora to the hospital. We can debrief later. You've done well here, it won't feel like it now. But being here and seeing this happen is a major positive. We just need to work with the police to get that container stopped."

Jones nodded and headed over to Jenny who was holding Isadora's hand as she was being helped onto a stretcher. Isadora looked pale and the blonde wig had gone. Jones could see Isadora was in a bad way, she had lost a lot of blood and Jenny was gripping tight to a tourniquet provided by the paramedics with one hand and holding onto Isadora with the other.

"Let's all go together," Isadora mumbled quietly and she closed her eyes as the pain hit. She was gripping tight onto Jenny's hand.

A helicopter whirred overhead as Isadora was loaded gently into the ambulance. Jones considered asking Spencer whether he needed to join the hunt for the container but suddenly felt immensely tired.

CHAPTER FORTY

It was 06.00am in the hotel in Bermondsey when the phone rang. Jones and Jenny had been at the hospital until the small hours. When they left her she'd already been in the operating theatre for three hours. Spencer had suggested they sleep in the hotel room and ensure MI5 removed the equipment Isadora had been supplied with.

The voice at the end of the phone cheered the weary couple as they were still struggling to come to terms with the events at the warehouse. It was Virginia, who had finally recovered from her blast injuries and they could hear Charles who was hovering in the background like a proud and interested Dad.

"Sorry to wake you so early. I'm afraid to say you have another busy day ahead. You'll have an early debrief in Thames House." Virginia explained.

"We'll get up now. What news of Isadora?" asked Jones.

"She's had the bullet removed and is in recovery. She's going to be fine but she'll be out of action for a month at least. She's been very lucky. So, Topaz is back to two again and we already have work to do. We'll need to meet you to discuss the next steps."

"Meet us? Are we on a flight back to Belfast?" Jenny asked.

"No, no," Virginia replied. "We're both back in England and I'm due at Milton College this afternoon. Perhaps you can join us? We'll expect you at about 2pm and we'll be having a conference call with the rest of the team beforehand. Spencer will be in touch soon to arrange the debrief. Life in the fast lane, eh?"

"What about the container, have they located it?" asked Jones, realising that was the major hole in the operation.

"The Met and MI5, working with GCHQ, have thrown the kitchen sink at it. The container and Joseph Armstrong have vanished off the face of the earth. Massey is re-interviewing Alexinsky now. Spencer will explain more later." Virginia signed off.

The two lay in bed together, Jones with his arm around Jenny. The hotel room was still dark from the black-out blinds and neither were in any rush to start their day. They had feasted on the mini-bar last night and they hadn't slept well. With light from a crack in the curtains, Jones kissed Jenny gently on the lips and smiled at her.

"I have never needed anyone more than you," he said, looking at her as she brushed her hair away from her face.

"I know," she replied, smiling. "I have a sense that we will make this work, despite everything. But we need to be careful. I can't risk losing you and we only really have each other now." They embraced, holding one another, almost not daring to let go. The very briefest moment of intimacy and love gave way to another call, this time on Jenny's handheld.

"I've sent a car to pick you up," Spencer said, shattering the moment. "Can you be outside the hotel in 15 minutes?"

"Absolutely. We'll be there." As she completed the call, Jenny leapt from the bed and ran into the bathroom. Through a crack in the door, she called out to Jones.

"You know, we'd be quicker if we shared the water."

"You don't have to ask me twice!" And Jones threw the covers off and ran into the bathroom.

Another black cab arrived outside the hotel for their transport to Thames House. Neither had been to the operational heart of MI5 before and neither cared. They were both mentally and physically drained from the emotion of everything, Jenny even slept during the journey.

Jube Spencer met them at the kerb side at the nearest taxi rank to Millbank and walked them to a side entrance where they were searched and tagged, before being escorted to a small meeting room. The whole place felt eerily well-thumbed and tired, even though it had only opened a year previously.

The meeting room already felt half full with a small team of people in business attire. Both Jones and Jenny were wearing grey un-ironed sweatshirts and jeans, as they had only packed the bare minimum, much to Jenny's chagrin.

At the top of the long rectangular table was a large muscular black man, who introduced himself as Clive and to his left an older lady, Janice.

"Big Clive," Jones mouthed silently to Jenny and she briefly smiled.

Both Clive and Janice were drinking espressos from unfeasibly tiny cups and had matching notepads. Clive smiled a great deal and looked attentively over to Jones and Jenny, in an attempt to put them at their ease. Janice was reading pages of notes over her half-moon glasses that had a long gold chain attached to them. The room was wood panelled and there was a green button on the wall, which seemed to alert junior staff to bring coffee or other provisions.

Spencer was sitting opposite the pair and he was joined by a young man, who wore a pink business shirt without a tie. He didn't introduce himself. Jones decided he was probably the notetaker. Clive coughed to clear his throat and Jones suspected a monologue was en route.

"We are delighted to meet you, Mr Jones and Miss Richmond. We are here today to listen to your take on the last few weeks and share our thoughts on the way ahead. Before we do so, I would like to bring you operationally up to speed on the current intelligence we have."

Jones noticed Clive assumed they knew exactly who he was and his role. Aside from the barest of mentions of Big Clive by Finch, back in Bangor, he was new to them both. He also noted Jube Spencer's unusual silence as he doodled circles on an exercise book. Jones suspected Clive might be very important.

"Joseph Armstrong killed both Stephen Finch and our operative Adam Masters yesterday and left the scene with over four tonnes of military-grade hardware and weaponry. We have an all-ports emergency in place and so far, we have drawn a blank, likewise our colleagues in Cheltenham and New Scotland Yard." Clive was looking through reams of paperwork.

"This could have been a national embarrassment and we have swerved that, thanks to journalists playing ball and some frank conversations with our American cousins. However, we haven't yet told them about the missing hardware and the possible Russian link. Therefore, we still have an enormous amount of work to do to salvage our credibility."

"Nevertheless, Gerard McMahon, largely due to your good work, is now safely in Paddington Hospital for observation before hopefully being released back home tomorrow. He appears in good health. I am also led to believe your colleague Isadora Brown is on a slow road to recovery. Is that correct Mr Spencer?" Jube nodded and continued his doodling.

"We are only just beginning the task of looking at Armstrong. He was a skilled marksman and served with great merit in the Balkans until quite recently. His part in the

Yugoslav conflict will need to be scrutinised as will his discharge in Serbia. This, as you might imagine, is a huge priority for us as Armstrong cannot be allowed to leave UK shores."

Afterwards, Clive effortlessly moved from Jones to Jenny checking and double-checking every part of their account whilst Janice noted their remarks. She occasionally interrupted to ensure clarity. He was very keen to understand their relationship, if any, with Armstrong and whether they had suspected him at any point. He didn't seem at all surprised when both underlined their shock at Armstrong's appearance in the warehouse. Jones admitted he assumed the Tipo was being driven by another of Finch's Red Line gang, which Clive rather pointedly corrected. He highlighted that Armstrong was indeed one of the Red Line terrorist network, but the whole thing was apparently a false flag operation created by the KGB. Clive was somewhat poker-faced throughout; the smile had gone.

Clive questioned them about McNally (who they agreed was resourceful and knowledgeable, especially during the Europa rescue), Massey (a bit of an unknown quantity to them but an inspiration to Jenny, understandably) and the Currys (parental figures, caring and massively intellectual). Jones felt as if he would be marked at the end and Jenny looked heavily fatigued.

Clive and Janice broke up the meeting after two hours and Spencer accompanied the pair to a yard at the back of the building where he bought them coffee and bacon sandwiches. He explained that such a de-brief was par for the course and they shouldn't be concerned. But as Jones and Jenny devoured their brunch his bulky mobile phone rang and he briefly left the pair.

Massey had concluded her re-interview with Alexinsky, with the threat of his own family hanging over his head, plus the possible incarceration in Belmarsh Prison, he admitted he was aware of another sleeper within the YCU set-up. But he flatly denied meeting him or knowing his identity. The golden egg was the potential link to a Russian operation in central America. Alexinsky admitted that both he and Finch had undergone training in a clandestine camp in Belize. He also admitted that there was a significant stash of Russian and ex-Soviet weaponry already in situ in Central America.

Belize, a former British colony where the British sovereign remains Head of State, had been called the last great tax haven on Earth for many different reasons. First, and perhaps most importantly, Belize had no capital gains taxes. Compared to the United States, where capital gains hovered around the 15 per cent mark, that offered a huge financial perk and therefore it was a useful place for corrupt entities to hide money. And where there's dubious finance, there's dubious people. Alexinsky explained that Russian officials, even steeped in communist rhetoric, store their ill-gotten gains in Belize and use it as a useful bolt-hole to syphon funds to sympathetic regimes in Colombia, Venezuela, Cuba and Mexico. When asked whether this was the likely location of the weaponry seized in the Docklands raid, Alexinsky clammed up again, although he suggested they were more than likely already sold before they were stolen. Massey thought this was a likely prospect.

Armed with this new information from the call, Spencer took the pair back to the small meeting room and Clive continued where he'd left off. But the smile had, at least partially, returned.

"Following an assessment of your work, we would like to offer you a twelve-month role with us as intelligence officers. You will remain aligned with the YCU and you will complete your studies accordingly. Your contact point will be Jube Spencer and you will immediately form part of the team working on the operation to capture the seized armaments and weaponry and to seek Joseph Armstrong. You may be amused to hear that we have called this Operation Topaz. Jube will take you through the next steps, assuming you agree to our proposals?" Both quickly signalled their agreement and, quick as a flash, another copy of the Official Secrets Act appeared.

"You'll both need to sign this. I have to say, in my twenty years in MI5, I have never admitted members of YCU so willingly. You have undertaken sterling work and I look forward to watching your success story." And with that, Clive and Janice left the room, pausing briefly to shake hands with both Jenny and Jones and seemingly ignoring Spencer.

Jones and Jenny arrived at Milton College at 2.15pm, they were late. The building somehow looked and smelt different, the streets seemed like visions from the past. As Jones walked up the steps to the College, he remembered his first visit, the trepidation and the anxiety. Jones had arrived as a failure in his own mind and was revisiting with a whole new future ahead. He and Jenny felt relaxed enough to hold hands as they entered the building and made their way to the reception.

"I'm Jones," he said. "I'm here to meet Virginia Curry."

The receptionist, without responding delved straight into a small box of messages in front of her. And handed him a small white envelope. It was in Virginia's beautiful handwriting.

"Jones and Jenny. Clearly, we can't openly celebrate what you've just achieved but let's have a drink and catch up somewhere you know well. V x"

It took less than five minutes for the pair to make their way to The Jericho. Where they opened the door to the sounds of laughing and the buzz of humanity. There, standing by the front bar was Virginia, still on crutches, Charles, Mr Singh and most surprisingly of all, Tom and Carl. Jones and Jenny embraced them all like old friends. Tom was keen to show Jones his long row of stitches stretching down from the centre of his head down past his neck. He'd been lucky. Carl was busily reading a Norwich City programme that his younger brother had sent him but was equally proud of his wounds. Importantly, both sat on either side of Mr Singh and he would undoubtedly be relieved that they were largely unscathed.

Jenny immediately befriended Mr Singh and explained how his genius had often saved the day. Charles joined in the plaudits for the former GCHQ reject. "Their loss was our gain" Charles underlined with his normal suaveness. Mr Singh couldn't hold back the emotion. They raised a glass to the missing member of the team, Isadora, and those from Alpha and Beta who had perished in Lennoxville and Limehall.

Jones didn't want to ruin the evening by drinking himself into oblivion. He wanted to feel every moment before the hard work started again. He savoured every drop and every look from Jenny and the team that had saved his life on many occasions. After a few hours, Jones looked at Jenny and they seemed to jointly decide it was time to leave and book a table somewhere. Before leaving, he noticed Virginia hobbling from the other bar, close to the exit door.

"Get yourself a suit, a shave and stop with all that drinking. Smarten yourself up and you might get somewhere." Jones said through a half-smile to Virginia.

"Did I really say that?" she asked.

"Yes," he nodded. "You were absolutely right and I can't thank you enough," Jones thought about hugging Virginia, but remembered himself, just in time. "I still need to smarten myself up, mind," he added.

He strolled over to the door and opened it wide for Jenny. Jones shook Virginia's hand and headed out. Jones wasn't stumbling in life anymore; the door of opportunity was ajar.

EPILOGUE

THE WALLS OF THE SHIPPING CONTAINER WERE DAMP WITH condensation and the motion of the vessel's gentle sway was beginning to unsettle Jones' stomach. It had been days since he'd last eaten and the seasickness and heat were getting to him. It was making him question why he'd been so eager to volunteer for the assignment and why the intelligence was so wrong.

The various viewing holes he'd painstakingly drilled along the inside of the container were useless now aside from providing fresh air as he found himself boxed in amongst thousands of similar but airtight units. His last view of the sea was some twelve days ago when he left Portugal and whilst his technical equipment told him exactly where he was, nothing could tell him what to do. And still, the ship rose and fell away against the tide.

There had been the occasional acrid smell of burning petrol, sometimes a shocking and thunderous alert sounded from the ship's hull and the constant clang of unsecured items in nearby units as they moved around inside, following the sway of the ship and keeping him awake and paranoid. The Portuguese-speaking crew were often audible as they walked around the perimeter of the ship and he could almost taste their cheap cigarettes as the smell wafted in through the air holes.

It was almost noon on day thirteen and Jones wondered what was smashing inside the neighbouring metal units. He wiped the torrent of sweat from his face against his forearm and saw it was dirty. He felt unwashed and uncomfortable. He was stripped down to his shorts and a plain grey t-shirt and sitting on the rivetted floor with his rolled-up green shirt acting as a cushion. It was getting hotter and hotter as they headed closer to North America and his nerves were frayed.

A half-full slops bucket sat in the corner of the room and food supplies were running low. Communications were sporadic but still regular enough to give him hope that a plan was imminent. Or that was his expectation. His team were trying hard to keep him in good spirits but the nicer they were, the more he realised the danger he faced. He wondered if this reckless voyage was even survivable.

The original strategy was a relatively simple one. Follow a shipment of arms on a low-capacity container ship from Viana do Castelo in Portugal to Belize by being part of the cargo. Technology wasn't enough. They needed a man on the inside. Then, attach a tracking device to the correct container and follow progress deep into Belize City using GPS back in Cheltenham and supported by local field agents. He would stay in situ in a pre-arranged safe house.

It was an awful long way and Jones would need to be extremely resilient. A hidden escape hatch at the top of the container was large enough to exit and crawl around the deck looking for the correct numbered unit. The immediate flaw was that the 'low capacity' vessel certainly wasn't low on anything. Against all intelligence, containers were stacked across the vast deck and on top and either side of Jones' container.

It was the worst of all scenarios. He was stuck in a sweltering container and the hatch was blocked from above. He had two days of water left and his only instinct was to survive.

Note from the author:

I would like to dedicate this book to my father, Barrie Robinson, who passed away in October 2020. It was the hole that was created in my life from his untimely death that made me want to write to escape from the torment and sadness of loss. One of my favourite places to hide had always been Northern Ireland. Its beauty, unique character and the incredible friendliness of those lucky enough to call it home has often made the difference for me. Visit it. I'd like to also thank my wife, Ali, and my cousin, Vince McLoughlin - both have been fantastic accidental developmental editors; my Mum (Jean) who keeps us in order at home; and Millie and Daisy, who might read this book one day.

Thanks to Veronica Gray, for ensuring I didn't embarrass myself with Irish references, to Hayley Webster for being the 'book doctor' and keeping things real and to the residents of Edwardstone and Boxford for harbouring me since 1996. It's been quite the journey.

Printed in Great Britain
by Amazon

25262429R00189